NEAL STEPHENSON

author of *Cryptonomicon*

"THRILLINGLY
CLEVER."
New York Times Book Review

ODALISQUE

THE BAROQUE CYCLE #3

"**L**ittered with treasure . . . noisy, impolite, exhausting, and beguiling . . . impressively entertaining over an impossible distance . . . Stephenson demonstrates a restless intellect . . . He's also consistently funny."

London Daily Telegraph

"**P**art romance, part picaresque adventure, part potboiler, part scientific treatise, part religious tome, part political saga—just about every literary genre around . . . A book that you don't want to end."

San Antonio Express-News

"**P**hilosophy, court intrigue, economics . . . wars, plagues, and natural disasters . . . Everyone who's anyone in late seventeenth-century or early eighteenth-century Europe and North America shows up in the story . . . Stephenson clearly never intended . . . one of those meticulously accurate historical novels that capture ways of thought of times gone by. Instead, it explores the philosophic concerns of today . . . Thrillingly clever, suspenseful, and amusing."

New York Times Book Review

"**E**laborate scene-setting on a grand stage . . . Stephenson [has an] irrepressible sense of humor—he wants us to have as much fun reading as he obviously did writing . . . The only thing more impressive than Stephenson's command of these seemingly disparate but interconnected subjects is the knowledge that he's only warming up."

Village Voice

"**T**he Baroque Cycle is great fun that never seems to end."

Columbus Dispatch

"[S]tephenson is] a visionary who sees into the past as easily as he spins scenarios of the future . . . Not merely a period piece but a book very much about today , . . with insights into our modern world."

Denver Rocky Mountain News

"The sort of book that lays waste your social life . . . It might also play merry havoc with whatever late seventeenth- and early eighteenth-century history you have, so skillfully does Stephenson mash together facts and flights of lurid fancy . . . Stephenson covers a terrific amount of theoretical, social, and geographical ground to persuade us that the period shaped the modern world. Bawdy, learned, hilarious, and utterly compelling, [it] is sprawling to the point of insanity and resoundingly, joyously good."

Times of London

"Because of his subject matter, Stephenson won't lose his usual science lovers. He'll pick up some history buffs as well, and his quirky characters, zestful pace, and wryly humorous tone will charm almost everyone else . . . But Stephenson's aim is more than an entertaining account of remarkable personalities. [His novel's] panoramic view encompasses the bitter religious and political struggles which gave rise to the scientific way of thought."

Seattle Times

"[S]tephenson] has one of those rare, fluid minds that push the boundaries of brilliance. With exuberant, intoxicating prose, he has written a lusty adventure tale that also seems to be scientifically accurate."

Lexington Herald Leader

"**A**we-inspiring . . . stuffed with heart-stopping action scenes, learned discussions on science, and a treasure of forgotten historical lore."

Book

"**T**ogether, the books of The Baroque Cycle form a sublime, immersive, brain-throttlingly complex marvel of a novel that will keep scholars and critics occupied for the next 100 years . . . It's the sort of work that quickly becomes an obsession . . . A reader's feast . . . There's something for everyone."

Toronto Star

"**A** tremendous gift to his fans, who will delve into a richly imagined world of intrigue, science, and plenty of name-dropping . . . A vast narrative that sweeps through a time of tremendous development in science, math, and discovery, not to mention a period of tremendous upheaval in the English monarchy . . . Stephenson's fantastic attention to detail is matched with lyrical descriptions and at times dark humor . . . It's a big world, and there's plenty of explaining to do . . . Stephenson is just the author to offer it."

Kansas City Star

"**W**onderfully inventive . . . Stephenson brings to life a cast of unforgettable characters in a time of breathtaking genius and discovery."

Contra Costa Times

"**S**prawling, irreverent, and ultimately profound."

Newsweek

"**A**rguably the most ambitious literary offering in this century... It is Dickensian potboiler and Baroque reader smashed into one hefty and masterfully paced [tale] told ... by a maddeningly talented writer ... It is a triumph."

Virginian Pilot

"**T**he late seventeenth century saw an explosion of intellectual brilliance that resembles nothing so much as it does an overflow from a boiling cauldron... As seen through Stephenson's eyes the [era] is endlessly fascinating, and so is the focus on the intersection of religion and science."

Salon.com

"**S**tephenson has been compared ... to Charles Dickens, Thomas Pynchon, Don DeLillo, William Gibson, Michael Crichton, and Isaac Asimov, which suggests what a broad range he covers... Both a whopping ... historical epic, filled with the usual trappings ... and a detail-packed history of science."

Atlanta Journal-Constitution

"**[S**tephenson] infuses old-school science and engineering with a badly needed dose of swashbuckling adventure ... Who knew the Natural Philosophers were so cool?"

Slate

"**S**parkling prose, subtle humor, and a superb knowledge of the period ... [a] grand feast."

Library Journal

THE BAROQUE CYCLE
by Neal Stephenson

QUICKSILVER: THE BAROQUE CYCLE #1
KING OF THE VAGABONDS: THE BAROQUE CYCLE #2
ODALISQUE: THE BAROQUE CYCLE #3

Coming Soon

THE CONFUSION, PART I: THE BAROQUE CYCLE #4
THE CONFUSION, PART II: THE BAROQUE CYCLE #5
SOLOMON'S GOLD: THE BAROQUE CYCLE #6
CURRENCY: THE BAROQUE CYCLE #7
THE SYSTEM OF THE WORLD: THE BAROQUE CYCLE #8

NEAL STEPHENSON

ODALISQUE

THE BAROQUE CYCLE #3

HarperTorch

An Imprint of HarperCollins*Publishers*

Odalisque: The Baroque Cycle #3 was originally published by HarperCollins in hardcover and trade paperback as part of the overall novel *Quicksilver: Volume One of the Baroque Cycle* by Neal Stephenson.

Map of 1667 London reproduced with changes courtesy of Historic Urban Plans, Inc.

Refracting sphere illustration from the facsimile edition of Robert Hooke's *Philosophical Experiments and Observations,* edited by W. Derham. Published by Frank Cass & Co., Ltd., London, 1967.

Illustrations from Isaac Newton's 1729 *Mathematical Principles of Natural Philosophy* courtesy of Primary Source Microfilm.

HARPERTORCH
An Imprint of HarperCollins*Publishers*
10 East 53rd Street
New York, New York 10022-5299

Copyright © 2003 by Neal Stephenson
Excerpt from *The Confusion, Part I* copyright © 2004 by Neal Stephenson
Maps by Nick Springer
Family trees created by Lisa Gold; illustrated by Jane S. Kim
Conic sections illustration, a digital recomposition of eight figures from Claude Richard's 1655 edition of Apollonius of Perga's *Conic Sections,* by Alvy Ray Smith
ISBN-13: 978-0-06-083318-3
ISBN-10: 0-06-083318-1

First HarperTorch paperback printing: April 2006
First Perennial printing: October 2004
First William Morrow hardcover printing: October 2003

HarperCollins®, HarperTorch™, and ♥™ are trademarks of HarperCollins Publishers Inc.

Printed in the United States of America

Visit HarperTorch on the World Wide Web at www.harpercollins.com

10 9 8 7 6 5 4 3 2 1

To the woman upstairs

✥

Acknowledgments

✣

THERE ARE MANY PEOPLE to be thanked for their help in the creation of The Baroque Cycle. Accordingly, please see the acknowledgments in *Quicksilver: The Baroque Cycle #1*.

Contents

Gunfleet House   Comstock House

Waterhouse

PICCADILLY

ST. JAMES STREET

St. James's Fields

St. Giles's Fields

St. James Palace

PALL MALL

Covent Garden

ST. MARTIN'S LANE

St. Martin-in-the-Fields

CHARING CROSS

LeFebure's

The New Exchange

THE STRAND

Holbein Gate

KING STREET

King St. Gate

Whitehall Palace

Westminster

LONDON

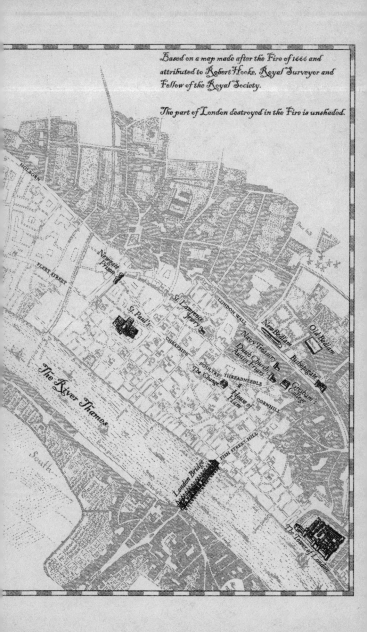

Based on a map made after the Fire of 1666 and attributed to Robert Hooke, Royal Surveyor and Fellow of the Royal Society.

The part of London destroyed in the Fire is unshaded.

HOLBORN

FLEET STREET

Newgate
Prison

St. Lawrence
Jewry

LONDON WALL

St. Paul's

CHEAPSIDE

New Bedlam

Navy Treasury
Dutch Church
Austin Friars

Bishopsgate

Old Bedlam

Gresham
College

POULTRY
THREADNEEDLE
The Change
House of
Ham

CORNHILL

The River Thames

Southwark

FISH STREET HILL

London Bridge

The Tower of London

BOOK THREE

Odalisque

In all times kings, and persons of sovereign
authority, because of their independency, are in
continual jealousies, and in the state and posture
of gladiators; having their weapons pointing, and
their eyes fixed on one another; that is, their
forts, garrisons, and guns upon the frontiers of
their kingdoms; and continual spies upon their
neighbors; which is a posture of war

—HOBBES, *Leviathan*

Whitehall Palace

FEBRUARY 1685

LIKE A HORSEMAN WHO REINS in a wild stallion that has
borne him, will he, nill he, across several counties; or a
ship's captain who, after scudding before a gale through a
bad night, hoists sail, and gets underway once more, navigat-
ing through unfamiliar seas—thus Dr. Daniel Waterhouse,
anno domini 1685, watching King Charles II die at Whitehall Palace.

Much had *happened* in the previous twelve years, but
nothing was really *different*. Daniel's world had been like a
piece of *caoutchouc* that stretched but did not rupture, and
never changed its true shape. After he'd gotten his Doctorate, there'd been nothing for him at Cambridge save lectur-
ing to empty rooms, tutoring dull courtiers' sons, and
watching Isaac recede further into the murk, pursuing his
quest for the Philosophic Mercury and his occult studies of
the Book of Revelation and the Temple of Solomon. So
Daniel had moved to London, where events went by him like
musket-balls.

John Comstock's ruin, his moving out of his house, and
his withdrawal from the Presidency of the Royal Society had
seemed epochal at the time. Yet within weeks Thomas More
Anglesey had not only been elected President of the Royal
Society but also bought and moved into Comstock's
house—the finest in London, royal palaces included. The
upright, conservative arch-Anglican had been replaced with

a florid Papist, but nothing was really different—which taught Daniel that the world was full of powerful men but as long as they played the same roles, they were as inter-changeable as second-rate players speaking the same lines in the same theatre on different nights.

All of the things that had been seeded in 1672 and 1673 had spent the next dozen years growing up into trees: some noble and well-formed, some curiously gnarled, and some struck down by lightning. Knott Bolstrood had died in exile. His son Gomer now lived in Holland. Other Bolstroods had gone over the sea to New England. This was all because Knott had attempted to indict Nell Gwyn as a prostitute in 1679, which had seemed sensational at the time. The older King Charles II had grown, the more frightened London had become of a return to Popery when his brother James ascended to the throne, and the more the King had needed to keep a nasty bleak Protestant—a Bolstrood—around to reassure them. But the more power Bolstrood acquired, the more he was able to whip people up against the Duke of York and Popery. Late in 1678, they'd gotten so whipped up that they'd commenced hanging Catholics for being part of a supposed Popish Plot. When they'd begun running low on Catholics, they had hanged Protestants for doubting that such a Plot existed.

By this point Anglesey's sons Louis, the Earl of Upnor, and Philip, Count Sheerness, had gambled away most of the family's capital anyway, and had little to lose except their creditors, so they had fled to France. Roger Comstock—who had been ennobled, and was now the Marquis of Ravenscar—had bought Anglesey (formerly Comstock) House. Instead of moving in, he had torn it down, plowed its gardens under, and begun turning it into "the finest piazza in Europe." But this was merely Waterhouse Square done bigger and better. Raleigh had died in 1678, but Sterling had stepped into his place just as easily as Anglesey had stepped into John Comstock's, and he and the Marquis of Ravenscar had set about doing the same old things with more capital and fewer mistakes.

The King had dissolved Parliament so that it could not murder any more of his Catholic friends, and had sent James off to the Spanish Netherlands on the "out of sight, out of mind" principle, and, for good measure, had gotten James's daughter Mary wedded to the Protestant Defender himself: William of Orange. And in case none of that sufficed, the Duke of Monmouth (who was Protestant) had been encouraged to parade around the country, tantalizing England with the possibility that he might be de-bastardized through some genealogical sleight-of-hand, and become heir to the throne.

King Charles II could still dazzle, entertain, and confuse, in other words. But his alchemical researches beneath the Privy Gallery had come to naught; he could not make gold out of lead. And he could not levy taxes without a Parliament. The surviving goldsmiths in Threadneedle Street, and Sir Richard Apthorp in his new Bank, had been in no mood to lend him anything. Louis XIV had given Charles a lot of gold, but in the end the Sun King turned out to be no different from any other exasperated rich in-law: he had begun finding ways to make Charles suffer in lieu of paying interest. So the King had been forced to convene Parliament. When he had, he had found that it was controlled by a City of London/friends of Bolstrood alliance (Foes of Arbitrary Government, as they styled themselves) and that the first item on their list had been, not to raise taxes, but rather to exclude James (and every other Catholic) from the throne. This Parliament had instantly become so unpopular with those who loved the King that the whole assembly—wigs, wool-sacks, and all—had had to move up to Oxford to be safe from London mobs whipped up by Sir Roger L'Estrange—who'd given up trying to suppress others' libels, and begun printing up his own. Safe (or so they imagined) at Oxford, these Whigs (as L'Estrange libelled them) had voted for Exclusion, and cheered for Knott Bolstrood as he proclaimed Nellie a whore.

A crier marching up Piccadilly had related this news to Daniel as he and Robert Hooke had stood in what had once

been Comstock's and then Anglesey's ballroom and was by
that point a field of Italian marble rubble open to a fine blue
October sky. As a work table they had been using the capital
of a Corinthian column that had plunged to earth when the
column had been jerked out from under it by Ravenscar's
merry Irish demolition men. The capital had half-embedded
itself in the soil and now rested at a convenient angle; Hooke
and Waterhouse had unrolled large sheets and weighed down
the corners with stray bits of marble: tips of angels' wings
and shards of acanthus leaves. These were surveyor's plats
laying out Ravenscar's scheme to embed a few square
blocks of Cartesian rationality on the pot-bound root-ball
that was the London street system. Surveyors and their ap-
prentices had stretched cords and hammered in stakes plotting the axes of three short parallel streets that, according to
Roger, would sport the finest shops in London: one was la-
beled Anglesey, one Comstock, and one Ravenscar. But that
afternoon, Roger had showed up, armed with an inky quill,
and scratched out those names and written in their stead
Northumbria,* Richmond,† and St. Alban's.‡

A month after that there'd been no Parliament and no
more Bolstroods in Britain. James had come home from exile, Monmouth had been removed from the King's service,
and England had become, effectively, a department of
France, with King Charles openly accepting a hundred thousand pounds a year, and most of the politicians in London—
Whigs and Tories alike—receiving bribes from the Sun
King as well. Quite a few Catholics who'd been tossed into
the Tower for supposed involvement in the Popish Plot had

---

*The Duke of Northumbria was the bastard son of Charles II by his mis-
tress Barbara Palmer, *nee* Villiers, Duchess of Castlemaine.

†The Duke of Richmond was the bastard son of Charles II by his mistress
Louise de Kéroualle, Duchess of Portsmouth.

‡The Duke of St. Alban's was the bastard son of Charles II by his mistress
Nell Gwyn, the nubile comedienne and apple-woman.

been released, making room for as many Protestants who had supposedly been involved in a Rye House Plot to put Monmouth on the throne. Just like many Popish Plotters before them, these had promptly begun to "commit suicide" in the Tower. One had even managed the heroic feat of cutting his own throat all the way to the vertebrae!

So Wilkins's work had been undone, at least for a while. Thirteen hundred Quakers, Barkers, and other Dissenters had been clapped into prison. Thus had Daniel spent a few months in a smelly place listening to angry men sing the same hymns he'd been taught as a boy by Drake.

It had been—in other words—a reign. Charles II's reign. He was the King, he loved France and hated Puritans and was always long on mistresses and short on money, and nothing ever really changed.

Now Dr. Waterhouse was standing on the King's Privy Stairs: a rude wooden platform clinging to a sheer vertical wall of limestone blocks that plunged straight into the Thames. All of the Palace buildings that fronted on the river were built this way, so as he gazed downriver, keeping watch for the boat that carried the chirurgeons, he found himself sighting down a long, continuous, if somewhat motley wall, interrupted by the occasional window or mock bastion. Three hundred feet downstream, a dock was thrust out into the river, and several intrepid watermen were walking to and fro on it in the lock-kneed gait of men trying to avoid freezing to death. Their boats were tied up alongside, awaiting passengers, but the hour was late, the weather cold, the King was dying, and no Londoners were availing themselves of the old right-of-way that ran through the Palace.

Beyond that dock, the river curved slowly around to the right, towards London Bridge. As the midday twilight had faded to an ashy afternoon, Daniel had seen a boat shove off from the Old Swan: a tavern at the northern end of the bridge that drew its clientele from those who did not like to gamble their lives by penetrating its turbulent arches. The boat had been struggling upstream ever since, and it was close enough now that, with the aid of the spyglass in Daniel's pocket, he could see it carried only two passengers.

Daniel had been remembering the night in 1670 when he'd come to Whitehall in Pepys's carriage, and wandered around the Privy Garden trying to act natural. At the time he'd thought it was cheeky and romantic, but now, remembering that he had ever been that fatuous made him grind his teeth, and thank God that the only witness had been Cromwell's severed head.

Recently he had spent a lot of time at Whitehall. The King had decided to relax his grip just a bit, and had begun letting a few Barkers and Quakers out of prison, and had decided to nominate Daniel as a sort of unofficial secretary for all matters having to do with mad Puritans: Knott Bolstrood's successor, that is, with all the same burdens, but much less power. Of Whitehall's two thousand or so rooms, Daniel had probably set foot in a few hundred—enough to know that it was a dirty, mildewed jumble, like the map of the inside of a courtier's mind, a slum in all but name. Whole sections had been taken over by the King's pack of semi-feral spaniels, who'd become inbred even by Royal standards and thus hare-brained even by Spaniel standards. Whitehall Palace was, in the end, a House: the house of a Family. It was a very strange old family. As of one week ago Daniel had already been somewhat better acquainted with that Family than anyone in his right mind would *want* to be. And *now,* Daniel was waiting here on the Privy Stairs only as an excuse to get out of the King's bedchamber—nay, his very *bed*—and to breathe some air that did not smell like the royal body fluids.

After a while the Marquis of Ravenscar came out and joined him. Roger Comstock—the least promising, and so far the most successful, of the men Daniel had gone to Cambridge with—had been in the north when the King had fallen ill on Monday. He was overseeing the construction of his manor house, which Daniel had designed for him. The news must've taken a day or two to reach him, and he must've set out immediately: it was now Thursday evening. Roger was still in his traveling-clothes, looking more drab than Daniel had ever seen him—almost Puritanical.

"My lord."

"Dr. Waterhouse."

From the expression on Roger's face, Daniel knew that he had stopped by the King's bedchamber first. In case there was any doubt of that, Roger tucked the long skirts of his coat behind him, clambered down onto both knees, bent forward, and threw up into the Thames.

"Will you please excuse me."

"Just like College days."

"I didn't imagine that a man could contain so many fluids and whatnot in his entire body!"

Daniel nodded toward the approaching boat. "Soon you'll witness fresh marvels."

"I could see from looking at His Majesty that the physicians have been quite busy?"

"They have done their utmost to hasten the King's departure from this world."

"Daniel! Lower your voice, I say," Roger huffed. "Some may not understand your sense of humor—if that is the correct word for it."

"Funny you should bring up the subject of Humours. It all began with an apoplectical fit on Monday. The King, hardy creature that he is, might've recovered—save that a Doctor happened to be in the very room, armed with a full complement of lancets!"

"Ugh! Worse luck!"

"Out came a blade—the Doctor found a vein—the King bade farewell to a pint or two of the Humour of Passion. But of course, he's always had plenty of that to go round—so he lived on through Tuesday, and had the strength to fend off the gathering swarm of Doctors on into yesterday. Then,

alas, he fell into an epileptical fit, and all of the Doctors
burst in at once. They'd been camped in his anterooms, arguing as to which humours, and how much of 'em, needed to
be removed. After going for a whole night and a day without
sleep, a sort of competition had arisen among them as to
who advocated the most heroic measures. When the King—
after a valorous struggle—finally lost his senses, and could
no longer keep 'em at bay, they fell on him like hounds. The
Doctor who had been insisting that the King suffered from
an excess of blood, had his lancet buried in the King's left
jugular before the others had even unpacked their bags. A
prodigious quantity of blood spewed forth—"

"I believe I saw it."

"Stay, I'm only beginning. The Doctor who had diagnosed an excess of *bile,* now pointed out that said imbalance
had only been worsened by the loss of so much *blood,* and
so he and a pair of bulky assistants sat the King up in bed,
hauled his mouth open, and began tickling his gorge with diverse feathers, scraps of whalebone, *et cetera.* Vomiting en-
sued. Now, a third Doctor, who had been insisting, most
tiresomely, that all the King's problems were owed to an ac-
cumulation of *colonic* humours, rolled his Majesty over and
shoved a prodigious long-necked calabash up the Royal
Anus. In went a mysterious, very expensive fluid—out
came—"

"Yes."

"Now a fourth Doctor set to work cupping him all over to
draw out other poisons through the skin—hence those gar-
gantuan hickeys, ringed by circular burns. The *first* doctor
was now in a panic, seeing that the adjustments made by the
other three had led to an excess of blood—it being all *relative,* you know. So he opened the *other* jugular, promising to
let out just a little. But he let out quite a bit. The other doctors became indignant now, and demanded the right to repeat
all of *their* treatments. But here's where I stepped in, and,
exercising—some would say, abusing—my full authority as

Secretary of the Royal Society, recommended a purging of *Doctors* rather than *humours* and kicked them out of the bedchamber. Threats were made against my reputation and my life, but I ejected them anon."

"But I heard news, as I came into London, that he was on the mend."

"After the Sons of Asclepius were finished with him, he did not really move for a full twenty-four hours. Some might've construed this as sleeping. He lacked the strength to pitch a fit—some might call it recovery. Occasionally I'd hold an ice-cold mirror in front of his lips and the reflection of the King's face would haze. In the middle of the day to-day, he began to stir and groan."

"His Majesty can scarcely be blamed for *that*!" Roger said indignantly.

"Nevertheless, more physicians got to him, and diagnosed a fever. They gave him a royal dose of the Elixir Proprietalis LeFebure."

"Now that must've improved the King's mood *to no end*!"

"We can only speculate. He has gotten worse. The sorts of Doctors who prescribe powders and elixirs have, consequently, fallen from favor, and the bleeders and purgers are upon us!"

"Then I'll add my weight as President, to yours as Secretary, of the Royal Society, and we'll see how long we can keep the lancets in their sheathes."

"Interesting point you raise there, Roger. . . ."

"Oh, Daniel, you have got that Waterhousian brooding look about you now, and so I fear you do not mean a *literal* point, as in *lancets*—"

"I was thinking—"

"Help!" Roger cried, waving his arms. But the watermen on yonder dock had all turned their backs on the Privy Stairs to watch the approach of the boat carrying those chirurgeons.

"D'you recall when Enoch Root made phosphorus from

horse urine? And the Earl of Upnor made a fool of himself supposing that it must have come from *royal* piss?"

"I'm *terrified* that you're about to say something *banal,* Daniel, about how the King's blood, bile, *et cetera* are no different from *yours.* So is it all right with you if I just *stipulate* that Republicanism makes *perfect sense,* seems to work well in Holland, and thereby *exempt* myself from this part of the conversation?"

"That is not precisely where I was going," Daniel demurred. "I was thinking about how easily your cousin was replaced with Anglesey—how disappointingly little difference it made."

"Before you corner yourself, Daniel, and force me to drag you out *as usual,* I would discourage any further usage of this similitude."

"Which similitude?"

"You are about to say that Charles is like Comstock and James is like Anglesey and that it will make no difference, in the end, which one is king. Which would be a dangerous thing for you to say—because the House where Comstock and Anglesey lived has been *razed* and *paved over.*" Roger jerked his head upwards towards Whitehall. "Which is not a fate we would wish on *yonder* house."

"But that is not what I was saying!"

"What were you saying, then? Something *not* obvious?"

"As Anglesey replaced Comstock, and Sterling replaced Raleigh, I replaced Bolstrood, in a way . . ."

"Yes, Dr. Waterhouse, we live in an orderly society and men replace each other."

"*Sometimes.* But some *can't* be replaced."

"I don't know that I agree."

"Suppose that, God forbid, Newton died. Who would replace him?"

"Hooke, or maybe Leibniz."

"But Hooke and Leibniz are *different.* I put it to you that some men really have unique qualities and cannot be replaced."

"Newtons come along so rarely. He is an exception to any rule you might care to name—really a very cheap rhetorical tactic on your part, Daniel. Have you considered running for Parliament?"

"Then I should have used a different example, for the point I'm wanting to make is that all round us, in markets and smithys, in Parliament, in the City, in churches and coalmines, there are persons whose departure really *would* change things."

"Why? What makes these persons different?"

"It is a very profound question. Recently Leibniz has been refining his system of metaphysics—"

"Wake me up when you are finished."

"When I first saw him at Lion Quay these many years ago, he was showing off his knowledge of London, though he'd never been here before. He'd been studying views of the city drawn by diverse artists from differing points of view. He went off on a rant about how the city itself has one form but it is perceived in different ways by each person in it, depending on their unique situation."

"Every *sophomore* thinks this."

"That was more than a dozen years ago. In his *latest* letter to me he seems to be leaning towards the view that the city does *not* have one absolute form *at all* . . ."

"Obvious nonsense."

". . . that the city is, in some sense, the result of the sum total of the perceptions of it by all of its constituents."

"I knew we never should have let him into the Royal Society!"

"I am not explaining it very well," Daniel admitted, "because I do not quite understand it, yet."

"Then why are you belaboring me with it *now* of all times?"

"The salient point has to do with perceptions, and how different parts of the world—different souls—perceive all of the other parts—the other souls. Some souls have perceptions that are confused and indistinct, as if they are peering through poorly ground lenses. Whereas others are like Hooke peering through his Microscope or Newton through his Reflecting Telescope. They have superior perceptions."

"Because they have better opticks!"

"No, even without lenses and parabolic mirrors, Newton and Hooke see things that you and I don't. Leibniz is proposing a strange inversion of what we normally mean when we describe a man as distinguished, or unique. Normally when we say these things, we mean that the man himself stands out from a crowd in some way. But Leibniz is saying that such a man's uniqueness is rooted in his ability to perceive *the rest of the universe* with unusual clarity—to distinguish one thing from another more effectively than ordinary souls."

Roger sighed. "All I know is that Dr. Leibniz has been saying some very rude things about Descartes lately—"

"Yes, in his *Brevis Demonstratio Erroris Memorabilis Cartesii et Aliorum Circa Legem Naturalem—*"

"And the French are up in arms."

"You said, Roger, that you would add your weight as President, to mine as Secretary, of the Royal Society."

"And I shall."

"But you flatter me by saying so. Some men *are* interchangeable, yes. Those two chirurgeons could be replaced with any other two, and the King would still die this evening. But could I—could *anyone*—fill *your* shoes so easily, Roger?"

"Why, Daniel, I do believe this is the first time in your life you've actually exhibited something akin to *respect* for me!"

"You are a man of parts, Roger."

"I am touched and of course I agree with the point you were trying to make—whatever the hell it might have been."

"Good—I am pleased to hear you agree with me in believing that James is no replacement for Charles."

Before Roger could recover—but after he mastered his anger—the boat was in earshot and the conversation, therefore, over.

"Long live the King, m'Lord, and *Doctor* Waterhouse,"

said one Dr. Hammond, clambering over the boat's gunwale onto the Privy Stairs. Then they all had to say it.

Hammond was followed by Dr. Griffin, who *also* greeted them with "Long live the King!" which meant that they all had to say it *again*.

Daniel must have said it with a noticeable lack of enthusiasm, for Dr. Hammond gave him a sharp look—then turned toward Dr. Griffin as if trolling for eyewitnesses. "It is very good that you have come in time, m'Lord," said Hammond to Roger Comstock, "as, between Jesuits on the one hand, and Puritans on t'other" (squirting long jets of glowing vitriol out of the pupils of his eyes, here, at Daniel), "some would say the King has had enough of bad advice."

Now Roger tended to say things after long pauses. When he'd been a clownish sizar at Trinity, this had made him seem not very intelligent; but now that he was a Marquis, and President of the Royal Society, it made him seem exceedingly sober and grave. So after they'd all climbed up the steps to the balcony that led into the part of Whitehall called the King's Apartments, he said: "A King's *mind* should never want for the counsel of learned *or* pious men, just as his *body* should never want for a bountiful supply of the diverse *humours* that sustain life and health."

Waving an arm at the shambling Palace above them, Dr. Hammond said to Roger, "This place is such a bazaar of rumor and intrigue, that your presence, m'Lord, will go far towards quelling any *whisperings* should the worst happen which Almighty God forbid." Favoring Daniel with another fearsome over-the-shoulder glare, as he followed the Marquis of Ravenscar into the King's Apartments.

"It sounds as if *some* have already gone far beyond *whispering,*" Daniel said.

"I'm certain that Dr. Hammond is solely concerned with preserving *your* reputation, Dr. Waterhouse," Roger said.

"What—it's been nigh on twenty years since His Majesty blew up my father—do people suppose I am still nursing a grudge?"

"That's not it, Daniel—"

"On the contrary! Father's departure from this plane was so brisk, so hot—leaving behind no physical remains—that it has been a sort of balm to my spirit to sit up with the King, night after night, imbrued in the royal gore, breathing it into my lungs, sopping it up with my flesh, and many other enjoyments besides, that I missed out on when my Father ascended . . ."

The Marquis of Ravenscar and the two other Doctors had slowed almost to a standstill and were now exchanging deeply significant looks. "Yes," Roger finally said, after another grand pause, "too much sitting up, in such a fœtid atmosphere, is not healthful for one's body, mind, or spirit . . . perhaps an evening's rest is in order, Daniel, so that when these two good Doctors have restored the King to health, you'll be ready to offer his Majesty your congratulations, as well as to re-affirm the profound loyalty you harbor, and have always harbored, in your breast, notwithstanding those events of two decades hence, which some would say have already been alluded to more than enough . . ."

He did not finish this sentence for a quarter of an hour. Before putting it to a merciful death, he'd managed to work in several enconiums for both Drs. Hammond and Griffin, likening one to Asclepius and the other to Hippocrates, while not failing to make any number of cautiously favorable remarks about every other Doctor who had come within a hundred yards of the King during the last month. He also (as Daniel noted, with a kind of admiration) was able to make it clear, to all present, just what a morbid catastrophe it would be if the King died and turned England over into the hands of that mad Papist the Duke of York whilst, practically in the same phrases—with the same *words*—asserting that York was really such a splendid fellow that it was almost imperative that all of them rush straight-away to the King's Bedchamber and smother Charles II under a mattress. In a sort of recursive fugue of dependent clauses he was, similarly, able to proclaim Drake Waterhouse to've been the finest Englishman who'd ever boiled beef whilst affirming that blowing him up with a ton of gunpowder had been an absolute touchstone of (depending on how you looked at it) monarchical genius that made Charles II such a colossal figure, (or) rampant despotism that augured so favorably for his brother's reign.

All of this as Daniel and the physicians trailed behind Roger through the leads, halls, galleries, antechambers, and chapels of Whitehall, rupturing stuck doors with shoulder-thrusts and beating back tons of dusty hangings. The Palace must have been but a single building at some point, but no one knew which bit had been put up first; anyway, other buildings had been scabbed onto that first one as fast as stones and mortar could be ferried in, and galleries strung like clothes-lines between wings of it that were deemed too far apart; this created courtyards that were, in time, subdivided, and encroached upon by new additions, and filled in. Then the builders had turned their ingenuity to bricking up old openings, and chipping out new ones, then bricking up the new ones and re-opening the old, or making newer ones yet. In any event, every closet, hall, and room was claimed by one nest or sect of courtiers, just as every snatch of Germany had its own Baron. Their journey from the Privy Stairs to the King's Bedchamber would, therefore, have been fraught with difficult border-crossings and protocol disputes if they'd made it in silence. But as the Marquis of Ravenscar was leading them surely through the maze, he went on, and on, with his Oration, a feat akin to threading needles while galloping on horseback through a wine cellar. Daniel lost track of the number of claques and cabals they burst in on, greeted, and left behind; but he did notice a lot of Catholics about, and more than a few Jesuits. Their route took them in a sort of jagged arc circumventing the Queen's Apartments, which had been turned into a sort of Portuguese nunnery quite a long time ago, furnished with prayer-books and ghastly devotional objects; yet it buzzed with its own conspiracies. Whenever they spied a door ajar, they heard brisk steps approaching it from the opposite side and saw it slammed and locked in their faces. They passed by the King's little chapel, which had been turned into a base-camp for this Catholic invasion, which didn't really surprise Daniel but would have ignited riots over nine-tenths of England had it been widely known.

Finally they arrived at the door to the King's Bedchamber, and Roger startled them all by finishing his sentence. He somehow contrived to separate Daniel from the physicians, and spoke briefly to the latter before showing them in to see the patient.

"What'd you tell them?" Daniel asked, when the Marquis came back.

"That if they unsheathed their lancets, I'd have their testicles for tennis-balls," Roger said. "I have an errand for you, Daniel: go to the Duke of York and report on his brother's condition."

Daniel took a breath, and held it. He could scarcely believe, all of a sudden, how tired he was. "I could say something obvious here, such as that *anyone* could do that, and *most* would do it better than *I,* and then you'd answer with something that'd make me feel a bit dim, such as—"

"In our concern for the *previous* king we must not forget to maintain good relations with the *next*."

" 'We' meaning—in this case—?"

"Why, the Royal Society!" said Roger, miffed to have been asked.

"Righto. What shall I tell him?"

"That London's finest physicians have arrived—so it shouldn't be much longer."

HE MIGHT HAVE SHIELDED HIMSELF from the cold and the wind by walking up the length of the Privy Gallery, but he'd had quite enough of Whitehall, so instead he went outside, crossed a couple of courts, and emerged at the front of the Banqueting House, directly beneath where Charles I had had his head lopped off, lo these many years ago. Cromwell's men had kept him prisoner in St. James's and then walked him across the Park for his decapitation. Four-year-old Daniel, sitting on Drake's shoulders in the plaza, had watched every one of the King's steps.

This evening, thirty-nine-year-old Daniel would be retracing that King's final walk—except backwards.

Now, Drake, twenty years ago, would have been the first to admit that most of Cromwell's work had been rolled back by the Restoration. But at least Charles II was a Protestant— or had the decency to pretend to be one. So Daniel oughtn't to make too much of an omen out of this walk—God forbid he should start thinking like Isaac, and find occult symbols in every little thing. But he couldn't help imagining that time was being rolled back even farther now, even past the reign of Elizabeth, all the way back to the days of Bloody Mary. In those days John Waterhouse, Drake's grandfather, had fled over the sea to Geneva, which was a hornets' nest of Calvinists. Only after Elizabeth was on the throne had he returned, accompanied by his son Calvin—Drake's father—and many other English and Scottish men who thought the way he did about religion.

In any event, now here was Daniel crossing the old Tilt Yard and descending the stairs into St. James's Park, going to fetch the man who had all the earmarks of the next Bloody Mary. James, the Duke of York, had lived at Whitehall Palace with the King and Queen until the tendency of Englishmen to riot and burn large objects in the streets at the least mention of his name had given the King the idea to pack him off to places like Brussels and Edinburgh. Since then he'd been a political comet, spending almost all of his time patrolling the liminal dusk, occasionally swooping back to London and scaring the hell out of everyone until the blaze of bonfires and burning Catholic churches drove him off into the darkness. After the King had finally lost patience, suspended Parliament, kicked out all the Bolstroods, and thrown the remaining Dissenters into jail, James had been suffered to come back and settle his household—but at St. James's Palace.

From Whitehall it was five minutes' walk across several gardens, parks, and malls. Most of the big old trees had been uprooted by the Devil's Wind that had swept over England on the day Cromwell had died. As a lad wandering up and down Pall Mall handing out libels, Daniel had watched new saplings being planted. He was dismayed, now, to see how large some of them had grown.

In spring and summer, royals and courtiers wore ruts in the paths that wound between these trees, going out for strolls that had become ritualized into processions. Now the terrain was empty, an unreadable clutter of brown and gray: a crust of frozen mud floating on a deep miasma of bog and horse-manure. Daniel's boots kept breaking through and plunging him into the muck. He learned to avoid stepping near the crescent-shaped indentations that had been made a few hours ago by the hooves of John Churchill's regiment of Guards drilling and parading on this ground, galloping hither and yon and cutting the heads off of straw men with sabers. Those straw men had not been dressed up as Whigs and Dissenters, but even so the message had been clear enough, for Daniel and for the crowds of Londoners gathered along the limit of Charing Cross burning bonfires for their King.

One Nahum Tate had recently translated into English a hundred-and-fifty-year-old poem by the Veronese astronomer Hieronymus Fracastorius, entitled (in the original) *Syphilis, Sive Morbvs Gallicvs* or (as Tate had it) *"Syphilis: or, a poetical history of the French Disease."* Either way, the poem told the tale of a shepherd named Syphilus who (like all shepherds in old myths) suffered a miserable and perfectly undeserved fate: he was the first person to be struck down by the disease that now bore his name. Inquiring minds might wonder why Mr. Tate had troubled himself to translate, at this moment, a poem about a poxy shepherd that had languished in Latin for a century and a half without any Englishman's feeling its lack: a poem about a disease, by an astronomer! Certain Londoners of a cynical turn of mind believed that the answer to this riddle might be found in certain uncanny similarities between the eponymous shepherd and James, the Duke of York. Viz. that all of said Duke's lovers, mistresses, and wives ended up with the said pestilence; that his first wife, Anne Hyde, had apparently died of it; that Anne Hyde's daughers, Mary and Anne, both had difficulties with their eyes, and with their wombs; that the Duke had obvious sores on his face and that he was either unbelievably stupid or out of his fucking mind.

Now (as Daniel the Natural Philosopher understood only too well) people had a habit of over-burdening explanations, and to do so was a bad habit—a kind of superstition. And yet the parallels between Syphilus the Shepherd and James the Heir to the English Throne were hard to ignore—and as if that weren't enough, Sir Roger L'Estrange had recently been leaning on Nahum Tate, asking him to perhaps find some *other* mildewy old Latin poems to translate. And everyone *knew* that L'Estrange was doing so, and understood why.

James was Catholic, and wanted to be a Saint, and that all fit together because he had been born in the Palace *of St. James's* some fifty-two years ago. It had always been his true home. In his tender years he'd been taught princely rudiments in this yard: fencing and French. He had been spirited up to Oxford during the Civil War, and more or less raised himself from that point on. Occasionally Dad would swing by and swoop him up and take him off to some battle-front to get creamed by Oliver Cromwell.

James had spent quite a bit of time hanging about with his cousins, the offspring of his aunt Elizabeth (the Winter Queen), a fecund but hapless alternate branch of the family. When the Civil War had been lost, he'd gone back to St. James's and lived there as a pampered hostage, wandering about this park and mounting the occasional boyish escape attempt, complete with encyphered letters spirited out to loyal confederates. One of those letters had been intercepted, and John Wilkins had been called in to decypher it, and Parliament had threatened to send James off to live in the decidedly less hospitable Tower. Eventually he'd slipped out across this park, disguised himself as a girl, and fled down the river and across the sea to Holland. Therefore he'd been out of the country when his father had been marched across this park to have his head lopped off. As the English Civil War had slowly ground to a halt, James had grown into a man, bouncing around between Holland, the Island of Jersey, and St. Germain (a royal suburb of Paris) and busying himself with the princely pastimes of riding, shooting, and screwing high-born Frenchwomen. But as Cromwell had continued to crush the Royalists at every turn, not only in England but Ireland and France as well, James had finally run out of money and become a soldier—a rather good one—under Marshal Turenne, the incomparable French general.

As HE TRUDGED ALONG Daniel occasionally swiveled his head to gaze north across Pall Mall. The view was different every time, as per the observations of Dr. Leibniz. But when the parallax of the streets was just right, he could see between the bonfires built there by nervous Protestants, up the lengths of the streets-named-after-royal-bastards, and all the way up to the squares where Roger Comstock and Sterling Waterhouse were putting up new houses and shops. Some of the larger ones were being made with great blocks of stone taken from the rubble of John Comstock's house—blocks that Comstock, in turn, had salvaged from the collapsed south transept of Old St. Paul's. Lights were burning in windows up there, and smoke drifting from chimneys. Mostly it was the mineral smoke of coal, but on the north wind Daniel caught the occasional whiff of roasting meat. Crunching and squelching across this wasted park, stepping over stuffed heads that had been lopped from straw men a few hours before, had given Daniel his appetite back. He wanted to be up there with a tankard in one hand and a drumstick in the other—but here he was, doing the sort of thing that he did. Which was what, exactly?

St. James's Palace was getting close, and he really ought to have an answer before he got there.

AT SOME POINT CROMWELL HAD, improbably, formed an alliance with the French, and then young James had had to go north to an impoverished, lonely, boring existence in the Spanish Netherlands. In the final years before the Restoration he'd knocked about Flanders with a motley army of exiled Irish, Scottish, and English regiments, picking fights with Cromwell's forces around Dunkirk. After the Restoration he'd come into his hereditary title of Lord High Admiral, and taken part in some rousing and bloody naval engagements against the Dutch.

However: the tendency of his siblings to die young, and the failure of his brother Charles to produce a legitimate heir, had made James the only hope for continuance of his mother's bloodline. While Mother had been living a good life in France, her sister-in-law, the Winter Queen, had been kicked around Europe like a stuffed pig's bladder at a county fair. Yet Elizabeth had pumped out babies with inhuman efficiency and Europe was bestrewn with her offspring. Many had come to naught, but her daughter Sophie seemed to have bred true, and was carrying on the tradition with seven surviving children. So, in the royal propagation sweepstakes, Henrietta Maria of France, the mother of James and Charles, seemed to be losing, in the long run, to the miserable Winter Queen. James was her only hope. And consequently, during James's various adventures she had used all of her wiles and connexions to keep him out of danger—leaving James with a simmering feeling of never having destroyed as many armies or sunk as many fleets as he *could* have.

Stymied, he'd spent much of the time since about 1670 doing—what, exactly? Mining Africa for gold, and, when that failed, Negroes. Trying to persuade English noblemen to convert to Catholicism. Sojourning in Brussels, and then in Edinburgh, where he had made himself useful by riding out to wild parts of Scotland to suppress feral Presbyterians in their rustic conventicles. Really he had been wasting his time, just waiting.

Just like Daniel.

A dozen years had flown by, dragging him along like a rider with one foot caught in the stirrup.

What did it mean? That he had best take matters in hand and get his life in order. Find something to do with his allotted years. He had been too much like Drake, waiting for some Apocalypse that would never come.

The prospect of James on the throne, working hand-in-glove with Louis XIV, was just sickening. This was an emergency, every bit as pressing as when London had burnt.

The realizations just kept coming—or rather they'd all appeared in his mind at once, like Athena jumping out of his skull in full armor, and he was merely trying to sort them out.

Emergencies called for stern, even desperate measures, such as blowing up houses with kegs of gunpowder (as King Charles II had personally done) or flooding half of Holland to keep the French out (as William of Orange had done). Or—dare he think it—overthrowing Kings and chopping their heads off as Drake had helped to. Men such as Charles and William and Drake seemed to take such measures without hesitation, while Daniel was either (a) a miserably pusillanimous wretch or (b) wisely biding his time.

Maybe this was why God and Drake had brought him into this world: to play some pivotal role in this, the final struggle between the Whore of Babylon, a.k.a. the Roman Catholic Church, and Free Trade, Freedom of Conscience, Limited Government, and diverse other good Anglo-Saxon virtues, which was going to commence in about ten minutes.

Romanists now swarming at Court with greater
confidence than had ever been seen since the
Reformation.

— *John Evelyn's Diary*

ALL OF THESE THOUGHTS terrified him so profoundly as to
nearly bring him to his knees before the entrance of St.
James's Palace. This wouldn't have been as embarrassing as
it sounded; the courtiers circulating in and out of the doors,
and the Grenadier Guards washing their hands in the blue,
wind-whipped flames of torchières, probably would have
pegged him as another mad Puritan taken in a Pentecostal
fit. However, Daniel remained on his feet and slogged up
stairs and into the Palace. He made muddy footprints on the
polished stone: making a mess of things as he went and leaving abundant evidence, which seemed a poor beginning for a
conspirator.

St. James's was roomier than the suite in Whitehall where
James had formerly dwelt, and (as Daniel only now apprehended) this had given him the space and privacy to gather
his own personal Court, which could simply be marched
across the Park and swapped for Charles's at the drop of a
crown. They'd seemed a queer swarm of religious cultists
and second-raters. Daniel now cursed himself for not having
paid closer attention to them. *Some* of them were players
who'd end up performing the same roles and prattling the
same dialogue as the ones they were about to replace, but (if
Daniel's ruminations on the Privy Stairs were not completely baseless) *others* had unique perceptions. It would be
wise for Daniel to identify these.

As he worked his way into the Palace he began to see
fewer Grenadier Guards and more shapely green ankles scis-
soring back and forth beneath flouncing skirts. James had
five principal mistresses, including a Countess and a
Duchess, and seven secondary mistresses, typically Merry
Widows of Important Dead Men. Most of them were Maids

of Honour, i.e., members of the ducal household, therefore
entitled to loiter around St. James's all they wanted. Daniel,
who made a sporting effort to keep track of these things, and
who could easily list the King's mistresses from memory,
had entirely lost track of the Duke's. But it was known empirically that the Duke would pursue any young woman who
wore green stockings, which made it much easier to sort
things out around St. James's, just by staring at ankles.

From the mistresses he could learn nothing, at least, until
he learned their names and gave them further study. What of
the courtiers? Some could be described exhaustively by saying "courtier" or "senseless fop," but others had to be known
and understood in the full variety of their perceptions.
Daniel recoiled from the sight of a fellow who, if he had not
been clad in the raiments of a French nobleman, might have
been taken for a shake-rag. His head seemed to have been
made in some ghastly Royal Society experiment by taking
two different men's heads and dividing them along the cen-
terline and grafting the mismatched halves together. He
jerked frequently to one side as if the head-halves were
fighting a dispute over what they should be looking at. From
time to time the argument would reach some impasse and
he'd stand frozen and mute for a few seconds, mouth open
and tongue exploring the room. Then he'd blink and resume
speaking again, rambling in accented English to a younger
officer—John Churchill.

The better half of this strange Frenchman's head looked
to be between forty and fifty years of age. He was Louis de
Duras, a nephew of Marshal Turenne but a naturalized Englishman. He had, by marrying the right Englishwoman and
raising a lot of revenue for Charles, acquired the titles Baron
Throwley, Viscount Sondes, and the Earl of Feversham.
Feversham (as he was generally called) was Lord of the
Bedchamber to King Charles II, which meant that he really
ought to have been over in Whitehall just now. His failure to
be there might be seen as proof that he was grossly incompetent. But he was also a Commander of Horse Guards. This

gave him an excuse for being here, since James, as a highly unpopular but healthy king-to-be, needed a lot more guarding than Charles, a generally popular king at death's door.

Around a corner and into another hall, this one so chilly that steam was coming from people's mouths as they talked. Daniel caught sight of Pepys and veered towards him. But then a wind-gust, leaking through an ill-fitting window-frame, blew a cloud of vapor away from the face of the man Pepys was talking to. It was Jeffreys. His beautiful eyes, now trapped in a bloated and ruddy face, fixed upon Daniel, who felt for a moment like a small mammal paralyzed by a serpent's hypnotic glare. But Daniel had the good sense to look the other way and duck through an opportune doorway into a gallery that connected several of the Duke's private chambers.

Mary Beatrice d'Este, a.k.a. Mary of Modena—James's second wife—would be sequestered back in these depths somewhere, presumably half out of her mind with misery. Daniel tried not to think of what it would be like for her: an Italian princess raised midway between Florence, Venice, and Genoa, and now stuck *here, forever,* surrounded by the mistresses of her syphilitic husband, surrounded in turn by Protestants, surrounded in turn by cold water, her only purpose in life to generate a male child so that a Catholic could succeed to the throne, but her womb barren so far.

Looking quite a bit more cheerful than that was Catherine Sedley, Countess of Dorchester, who'd been rich to begin with and had now secured her pension by producing two of James's innumerable bastard sons. She was not an attractive woman, she was not Catholic, and she hadn't even bothered to pull on green stockings—yet she had some mysterious unspecified hold over James exceeding that of any of his other mistresses. She was strolling down the gallery *tête-à-tête* with a Jesuit: Father Petre, who among other duties was responsible for bringing up all of James's bastards to be good Catholics. Daniel caught a moment of genuine amusement on Miss Sedley's face and guessed that the Jesuit was

relating some story about her boys' antics. In this windowless gallery, lit feebly by some candles, Daniel could not
have been more than a dim apparition to them—a pale face
and a lot of dark clothing—a Puritan Will-o'-the-wisp, the
sort of bad memory that forever haunted the jumpy Royals
who'd survived the Civil War. The affectionate smiles were
replaced by alert looks in his direction: was this an invited
guest, or a Phanatique, a *hashishin*? Daniel was grotesquely
out of place. But his years at Trinity had made him accustomed to it. He bowed to the Countess of Dorchester and exchanged some sort of acrid greeting with Father Petre.
These people did not like him, did not want him here, would
never be friendly to him in any sense that counted. And yet
there was a symmetry here that unnerved him. He'd seen
wary curiosity on their faces, then recognition, and now polite masks had fallen over their covert thoughts as they wondered why he was here, and tried to fit Daniel Waterhouse
into some larger picture.

But if Daniel had held a mirror up to his own face he'd
have seen just the same evolution.

He was one of them. Not as powerful, not as highly
ranked—in fact, completely unranked—but he was *here,
now,* and for these people that was the only sort of rank that
amounted to anything. To be here, to smell the place, to bow
to the mistresses, was a sort of initiation. Drake would have
said that merely to set foot in such people's houses and show
them common courtesy was to be complicit in their whole
system of power. Daniel and most others had scoffed at such
rantings. But now he knew it was true, for when the Countess had acknowledged his presence and known his name,
Daniel had felt important. Drake—if he'd had a grave—
would have rolled over in it. But Drake's grave was the air
above London.

An ancient ceiling beam popped as the Palace was hit by
another gust.

The Countess was favoring Daniel with a knowing smile.
Daniel had had a mistress, and Miss Sedley knew it: the in-

comparable Tess Charter, who had died of smallpox five
years ago. Now he *didn't* have a mistress, and Catherine
Sedley probably knew *that,* too.

He had slowed almost to a stop. Steps rushed toward him
from behind and he cringed, expecting a hand on his
shoulder, but two courtiers, then two more—including
Pepys—divided around him as if he were a stone in a
stream, then converged on a large Gothic door whose wood
had turned as gray as the sky. Some protocol of knocking,
throat-clearing, and doorknob-rattling got underway. The
door was opened from inside, its hinges groaning like a
sick man.

St. James's was in better upkeep than Whitehall, but still
just a big old house. It was quite a bit shabbier than Com-
stock/Anglesey House. But that House had been brought
down. And what had brought it down had not been revolution, but the movings of markets. The Comstocks and An-
gleseys had been ruined, not by lead balls, but by golden
coins. The neighborhood that had been built upon the ruins
of their great House was now crowded with men whose
vaults were well-stocked with that kind of ammunition.

To mobilize those forces, all that was needed was some of
that kingly ability to decide, and to act.

He was being beckoned forward. Pepys stepped toward
him, holding out one hand as if to take Daniel's elbow. If
Daniel were a Duke, Pepys would be offering sage advice to
him right now.

"What should I say?" Daniel asked.

Pepys answered immediately, as if he'd been practicing
the answer for three weeks in front of a mirror. "Don't fret
so much over the fact that the Duke loathes and fears Puritans, Daniel. Think instead of those men that the Duke
loves: Generals and Popes."

"All right, Mr. Pepys, I am thinking of them . . . and it is
doing me no good."

"True, Roger may have sent you here as a sacrificial lamb,
and the Duke may see you as an assassin. If he does, then

any attempt you make to sweeten and dissemble will be taken the wrong way. Besides, you're no good at it."

"So . . . if my head's to be removed, I should go lay my head on the chopping-block like a man . . ."

"Belt out a hymn or two! Kiss Jack Ketch and forgive him in advance. Show these fops what you're made of."

"Do you *really* think Roger sent me here to . . ."

"Of course not, Daniel! I was being *jocular*."

"But there is a certain tradition of killing the messenger."

"Hard as it might be for you to believe, the Duke admires certain things about Puritans: their sobriety, their reserve, their flinty toughness. He saw Cromwell fight, Daniel! He saw Cromwell mow down a generation of Court fops. He has not forgotten it."

"What, you're suggesting I'm to emulate *Cromwell* now!?"

"Emulate *anything* but a courtier," said Samuel Pepys, now gripping Daniel's arm and practically shoving him through the doorway.

Daniel Waterhouse was now in the Presence of James, the Duke of York.

The Duke was wearing a blond wig. He had always been pale-skinned and doe-eyed, which had made him a bonny youth, but a somewhat misshapen and ghastly adult. A dim circle of courtiers ringed them, hemming into their expensive sleeves and shuffling their feet. The occasional spur jingled.

Daniel bowed. James seemed not to notice. They looked at each other for a few moments. Charles would already have made some witty remark by this point, broken the ice, let Daniel know where he stood, but James only looked at Daniel expectantly.

"How is my brother, Dr. Waterhouse?" James asked.

Daniel realized, from the way he asked it, that James had no idea just how sick his brother really was. James had a temper; everyone knew it; no one had the courage to tell him the truth.

"Your brother will be dead in an hour," Daniel announced.

Like a barrel's staves being drawn together in a cooper's shop, the ring of courtiers tensed and drew inwards.

"He has taken a turn for the worse, then!?" James exclaimed.

"He has been at death's door the whole time."

"Why was this never said plainly to me until this instant?"

The correct answer, most likely, was that it *had* been, and he simply hadn't gotten it; but no one could say this.

"I have no idea," Daniel answered.

ROGER COMSTOCK, SAMUEL PEPYS, and Daniel Waterhouse were in the antechamber at Whitehall.

"He said, 'I am surrounded by men who are afraid to speak truth to my face.' He said, 'I am not as complicated as my brother—not complicated enough to be a king.' He said, 'I need your help and I know it.'"

"He said all of that!?" Roger blurted.

"Of course not," Pepys scoffed, "but he *meant* it."

The antechamber had two doors. One led to London, and half of London seemed to be gathered on the other side of it. The other door led to the King's bedchamber, where, surrounding the bed of the dying monarch, were James, Duke of York; the Duchess of Portsmouth, who was Charles's primary mistress; Father Huddlestone, a Catholic priest; and Louis de Duras, the Earl of Feversham.

"What else did he say?" Roger demanded. "Or more to the point, what else did he *mean*?"

"He is dim and stiff, and so he needs someone clever and flexible. Apparently I have a reputation for being both."

"Splendid!" Roger exclaimed, showing a bit more merriment than was really appropriate in these circumstances. "You have Mr. Pepys to thank for it—the Duke trusts Mr. Pepys, and Mr. Pepys has been saying good things about you."

"Thank you, Mr. Pepys . . ."

"You're welcome, Dr. Waterhouse!"

". . . for telling the Duke that I have a cowardly willingness to bend my principles."

"As much as it offends me to tell such beastly lies about you, Daniel, I'm willing to do it, as a personal favor to a good friend," Pepys answered instantly.

Roger ignored this exchange, and said: "Did his royal highness ask you for any advice?"

"I told him, as we trudged across the park, that this is a Protestant country, and that he belongs to a religious minority. He was astounded."

"It must have come as a grievous shock to him."

"I suggested that he turn his syphilitic dementia into an asset—it shows off his humane side while providing an excuse for some of his behavior."

"You didn't really say that!"

"Dr. Waterhouse was just seeing if you were paying attention, m'Lord," Pepys explained.

"He told me he had syphilis twenty years ago at Epsom," Daniel said, "and the secret—it was a secret in those days—did not get out *immediately*. Perhaps this is why he trusts me."

Roger had no interest whatever in such old news. His eyes were trained to the opposite corner of the room, where Father Petre was shoulder-to-shoulder with Barrillon, the French Ambassador.

One of the doors opened. Beyond it, a dead man was lying in a stained bed. Father Huddlestone was making the sign of the cross, working his way through the closing stanzas of the rite of extreme unction. The Duchess of Portsmouth was weeping into a hanky and the Duke of York—no, the King of England—was praying into clasped hands.

The Earl of Feversham tottered out and steadied himself against the doorjamb. He looked neither happy nor sad, but vaguely lost. This man was now Commander in Chief of the Army. Paul Barrillon had a look on his face as if he were sucking on a chocolate truffle and didn't want anyone to know. Samuel Pepys, Roger Comstock, and Daniel Waterhouse shared an uneasy look.

"M'Lord? What news?" Pepys said.

"What? Oh! The King is dead," Feversham announced. His eyes closed and he leaned his head on his upraised arm for a moment, as if taking a brief nap.

"Long live . . ." Pepys prompted him.

Feversham awoke. "Long live the King!"

"Long live the King!" everyone said.

Father Huddlestone finished the rite and turned towards the door. Roger Comstock chose that moment to cross himself.

"Didn't know you were Catholic, m'lord," Daniel said.

"Shut up, Daniel! You know I'm a Freedom of Conscience man—have I ever troubled you about *your* religion?" said the Marquis of Ravenscar.

Versailles

SUMMER 1685

For the market is against our sex just now; and if a young woman has beauty, birth, breeding, wit, sense, manners, modesty, and all to an extreme, yet if she has not money she's nobody, she had as good want them all; nothing but money now recommends a woman; the men play the game all into their own hands.

— DANIEL DEFOE, *Moll Flanders*

To M. le comte d'Avaux
12 July 1685
Monseigneur,

As you see I have encyphered this letter according to your instructions, though only you know whether this is to protect it from the eyes of Dutch spies, or your rivals at Court. Yes, I have discovered that you have rivals.

On my journey I was waylaid and ill-used by some typically coarse, thick Dutchmen. Though you would never have guessed it from their looks and manners, these had something in common with the King of France's brother: namely, a fascination with women's undergarments. For they went through my baggage thoroughly, and left it a few pounds lighter.

Shame, shame on you, monseigneur, for placing

those letters among my things! For a while I was
afraid that I would be thrown into some horrid Dutch
work-house, and spend the rest of my days scrubbing
sidewalks and knitting hose. But from the questions
they asked me, it soon became obvious that they were
perfectly baffled by this French cypher of yours. To
test this, I replied that I could read those letters as well
as *they* could; and the dour looks on the faces of my
interrogators demonstrated that their incompetence
had been laid bare, and my innocence proved, in the
same moment.

I will forgive you, monseigneur, for putting me
through those anxious moments if you will forgive me
for believing, until quite recently, that you were utterly
mad to send me to Versailles. For how could a common girl such as I find a place in the most noble and
glorious palace in the world?

But now I know things and I understand.

There is a story making the rounds here, which you
must have heard. The heroine is a girl, scarcely better
than a slave—the daughter of a ruined petty noble
fallen to the condition of a Vagabond. Out of desperation this waif married a stunted and crippled writer in
Paris. But the writer had a *salon* that attracted certain
Persons of Quality who had grown bored with the insipid discourse of Court. His young wife made the acquaintance of a few of these noble visitors. After he
died, and left this girl a penniless widow, a certain
Duchess took pity on her, brought her out to Versailles, and made her a governess to some of her illegitimate children. This Duchess was none other than
the *maîtresse déclarée* to the King himself, and her
children were royal bastards. The story goes that King
Louis XIV, contrary to the long-established customs
of Christian royalty, considers his bastards to be only
one small step beneath the Dauphin and the other *Enfants de France*. Protocol dictates that the governess

of *les Enfants de France* must be a duchess; accordingly, the King made the governess of his bastards into a marquise. In the years since then, the King's *maîtresse déclarée* has gradually fallen from favor, as she has grown fat and histrionic, and it has been the case for some time that when the King went every day to call upon her at one o'clock in the afternoon, just after Mass, he would simply walk through her apartment without stopping, and go instead to visit this widow—the Marquise de Maintenon, as she was now called. Finally, Monseigneur, I have learned what is common knowledge at Versailles, namely that the King secretly married the Marquise de Maintenon recently and that she is the Queen of France in all but name.

It is plain to see that Louis keeps the powerful of France on a short leash here, and that they have nothing to do but gamble when the King is absent and ape his words and actions when he is present. Consequently every Duke, Count, and Marquis at Versailles is prowling through nurseries and grammar-schools, disrupting the noble children's upbringing in the hunt for nubile governesses. No doubt you knew this when you made arrangements for me to work as a governess to the children of M. le comte de Béziers. I cringe to think what awful debt this poor widower must have owed you for him to consent to such an arrangement! You might as well have deposited me in a bordello, Monseigneur, for all the young blades who prowl around the entrance of the count's apartment and pursue me through the gardens as I try to carry out my nominal duties—and not because of any native attractiveness I may possess but simply because it is what the King did.

Fortunately the King has not seen fit to grace me with a noble title yet or I should never be left alone long enough to write you letters. I have reminded some of these loiterers that Madame de Maintenon is a famously pious woman and that the King (who could have any woman in the world, and who ruts with disposable damsels two or three times a week) fell in love with her because of her intelligence. This keeps most of them at bay.

I hope that my story has provided you with a few moments' diversion from your tedious duties in the Hague, and that you will, in consequence, forgive me for not saying anything of substance.

> Your obedient servant,
> Eliza

P.S. M. le comte de Béziers' finances are in comic disarray—he spent fourteen percent of his income last year on wigs, and thirty-seven percent on interest, mostly on gambling debts. Is this typical? I will try to help him. Is this what you wanted me to do? Or did you want him to remain helpless? That is easier.

> My dark and cloudy words they do but hold
> The truth, as cabinets enclose the gold.
> —JOHN BUNYAN, *The Pilgrim's Progress*

To Gottfried Wilhelm Leibniz
4 August 1685
Dear Doctor Leibniz,

Difficulty at the beginning* is to be expected in any new venture, and my move to Versailles has been no exception. I thank God that I lived for several years in the *harim* of the Topkapi Palace in Constantinople, being trained to serve as a consort to the Sultan, for only this could have prepared me for Versailles. Unlike Ver-

---

* ☷ The name of Hexagram 3 of the *I Ching*, or 010001, that being the encryption key for the subliminal message embedded in the script of this letter.

sailles, the Sultan's palace grew according to no coherent plan, and from the outside looks like a jumble
of domes and minarets. But seen from the inside both
palaces are warrens of stuffy windowless rooms created by subdividing other rooms. This is a mouse's-
eye view, of course; just as I was never introduced to
the domed pavilion where the Grand Turk deflowers
his slave-girls, so I have not yet been allowed to enter
the Salon of Apollo and view the Sun King in his radiance. In both Palaces I have seen mostly the wretched
closets, garrets, and cellars where courtiers dwell.

Certain parts of this Palace, and most of the gardens, are open to anyone who is decently dressed. At
first this meant they were closed to me, for William's
men ripped up all of my clothes. But after I arrived,
and word of my adventures began to circulate, I received cast-offs from noblewomen who either sympa-
thized with my plight or needed to make room in their
tiny closets for next year's fashions. With some needle-
work I have been able to make these garments over
into ones that, while not quite fashionable, will at least
not expose me to ridicule as I lead the son and daughter of M. le comte de Béziers through the gardens.

To describe this place in words is hopeless. Indeed I
believe it was meant to be so, for then anyone who
wants to know it must come here in person, and that is
how the King wants it. Suffice it to say that here, every
dram of water, every leaf and petal, every square inch
of wall, floor, and ceiling bear the signature of Man;
all have been thought about by superior intellects,
nothing is accidental. The place is pregnant with Intention and wherever you look you see the gaze of the
architects—and by extension, Louis—staring back at
you. I am contrasting this to blocks of stone and
beams of wood that occur in Nature and, in most
places, are merely harvested and shaped a bit by arti-
sans. Nothing of that sort is to be found at Versailles.

At Topkapi there were magnificent carpets everywhere, Doctor, carpets such as no one in Christendom has ever seen, and all of them were fabricated thread by thread, knot by knot, by human hands. That is what Versailles is like. Buildings made of plain stone or wood are to this place what a sack of flour is to a diamond necklace. Fully to describe a routine event, such as a conversation or a meal, would require devoting fifty pages to a description of the room and its furnishings, another fifty to the clothing, jewelry, and wigs worn by the participants, another fifty to their family trees, yet another to explaining their current positions in the diverse intrigues of the Court, and finally a single page to setting down the words actually spoken.

Needless to say this will be impractical; yet I hope you will bear with me if I occasionally go on at some length with florid descriptions. I know, Doctor, that even if you have not seen Versailles and the costumes of its occupants, you have seen crude copies of them in German courts and can use your incomparable mind to imagine the things I see. So I will try to restrain myself from describing every little detail. And I know that you are making a study of family trees for Sophie, and have the resources in your library to investigate the genealogy of any petty nobleman I might mention. So I will try to show restraint there as well. I will try to explain the current state of Court intrigue, since you have no way of knowing about such things. For example, one evening two months ago, my master M. le comte de Béziers was given the honor of holding a candle during the King's going-to-bed ceremony, and consequently was invited to all the best parties for a fortnight. But lately his star has been in eclipse, and his life has been very quiet.

If you are reading this it means you detected the key from the I Ching. *It appears that French cryptography is not up to the same standard as French interior deco-*

ration; their diplomatic cypher has been broken by the Dutch, but as it was invented by a courtier highly thought of by the King, no one dares say anything against it. If what they say about Colbert is true, he never would have allowed such a situation to arise, but as you know he died two years ago and cyphers have not been upgraded since. I am writing in that broken cypher to d'Avaux in Holland on the assumption that everything I write will be decyphered and read by the Dutch. But as is probably obvious already, I write to you on the assumption that your cypher affords us a secure channel.

Since you employ the Wilkins cypher, which uses five plaintext letters to encrypt one letter of the actual message, I must write five words of drivel to encypher one word of pith, and so you may count on seeing lengthy descriptions of clothing, etiquette, and other tedious detail in future letters.

I hope I do not seem self-important by presuming that you may harbor some curiosity concerning *my* position at Court. Of course I am a nothing, invisible, not even an ink-speck in the margin of the Register of Ceremonies. But it has not escaped the notice of the nobles that Louis XIV chose most of his most important ministers (such as Colbert, who bought one of your digital computers!) from the middle class, and that he has (secretly) married a woman of low degree, and so it is fashionable in a way to be seen speaking to a commoner if she is clever or useful.

Of course hordes of young men want to have sex with me, but to relate details would be repetitious and in poor taste.

Because M. le comte de Béziers' bolt-hole in the south wing is so uncomfortable, and the weather has been so fine, I have spent several hours each day going on walks with my two charges, Beatrice and Louis, who have 9 and 6 years of age, respectively. Versailles has vast gardens and parks, most of which are deserted except when the King goes to hunt or promenade, and then they are crowded with courtiers. Until very recently they were also filled with common people who would come all the way from Paris to see the sights, but these pressed around the King so hotly, and made such a shambles of the statues and waterworks, that recently the King banned the *mobile* from all of his gardens.

As you know, it is the habit of all well-born ladies to cover their faces with masks whenever they venture out of doors, so that they will not be darkened by the sun. Many of the more refined men do likewise—the King's brother Philippe, who is generally addressed as Monsieur, wears such a mask, though he frets that it smears his makeup. On such warm days as we have had recently, this is so uncomfortable that the ladies of Versailles, and by extension their attendants, households, and gallants, prefer simply to remain indoors. I can wander for hours through the park with Beatrice and Louis in train and encounter only a few other people: mostly gardeners, occasionally lovers on their way to trysts in secluded woods or grottoes.

The gardens are shot through with long straight paths and avenues that, as one steps into certain intersections, provide sudden unexpected vistas of fountains, sculpture groups, or the château itself. I am teaching Beatrice and Louis geometry by having them draw maps of the place.

If these children are any clue as to the future of the nobility, then France as we know it is doomed.

Yesterday I was walking along the canal, which is a cross-shaped body of water to the west of the château; the long axis runs east–west and the crossbar north–south, and since it is a single body of water its surface is, of course, level, that being a known prop-

erty of water. I put a needle in one end of a cork and
weighted the other end (with a corkscrew, in case you
are wondering!) and set it afloat in the circular pool
where these canals intersect, hoping that the needle
would point vertically upwards—trying (as you have
no doubt already perceived) to acquaint Beatrice and
Louis with the idea of a third spatial dimension per-
pendicular to the other two. Alas, the cork did not float
upright. It drifted away and I had to lie flat on my
belly and reach out over the water to rake it in, and the
sleeves of my hand-me-down dress became soaked
with water. The whole time I was preoccupied with the
whining of the bored children, and with my own pas-
sions as well—for I must tell you that tears were running down my sunburned cheeks as I remembered the
many lessons I was taught, as a young girl in Algiers,
by Mummy and by the Ladies' Volunteer Sodality of
the Society of Britannic Abductees.

At some point I became aware of voices—a man's
and a woman's—and I knew that they had been conversing nearby for quite some time. With all of these
other concerns and distractions I had taken no note of
them. I lifted my head to gaze directly across the canal
at two figures on horseback: a tall magnificent well-
built man in a vast wig like a lion's mane, and a
woman, built something like a Turkish wrestler,
dressed in hunting clothes and carrying a riding crop.
The woman's face was exposed to the sun, and had
been for a long time, for she was tanned like a saddlebag. She and her companion had been talking about
something else, but when I looked up I somehow drew
the notice of the man; instantly he reached up and
doffed his hat to me, from across the canal! When he
did, the sun fell directly on his face and I recognized
him as King Louis XIV.

I simply could not imagine any way to recover from
this indignity, and so I pretended I had not seen him.

As the crow flies we were not far apart, but by land we were far away to reach me, the King and his Diana-like hunting-companion would have had to ride west for some distance along the bank of the canal; circum-navigate the large pool at that end; and then go the same distance eastwards along the opposite bank. So I convinced myself that they were far away and I pre-tended not to see them; God have mercy on me if I chose wrong. I tried to cover my embarrassment by ranting to the children about Descartes and Euclid.

The King put his hat back on and said, "Who is she?"

I closed my eyes and sighed in relief; the King had decided to play along, and act as if we had not seen each other. Finally I had coaxed the floating cork back into my hands. I drew myself up and sat on the brink of the canal with my skirts spread out around me, in profile to the King, and quietly lectured the children.

Meanwhile I was praying that the woman would not know my name. But as you will have guessed, Doctor, she was none other than his majesty's sister-in-law, Elisabeth Charlotte, known to Versailles as Madame, and known to Sophie—her beloved aunt—as Lisel-otte.

Why didn't you tell me that the Knight of the Rustling Leaves was a clitoriste? *I suppose this should come as no surprise given that her husband Philippe is a homosexual, but it caught me somewhat off guard. Does she have lovers? Hold, I presume too much; does she even know what she is?*

She gazed at me for a languid moment; at Ver-sailles, no one of importance speaks quickly and spontaneously, every utterance is planned like a move in a chess game. I knew what she was about to say: "I do not know her." I prayed for her to say it, for then the King would know that I was not a person, did not ex-ist, was no more worthy of his attention than a fleeting ripple in the surface of the canal. Then finally I heard Madame's voice across the water: "It looks like that girl who was duped by d'Avaux and molested by the Dutchmen, and showed up dishevelled and expecting sympathy."

It strikes me as unlikely that Liselotte could have recognized me in this way without another channel of information; did you write a letter to her, Doctor? It is never clear to me how much you are acting on your own and how much as a pawn—or perhaps I should say "knight" or "rook"—of Sophie.

These cruel words would have brought me to tears if I'd been one of those rustic countesses who flock to Versailles to be deflowered by men of rank. But I had already seen enough of this place to know that the only truly cruel words here are "She is nobody." And Madame had not said that. Consequently, the King had to look at me for a few moments longer.

Louis and Beatrice had noticed the King, and were frozen with a mixture of awe and terror—like statues of children.

Another one of those pauses had gone by. I heard the King saying, "That story was told in my presence." Then he said, "If d'Avaux would only put his letters into the bodice of some poxy old hag he could be assured of absolute secrecy, but what Dutchman would not want to break the seal on *that* envelope?"

"But, Sire," said Liselotte, "d'Avaux is a Frenchman—and what Frenchman *would*?"

"He is not as refined in his tastes as he would have you think," the King returned, "and *she* is not as coarse as *you* would have *me* think."

At this point little Louis stepped forward so suddenly that I was alarmed he would topple into the Canal and oblige me to swim; but he stopped on the brink, thrust out one leg, and bowed to the King just like a courtier. I pretended now to notice the King for the first time, and scrambled to my feet. Beatrice and I made curtseys across the canal. Once more the King acknowledged us by doffing his hat, perhaps with a certain humorous exaggeration.

"I see that look in your eye, *vôtre majesté*," said Liselotte.

"I see it in yours, Artemis."

"You have been listening to gossip. I tell you that these girls of low birth who come here to seduce noblemen are like mouse droppings in the pepper."

"Is *that* what she wants us to believe? How banal."

"The best disguises are the most banal, Sire."

This seemed to be the end of their strange conversation; they rode slowly away.

The King is said to be a great huntsman, but he was riding in an extremely stiff posture—I suspect he is suffering from hemorrhoids or possibly a bad back.

I took the children back straightaway and sat down to write you this letter. For a nothing like me, today's events are the pinnacle of honor and glory, and I wanted to memorialize them before any detail slipped from my memory.

To M. le comte d'Avaux
1 September 1685
Monseigneur,

I have as many visitors as ever (much to the annoyance of M. le comte de Béziers), but since I got a deep tan and took to wearing sackcloth and quoting from the Bible a lot, they are not as interested in romance. Now they come asking me about my Spanish uncle. "I am sorry that your Spanish uncle had to move to Amsterdam, mademoiselle," they say, "but it is rumored that hardship has made him a wise man." The first time some son of a marquis came up to me spouting such nonsense I told him he must have me mixed up with some other wench, and sent him packing! But the next one dropped your name and I understood that he had in some sense been dispatched by you—or, to be more precise, that his coming to me under the delusion of my having a wise Spanish uncle was a consequence or ramification of some chain of events that had been set in motion by you. On that assumption, I began to play along, quite cautiously, as I did not know what sort of game might be afoot. From the way this fellow talked I soon understood that he believes me to be a sort of crypto-Jew, the bastard offspring of a swarthy Spanish Kohan and a butter-haired Dutch-woman, which might actually seem plausible as the sun has bleached my hair and darkened my skin.

These conversations are all the same, and their particulars are too tedious to relate here. Obviously you have been spreading tales about me, Monseigneur, and half the petty nobles of Versailles now believe that I (or, at any rate, my fictitious uncle) can help them get out from under their gambling debts, pay for the remodeling of their châteaux, or buy them splendid new carriages. I can only roll my eyes at their avarice. But if the stories are to be believed, their fathers and grandfathers used what money they had to raise private armies and fortify their cities against the father and grandfather of the present King. I suppose it's better for the money to go to dressmakers, sculptors, painters, and *chefs de cuisine* than to mercenaries and musket-makers.

Of course it is true that their gold would fetch a higher rate of return wisely invested in Amsterdam than sitting in a strong-box under their beds. The only difficulty lies in the fact that I cannot manage such investments from a closet in Versailles while at the same time teaching two motherless children how to read and write. My Spanish uncle is a fiction of yours, presumably invented because you feared that these French nobles would never entrust their assets to a woman. This means that I must do the work personally, and this is impossible unless I have the freedom to travel to Amsterdam several times a year . . .

To Gottfried Wilhelm Leibniz
12 Sept. 1685

This morning I was summoned to the comparatively spacious and splendid apartments of a Lady in Waiting to the Dauphine, in the South Wing of the palace adjacent to the apartments of the Dauphine herself.

The lady in question is the duchesse d'Oyonnax. She has a younger sister who is the marquise d'Ozoir and who happens to be visiting Versailles with her daughter of nine years.

The girl seems bright but is half dead with asthma. The marquise ruptured something giving birth to her and cannot have any more children.

The d'Ozoirs are one of the rare exceptions to the general rule that all French nobles of any consequence must dwell at Versailles—but only because the Marquis has responsibilities at Dunkirk. In case you have not been properly maintaining your family trees of the European nobility, Doctor, I will remind you that the Marquis d'Ozoir is the bastard son of the duc d'Arcachon.

Who, when he was a stripling of fifteen, begat the future marquis off his grandmama's saucy maid-companion—the poor girl had been dragooned into teaching the young Duke his first love-lesson.

The duc d'Arcachon did not actually take a wife until he was twenty-five, and she did not produce a viable child (Étienne d'Arcachon) for three years after that. So the bastard was already a young man by the time his legitimate half-brother was born. He was shipped off to Surat as an aide to Boullaye and Beber, who tried to establish the French East India Company there around 1666.

But as you may know the French E.I.C. did not fare
quite as well as the English and Dutch have done.
Boullaye and Beber began to assemble a caravan in
Surat but had to depart before all preparations had
been made, because the city was in the process of
falling to the Mahratta rebels. They traveled into the
interior of Hindoostan, hoping to establish trade
agreements. As they approached the gates of a great
city, a delegation of banyans—the richest and most in-
fluential *commerçants* of that district—came out to
greet them, carrying small gifts in bowls, according to
the local custom. Boullaye and Beber mistook them
for beggars and thrashed them with their riding-whips
as any self-respecting upper-caste Frenchmen would
do when confronted by pan-handling Vagabonds on
the road.

The gates of the city were slammed in their faces.
The French delegation were left to wander through the
hinterland like out-castes. Quickly they were abandoned by the guides and porters they had hired at
Surat, and began to fall prey to highwaymen and
Mahratta rebels. Eventually they found their way to
Shahjahanabad, where they hoped to beg for succor
from the Great Mogul Aurangzeb, but they were informed he had retired to the Red Fort at Agra. They
traveled to Agra only to be told that the officials they
needed to prostrate themselves before, and to shower
with gifts, in order to gain access to the Great Mogul,
were stationed in Shahjahanabad. In this way they
were shuttled back and forth along one of Hindoostan's most dangerous roads until Boullaye had
been strangled by dacoits and Beber had succumbed to
disease (or perhaps it was the other way round) and
most of their expedition had fallen victim to more or
less exotic hazards.

The bastard son of the duc d'Arcachon survived all
of them, made his way out to Goa, talked his way

aboard a Portuguese ship bound for Mozambique, and pursued a haphazard course to the slave coast of Africa, where finally he spied a French frigate flying the coat of arms of the Arcachon family: fleurs-de-lis and Neeger-heads in iron collars. He persuaded some Africans to row him out to that ship in a long-boat and identified himself to her captain, who of course was aware that the duc's illegitimate son was lost, and had been ordered to keep an ear to the ground for any news. The young man was brought aboard the ship.

And the Africans who had brought him out were rewarded with baptisms, iron jewelry, and a free trip to Martinique to spend the rest of their lives working in the agricultural sector.

This led to a career running slaves to the French West Indies. During the course of the 1670s the young man amassed a modest fortune from this trade and purchased, or was rewarded by the King with, the title of Marquis. Immediately he settled in France and married. For several reasons he and his wife have not established themselves near Versailles. For one thing, he is a bastard whom the duc d'Arcachon prefers to keep at arm's length. For another, his daughter has asthma and needs to breathe sea-air. Finally, he has responsibilities along the sea-coast. You may know, Doctor, that the people of India believe in the perpetual re-incarnation of souls; likewise, the French East India Company might be thought of as a soul or spirit that goes bankrupt every few years but is always re-incarnated in some new form. Recently it has happened one more time. Naturally many of its operations are centered at Dunkirk, le Havre, and other sea-ports, and so that is where the Marquis and his family spend most of their time. But the Marquise comes to visit her sister the duchesse d'Oyonnax frequently, and brings the daughter with her.

As I mentioned, Oyonnax is a lady-in-waiting to the

Dauphine, which is looked on as an extremely desirable position. The Queen of France died two years ago, and had been estranged from the King for many years at the time of her death. The King has Mme. de Maintenon now, but she is not officially his wife. Therefore, the most important woman at Versailles *not really, but nominally, according to the rules of precedence* is the Dauphine, wife of the King's eldest son and heir apparent. Competition among the noble ladies of France for positions in her household is intense . . .

So intense that it has resulted in no fewer than four poisonings. I do not know if the sister of d'Ozoir poisoned anyone herself, but it is generally understood that she did allow her naked body to be used as a living altar during black masses held at an abandoned country church outside of Versailles. This was before the King became aware that his court was infested with homicidal Satanists, and instituted the chambre ardente *to investigate these doings. She was indeed among the 400-odd nobles arrested and interrogated, but nothing was ever proved against her.*

All of which is to say that Mme. la duchesse d'Oyonnax is a great lady indeed, who entertains her sister Mme. la marquise d'Ozoir in grand style.

When I entered her salon I was surprised to see my employer, M. le comte de Béziers, seated on a stool so low and tiny it seemed he was squatting on his haunches like a dog. And indeed he had hunched his shoulders and was gazing sidelong at the Marquise like an old peasant's cur anticipating the descent of the cudgel. The Duchess was in an armchair of solid silver and the Marquise was in a chair without arms, also in silver.

I remained standing. Introductions were made—here I elide all of the tedious formalities and small talk—and the Marquise explained to me that she had been looking for a tutor to educate her daughter. The girl already has a governess, mind you, but that woman is quite close to being illiterate and consequently the child's mental development has been retarded *or perhaps she is simply an imbecile*. Somehow she had settled on me as being the most likely candidate *this is the work of d'Avaux*.

I was *pretended to be* astonished, and went on at some length protesting the decision on grounds that I was not equal to such a responsibility. I wondered aloud who would look after poor little Beatrice and Louis. M. le comte de Béziers gave me the happy news that he'd found an opportunity in the south and would soon be leaving Versailles.

You may not know that one of the only ways for a French nobleman to make money without losing caste is by serving as an officer on a merchant ship. Béziers has taken such a position on a French E.I.C. vessel that will be sailing out of the Bassin d'Arcachon come spring, bound for the Cape of Good Hope; points east; and if I'm any judge of such matters, David Jones's Locker.

Although, if Mme. de Maintenon opens her school for poor girls of the French nobility at St. Cyr next year *her personal obsession—St. Cyr lies within sight of Versailles, to the southwest, just beyond the walls*, then Beatrice might be shipped there to be groomed for life at Court.

Under the circumstances I could hardly show the tiniest degree of reluctance, let alone decline this offer, and so I write you this letter from my new lodging in an attic room above the Duchess's apartments. Only God in Heaven knows what new adventures await me now! The Marquise hopes to remain at Versailles until the end of the month *the King will spend October at Fontainebleu as is his custom, and there is no point remaining at Versailles when he is not here* and then re-

pair to Dunkirk. I shall, of course, go with her. But I
will certainly write another letter to you before then.

To M. le comte d'Avaux
25 September 1685

It is two weeks since I entered the service of the
Marquis and the Marquise d'Ozoir, and another week
until we leave for Dunkirk, so this is the last letter I
will send from Versailles.

If I am reading your intentions correctly, I'll remain
in Dunkirk only as long as it takes to walk across the
gangplank of a Holland-bound ship. If that comes to
pass, any letters I send after today will reach Amsterdam after I do.

When I came down here some months ago, I
stopped over in Paris for a night and witnessed the following from my window: in the market-square before
that *pied-à-terre* where you were so kind as to let me
stay, some common people had erected a cantilever, a
beam projecting out into space, like the cranes used by
merchants to hoist bales up into their warehouses. On
the pavement beneath the end of this beam they kindled a bonfire. A rope was thrown over the end of the
beam.

These preparations had drawn a crowd and so it was
difficult for me to see what happened next; but from
the laughter of the crowd and the thrashing of the
rope, I inferred that some antic, hilarious struggle was
taking place on the street. A stray cat dashed away and
was half-heartedly pursued by a couple of boys. Finally the other end of the rope was drawn tight, hoist-
ing a great, lumpy sack into the air; it swung to and fro
high above the fire. I guessed it was full of some
sausages to be cooked or smoked.

Then I saw that something was moving inside the
sack.

The rope was let out and the writhing bag descended until its underside glowed red from the flames underneath. A horrible yowling came out of it and the bag began to thrash and jump. I understood now that it was filled with dozens of stray cats that had been caught in the streets of Paris and brought here to amuse the crowd. And believe me, Monseigneur, they were amused.

If I had been a man, I could have ridden out into that square on horseback and severed that rope with a sword-blow, sending those poor animals down to perish quickly in the roaring flames. Alas, I am not a man, I lack a mount and a sword, and even if I had all of these I might lack courage. In all my life I have only known one man brave or rash enough to do such a deed, but he lacked moral fiber and probably would have reveled in the spectacle along with all those others. All I could do was to close up the shutters and plug my ears; though as I did, I noticed that many windows around the square were open. Merchants and persons of quality were watching it, too, and even bringing their children out.

During the dismal years of the Fronde Rebellion, when the young Louis XIV was being hounded through the streets of Paris by rebellious princes and starving mobs, he must have witnessed one of these cat-burnings, for at Versailles he has created something similar: all the nobles who tormented him when he was a scared little mouse have been rounded up and thrown into this bag and suspended in the air; and the King holds the end of the rope. I am in the sack now, Monseigneur, but as I am only a kitten whose claws have not grown in, all I can do is remain as close as possible to much bigger and more dangerous cats.

Mme. la duchesse d'Oyonnax runs her household like a Ship of the Line: everything trim, all the time. I have not been out of doors since I entered the service of her sister. My tan has faded, and all of the patched-

together clothes in my wardrobe have been torn up for
rags and replaced with better. I will not call it finery,
for it would never do to outshine these two sisters in
their own apartment. But neither would it do to em-
barrass them. So I will venture to say that the Duchess
no longer cringes and grimaces when she catches
sight of me.

In consequence I am now catching the eyes of the
young blades again. If I still served M. le comte de
Béziers I would never get a moment's peace, but
Mme. la duchesse d'Oyonnax has claws—some would
say, poison-tipped ones—and fangs. So the lust of the
courtiers has been channelled into spreading the usual
rumors and speculations about me: that I am a slut,
that I am a prude, that I am a Sapphist, that I am an un-
tutored virgin, that I am a past mistress of exotic sexual practices. An amusing consequence of my
notoriety is that men come to call on the Duchess at all
hours, and while most of them only want to bed me,
some bring bills of exchange or little purses of dia-
monds, and instead of whispering flattery and lewd
suggestions they say, "What rate of return could this
bring in Amsterdam?" I always answer, "Why, it all
depends on the whim of the King; for do the markets
of Amsterdam not fluctuate according to the wars and
treaties that only His Majesty has the power to make?"
They think I am only being coy.

Today the King came to see me; but it is not what
you think.

I had been warned of His Majesty's coming by the
cousin of the Duchess: a Jesuit priest named Édouard de
Gex, who has come here on a visit from the *pays* in the
southeast where this family maintains its ancestral
seat. Father Édouard is a very pious man. He had been
invited to play a minor role in the King's getting-out-
of-bed ceremony, and had overheard a couple of
courtiers speculating as to which man would claim my

maidenhead. Then another offered to wager that I didn't *have* a maidenhead, and yet another wagered that if I did it would be claimed by a woman, not a man—two likely candidates being the Dauphine, who is having an affair with her maid, and Liselotte.

At some point, according to Father Édouard, the King took notice of this conversation and inquired as to what lady was being talked about. "It is no lady, but the tutor of the daughter of the d'Ozoirs," said one of them; to which the King replied, after a moment's thought, "I have heard of her. They say she is beautiful."

When Father Édouard told me this story I understood why not a single young courtier had come sniffing around after me that day. They thought the King had conceived an interest in me, and were now afraid to come anywhere near!

Today the Duchess, the Marquise, and all their household took the unusual measure of attending Mass at half past noon. I was left alone in the apartment under the pretext that I needed to pack some things for the upcoming journey to Dunkirk.

At one o'clock the chapel bells rang, but my mistresses did not return to the apartment. Instead a gentleman—the most famous chirurgeon in Paris—let himself in through the servants' entrance, followed by a retinue of assistants, as well as a priest: Father Édouard de Gex. Moments later King Louis XIV of France entered *solus* through the front, slamming a gilded door in the faces of his courtiers, and greeted me in a very polite way.

The King and I stood in a corner of the Duchess's salon and (as bizarre as this must sound) exchanged trivial conversation while the surgeon's assistants worked furiously. Even one who is as unschooled in Court etiquette as I knew that in the presence of the King no other person may be acknowledged, and so I pretended not to notice as the assistants dragged the massive silver chairs to the edges of the room, rolled up the carpets, laid down canvas drop-cloths, and carried in a heavy wooden bench. The chirurgeon was arranging some very unpleasant-looking tools on a side table, and muttering occasional commands; but all of this took place in nearly perfect silence.

"D'Avaux says you are good with money," the King said.

"I say d'Avaux is good at flattering young ladies," I answered.

"It is an error for you to feign modesty when you are talking to me," the King said, firmly but not angrily.

I saw my error. We use humility when we fear that someone will consider us a rival or a threat; and while this may be true of common or even noble men, it can never be true of *le Roi* and so to use humility in His Majesty's presence is to imply that the King shares the petty jealousies and insecurities of others.

"Forgive me for being foolish, Sire."

"Never; but I forgive you for being inexperienced. Colbert was a commoner. He was good with money; he built everything you see. He did not know how to speak to me at first. Have you ever experienced a sexual climax, mademoiselle?"

"Yes."

The King smiled. "You have learned quickly how to answer my questions. That pleases me. You will please me more by now making the sounds that you made when you had this climax. You may have to make those sounds for a long time—possibly a quarter of an hour."

I must have clutched my hands together in front of my bosom, or put on some such show of girlish anxiety. The King shook his head and smiled in a knowing way. "To see a certain *déshabille,* in a quarter of an hour, would please me—only that it might be glimpsed, through the door, by the ones who wait in the gallery." The King nodded toward the door through which he had entered. "Now if you will excuse me, mademoiselle. You may begin at any time." He turned away from me, doffing his coat and handing it to one of the chirurgeon's assistants as he moved toward the heavy bench, now draped in white linen, that sat in the middle of the room on a carpet of sailcloth. The chirurgeon and his assistants closed in on the King like flies on a piece of meat. Suddenly—to my indescribable shock—the King's breeches were down around his ankles. He lay down on his stomach on the bench. For a moment I fancied he was one of those men who likes to be struck on the buttocks. But then he spread his legs apart, bracing his feet against the floor to either side of the bench, and I saw a frightful purplish swelling in the crevice of his buttocks.

"Father Édouard," the King said quietly, "you are among the most learned men of France. Even among your fellow Jesuits you are respected as one to whom no detail is unnoticed. Since I cannot view the operation, you will please me by paying the closest attention, and telling me the story later, so that I will know whether this chirurgeon is to be counted a friend or an enemy of France."

Father Édouard nodded and said something I could not hear.

"Your Majesty!" the chirurgeon exclaimed. "To perfect my skills, I have performed a hundred of these operations, in the last six months, since I was made aware of your complaint—"

"Those hundred are not of interest to me."

Father Édouard had noticed me standing in the corner. I prefer not to speculate what sort of expression was on my face! He locked his dark eyes on mine—he is a handsome man—and then glanced significantly toward the door, through which I could hear a low hubbub of ribald conversation among the dozen or so courtiers biding their time.

I moved closer to that door—not too close—and let out a throaty sigh. "Mmm, *Vôtre Majesté!*" The courtiers outside began shushing one another. In my other ear I heard a faint ringing noise as the chirurgeon picked a knife up off his table.

I let out a groan.

So did the King.

I let out a scream.

So did the King.

"Oh, gentle, it is my first time!" I shouted, as the King shouted curses at the chirurgeon, muffled by a silken pillow Father Édouard was holding to his face.

So it went. For a while I continued screaming as if suffering great discomfort, but as the minutes wore on, I changed over to moans of pleasure. It seemed to go on for much longer than a quarter of an hour. I lay down on a rolled-up carpet and tore at my own clothes, pulled the ribbons and braids from my hair, and breathed as heavily as I could, to make my face flushed and sweaty. Towards the end, I closed my eyes: partly to block out the hellish things I was beginning to see in the middle of the room, and partly to play my role more convincingly. Now I could clearly hear the courtiers in the gallery.

"She's a screamer," said one of them admiringly. "I like that, it makes my blood hot."

"It is most indiscreet," said another scornfully.

"The mistress of a King does not *have* to be discreet."

"Mistress? He'll throw her away soon, then where will she be?"

"In my bed, I hope!"

"Then you had best invest in a set of earplugs."

"He had best learn to fuck like a King before he'll need them!"

A drop of moisture struck me on the forehead. Fearing that it was a splash of blood, I opened my eyes and looked vertically upwards into the face of Father Édouard de Gex. He was indeed all spattered with the blood royal, but what had fallen on me was a bead of sweat from his brow. He was glaring straight down into my face. I have no idea how long he had been watching me thus. I glanced over towards the bench and saw blood everywhere. The chirurgeon was sitting on the floor, drained. His assistants were packing rags between the King's buttocks. To stop all of a sudden would be to give the ruse away, and so I closed my eyes again and brought myself to a screaming—if simulated—climax, then exhaled one long last moan, and opened my eyes again.

Father Édouard was still standing there above me, but his eyes were closed and his face slack. It is an expression I have seen before.

The King was standing up, flanked between a pair of assistants who stood ready to catch him if he should faint. He was deathly pale and tottering from side to side, but—somewhat incredibly—he was alive, and awake, and buttoning up his own breeches. Behind him other assistants were bundling up the bloody sheets and drop-cloths and rushing them out through the back door.

Here is what the King said to me as he was leaving:

"Nobles of France enjoy my esteem and confidence as a birthright, and make themselves common by their failures. Commoners may earn my esteem and confidence by pleasing me, and thereby ennoble themselves. You may please me by showing discretion."

"What of d'Avaux?" I asked.

"You may tell him everything," said the King, "so that he may feel pride, inasmuch as he is my friend, and fear, inasmuch as he is my foe."

Monseigneur, I do not know what His Majesty meant by this, but I am sure you do . . .

To Gottfried Wilhelm Leibniz
29 September 1685
Doctor,

   The season has turned and brought a noticeable darkening of the light.* In two days the sun will sink farther beneath the southern horizon as I journey with Mme. la marquise d'Ozoir to Dunquerque at the extreme northern limit of the King's realm *and thence God willing to Holland.* I have heard that the sun has been shining very hot in the South, in the country of Savoy *more on this later.*

   The King is at war—not only with the Protestant heretics who infest his realms, but with his own doctors. A few weeks ago he had a tooth pulled. Any tooth-puller chosen at random from the Pont-Neuf could have handled this operation, but d'Aquin, the King's doctor, got it wrong, and the resulting wound became abscessed. D'Aquin's solution to this problem was to pull out every last one of the King's upper teeth. But while he was doing this he somehow managed to rip out part of the King's palate, creating a horrendous wound which he then had to close up by the application of red-hot irons. Nonetheless, it too abscessed and had to be cauterized several more times. *There is another story, too, concerning the King's health, which I will have to tell you some other time.*

   It is nearly beyond comprehension that a King should suffer so, and if these facts were generally known among the peasantry they would doubtless be misconstrued as an omen of Divine misfavor. In the corridors of Versailles, where most *but not all!* of the King's sufferings are common knowledge, there are a few weak-minded ninehammers who think this way; but fortunately this château has been graced, for the

---

* ☷ Darkening of the Light: Hexagram 36 of the *I Ching,* or 000101.

last few weeks, by the presence of Father Édouard de Gex, a vigorous young Jesuit of a good family *when Louis seized the Franche-Comté in 1667 this family betrayed their Spanish neighbors and flung open their gates to his army; Louis has rewarded them with titles* and a great favorite of Mme. de Maintenon, who looks to him as a sort of spiritual guide. Where most of our fawning courtier-priests would prefer to avoid the theological questions raised by the King's sufferings, Father Édouard has recently taken this bull by the horns, and both asked and answered these questions in a most forthright and public way. He has given lengthy homilies at Mass, and Mme. de Maintenon has arranged for his words to be printed and distributed around Versailles and Paris. I will try to send you a copy of his booklet. The gist of it is that the King is France and that his ailments and sufferings are reflections of the condition of the realm. If various pockets of his flesh have become abscessed it is a sort of carnal metaphor for the continued existence of heresy within the borders of France—meaning, as everyone knows, the R.P.R., the *religion prétendue réformée*, or Huguenots as they are known by some. The points of similarity between R.P.R. communities and suppurating abscesses are many, viz. . . .

    Forgive this endless homily, but I have much to tell and am weary of writing endless descriptions of gowns and jewels to cover my traces. This family of Fr. de Gex, Mme. la duchesse d'Oyonnax, and Mme. la marquise d'Ozoir have long dwelt in the mountains of Jura between Burgundy and the southern tip of the Franche-Comté. It is a territory where many things come together and accordingly it is a sort of cornucopia of enemies. For generations they looked on with envy as their neighbor the Duke of Savoy reaped a harvest of wealth and power by virtue of sitting astride the route joining Genoa and Lyons—the finan-

cial aorta of Christendom. And from their châteaux in
the southern Jura they can literally gaze down into the
cold waters of Lake Geneva, the wellspring of Protes-
tantism, where the English Puritans fled for refuge
during the reign of Bloody Mary and where the French
Huguenots have enjoyed a safe haven from the repres-
sions of their Kings. I have seen much of Father
Édouard lately because he pays frequent visits to the
apartments of his cousines, and I have witnessed in
his dark eyes a hatred of the Protestants that would
make your flesh crawl if you saw it.

This family's opportunity finally came when Louis
conquered the Franche-Comté, as I said, and they
have not failed to take full advantage of it. Last year
brought them more good fortune: the Duke of Savoy
was forced to take as his wife Anne Marie, the daughter of Monsieur by his first wife, Minette of England,
and hence the niece of King Louis XIV. So the Duke—
hitherto independent—became a part of the Bourbon
family, and subject to the whims of the patriarch.

Now Savoy also borders on that troublesome Lake
and it has long been the case that Calvinist proselytiz-
ers would come up the valleys to preach to the common folk, who have followed the example of their
Duke in being independent-minded and have been re-
ceptive to the rebel creed.

You can almost finish the story yourself now, Doctor. Father Édouard has been telling his disciple, Mme.
de Maintenon, all about how Protestants have been
running rampant in Savoy, and spreading the infection
to their R.P.R. brethren in France. De Maintenon re-
peats all of this to the suffering King, who even in the
best of times has never hesitated to be cruel to his subjects, or even his own family, for the good of the realm.
But these are not the best of times for the King—there
has been a palpable darkening of the light, which is

why I chose this hexagram as my encryption key. The King has told the Duke of Savoy that the "rebels" as he considers them are not merely to be suppressed— they are to be exterminated. The Duke has temporized, hoping that the King's mood will improve as his ailments heal. He has proffered one excuse after another. But very recently the Duke made the error of claiming that he cannot carry out the King's commands because he does not have enough money to mount a military campaign. Without hesitation the King generously offered to undertake the operation out of his own pocket.

As I write this Father Édouard is preparing to ride south as chaplain of a French army with Maréchal de Catinat at its head. They will go into Savoy whether the Duke likes it or not, and enter the valleys of the Protestants and kill everyone they see. Do you know of any way to send warnings to that part of the world?

The King and all who know of his late sufferings take comfort in the understanding that Father Édouard has brought us: namely that the measures taken against the R.P.R., cruel as they might seem, are more painful to the King than to anyone; but that this pain must be endured lest the whole body perish.

I must go—I have responsibilities below. My next letter will come from Dunquerque, God willing.

>   Your most affectionate student and servant,
>   Eliza

London

Philosophy is written in this immense book that stands ever open before our eyes (I speak of the Universe), but it cannot be read if one does not first learn the language and recognize the characters in which it is written. It is written in mathematical language, and the characters are triangles, circles, and other geometrical figures, without the means of which it is humanly impossible to understand a word; without these philosophy is confused wandering in a dark labyrinth.

—GALILEO GALILEI, *Il Saggiatore*
(THE ASSAYER) TRANSLATED BY
JULIAN BARBOUR IN *Absolute or Relative Motion?*
Volume 1: The Discovery of Dynamics

THE AIR IN THE COFFEE-HOUSE made Daniel feel as if he'd been buried in rags.

Roger Comstock was peering down the stem of his clay pipe like a drunken astronomer drawing a bead on something. In this case the target was Robert Hooke, Fellow of the Royal Society, visible only barely (because of gloom and smoke) and sporadically (because of table-flitting patrons). Hooke had barricaded himself behind a miniature apothecary shop of bottles, purses, and flasks, and was mixing up his dinner: a compound of mercury, iron filings, flowers of sulfur, purgative waters from diverse springs, many of which were Lethal to Waterfowl; and extracts of several plants, including the rhubarb and the opium poppy. "He is still alive, I see," Roger mused. "If Hooke spent any more time lingering at Death's door, Satan himself would have the man ejected for vagrancy. Yet just as I am wondering whether I can make time for his funeral, I learn from Sources that he is campaigning like a French regiment through every whorehouse in Whitechapel."

Daniel could think of nothing to add.

"What of Newton?" Roger demanded. "You *said* he was going to *die*."

"Well, I was the only way he ever got food," Daniel said weakly. "From the time we began rooming together until my ejection in '77, I kept him alive like a nursemaid. So I had good reasons for making that prediction."

"Someone else must have been bringing him food since then—one of his students?"

"He *has* no students," Daniel pointed out.

"*But he must eat*," Roger countered.

Daniel glimpsed Hooke stirring up his concoction with a glass rod. "Perhaps he has concocted the *Elixir Vitae* and is immortal now."

"Judge not lest ye be judged! I believe that is your third helping of *usquebaugh*," Roger said sternly, glaring at the amber dram in front of Daniel. Daniel reached out to guard it in the curled fingers of his left hand.

"I am entirely serious," Roger continued. "Who looks after him?"

"Why does it matter, as long as *someone* does?"

"It matters who the someone is," Roger said. "You told me that when he was a student Newton would lend out money, and keep track of his loans like a Jew!"

"Actually I believe that Christian lenders *also* prefer to be paid back . . ."

"Never mind, you know what I mean. In the same way, Daniel, if someone is providing for Newton's upkeep and maintenance, they may be expecting favors in return."

Daniel sat up straighter. "You think it's the esoteric brotherhood."

Roger raised his eyebrows in a cruel parody of innocence. "No, but evidently *you* think so."

"For a while Upnor was trying to get his barbs into Isaac," Daniel admitted, "but that was a long time ago."

"Let me remind you that among people who *keep track* of debts—as opposed to *forgiving* 'em—'a long time ago' means 'lots and lots of compound interest.' Now, you told me he vanishes several weeks out of each year."

"Not necessarily for sinister purposes. He has land in Lincolnshire that needs looking after."

"*You* made it sound sinister, when you told me of it."

Daniel sighed, forsook his dram, clamped his temples between the thumb and fingertips of one hand. All he could see now was his pink palm—cratered from smallpox, now. The disease had converted perhaps a quarter of Tess's body to pustules, and removed most of the skin from her face and torso, before she'd finally given up the ghost. "To be quite honest with you, I do not care," he said. "I tried to hold him back. Tried to turn his attention toward astronomy, dynamics, physics—natural philosophy as opposed to unnatural theology. I failed; I left; here I am."

"You left? Or were ejected?"

"I misspoke."

"Which time?"

"I meant it in a sort of metaphorical way, when I used the word 'ejected.' "

"You are a damned liar, Daniel!"

"What did you say!?"

"Oh, sorry, I was speaking in a sort of metaphorical way."

"Try to understand, Roger, that the circumstances of my

break with Isaac were—are—complicated. As long as I try to express it with a single verb, *videlicet,* 'to leave,' 'to be ejected,' I'll be in some sense a liar, and inasmuch as a liar, damnable."

"Give me more verbs, then," said Roger, catching the eye of a serving-girl and giving her a look that meant *I have him going now, keep it coming and keep the sleeve-tuggers away from us.* Then he leaned forward, looming in an alarming way through the smoke above the table, catching the light of a candle on the underside of his chin. "It is sixteen seventy-six!" Roger thundered. "Leibniz has come to London for the second time! Oldenburg is furious with him because he has failed to bring the digital computer, as promised! Instead Leibniz has devoted the last four years to fooling around with mathematics in Paris! Now he is asking extremely awkward questions about some maths work that Newton did years ago. Something mysterious is afoot—Newton has you, Doctor Waterhouse, copying out papers and encrypting arcane mathematical formulae—Oldenburg is beside himself—Enoch Root is mixed up in it somehow—there are *rumors* of letters, and even conversations, between Newton and Leibniz. Then Oldenburg dies. Not long afterwards there is a fire in your chambers at Trinity, and many of Newton's alchemical papers go up in particolored flames. Then you move to London and refuse to say why. What is the correct verb? 'To leave' or 'to be ejected?' "

"There was simply no room for me there—my bed took up space that could have been used for another furnace."

"To conspire? To plot?"

"The mercury fumes were making me jumpy."

"To burn? To torch?"

Daniel now gripped the arms of his chair, threatening to get up and leave. Roger held up a hand. "I'm President of the Royal Society—it is my duty to be curious."

"I'm Secretary, and it is my duty to hold it all together when the President is being a fool."

"Better a fool in London than fuel in Cambridge. You will forgive me for wondering what went on."

"Since you're pretending to be a Catholic now, you may expect cheap grace from your French priests, but not from me."

"You are showing the self-righteousness I associated with upright men who've secretly done something very wrong—which is not to assert that you have any dark secrets, Daniel, only that you *act* that way."

"Does this conversation have any purpose other than to make me want to kill you, Roger?"

"I simply want to know what the hell Newton is doing."

"Then why harry me with these questions about what happened in '77?"

Roger shrugged. "You won't talk about *now,* so I thought I would try my luck with *then.*"

"Why the sudden interest in Isaac?"

"Because of *De Motu Corporum in Gyrum.* Halley says it is stupendous."

"No doubt."

"He says that it is only a sketch for a vast work that is consuming all of Newton's energies now."

"I am pleased that Halley has an explanation for the orbit of his comet, and even more pleased that he has taken over responsibility for the care and feeding of Isaac. What do you want of me?"

"Halley is blinded by comet-light," Roger scoffed. "If Newton decides to work out the mysteries of gravity and of planetary motion then Halley cares not why—he is a happy astronomer! And with Flamsteed around to depress the statistics, we need more happiness in the astronomical profession."

In *anno domini* 1674, the Sieur de St. Pierre (a French courtier, never mind the details) had been at some excellent Royal soiree when Louise de Kéroualle and her cleavage had hove into view above the rim of his goblet. Like most men who found themselves in her presence, the Sieur had been seized by an unaccountable need to impress her, somehow, some way. Knowing that Natural Philosophy was a big deal at the Court of Charles II, he had employed the following gambit: he had remarked that one could solve the problem of finding the Longitude by plotting the motions of the moon against the stars and using the heavens as a big clock. Kéroualle had relayed this to the King during some sort of Natural-Philosophic pillow talk, and his majesty had commissioned four Fellows of the Royal Society (the Duke of Gunfleet, Roger Comstock, Robert Hooke, and Christopher Wren) to find out if such a thing were really possible. They had asked one John Flamsteed. Flamsteed was the same age as Daniel. Too sickly to attend school, he had stayed home and taught himself astronomy. Later his health had improved to the point where he'd been able to attend Cambridge and learn what could be taught there, which was not much, at the time. When he had received this inquiry from the aforementioned four Fellows of the Royal Society, he had been just finishing up his studies, and looking for something to do. He had shrewdly written back saying that the proposal of the Sieur de St. Pierre, though it might be possible in theory, was perfectly absurd in practice, owing to a want of reliable astronomical data—*which could only be remedied by a lengthy and expensive research program.* It was the first and the last politic thing that Flamsteed had ever done. Without delay Charles II had appointed him Astronomer Royal and founded the Royal Observatory.

Flamsteed's temporary quarters, for the first couple of years, were in the Tower of London, atop the round turret of the White Tower. He made his first observations there while a permanent facility was being constructed on a patch of disused royal property at Greenwich.

Henry VIII, not satisfied with six wives, had maintained any number of mistresses, storing them, when not in use, in a sort of bolt-hole on the top of a hill above Greenwich Palace. His successors had not shared his appetites, and so the royal fuck-house had largely fallen into ruin. The foundations, however, were still sound. Atop them, Wren and

Hooke, working in a hurry, and on a tiny budget, had built some apartments, which served as plinth for an octagonal salt-box. Atop that was a turret, an allusion in miniature to the Norman turrets of the Tower of London. The apartments were for Flamsteed to live in. The octagon above was constructed essentially so that the court-fop contingent of the Royal Society would have a place to go and peer learnedly through telescopes. But because it had been built on the foundations of Henry VIII's hilltop love shack, the whole building was oriented the wrong way. To make real observations, it had been necessary to construct an alienated limestone wall in the garden out back, oriented north–south. This was partly sheltered by a sort of roofless shack. Bolted to it were a pair of Hooke-designed quadrants, one looking north and the other looking south, each equipped with a sighting-tube. Flamsteed's life, thereafter, consisted of sleeping all day, then going out at night, leaning against this wall, peering through the sighting-tubes at stars swinging past, and noting their positions. Every few years, the work was enlivened by the appearance of a comet.

"What was Newton doing one year ago, Daniel?"

"Sources tell me he was calculating the precise date and hour of the Apocalypse, based upon occult shreds of data from the Bible."

"We must have the same sources," Roger said agreeably. "How much do *you* pay them?"

"I say things to them in return. It is called having conversations, and for some it is payment enough."

"You must be right, Daniel. For, several months ago, Halley shows up and has a conversation with Newton: 'Say, old chap, what about comets?' And Newton drops the Apocalypse and turns to Euclid. Within a few months he's got *De Motu* out."

"He worked out most of it in '79, during his *last* feud with Hooke," Daniel said, "and mislaid it, and had to work it out a second time."

"What—Doctor Waterhouse—do alchemy, the Apocalypse, and the elliptical orbits of heavenly bodies have in common? Other than that Newton is obsessed with all of them."

Daniel said nothing.

"Anything? Everything? Nothing?" Roger demanded, and slapped the edge of the table. "Is Newton a billiard ball or a comet?"

"I beg your pardon?"

"Oh, come here, Daniel," Roger clucked, going into sudden motion. Rather than standing up first, *then* walking, he lowered his wig, raised his hindquarters, and lunged off into the crowd like a bull, and in spite of bulk, middle age, gout, and drink, forged a path through the coffee-house faster than Daniel could follow. When Daniel next caught sight of Roger, the Marquis was shouldering his way past a fop. The fop was gripping a wooden implement shaped vaguely like a long-handled flour-scoop, and taking aim at a painted wooden sphere at rest on a green baize firmament. "Behold!" Roger exclaimed, and shoved at the ball with his bare hand. It rolled into another ball and stopped; the second ball rolled away. The fop was gripping his stick with both hands and winding up to break it over Roger's head, when Roger adroitly turned his back on the table, giving the fop a clear view of his face. The stick fell from the fop's hands. "Excellent shot, m'Lord," he began, "though not wholly in line with the spirit or the letter of the rules . . ."

"I am a Natural Philosopher, and my Rules are the God-given Rules of the Universe, not the arbitrary ones of your insipid sport!" Roger thundered. "The ball transfers its *vis viva* into another ball, the quantity of motion is conserved, all is more or less orderly." Roger now opened one hand to reveal that he had snatched another ball. "Or, I may toss it into the air thus—" he did so "—and it describes a Galilean trajectory, a parabola." The ball plonked down squarely into a mug of chocolate, halfway across the room; its owner recovered quickly, raising the mug to Roger's health. "But comets adhere to no laws, they come from God only knows where, at unpredictable times, and streak through the cosmos on their own unfathomable trajectories. So, I ask you, Daniel: Is Newton like a comet? Or, like a billiard ball, is he following some rational trajectory I have not the wit to understand?"

"I understand your question now," Daniel said. "Astronomers used to explain the seeming retrograde movements of the planets by imagining a phantastic heavenly axle-tree fitted out with crystalline spheres. *Now* we know that in fact the planets move in smooth ellipses and that retrograde motion is an *illusion* created by the fact that we are making our observations from a moving platform."

"Viz. the Earth."

"If we could see the planets from some fixed frame of reference, the retrograde motion would disappear. And you, Roger, observing Newton's wandering trajectory—one year devising new receipts for the Philosophic Mercury, the next hard at work on Conic Sections—are trying to figure out whether there might be some Reference Frame within which all of Isaac's moves make some kind of damned sense."

"Spoken like Newton himself," Roger said.

"You want to know whether his recent work on gravitation is a change of subject, or merely a new point of view—a new way of perceiving the same old Topic."

"*Now* you are talking like Leibniz," Roger said grumpily.

"And with good reason, for Newton and Leibniz are both working on the same problem, and have been since at least '77," Daniel said. "It is the problem that Descartes could not solve. It comes down to whether the collisions of those billiard balls can be explained by geometry and arithmetic—or do we need to go beyond pure thought and into Empirical and/or Metaphysical realms?"

"Shut up," Roger said, "I'm working on a murderous headache *as it is*. I do not want to hear of metaphysics." He seemed partly sincere—but he was keeping one eye on someone who was coming up behind Daniel. Daniel turned around and came face to face with—

"Mr. Hooke!" Roger said.

"M'lord.

"You, sir, taught this fellow to make thermometers!"

"So I did, m'lord."

"I was just explaining to him that I wanted him to go up to Cambridge and gauge the heat of that town."

"The entire country seems warm to me, m'lord," said Hooke gravely, "in particular the eastern limb."

"I hear that the warmth is spreading to the West country."

"Here is a *pretext*," said the Marquis of Ravenscar, stuffing a sheaf of papers into Daniel's right hip pocket, "and here is something for you to peruse on your journey—the latest from Leipzig." He shoved something rather heavier into the left pocket. "Good night, fellow Philosophers!"

"Let us go and walk in the streets of London," Hooke said to Daniel. He did not need to add: *Most of which I laid out personally.*

"RAVENSCAR HATED HIS COUSIN John Comstock, ruined him, bought his house, and tore it down," Hooke said, as if he'd been backed into a corner and forced to admit it, "but learned from him all the same! Why did John Comstock back the Royal Society in its early days? Because he was curious as to Natural Philosophy? Perhaps. Because Wilkins talked him into it? In part. But it cannot have escaped your notice that most of our experiments in those days—"

"Had something to do with gunpowder. Obviously."

"*Roger* Comstock owns no gunpowder-factories. But his interest in the doings of our Society is no less pragmatic. Make no mistake. The French and the Papists are running the country now—are they running Newton?"

Daniel said nothing. After years of sparring with Hooke over gravitation, Isaac had soared far beyond Hooke's reach since Halley's visit.

"I see," Daniel said finally. "Well, I must go north anyway, to play at being the Puritan Moses."

"It would be worth an excursion to Cambridge, then, in order to—"

"In order to clear Newton's name of any scurrilous accusations that might be made against him by jealous rivals," Daniel said.

"I was going to say, in order to disentangle him from the foreign supporters of a doomed King," Hooke said. "Good night, Daniel." And with a few dragging steps he was swallowed up in the sulfurous fog.

THE ENTIRE COUNTRY SEEMS WARM *to me . . . in particular the eastern limb.* Hooke might throw accusations carelessly, but not words. Among men who peered through telescopes, "limb" meant the edge of a heavenly body's disk, such as the moon's crescent when it was illumined from the side. Setting out to the northeast the next day, Daniel glanced at a map of Essex, Suffolk, and Norfolk and noticed that they formed a semicircular limb, bounded by the Thames on the south and the Wash on the north, and in between them, bulging eastwards into the North Sea. A bright light kindled above the Hague would shine a hundred nautical miles across the sea and light up that entire sweep of coastline, setting it aglow like a crescent moon, like the alchemist's symbol for silver. Silver was the element of the Moon, the complement and counterpart of the Sun, whose element was gold. And as the Sun King was now pouring much gold into England, the possible existence of a silvery lunar crescent just to the north of London had import. Roger had no patience with alchemical suppositions and superstitions, but politics he knew well.

The fifty-second parallel ran directly from Ipswich to the Hague, so any half-wit with a backstaff and an ephemeris could sail unerringly from one to the other and back. Daniel knew the territory well—the North Sea infiltrated the Suffolk coast with so many spreading rays of brackish water that when you gazed east at sunrise the terrain seemed to be crazed with rivers of light. It was impossible to travel up the coast proper. The road from London was situated ten to twenty miles inland, running more or less straight from Chelmsford to Colchester to Ipswich, and everything to the right side—between it and the sea—was hopeless, from the point of view of a King or anyone else who wanted to rule it: a long strip of fens diced up by estuaries and therefore equally impassable to horses and boats, easier to reach from Holland than from London. *Staying* there wasn't so bad, and staying out was even better, but *movement* was rarely worth the trouble. Objects would not move in a resistive medium unless impelled by a powerful force—ergo, any travelers in that coastal strip had to be smugglers, drawn by profit and repulsed by laws, shipping England's rude goods to Holland and importing Holland's finished ones. So Daniel, like his brothers Sterling and Oliver and Raleigh before him, had spent much time in this territory as a youth, loading and unloading flat-bottomed Dutch boats lurking beneath weeping willows in dark river-courses.

The first part of the journey was like being nailed, with several other people, into a coffin borne through a coal-mine by epileptic pallbearers. But at Chelmsford some passengers got out of the carriage and thereafter the way became straight and level enough that Daniel could attempt to read. He took out the printed document that Roger had given him in the coffee-house. It was a copy of *Acta Eruditorum,* the scholarly rag that Leibniz had founded in his home town of Leipzig.

Leibniz had been trying for a long time to organize the smart Germans. The smart Britons tended to see this as a shabby mockery of the Royal Society, and the smart Frenchmen viewed it as a mawkish effort by the Doctor (who'd been living in Hanover since '77) to hold up a flawed and tarnished mirror to the radiant intellectual life of Paris. While Daniel (reluctantly) saw some justice in these opinions, he suspected that Leibniz was *mostly* doing it simply because it was a good idea. At any rate *Acta Eruditorum* was Leibniz's (hence Germany's) answer to *Journal des Savants,* and it tended to convey the latest and best ideas coming from Germany—i.e., whatever Leibniz had been thinking about lately.

This particular issue had been printed several months earlier and contained an article by Leibniz on mathematics. Daniel began skimming it and right away saw distinctly familiar terms—the likes of which he had not glimpsed since '77—

"Stab me in the vitals," Daniel muttered, "he's finally done it!"

"Done what!?" demanded Exaltation Gather, who was sitting across from Daniel hugging a large box full of money.

"Published the calculus!"

"And what, pray tell, is that, Brother Daniel? Other than something that grows on one's teeth." The hoard of coins in Exaltation Gather's strong-box made dim muffled chinking noises as the carriage rocked from side to side on its Suspension—one of those annoyingly good French ideas.

"New mathematics, based upon the analysis of quantities that are infinitesimal and evanescent."

"It sounds very *metaphysical*," said the Reverend Gather. Daniel looked up at him. No one and nothing had ever been less metaphysical than he. Daniel had grown up in the company of men like this and for a while had actually considered them to be normal-looking. But several years spent in London coffee-houses, theatres, and royal palaces had insensibly altered his tastes. Now when he gazed upon a member of a Puritan sect he always cringed inside. Which was just the effect that the Puritans were aiming for. If the Rev. Gather's Christian name had been Exultation his garb would have been wildly inappropriate. But Exaltation it was, and for these people exaltation was a grim business.

Daniel had finally convinced King James II that His Majesty's claims to support all religious dissidents would seem a lot more convincing if he would take Cromwell's skull down from the stick where it had been posted all through Charles II's quarter-century-long reign, and put it back in the Christian grave with the rest of Cromwell. To

Daniel and certain others, a skull on a stick was a conspicuous object and the request to take it down wholly reasonable.
But His Majesty and every courtier within earshot had
looked startled: they'd forgotten it was there! It was part of
the London landscape, it was like the bird-shit on a windowpane you never notice. Daniel's request, James's ensuing de-
cree, and the fetching down and re-interment of the skull had
only drawn attention to it. Attention, in a modern Court,
meant cruel witticisms, and so it had been a recent vogue to
address wandering Puritan ministers as "Oliver," the joke
being that many of them—being wigless, gaunt, and sparely
dressed—looked like skulls on sticks. Exaltation Gather
looked so much like a skull on a stick that Daniel almost had
to physically restrain himself from knocking the man down
and shoveling dirt on him.

"Newton seems to agree with you," Daniel said, "or else
he's afraid that some Jesuit will *say* so, which amounts to the
same thing."

"One need not be a Jesuit to be skeptical of vain imaginings—" began the now miffed Gather.

"*Something* must be there," Daniel said. "Look out the
window, yonder. That fen is divided into countless small
plots by watercourses—some natural, some carved out by
industrious farmers. Each rectangle of land could be made
into two smaller ones—just drag a stick across the muck and
the water will fill up the scratch in the ground, like the æther
filling the void between particles of matter. Is that metaphysical yet?"

"Why no, it is a good similitude, earthy, concrete, like
something from the Geneva Bible. Have you looked into the
Geneva Bible recently, or—"

"What happens then if we continue subdividing?" Daniel
asked. "Is it the same all the way down? Or is it the case that
something happens eventually, that we reach a place where
no further subdivision is possible, where fundamental properties of Creation are brought into play?"

"Er—I have no idea, Brother Daniel."

"Is it vanity for us to consider the question? Or did God give us brains for a reason?"

"No religion, with the possible exception of Judaism, has ever been more favorably disposed towards education than ours," said Brother Exaltation, "so that question is answered before 'twas asked. But we must consider these, er, infinitesimals and evanescents in a way that is rigorous, pure, free from heathenish *idolatry* or French *vanity* or the metaphysical infatuations of the Papists."

"Leibniz agrees—and the result of applying just the approach you have prescribed, in the mathematical realm, is here, and it is called the calculus," said Daniel, patting the document on his knee.

"Does Brother Isaac agree?"

"He did twenty years ago, when he *invented* all of this," Daniel said. "Now I have no idea."

"I have heard from one of our brethren in Cambridge that Brother Isaac's comportment in church has raised questions as to his faith."

"Brother Exaltation," said Daniel sharply, "before you spread rumors that may get Isaac Newton thrown into prison, let's see about getting a few of our brethren *out*—shall we?"

IPSWICH HAD BEEN A CLOTH port forever, but that trade had fallen on hard times because of the fatal combination of cheap stuff from India and Dutch shipping that could bring it to Europe. It was the prototype of the ridiculously ancient English town, situated at the place where the River Orwell broadened into an estuary, the obvious spot where anyone from a cave-man to a Cavalier would drive a stake into the muck and settle. Daniel judged that the gaol had been the first structure to go up, some five or six thousand years ago perhaps, and that the rats had moved in a week or two later. Ipswich was the county seat, and so when Charles II had whimsically decided to enforce the Penal Laws, all of Suffolk's most outstanding Quakers, Barkers, Ranters, Congregationalists, Presbyterians, and the odd Jew had been rounded up and been deposited here. They might just as well have been released a month ago, but it was important to the King that Daniel, his chosen representative, come out and handle the matter in person.

The carriage pulled up in front of the gaol and Exaltation Gather sat in it nervously gripping his strong-box while Daniel went inside and scared the gaoler half to death by brandishing a tablecloth-sized document with a wax seal as big as a man's heart dangling from it. Then Daniel went into the gaol, interrupting a prayer meeting, and spouted an oration he'd already used in half a dozen other gaols, a wrung-out rag of a speech so empty and banal that he had no idea whether he was making any sense at all, or just babbling in tongues. The startled, wary looks on the faces of the imprisoned Puritans suggested that they were extracting *some* meaning from Daniel's verbalizations—he had no idea *what* exactly. Daniel did not really know how his speech was being interpreted until later. The prisoners had to be released one at a time. Each of them had to pay the bill for his meals and other necessaries—and many had been here for years.

Hence Exaltation Gather and his box of money. The King's gesture would fall flat if half the prisoners remained in pokey for debts accumulated during their (unjust and un-Christian) imprisonment and so the King had (through Daniel) encouraged special collections to be taken up in sympathetic churches and had (though this was supposed to be grievously secret) supplemented that money with some from his own reserves to make sure it all came off well. In practice it meant that the nonconformists of London and the King of England had used Exaltation Gather's strong-box as a dust-bin for disposal of all their oldest, blackest, lightest in weight, most clipped, worn, filed-down, and adulterated coins. The true value of each one of these objects had to be debated between the gaoler of Ipswich on one hand, and on the other, Exaltation Gather and any recently freed Puritans who (a) were sharp when it came to money and (b) enjoyed verbal disputes—i.e., all of them.

Daniel staged an orderly retreat to a church-yard with a view down to the harbor, where the sound of the argument was partly masked by the rushing and slapping of the surf. Various Puritans found him, and lined up to give him pieces of their minds. This went on for most of the day—but as an example, Edmund Palling came up and shook Daniel's hand.

Edmund Palling was a perpetual old man. So it had always seemed to Daniel. Admittedly his strategy of radical hairlessness made it difficult to guess his age. But he'd seemed an old man running around with Drake during the Civil War, and as an old man he had marched in Cromwell's funeral procession. As an old trader he had frequently showed up at Stourbridge Fair peddling this or that, and had walked into Cambridge to inflict startling visitations on Daniel. Old Man Palling had attended the memorial service for Drake, and during his years living in London, Daniel had occasionally bumped into this elderly man on the streets of London.

Now here he was: "Which is it, Daniel, stupid or insane? You know the King."

Edmund Palling was a sensible man. He was, as a matter of fact, one of those Englishmen who was so sensible that he was daft. For as any French-influenced courtier could explain, to insist on everything's being reasonable, in a world that *wasn't,* was, in itself, unreasonable.

"Stupid," Daniel said. Until now he had been every inch the Court man, but he could not dissimulate to such as Edmund Palling. To be with this old man was to be thrown back four decades, to a time when it had become common for ordinary sensible Englishmen to speak openly the widely agreed-upon, but previously unmentionable fact that monarchy was a load of rubbish. The fact that, since those days, the Restoration had occurred and that Europe was in fact ruled by great Kings was of no consequence. At any rate, Daniel felt perfectly at home and at peace among these men, which was a bit alarming given that he was a close advisor to King James II. He could no more defend that King, or any monarch, to Edmund Palling than go to a meeting of the Royal Society and assert that the Sun revolved around the Earth.

Edmund Palling was fascinated, and nodded sagely. "Some have been saying insane, you know—because of the syphilis."

"Not true."

"That is extraordinary, because *everyone* is convinced he has syphilis."

"He *does*. But having gotten to know His Majesty reasonably well, Mr. Palling, it is my opinion, as Secretary of the Royal Society, that when he, er . . ."

"Does something that is just amazingly ludicrous."

"As some would say, Mr. Palling, yes."

"Such as letting us out of gaol in the hopes that we'll not perceive it as a cynical ploy, and supposing that we'll rally about his standard as if he really gives a farthing for Freedom of Conscience!"

"Without staking myself to any position concerning what you've just said, Mr. Palling, I would encourage you to look towards mere stupidity in your quest for explanations. Not to rule out fits of syphilitic insanity *altogether,* mind you . . ."

"What's the difference then? Or is it a distinction without a difference?"

"*This* sort of thing," Daniel said, waving towards the Ipswich gaol, "is *stupidity.* By contrast, a fit of syphilitic insanity would lead to results of a different character entirely: spasms of arbitrary violence, mass enslavements, beheadings."

Mr. Palling shook his head, then turned toward the water. "One day soon the sun will rise from across yonder sea and chase the fog of stupidity and the shadows of syphilitic insanity away."

"Very poetic, Mr. Palling—but I have met the Duke of Monmouth, I have roomed with the Duke of Monmouth, I have been vomited on by the Duke of Monmouth, and I am telling you that the Duke of Monmouth is no Charles II! To say nothing of Oliver Cromwell."

Mr. Palling rolled his eyes. "Very well, then—if Monmouth fails I'm on the next ship to Massachusetts."

STRETCH A LINE, and another intersecting it, and rotate the former about the latter and it will sweep out a cone. Now shove this cone through a plane (fig. 1) and mark every point on the plane where the cone touches it. Commonly the result is an ellipse (fig. 2), but if the cone's slope is parallel to the plane it makes a parabola (fig. 3), and if it's parallel to the axis it makes a two-part curve called a hyperbola (fig. 4).

An interesting feature of all of these curves—the ellipse, the parabola, and the hyperbola—was that they were generated by straight things, viz. two lines and a plane. An interesting feature of the hyperbola was that far away its legs came very close to being straight lines, but near the center there was dramatic curvature.

Greeks, e.g., Euclid, had done all of these things long ago and discovered various more or less interesting properties of conic sections (as this family of curves was called) and of other geometric constructions such as circles and triangles. But they'd done so as an exploration of pure thought, as a mathematician might compute the sum of two numbers. Every assertion that Euclid, *et al.,* made concerning geometry was backed up by a chain of logical proofs that could be followed all the way back to a few axioms that were obviously true, e.g., "the shortest distance between two points is a straight line." The truths of geometry were *necessary* truths; the human mind could imagine a universe in which Daniel's name was David, or in which Ipswich had been built on the other side of the Orwell, but geometry and math *had* to be true, there was no conceivable universe in which 2 + 3 was equal to 2 + 2.

Occasionally one discovered correspondences between things in the real world and the figments of pure math. For

LIBRI I. CONICORVM APOLLONII

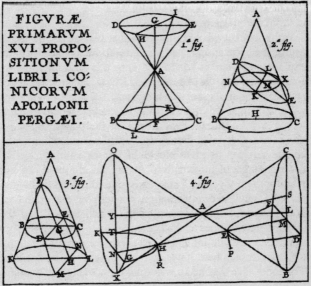

FIGVRÆ
PRIMARVM.
XVI. PROPO·
SITIONVM.
LIBRI I. CO·
NICORVM
APOLLONII
PERGÆI.

example: Daniel's trajectory from London to Ipswich had run in nearly a straight line, but after every one of the Dissenters had been let out of gaol, Daniel had executed a mighty change in direction and the next morning began riding on a rented horse towards Cambridge, following a trajectory that became straighter the farther he went. He was, in other words, describing a hyperbolic sort of path across Essex, Suffolk, and Cambridgeshire.

But he was not doing so *because* it was a hyperbola, or (to look at it another way) it was not a hyperbola because he was doing so. This was simply the route that traders had always taken, going from market to market as they traveled up out of Ipswich with wagon-loads of imported or smuggled goods. He could have followed a *zigzag* course. That it looked like a hyperbola when plotted on a map of England was *luck*. It was a *contingent* truth.

It did not *mean* anything.

In his pocket were some notes that his patron, the good Marquis of Ravenscar, had stuffed into his pocket with the explanation "Here is a pretext." They'd been written out by John Flamsteed, the Astronomer Royal, apparently in response to inquiries sent down by Isaac. Daniel dared not unwrap and read this packet—the uncannily sensitive Isaac would smell Daniel's hand-prints on the pages, or something. But the cover letter was visible. Wedged into the chinks between its great blocks of Barock verbiage were a few dry stalks of information, and by teasing these out and plaiting them together Daniel was able to collect that Newton had requested information concerning the comet of 1680; a recent conjunction of Jupiter and Saturn; and the ebb and flow of tides in the ocean.

If any other scholar had asked for data on such seemingly disparate topics he'd have revealed himself to be a crank. The mere fact that Isaac was thinking about all of them at the same time was as good as proof that they were all related. Tides obviously had something to do with the moon because the formers' heights were related to the latter's phase; but what influence could connect the distant sphere of rock to every sea, lake, and puddle on the earth? Jupiter, orbiting along an inside track, occasionally raced past Saturn, lumbering along on the outer boundary of the solar system. Saturn had been seen to slow down as Jupiter caught up with it, then to speed up after Jupiter shot past. The distance separating Jupiter from Saturn was, at best, two thousand times that between the moon and the tides; what influence could span such a chasm? And comets, almost by definition, were above and outside of the laws (whatever they might be) that governed moons and planets—comets were not astronomical bodies, or indeed natural phenomena at all, so much as metaphors for the alien, the exempt, the transcendent—

they were monsters, thunderbolts, letters from God. To bring them under the jurisdiction of any system of natural laws was an act of colossal hubris and probably asking for trouble.

But a few years earlier a comet had come through inbound, and a bit later an outbound one had been tracked, each moving on a different line, and John Flamsteed had stuck his neck out by about ten miles and asked the question, What if this was not *two* comets but one?

The obvious rejoinder was to point out that the two lines were different. One line, one comet; two lines, two comets. Flamsteed, who was as painfully aware of the vagaries and limitations of observational astronomy as any man alive, had answered that comets *didn't* move along lines and *never had;* that astronomers had observed only short segments of comets' trajectories that might actually be relatively straight excerpts of vast curves. It was known, for example, that most of a hyperbola was practically indistinguishable from a straight line—so who was to say that the supposed two comets of 1680 might not have been one comet that had executed a sharp course-change while close to the Sun, and out of astronomers' view?

In some other era this would have ranked Flamsteed with Kepler and Copernicus, but he was living now, and so it had made him into a sort of data cow to be kept in a stall in Greenwich and milked by Newton whenever Newton became thirsty. Daniel was serving in the role of milk-maid, rushing to Cambridge with the foaming pail.

There was much in this that demanded the attention of any European who claimed to be educated.

(1) Comets passed freely through space, their trajectories shaped only by (still mysterious) interactions with the Sun. If they moved on conic sections, it was no accident. A comet following a precise hyperbolic trajectory through the æther was a completely different thing from Daniel's *just happening* to trace a roughly hyperbolic course through the English

countryside. If comets and planets moved along conic sections, it had to be some kind of *necessary* truth, an intrinsic
feature of the universe. It *did* mean something. What exactly?

(2) The notion that the Sun exerted some centripetal force
on the planets was now becoming pretty well accepted, but
by asking for data on the interactions of moon and sea, and
of Jupiter and Saturn, Isaac was as much as saying that these
were all of a piece, that *everything* attracted *everything*—that
the influences on (say) Saturn of the Sun, of Jupiter, and of
Titan (the moon of Saturn that Huygens had discovered)
were different only insofar as they came from different directions and had different magnitudes. Like the diverse
goods piled up in some Amsterdam merchant's warehouse,
they might come from many places and have different val-
ues, but in the end all that mattered was how much gold they
could fetch on the Damplatz. The gold that paid for a pound
of Malabar pepper was melted and fused with the gold that
paid for a boat-load of North Sea herring, and all of it was
simply gold, bearing no trace or smell of the fish or the spice
that had fetched it. In the case of Cœlestial Dynamics, the
gold—the universal medium of exchange, to which everything was reduced—was force. The force exerted on Saturn
by the Sun was no different from that exerted by Titan. In
the end, the two forces were added together to make a vector, a combined resultant force bearing no trace of its ori-
gins. It was a powerful kind of alchemy because it took the
motions of heavenly bodies down from inaccessible realms
and brought them within reach of men who had mastered the
occult arts of geometry and algebra. Powers and mysteries
that had been the exclusive province of Gods, Isaac was now
arrogating to himself.

A SAMPLE CONSEQUENCE OF THIS alchemical fusing of forces
would be that a comet fleeing the Sun on the out-bound limb
of a hyperbola, traveling an essentially straight line, would,
if it happened to pass near a planet, be drawn towards it. The

Sun was not an absolute monarch. It did not have any special God-given power. The comet did not have to respect its force more than the forces of mere planets—in fact, the comet could not even perceive these two influences as being separate, they'd already been converted to the universal currency of force, and fused into a single vector. Far from the Sun, close to the planet, the latter's influence would predominate, and the comet would change course smartly.

And so did Daniel, after riding almost straight across the fenny country northeast of Cambridge for most of a day, and traversing the pounded, shit-permeated mud flat where Stourbridge Fair was held, suddenly swing round a bend of the Cam and drop into an orbit whose center was a certain suite of chambers just off to the side of the Great Gate of Trinity College.

Daniel still had a key to the old place, but he did not want to go there just yet. He stabled his horse out back of the college and came in through the rear entrance, which turned out to be a bad idea. He knew that Wren's library had started building, because Trinity had dunned him, Roger, and everyone else for contributions. And from the witty or despairing status reports that Wren gave the R.S. at every meeting, he was aware that the project had stopped and started more than once. But he hadn't thought about the practical consequences. The formerly smooth greens between the Cam and the back of the College were now a rowdy encampment of builders, their draft-animals, and their camp-followers (and not just whores but itinerant publicans, tool-sharpeners, and errand-boys, too). So there was a certain amount of wading through horse-manure, wandering into blind alleys that had once been bowling-greens, tripping over hens, and declining more or less attractive carnal propositions before Daniel could even get a clear view of the library.

Most of Cambridge had fallen into twilight while Daniel had been seeking a route through the builders' camp. Not that it made much of a difference, since the skies had looked like hammered lead all day. But the upper story of the Wren

Library was high enough to look west into tomorrow's weather, which would be fine and clear. The roof was mostly on, and where it wasn't, its shape was lofted by rafters and ridge-beams of red oak that seemed to resonate in the warm light of the sunset, not merely blocking the rays but humming in sympathy with their radiance. Daniel stood and looked at it for a while because he knew that any moment of such beauty could never last, and he wanted to describe it to the long-suffering Wren when he got back to London.

The bell began to toll, calling the Fellows to the dining hall, and Daniel slogged forward through the Library's vacant arches and across Neville's Court just in time to throw on a robe and join his colleagues at the High Table.

The faces around that table were warmed by port and candlelight, and exhibiting a range of feelings. But on the whole they looked satisfied. The last Master who'd tried to enforce any discipline on the place had suffered a stroke while hollering at some rowdy students. There was no preventing students and faculty from drawing weighty conclusions from such an event. His replacement was a friend of Ravenscar, an Earl who'd showed up reliably for R.S. meetings since the early 1670s and reliably fallen asleep halfway through them. He came up to Cambridge only when someone more important than he was there. The Duke of Monmouth was no longer Chancellor; he'd been stripped of all such titles during one of his banishments, and replaced by the Duke of Tweed—a.k.a. General Lewis, the L in Charles II's CABAL.

Not that he or any other Chancellor made any difference. The college was run by the Senior Fellows. Twenty-five years earlier, just at the moment Daniel and Isaac had entered Trinity, Charles II had kicked out the Puritan scholars who had nested there under Wilkins and replaced 'em with Cavaliers who could best be described as gentlemen-scholars—in that order. While Daniel and Isaac had been educating themselves, these men had turned the college into their own personal termite-mound. Now they were Senior

Fellows. The High Table diet of suet, cheese, and port had had its natural effect, and it was a toss-up as to whether their bodies or their minds had become softer.

No one could recollect the last time Isaac had set foot in this Hall. His lack of interest was looked on as proving not that something was wrong with Trinity but that something was wrong with Isaac. And in a way, this was just; if a College's duty was to propagate a certain way of being to the next generation, this one was working perfectly, and Isaac would only have disrupted the place by bothering to participate.

The Fellows seemed to know this (this was how Daniel thought of them: not as a roomful of individuals but as The Fellows, a sort of hive or flock, an aggregate. The question of aggregates had been vexing Leibniz to no end. A flock of sheep consisted of several individual sheep and was a flock only by convention—the quality of flockness was put on it by humans—it existed only in some human's mind as a perception. Yet Hooke had found that the human body was made up of cells—therefore, just as much an aggregate as a flock of sheep. Did this mean that the body, too, was just a figment of perception? Or was there some unifying influence that made those cells into a coherent body? And what of High Table at Trinity College? Was it more like a flock of sheep or a body? To Daniel it seemed very much like a body at the moment. To carry out the assignment given him by Roger Comstock he'd have to interrupt that mysterious unifying principle somehow, disaggregate the College, then cut a few sheep from the flock). The aggregate called Trinity noticed that Isaac only came to church once a week, on Sunday, and his behavior in the chapel was raising Trinity's eyebrows, though unlike Puritans these High Church gentles would never come out and say what they were thinking about religion. That was all right with Daniel, who knew perfectly well what Newton was doing and what these men were thinking about it.

But later, after Daniel and several of the Fellows had filed out of the Hall and gone upstairs to a smaller room, to sit around a smaller table and drink port, Daniel used this as a sort of lure, dragging it through the pond to see if anything would rise up out of the murk and snap at it: "Given the company Newton's been known to keep, I can't help but wonder if he has become attracted to Popery."

Silence.

"Gentlemen!" Daniel continued, "there's nothing *wrong* with it. Remember, our King is a Catholic."

There were thirteen other men in the room. Eleven of them found his remark to be in unspeakably poor taste (which was true) and said nothing. Daniel did not care; they'd forgive him on grounds that he'd been drinking and was well-connected. One of them understood immediately what Daniel was up to: this was Vigani, the alchemist. If Vigani had been following Isaac as closely, and listening to him as intently, as he had followed and listened to Daniel this evening, he would know a lot. For now, the ends of his mustache curled up wickedly and he hid his amusement in a goblet.

But one man, the youngest and drunkest in the room—a man who'd made no secret of the fact that he desperately wanted to get into the Royal Society—rose to the bait.

"I'd sooner expect all of Mr. Newton's nocturnal visitors to convert to *his* brand of religion than *he* to *theirs*!"

This produced a few stiff chuckles, which only encouraged him. "Though God help 'em if they tried to get back into France afterwards—considering what King Louis does to Huguenots, imagine what kind of welcome he'd give to a full-blown—"

"To say nothing of Spain with the Inquisition," said Vigani drolly. Which was a heroic and well-executed bid to change the topic to something so banal as to be a complete waste of breath—after all, the Spanish Inquisition had few defenders locally.

But Daniel had not endured years among courtiers without developing skills of his own. "I'm afraid we'll have to wait for an English Inquisition to find out what our friend was just about to say!"

"*That* should be coming along any day now," someone muttered.

They were beginning to break ranks! But Vigani had recovered: "Inquisition? Nonsense! Freedom of Conscience is the King's byword—or so Dr. Waterhouse has been telling everyone."

"I have been a mere conduit for what the King says."

"But you have just come from releasing a lot of Dissenters from prison, have you not?"

"Your knowledge of my pastimes is uncanny, sir," Daniel said. "You are correct. There are plenty of empty cells available just now."

"Shame to waste 'em," someone offered.

"The King will find some use for those vacancies," predicted someone else.

"An easy prediction to make. Here's a more difficult: what will that King's name be?"

"England."

"I meant his Christian name."

"You're assuming he's going to be a Christian, then?"

"You're assuming he's one now?"

"Are we speaking of the King who lives in Whitehall, or the one who has been spotted in the Hague?"

"The one in Whitehall has been *spotted* ever since his years in France: spotted on his face, on his hands, on his—"

"Gentlemen, gentlemen, this room is too warm and close for your wit, I beg you," said the most senior of the Fellows present, who looked as if he might be on the verge of having a stroke of his own. "Dr. Waterhouse was merely enquiring about his old friend, our colleague, Newton—"

"Is this the version we're all going to relate to the English Inquisition?"

"You are merry, too merry!" protested the Senior Fellow, now red in the face, and not with embarrassment. "Dr. Newton might serve as an example to you, for he goes about his work with *gravity,* and it is *sound* work in geometry, mathematics, astronomy . . ."

"Eschatology, astrology, alchemy . . ."

"No! No! Ever since Mr. Halley came up to enquire on the subject of Comets, Newton has had many fewer visitors from outside, and Signore Vigani has had to seek companionship in the Hall."

"I need only *enter* the Hall and companionship is *found,*" said Vigani smoothly, "there is never *seeking.*"

"Please excuse me," Daniel said, "it sounds as if Newton might welcome a visitor."

"He might welcome a crust of bread," someone said, "lately he has been scratching in his garden like a peckish hen."

> I cannot choose but condemn those Persons, who suffering themselves to be too much dazzled with the Lustre of the noble Actions of the Ancients, make it their Study to Extol them to the Skies; without reflecting, that these later Ages have furnished us with others more Heroick and Wonderful.
>
> —GEMELLI CARERI

PASSING THROUGH the Great Gate, he borrowed a lantern from a porter and exited onto a walkway that led to the street, hemmed in by crenellated walls. The wall to his left had a narrow gate let into it. Using his old key, Daniel opened the lock on this gate and stepped through into a sizable garden. It was laid out as a grid of gravel walkways with squares of greenery between. Some of the squares were planted with small fruit trees, others with shrubs or grass. To his left a line of taller trees screened the windows of the row of chambers that filled the space between the Great Gate and the Chapel. The buds in their branches were just evolving to nascent leaves, and where light shone from Isaac's windows they glowed like stopped explosions, phosphorus-green. But most of the windows were dark, and the stars above the muzzles of the chimneys were sharp and crystalline, not blurred by heat or dimmed by smoke. Isaac's furnaces were cold, the stuff in their crucibles congealed. Their heat had all gone into his skull.

Daniel let his lantern-hand fall to his side so that the light shone across the gravel path from the altitude of his knee. This made Isaac's chicken-scratchings stand out in high relief.

Every one had started the same way: with Isaac slashing the toe of his shoe, or the point of his stick, across the ground to make a curve. Not a specific curve—not a circle or a parabola—but a representative curve. Everything in the universe was curved, and those curves were evanescent and fluxional, but with this gesture Isaac snatched a particular curve—it didn't matter which—down from the humming cosmos, like a frog flicking its tongue out to filch a gnat from a swarm. Once trapped in the gravel, it was frozen and helpless. Isaac could stand and look at it for as long as he wanted, like Sir Robert Moray gazing at a stuffed eel in a glass box. After a while Isaac would begin to slash straight lines into the gravel, building up a scaffold of rays, perpendiculars, tangents, chords, and normals. At first this would seem to grow in a random way, but then lines would intersect with others to form a triangle, which would miraculously turn out to be an echo of another triangle in a different place, and this fact would open up a sort of sluice-gate that would free information to flood from one part of the diagram to another, or to leap across to some other, completely different diagram—but the results never came clear to Daniel's mind because here the diagram would be aborted and a series of footsteps—lunar craters in the gravel—would plot Isaac's hasty return to his chambers, where it could be set down in ink.

Daniel followed these footsteps into the chambers he had once shared. The ground floor was cluttered with alchemical droppings, but not as dangerous as usual, since everything

was cold. Daniel shone his lantern around one quiet room
and then another. Everything that gave light back was hard
mineral stuff, the inert refractory elements to which nature
always returned: crusty crucibles, sooty retorts, corroded
tongs, black crystals of charcoal, globs of quicksilver
trapped in floor-cracks, a box of golden guineas left open
next to a window as if to prove to all passers-by that the man
who lived here cared nothing for gold.

On a desk he saw letters in Latin from gentlemen in
Prague, Naples, St.-Germain, addressed to JEOVA SANC-
TUS UNUS. Through gaps between them Daniel saw parts
of a large drawing that had been pinned down to the surface of the table. It looked like a floor plan of a building.
Daniel moved some papers and books out of the way to expose more of it. He was wondering whether Isaac—like
Wren, Hooke, and Daniel himself—had gone into Architecture.

Isaac appeared to be designing a square, walled court with
a rectangular structure in the middle. Sweeping a trapezoid
of lantern-light over a block of writing, Daniel read the following: *The same God gave the dimensions of the Taberna-
cle to Moses and Temple with its Courts to David & Ezekiel
& altered not the proportion of the areas but only doubled
them in the Temple . . . So then Solomon and Ezekiel agree,
and are double to Moses.*

"I am only trying to recover what Solomon knew," Isaac
said.

Knowing that the lantern would blind Isaac's burnt eyes,
Daniel raised it up and blew it out before turning around.
Isaac had come in silence down a stone staircase. His atelier
on the first story had candles burning, and these warmed the
stone behind Isaac with orange light. He was a black silhouette robed in a dressing-gown, his head cloaked with silver.
He had not grown any heavier since College days, which
was no surprise if the rumors about his dining habits were to
be credited.

"I can't help but wonder if you—perhaps even *I*—don't

know a hell of a lot more about practically every subject than Solomon ever did," Daniel said.

Isaac said nothing for a moment, but something about his silhouette looked wounded, or sad.

"It's right there in the Bible, Daniel. First chapter: the Garden of Eden. Last chapter: the Apocalypse."

"I know, I know, the world started out perfectly good and has gotten worse and worse since then, and the only question is how bad will it get before God brings down the curtain. I was raised to believe that this tendency was as fixed and un-avoidable as gravity, Isaac. But the Apocalypse did not come in 1666."

"It will occur not long after 1867," Isaac said. "That is the year when the Beast will fall."

"Most Anglican cranks are guessing 1700 for the demise of the Catholic Church."

"It is not the only way that the Anglicans are wrong."

"Could it be, Isaac, that things are getting *better,* or at worst remaining more or less *the same,* rather then getting *worse* all the time? Because I really think you may know cer-tain things that never entered Solomon's head."

"I am working out the System of the World upstairs," Isaac said offhandedly. "It is not beyond reason to think that Solomon and other ancients knew that System, and en-crypted it in the design of their Temples."

"But according to the Bible those designs were given to them directly by God."

"But go outside and look up at the stars and you see God trying to give you the same thing, if only you will pay atten-tion."

"If Solomon knew all of this, why didn't he just come out and say, 'The sun is in the middle of the solar system and planets go round about it in ellipses?'"

"I believe he did say so, in the design of his temple."

"Yes, but why are God and Solomon alike so damned oblique in everything? Why not just come out and say it?"

"It is good that you do not waste my time with tedious letters," Isaac said. "When I read a letter I can follow the words, but I cannot fathom the mind, of him who sent it. It is better that you come to visit me in the night-time."

"Like an alchemist?"

"Or an early Christian in pagan Rome . . ."

"Scratching curves in the dust?"

". . . or any Christian who dares oppose the idolators. If you were to use me thus in a letter, I would conclude you were in the employ of the Beast, as some say you are."

"What, merely for suggesting that the world does something other than rot?"

"Of course it rots, Daniel. There is no perpetual motion machine."

"Except for the heart."

"The heart rots, Daniel. Sometimes it even begins to rot while its owner still lives."

Daniel dared not follow that one up. After a silence Isaac continued, in a throatier voice: "Where do we find God in the world? That is all I want to know. I have not found Him yet. But when I see anything that does *not* rot—the workings of the solar system, or a Euclidean proof, or the perfection of gold—I sense I am drawing nearer to the Divine."

"Have you found the Philosophick Mercury yet?"

"In '77, Boyle was certain he had it."

"I remember."

"I agreed with him for a short time—but it was wishful thinking. I am seeking it in geometry now—or rather I am seeking it where geometry fails."

"Fails?"

"Come upstairs with me Daniel."

DANIEL RECOGNIZED THE first proof as easily as his own signature. "Objects governed by a centripetal force conserve angular

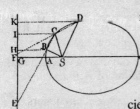

momentum and sweep out equal areas in equal times."

"You have read my *De Motu Corporum in Gyrum?*"

"Mr. Halley has made its contents known to the Royal Society," Daniel said drily.

"Some supporting lemmas come out of this," Isaac said, pulling another diagram over the first.

"and thence we can move on immediately to"

"That is the great one," Daniel said. "If the centripetal force is governed by an inverse-square law, then the body moves on an ellipse, or at any rate a conic section."

"I would say, 'That heavenly bodies *do* move on conic sections proves the inverse-square law.' But we are only speaking of fictions, so far. These proofs only apply to infinitesimal concentrations of mass, which do not exist in the real world. *Real* heavenly bodies possess geometry—they comprise a vast number of tiny particles arranged in the shape of a sphere. If Universal Gravitation exists, then each of the motes that make up the Earth attracts every other, and attracts the moon as well, and vice versa. And each of the moon's particles attracts the water in Earth's oceans to create tides. But how does the spherical geometry of a planet inform its gravity?"

Isaac produced another sheet, much newer-looking than the rest.

Daniel did not recognize this one. At first he thought it was a diagram of an eyeball, like the ones Isaac had made as a student. But Isaac was speaking of planets, not eyes.

A few awkward moments followed.

"Isaac," Daniel finally said, "*you* can draw a diagram like this one and say, 'Behold!' and the proof is finished. *I* require a bit of explanation."

"Very well." Isaac pointed to the circle in the middle of the diagram. "Consider a spherical body—actually an aggregate of countless particles, each of which produces gravitational attraction according to an inverse square law." Now he reached for the nearest handy object—an inkwell—and set it on the corner of the page, as far away from the "spherical body" as it could go. "What is felt by a satellite, here, on the outside, if the separate attractions of all of those particles are summed and fused into one aggregate force?"

"Far be it from me to tell you how to do physics, Isaac, but this strikes me as an ideal problem for the integral calculus—so why are you solving it geometrically?"

"Why not?"

"Is it because Solomon didn't have the calculus?"

"The calculus, as *some* call it, is a harsh method. I prefer to develop my proofs in a more geometric way."

"Because geometry is ancient, and everything ancient is good."

"This is idle talk. The result, as anyone can see from contemplating my diagram, is that a spherical body—a planet, moon, or star—having a given quantity of matter, produces a gravitational attraction that is the same as if all of its matter were concentrated into a single geometric point at the center."

"The *same*? You mean *exactly* the same?"

"It is a geometrical proof," Isaac merely said. "That the particles are spread out into a sphere *doesn't make any difference* because the geometry of the sphere is what it is. The gravity is the same."

Daniel now had to locate a chair; all the blood in his legs seemed to be rushing into his brain.

"If that is true," he said, "then everything you proved *before* about point objects—for example that they move along conic section trajectories—"

"Applies without alteration to spherical bodies."

"To *real things*." Daniel had a queer vision just then of a shattered Temple reconstituting itself: fallen columns rising up from the rubble, and the rubble re-aggregating itself into cherubim and seraphim, a fire sparking on the central altar. "You've done it then . . . created the System of the World."

"*God* created it. I have only *found* it. Rediscovered what was forgot. Look at this diagram, Daniel. It is *all here,* it is Truth made manifest, *epiphanes*."

"Now you said before that you were looking for God where Geometry failed."

"Of course. There is no *choice* in this," Isaac said, patting his diagram with a dry hand. "Not even God could have made the world otherwise. The only God here—" Isaac slammed the page hard "—is the God of Spinoza, a God that is everything and therefore nothing."

"But it seems as if you've explained everything."

"I've not explained the inverse square law."

"You've a proof right there saying that if gravity follows an inverse square law, satellites move on conic sections."

"And Flamsteed says that they do," Isaac said, yanking the sheaf of notes out of Daniel's hip pocket. Ignoring the cover letter, he tore the ribbon from the bundle and began to scan the pages. "Therefore gravity does indeed follow an inverse square law. But we may only say so because it is consistent with Flamsteed's observations. If tonight Flamsteed notices a comet moving in a spiral, it shows that all my work is wrong."

"You're saying, why do we need Flamsteed at all?"

"I'm saying that the fact that we do need him proves that God is making choices."

"Or has made them."

This caused a sort of queasy sneer to come across Isaac's face. He closed his eyes and shook his head. "I am not one of those who believes that God made the world and walked away from it, that He has no further choices to make, no on-going presence in the world. I believe that He is everywhere, making choices all the time."

"But only because there are certain things you have not explained yet with geometric proofs."

"As I told you, I seek God where Geometry fails."

"But perhaps there is an undiscovered proof for the inverse square law. Perhaps it has something to do with vortices in the æther."

"No one has been able to make sense of vortices."

"Some interaction of microscopic particles, then?"

"Particles traversing the distance from the Sun to Saturn and back, at infinite speed, without being hindered by the æther?"

"You're right, it is impossible to take seriously. What is *your* hypothesis, Isaac?"

"*Hypothesis non fingo.*"

"But that's not really true. You begin with a hypothesis—I saw several of them scratched in the gravel out there. Then you come up with one of these diagrams. I cannot explain how you do that part, unless God is using you as a conduit. When you are finished, it is no longer a hypothesis but a demonstrated truth."

"Geometry can never explain gravity."

"Calculus then?"

"The calculus is just a convenience, a short-hand way of doing geometry."

"So what is beyond geometry is also beyond calculus."

"Of course, by definition."

"The inner workings of gravity, you seem to be saying,

are beyond the grasp, or even the reach, of Natural Philosophy. To whom should we appeal, then? Metaphysicians? Theologians? Sorcerers?"

"They are all the same to me," Isaac said, "and I am one."

Beach North of Scheveningen

OCTOBER 1685

⚕

IT WAS AS IF WILLIAM of Orange had searched the world over to find the place most different from Versailles, and had told Eliza to meet him there. At Versailles, everything had been designed and made by men. But here was nothing to see but ocean and sand. Every grain of sand had been put where it was by waves that formed up in the ocean according to occult laws that might have been understood by the Doctor, but not by Eliza.

She had dismounted and was leading her horse northwards up the beach. The sand was hard-packed and solid and wet, speckled all over with cockle shells in colors and patterns of such profusion and variety that they must have given the first Dutchmen the idea to go out into the sea and bring back precious things from afar. They made a welcome contrast against the extreme flatness and sameness of beach, water, and misty sky, and exerted a hypnotic effect on her. She forced herself to look up from time to time. But the only feature of the view that ever changed was the signatures of foam deposited on the beach by the waves.

Each breaker, she supposed, was as unique as a human soul. Each made its own run up onto the shore, being the very embodiment of vigor and power at the start. But each slowed, spread thin, faltered, dissolved into a hissing ribbon of gray foam, and got buried under the next. The end result of all their noisy, pounding, repetitious efforts was the beach. Seen through a lens, the particular arrangement of sand-grains that made up the beach presumably was complicated, and reflected the individual contributions of every single wave that had ended its life here; but seen from the level of Eliza's head it was unspeakably flat, an "abomination of desolation in a dark place," as the Bible would put it.

She heard a ripping noise behind her and turned around to look to the south, toward the dent in the beach, several miles distant, that formed the harbor of Scheveningen. The last time she'd looked back, a few minutes ago, there had been nothing between her and the anchorage but a few clam-diggers. But now there was a sail on the sand: a triangle of canvas, stretched drum-tight by the wet wind off the sea. Below it hovered a spidery rig of timbers with spoked wagon-wheels at their ends. One wheel was suspended in the air by the heeling of the vehicle. Taken together with the speed of its progress up the beach, this created the impression that it was flying. The wheel spun slowly in the air, dripping clots of wet sand from its rim, which was very wide so that it rolled over, instead of cutting into, the sand and its gay mosaic of cockle shells. The opposite wheel was scribing a long fat track down the beach, slaloming between the dark hunched forms of the diggers; though, a hundred yards in its wake, this trace had already been erased by the waves.

A fishing-boat had eased in to shore as the tide ebbed, pulled up her sideboards, and allowed herself to be stranded there. The fishermen had chocked her upright with baulks of wood, brought their catch up out of the hold, and laid it out on the sand, creating a little fish-market that would last until the tide flowed in again, chased away the customers, and floated the boat. People had carried baskets out from town, or driven out in carriages, to carry out disputes with the fishermen over the value of what they'd brought back from the deep.

Some of them turned to look at the sand-sailer. It rushed past Eliza, moving faster than any horse could gallop. She recognized the man operating the tiller and manipulating the lines. Some of the fish-buyers did, too, and a few of those bothered to doff their hats and bow. Eliza mounted her horse and rode in pursuit.

The view inland was blocked by dunes. Not dunes such as Eliza had once seen in the Sahara, but hybrids of dunes and hedges. For these were covered by, and anchored in, vegetation that was light green in the lower slopes, but in other places deepened to a bluish cast, and formed up into great furry dark eyebrows frowning at the sea.

A mile or so north of where the fishing-boat had been beached, the sight-line from the town was severed by a gradual bend in the coastline, and a low spur flung seawards by a dune. From here, the only sign that Holland was a settled country was a tall watchtower with a conical roof, built atop a dune, perhaps half a mile distant. The sand-sailer had come to rest, its sheets loosened so that the sail reached and weathercocked.

"I am probably meant to ask, 'Where is your Court, O Prince, your entourage, your bodyguards, your train of painters, poets, and historians?' Whereupon you'd give me a stern talking-to about the decadence of France."

"Possibly," said William, Prince of Orange and Stadholder of the Dutch Republic. He had extricated himself from the canvas seat of the sailer and was standing on the beach facing out to sea, layers of sand-spattered leather and spray-soaked wool giving his body more bulk than it really had. "Or perhaps I like to go sand-sailing by myself, and your reading so much into it is proof you've been too long at Versailles."

"Why is this dune here, I wonder?"

"I don't know. Tomorrow it may not be. Why do you mention it?"

"I look at all these waves, spending so much effort to accomplish so little, and wonder that from time to time they can raise something as interesting as a dune. Why, this hill of sand is equivalent to Versailles—a marvel of ingenuity. Waves from the Indian Ocean, encountering waves of Araby

off the Malabar Coast, must gossip about this dune, and ask
for the latest tidings from Scheveningen."

"It is normal for women, at certain times of the month,
and in certain seasons of the year, to descend into moods
such as this one," the prince mused.

"A fair guess, but wrong," Eliza said. "There are Christian
slaves in Barbary, you know, who expend vast efforts to accomplish tiny goals, such as getting a new piece of furniture
in their *banyolar* . . ."

"Banyolar?"

"Slave-quarters."

"What a pathetic story."

"Yes, but it is all right for them to achieve meager results
because they are in a completely hopeless and desperate situation," Eliza said. "In a way, a slave is fortunate, because
she has more head-room for her dreams and phant'sies,
which can soar to dizzying heights without bumping up
'gainst the ceiling. But the ones who live at Versailles are as
high as humans can get, they practically have to go about
stooped over because their wigs and head-dresses are scraping the vault of heaven—which consequently seems low and
mean to them. When they look up, they see, not a vast beckoning space above, but rather—"

"The gaudy-painted ceiling."

"Just so. You see? There is no head-room. And so, for one
who has just come from Versailles, it is easy to look at these
waves, accomplishing so little, and to think that no matter
what efforts we put forth in our lives, all we're really doing
is rearranging the sand-grains in a beach that in essence
never changes."

"Right. And if we're really brilliant, we can cast up a little
dune or hummock that will be considered the Eighth Wonder of the World."

"Just so!"

"Lass, it's very poetic, albeit in a bleak Gothic sort of
way, but, begging your pardon, I look up and I don't see the
ceiling. All I see is a lot of damned Frenchmen looking

down their noses at me from a mile high. I must pull them all down to my level, or draw myself up to theirs, before I can judge whether I have succeeded in making a dune, or what-have-you. So let us turn our attentions thither."

"Very well. There is little to hold our attention *here*."

"What do you imagine was the point of the King's admonition, at the end of your most recent letter?"

"What—you mean, what he said to me after his operation?"

"Yes."

"Fear me inasmuch as you are my foe, be proud inasmuch as my friend? That one?"

"Yes, that one."

"Seems self-explanatory to me."

"But why on earth would the King feel the need to deliver such a warning to d'Avaux?"

"Perhaps he has doubts as to the count's loyalty."

"That is inconceivable. No man could be more his King's creature than d'Avaux."

"Perhaps the King is losing his grip, and perceiving enemies where none exist."

"Very doubtful. He has too many real enemies to indulge himself so—and besides, he is very far from losing his grip!"

"Hmph. None of *my* explanations is satisfactory, it seems."

"Now that you are out of France you must shed the habit of pouting, my Duchess. You do it exquisitely, but if you try it on a Dutchman he'll only want to slap you."

"Will you share *your* explanation with me, if I promise not to pout?"

"Obviously the King's admonition was intended for someone other than the comte d'Avaux."

This left Eliza baffled for a minute. William of Orange fussed with the rigging of his sand-sailer while she turned it over in her head. "You are saying then that the King knows my letters to d'Avaux are being deciphered and read by Dutch agents . . . and that his warning was intended for *you*. Have I got it right?"

"You are only starting to get it right . . . and this is becoming tedious. So let me explain it, for until you understand this, you will be useless to me. Every letter posted abroad from Versailles, whether it originates from you, or Liselotte, or the Maintenon, or some chambermaid, is opened by the Postmaster and sent to the *cabinet noir* to be read."

"Heavens! Who is in the *cabinet noir*?"

"Never mind. The point is that they have read all of your letters to d'Avaux and conveyed anything important to the King. When they are finished they give the letters back to the Postmaster, who artfully re-seals them and sends them north . . . *my* Postmaster then re-opens them, reads them, re-seals them, and sends them on to d'Avaux. So the King's admonition could have been intended for anyone in that chain: d'Avaux (though probably not), me, my advisors, the members of his own *cabinet noir* . . . or *you*."

"Me? Why would he want to admonish a little nothing like me?"

"I simply mention you for the sake of completeness."

"I don't believe you."

The Prince of Orange laughed. "Very well. Louis' entire system is built on keeping the nobility poor and helpless. Some of them enjoy it, others don't. The latter sort look for ways of making money. To whatever degree they succeed, they threaten the King. Why do you think the French East India Company fails time and again? Because Frenchmen are stupid? They are not stupid. Or rather, the stupid ones get despatched to India, because Louis wants that company to fail. A port-city filled with wealthy *commerçants*—a London or an Amsterdam—is a nightmare to him."

"Now, some of those nobles who desire money have turned their attentions toward Amsterdam and begun to engage the services of Dutch brokers. This was how your former business associate, Mr. Sluys, made his fortune. The King is pleased that you ruined Sluys, because he took some French counts down with him, and they serve as object lessons to any French nobles who try to build fortunes in the market of Amsterdam. But now you are being approached, yes? Your 'Spanish Uncle' is the talk of the town."

"You can't possibly expect me to believe that the King of France views *me* as a threat."

"Of course not."

"*You,* William of Orange, the Protestant Defender, are a threat."

"I, William, whatever titles you wish to hang on me, am an *enemy,* but not a *threat.* I may make war on him, but I will never imperil him, or his reign. The only people who can do that are all living at Versailles."

"Those dreadful dukes and princes and so on."

"And duchesses and princesses. Yes. And insofar as you might help these do mischief, you are to be watched. Why do you imagine d'Avaux put you there? As a favor? No, he put you there to be watched. But insofar as you may help Louis maintain his grip, you are a tool. One of many tools in his toolbox—but a strange one, and strange tools are commonly the most useful."

"If I am so useful to Louis—your enemy—then what am I to *you?*"

"To date, a rather slow and unreliable pupil," William answered.

Eliza heaved a sigh, trying to sound bored and impatient. But she could not help shuddering a bit as the air came out of her—a premonition of sobs.

"Though not without promise," William allowed.

Eliza felt better, and hated herself for being so like one of William's hounds.

"None of what I have written in any of my letters to d'Avaux has been of any use to you at all."

"You have only been learning the ropes, so far," William

said, plucking like a harp-player at various lines and sheets in the rigging of his sand-sailer. He climbed aboard and settled himself into the seat. Then he drew on certain of those ropes while paying out others, and the vehicle sprang forward, rolling down the slope of the dune, and building speed back towards Scheveningen.

ELIZA MOUNTED HER HORSE and turned around. The wind off the sea was in her face now, like a fine mixture of ice and rock salt fired out of blunderbusses. She decided to cut inland to get out of the weather. Riding up over the crest of the dune was something of a project, for it had grown to a considerable height here.

In the scrubby plants of the beach—shrubs as tall as a man, with wine-colored leaves and red berries—spiders had spun their webs. But the mist had covered them with strings of gleaming pearls so that she could see them from a hundred feet away. So much for being stealthy. Though a stealthy human, crouching among those same shrubs to look down on the beach, would be perfectly invisible. Farther up the slopes grew wind-raked trees inhabited by raucous, irritable birds, who made it a point to announce, to all the world, that Eliza was passing through.

Finally she reached the crest. Not far away was an open sea of grass that would take her to the polders surrounding the Hague. To reach it, she'd have to pass through a forest of scrubby gnarled trees with silvery gray foliage, growing on the lee side of the dune. She stopped for a moment there to get her bearings. From here she could see the steeples of the Hague, Leiden, and Wassenaar, and dimly make out the etched rectangles of formal gardens in private compounds built in the countryside along the coast.

As she rode down into the woods the susurration of the waves was muted, and supplanted by the hissing of a light, misty rain against the leaves. But she did not enjoy the sudden peace for very long. A man in a hooded cloak rose up from behind one of those trees and clapped his hands in the horse's face. The horse reared. Eliza, completely unready, fell off and landed harmlessly in soft sand. The cloaked man gave the horse a resounding slap on the haunches as it returned to all fours, and it galloped off in the direction of home.

This man stood with his back to Eliza for a moment, watching the horse run away, then looked up at the crest of the dune, and down the coast to that distant watch-tower, to see if anyone had seen the ambuscade. But the only witnesses were crows, flapping into the air and screaming as the horse charged through their sentry-lines.

Eliza had every reason to assume that something very bad was planned for her now. She had barely seen this fellow coming in the corner of her eye, but his movements had been brisk and forceful—those of a man accustomed to action, without the affected grace of a gentleman. This man had never taken lessons in dancing or fencing. He moved like a Janissary—like a soldier, she corrected herself. And that was rather bad news. A fair proportion of the murder, robbery, and rape committed in Europe was the work of soldiers who had been put out of work, and just now there were thousands of those around Holland.

Under the terms of an old treaty between England and Holland, six regiments of English and Scottish troops had long been stationed on Dutch soil, as a hedge against invasion from France (or, much less plausibly, the Spanish Netherlands). A few months earlier, when the Duke of Monmouth had sailed to England and mounted his rebellion, his intended victim, King James II, had sent word from London that those six regiments were urgently required at home. William of Orange—despite the fact that his sympathies lay more with Monmouth than with the King—had complied without delay, and shipped the regiments over. By the time they had arrived, the rebellion had been quashed, and there had been nothing for them to do. The King had been slow to send them back, for he did not trust his son-in-law (William of Orange) and suspected that those six regiments might one day return as the vanguard of a Dutch invasion. He had wanted to station them in France instead. But King Louis— who had plenty of his own regiments—had seen them as an unnecessary expense, and William had insisted that the treaty be observed. So the six regiments had come back to Holland.

Shortly thereafter, they had been disbanded. So now the Dutch countryside was infested with unpaid and unled foreign soldiers. Eliza guessed that this was one of them; and since he had not bothered to steal her horse, he must have other intentions.

She rolled onto her elbows and knees and gasped as if she'd had the wind knocked out of her. One arm was supporting her head, the other clutching at her abdomen. She was wearing a long cape that had spread over her like a tent. Propping her forehead against her wrist, she gazed upside-down into the hidden interior of that tent, where her right hand was busy in the damp folds of her waist-sash.

One of the interesting bits of knowledge she had picked up in the Topkapi Palace was that the most feared men in the Ottoman Empire were not the Janissaries with their big scimitars and muskets, but rather the *hashishin:* trained murderers who went unarmed except for a small dagger concealed in the waistband. Eliza did not have the skills of a *hashishin,* but she knew a good idea when she saw one, and she was never without the same kind of weapon. To whip it out now would be a mistake, though. She only made sure it was ready to hand.

Then she lifted her head, pushed herself up to a kneeling position, and gazed at her attacker. At the same moment, he turned to face her and threw back his hood to reveal the face of Jack Shaftoe.

ELIZA WAS PARALYZED for several moments.

Since Jack was almost certainly dead by now, it would be conventional to suppose that she was looking upon his ghost. But this was the reverse of the truth. A ghost ought to be paler than the original, a drawn shadow. But Jack—at least, the Jack she'd most recently seen—had been like the ghost of *this* man. This fellow was heavier, steadier, with better color and better teeth . . .

"Bob," she said.

He looked slightly startled, then made a little bow. "Bob Shaftoe it is," he said, "at your service, Miss Eliza."

"You call knocking me off my horse being at my service?"

"You *fell* off your horse, begging your pardon. I apologize. But I did not wish that you would gallop away and summon the Guild."

"What are you doing here? Was your regiment one of those that was disbanded?"

His brain worked. Now that Bob had begun talking, and reacting to things, his resemblance to Jack was diminishing quickly. The physical similarity was strong, but this body was animated by a different spirit altogether. "I see Jack told you something of me—but skipped the details. No. My regiment still exists, though it has a new name now. It's guarding the King in London."

"Then why're you not with it?"

"John Churchill, the commander of my regiment, sends me on odd errands."

"This one must be very odd indeed, to bring you to the wrong shore of the North Sea."

"It is a sort of salvage mission. No one expected the regiments here to be disbanded. I am trying to track down certain sergeants and corporals who are well thought of, and recruit them into the service of my master before they get hanged in Dutch towns for stealing chickens, or press-ganged on India ships, or recruited by the Prince of Orange . . ."

"Do I looked like a grizzled sergeant to you, Bob Shaftoe?"

"I am laying that charge to one side for a few hours to speak to you about a private matter, Miss Eliza. The time it will take to walk back to the Hague should suffice."

"Let's walk, then, I am getting cold."

༜

Dorset
JUNE 1685

⚜

I never justify'd cutting off the King's Head,
yet the Disasters that befel Kings when they begun to be Arbitrary, are not without their use,
and are so many Beacons to their Successors to
mark out the Sands which they are to avoid.

— *The Mischiefs That Ought Justly*
to Be Apprehended from a
Whig-Government, ANONYMOUS,
ATTRIBUTED TO BERNARD MANDEVILLE, 1714

IF POOR JACK'S RAVINGS have any color of truth in them, then
you have been among Persons of Quality. So you have learnt
how important Family is to such people: that it gives them
not only name but rank, a house, a piece of land to call
home, income and food, and that it is the windowpane
through which they look out and perceive the world. It
brings them troubles, too: for they are born heirs to superiors
who must be obeyed, roofs that want fixing, and diverse local troubles that belong to them as surely as their own
names.

Now, in place of "Persons of Quality" substitute "common men of soldier type" and in place of "Family" say
"Regiment," and you will own a fair portrait of my life.

You seem to've spent a lot of time with Jack and so I'll

spare you the explanation of how two mudlark boys found themselves in a regiment in Dorset. But my career has been like his in a mirror, which is to say, all reversed.

The regiment he told you of was like most old English ones, which is to say, 'twas *militia*. The soldiers were common men of the shire and the officers were local gentlemen, and the big boss was a Peer, the Lord Lieutenant—in our case, Winston Churchill—who got the job by living in London, wearing the right clothes, and saying the right things.

Those militia regiments once came together to form Cromwell's New Model Army, which defeated the Cavaliers, slew the King, abolished Monarchy, and even crossed the Channel to rout the Spaniards in Flanders. None of this was lost on Charles II. After he came back, he made a practice of keeping *professional* soldiers on his payroll. They were there *to keep the militias in check*.

You may know that the Cavaliers who brought Charles II back made their landfall in the north and came down from Tweed, crossing the Cold Stream with a regiment under General Lewis. That regiment is called the Coldstream Guards, and General Lewis was made the Duke of Tweed for his troubles. Likewise King Charles created the Grenadier Guards. He probably would have abolished the militia altogether if he could have—but the 1660s were troublous times, what with Plague and Fire and bitter Puritans roaming the country. The King needed his Lords Lieutenant to keep the people down—he granted 'em the power to search homes for arms and to throw troublesome sorts in prison. But a Lord Lieutenant could not make use of such powers save through a local militia and so the militias endured. And 'twas during those times that Jack and I were plucked out of a Vagabond-camp and made into regimental boys.

A few years later John Churchill reached an age—eighteen years—when he was deemed ready to accept his first commission, and was given a regiment of Grenadier Guards. It was a new regiment. Some men and armaments and other necessaries were made available to him, but he had to raise the rest himself, and so he did the natural thing and recruited many soldiers and non-commissioned officers from his father's militia regiment in Dorset—including me and Jack. For there is a difference 'twixt Families and Regiments, which is that the latter have no female members and cannot increase in the natural way—new members must be raised up out of the soil like crops, or if you will, taxes.

Now I'll spare you a recitation of my career under John Churchill, as you've no doubt heard a slanderous version of it from brother Jack. Much of it consisted of long marches and sieges on the Continent—very repetitive—and the rest has been parading around Whitehall and St. James, for our nominal purpose is to guard the King.

Lately, following the death of Charles II, John Churchill spent some time on the Continent, going down to Versailles to meet with King Louis and biding in Dunkirk for a time to keep a weather eye on the Duke of Monmouth. I was there with him and so when Jack came through aboard his merchant-ship full of cowrie-shells I went out to have a brotherly chat with him.

Here the tale could turn ghastly. I'll not describe Jack. Suffice it to say I have seen better and worse on battle-fields. He was far gone with the French Pox and not of sound mind. I learnt from him about you. In particular I learnt that you have the strongest possible aversion to Slavery—whereof I'll say more anon. But first I must speak of Monmouth.

There was a Mr. Foot aboard *God's Wounds,* one of those pleasant and harmless-seeming fellows to whom anyone will say anything, and who consequently knows everyone and everything. While I was waiting for Jack to recover his senses I passed a few hours with him and collected the latest gossip—or, as we say in the military, intelligence—from Amsterdam. Mr. Foot told me that Monmouth's invasion-force was massing at Texel and that it was certainly bound for the port of Lyme Regis.

When I was finished saying my good-byes to poor Jack I went ashore and tried to seek out my master, John Churchill,

to give him this news. But he had just sailed for Dover,
London-bound, and left orders for me to follow on a slower
boat with certain elements of the regiment.

Now I've probably given you the impression that the
Grenadier Guards were in Dunkirk, which is wrong. They
were in London guarding the King. Why was I not with my
regiment? To answer I would have to explain what I am to
John Churchill and what he is to me, which would take more
time than it would be worth. Owing to my advanced age—
almost thirty—and long time in service, I am a very senior
non-commissioned officer. And if you knew the military this
would tell you much about the peculiar and irregular nature
of my duties. I do the things that are too difficult to explain.

Not very clear, is it? Here is a fair sample: I ignored my
orders, cast off my uniform, borrowed money on my master's good name, and took passage on a west-bound ship that
brought me eventually to Lyme Regis. Before I embarked I
sent word to my master that I was making myself useful in
the West, where I had heard that some Vagabonds wanted
hanging. As I'm certain you have perceived, this was both a
prophecy of what was soon to come, and a reminder of
events long past. Monmouth had set sail for Dorset because
it was a notorious hotbed of Protestant rebellion. Ashe
House, which was the seat of the Churchill family, looked
down into the harbor of Lyme Regis, which had been the site
of a dreary siege during the Civil War. Some of the
Churchills had been Roundheads, others Cavaliers. Winston
had taken the Cavalier side, had brought this riotous place to
heel, and he and his son had been made important men for
their troubles. Now Monmouth—John's old comrade-in-
arms from Siege of Maestricht days—was coming to make a
bloody mess of the place. It would make Winston look either
foolish or disloyal in the eyes of the rest of Parliament, and it
would cast doubts on John's loyalty.

For some years, John has been in the household of the
Duke of York—now King James II—but his wife Sarah is
now Lady of the Bedchamber to the Duke's daughter, the

Princess Anne: a Protestant who might be Queen someday.
And among those Londoners who whisper into each other's
ears for a living, this has been taken to mean that John's
merely putting on a show of loyalty to the King, biding his
time until the right moment to betray that Papist and bring a
Protestant to the throne. Nothing more than Court gossip—
but if Monmouth used John's very home ground as the
beach-head of a Protestant rebellion, how would it look?

Monmouth's little fleet dropped anchor in the harbor of
Lyme Regis two days after I had arrived. The town was
giddy—they thought Cromwell had been re-incarnated.
Within a day, fifteen hundred men had rallied to his standard. Almost the only one who did not embrace him was the
Mayor. But I had already warned him to keep his bags
packed and horses saddled. I helped him and his family slip
out of town, following covert trails of Vagabonds, and he
despatched messengers to the Churchills in London. This
way Winston could go to the King and say, "My constituents
are in rebellion and here is what my son and I are doing
about it" rather than having the news sprung on him out of
the blue.

It would be a week at the earliest before my regiment
could come out from London—which amounts to saying
that Monmouth had a week to raise his army, and that I had
a week in which to make myself useful. I waited in a queue
in the market-square of Lyme Regis until the clerk could
prick my name down in his great book; I told him I was Jack
Shaftoe and under that name I joined Monmouth's army.
The next day we mustered in a field above the town and I
was issued my weapon: a sickle lashed to the end of a stick.

The next week's doings were of some moment to John
Churchill, when I told him the tale later, but would be tedious to you. There is only one part you might take an interest in, and that is what happened at Taunton. Taunton is an
inland town. Our little army reached it after several days'
straggling through the countryside. By that time we were
three thousand strong. The town welcomed us even more

warmly than Lyme Regis; the school girls presented Monmouth with a banner they had embroidered for him, and served us meals in a mess they had set up in the town square. One of these girls—a sixteen-year-old named Abigail Frome . . .

Shall I devote a thousand words, or ten thousand, to how I fell in love with Abigail Frome? "I fell in love with her" does not do it justice, but ten thousand words would be no better, and so let us leave it at that. Perhaps I loved her because she was a rebel girl, and my heart was with the rebellion. My mind could see it was doomed, but my heart was listening to the Imp of the Perverse. I had chosen the name of Jack Shaftoe because I reckoned my brother was dead by now and would not be needing it. But being "Jack Shaftoe" had awakened a lust I had long forgotten: I wanted to go a-vagabonding. And I wanted to take Abigail Frome with me.

That was true the first and possibly the second day of my infatuation. But in between those long sunny June days were short nights of broken and unrestful sleep, when fretful thoughts would dissolve into strange dreams that would end with me shocked upright in my bed, like a sailor who has felt his ship hit a reef, and who knows he ought to be doing somewhat other than just lying there. I'd not bedded the girl or even kissed her. But I believed we were joined together now, and that I needed to make preparations for a life altogether different. Vagabonding and rebellion could not be part of that life—they are fit for men, but men who try to bring their women and children along on that life are bastards plain and simple. If you spent any time on the road with Jack, you will take my meaning.

So my Vagabond-passion for this rebel girl made me turn against the rebellion finally. I could flirt with one or the other but not with both; and flirting with Abigail was more rewarding.

Now came word that the militia—my old regiment of local commoners—was being called up to perform its stated function, namely, to put down the rebellion. I deserted my rebel regiment, crept out of Taunton, and went to the mustering-place. Some of the men were ready to throw in their lot with Monmouth, some were loyal to the King, and most were too scared and amazed to do anything. I rallied a company of loyal men, little better than stragglers, and marched them to Chard, where John Churchill had at last arrived and set up an encampment.

This is as good a time as any to mention that while sneaking through the rebel lines at Taunton I had been noticed— not by the sentry, a dozing farmhand, but by his dog. The dog had come after me and seized me by the leg of my breeches and held me long enough for the farmer to come after me with a pitchfork. As you can see, I had let things get out of hand. It was because I have a fatuous liking for dogs, and always have, ever since I was a mudlark boy and Persons of Quality would call me a dog. I had removed the sickle from the end of my stick and left it in Taunton, but the stick I still had, so I raised it up and brought the butt down smartly between the dog's brown eyes, which I remember clearly glaring up at me. But it was a dog of terrier-kind and would on no account loosen its bite. The farmer thrust at me with his pitchfork. I spun away. One tine of the fork got under the skin of my back and tunneled underneath for about a hand's breadth and then erupted somewhere else. I made a backhand swing of my stick and caught him across the bridge of the nose. He let go the pitchfork and put his hands to his face. I pulled the iron out of my flesh, raised it up above the dog, and told the farmer that if he would only call the damned creature off I would not have to spill any blood here, other than my own.

He saw the wisdom of this. But now he had recognized me. "Shaftoe!" he said, "have you lost your nerve so soon?" I recognized him now as a fellow I had passed time with while we waited in the queue in Lyme Regis to enlist in Monmouth's army.

I am accustomed to the regular and predictable evolutions of the march, the drill, and the siege. Yet now within a few days of my conceiving a boyish infatuation with Abigail Frome, I had worked my way round to one of those farcical muddles you see in the fourth act of a comedy. I was forsaking the rebellion in order to forge a new life with a rebel lass, who had fallen in love, not with me, but with my brother, who was dead. I who have slain quite a few men had been caught and recognized because I would not hurt a mongrel. And I who was—if I may say so—doing something that demanded a whiff of courage or so, and that demonstrated my loyalty, would now be denounced as a coward and traitor, and Abigail would consider me in those terms forever.

A civilian—by your leave—would have been baffled, amazed. My soldier's mind recognized this immediately as a screw-up, a cluster-fuck, a Situation Normal. This sort of thing happens to us all the time, and generally has worse consequences than a pretty girl deciding that she despises you. Fermented beverages and black humor are how we cope. I extricated myself without further violence. But by the time I made my way into the camp of John Churchill, the pitchfork-wound on my back had suppurated, and had to be opened up and aired out by a barber. I could not see it myself, but all who gazed upon it were taken a-back. Really 'twas a shallow wound, and it healed quickly once I became strong enough to fend off the barber. But that I had staggered into the camp bleeding and feverish at the head of a column of loyal militia troops was made into something bigger than it really was. John Churchill heaped praise and honor upon me, and gave me a purse of money. When I related the entire tale to him, he laughed and mused, "I am doubly indebted to your brother now—he has furnished me with an excellent horse and a vital piece of intelligence."

Jack tells me you are literate and so I will let you read about the details of the fighting in a history-book. There are a few particulars I will mention because I doubt that historians will consider them meet to be set down in print.

The King declined to trust John Churchill, for the reasons I stated earlier. Supreme command was given to Feversham, who despite his name is a Frenchman. Years ago Feversham undertook to blow up some houses with gunpowder, supposedly to stop a fire from spreading, but really, I suspect, because he was possessed of that urge, common to all men, to blow things up for its own sake. Moments after he satisfied that urge, he was brained by a piece of flying debris, and left senseless. His brain swelled up. To make room for it, the chirurgeons cut a hole in his skull. You can imagine the details for yourself—suffice it to say that the man is a living and breathing advertisement for the Guild of Wigmakers. King James II favors him, which, if you knew nothing else about His Majesty, would give you knowledge sufficient to form an opinion about his reign.

It was this Feversham who had been placed in command of the expedition to put down the Duke of Monmouth's rebellion, and he who received credit for its success, but it was John Churchill who won the battles, and my regiment, as always, that did the fighting. The Duke of Grafton came out at the head of some cavalry and did battle with Monmouth at one point. The engagement was not all that important, but I mention it to add some color to the story, for Grafton is one of Charles II's bastards, just like Monmouth himself!

The campaign was made exciting only by Feversham's narcolepsy. That, combined with his inability to come to grips with matters even when he was awake, made it seem for a day or two as if Monmouth had a chance. I spent most of the time lying on my stomach recovering from the pitchfork-wound. And I count myself fortunate in that, because I had, and have, no love for the King, and I liked those rustic Nonconformists with their sickles and blunderbusses.

In the end Monmouth deserted those men even as they were fighting and dying for him. We found him cowering in a ditch. He was shipped off to the Tower of London and died groveling.

The farmers and tradesmen of Lyme Regis and Taunton who had made up Monmouth's army were Englishmen through and through, which is to say not only were they level-headed decent sensible moderate folk, but they could not conceive of, and did not know about, any other way of being. It simply did not occur to them that Monmouth would abandon them and try to flee the island. But it had occurred to me, because I had spent years fighting on the Continent.

Likewise they never imagined the repression that followed. Living in that open green countryside or settled in their sleepy market-towns, they had no understanding of the feverish minds of the Londoners. If you go to a lot of plays, as Jack and I used to do, you notice, soon enough, that the playwrights only have so many stories to go around. So they use them over and over. Oftimes when you sneak into a play that has just opened, the characters and situations will seem oddly familiar, and by the time the first scene has played out, you will recall that you've already seen this one several times before—except that it was in Tuscany instead of Flanders, and the schoolmaster was a parson, and the senile colonel was a daft admiral. In like manner, the high and mighty of England have the story of Cromwell stuck in their heads, and whenever anything the least bit upsetting happens—especially if it's in the country, and involves Nonconformists—they decide, in an instant, that it's the Civil War all over again. All they want is to figure out which one is playing the role of Cromwell, and put his head on a stick. The rest must be put down. And so it will continue until the men who run England come up with a new story.

Worse, Feversham was a French nobleman to whom peasants (as he construed these people) were faggots to be stuffed into the fireplace. By the time he was finished, every tree in Dorset had dead yeomen, wheelwrights, coopers, and miners hanging from its branches.

Churchill wanted no part of this. He got himself back to London as directly as possible, along with his regiments—myself included. Feversham had not been slow to spread tales of the glorious fight. He had already made himself into a hero, and every other part of the tale was likewise made into something much grander than it really was. The ditch in

which we captured Monmouth was swollen, by the tale-
tellers, into a raging freshet called the Black Torrent. The
King was so taken with this part of the story that he has
given my regiment a new name: we are now, and forever, the
King's Own Black Torrent Guards.

Now at last I can speak to you of slavery, which according
to Jack is a practice on which you harbor strong opinions.

The Lord Chief Justice is a fellow name of Jeffreys, who
was reputed for cruelty and bloody-mindedness even in the
best of times. He has spent his life currying favor with the
Cavaliers, the Catholics, and the Frenchified court, and
when King James II came to the throne Jeffreys got his reward and became the highest judge of England. Monmouth's
rebellion brought a whiff of blood on the west wind, and Jeffreys followed it like a slavering hound and established a
Court of Assizes in that part of the country. He has executed
no fewer than four hundred persons—that is, four hundred in
addition to those slain in battle or strung up by Feversham.
In some parts of the Continent, four hundred executions
would go nearly unnoticed, but in Dorset it is reckoned a
high figure.

As you can see, Jeffreys has been ingenious in finding
grounds for putting men to death. But there are many cases
where not even he could justify capital punishment, and so
instead the defendants were sentenced to slavery. It says
something about his mind that he considers slavery a lighter
punishment than death! Jeffreys has sold twelve hundred ordinary West Country Protestants into chattel slavery in the
Caribbean. They are on their way to Barbados even now,
where they and their descendants will chop sugar cane forever among neegers and Irishmen, with no hope of ever
knowing freedom.

The girl I love, Abigail Frome, has been made a slave. All
the schoolgirls of Taunton have been. For the most part these
girls have not been sold to sugar plantations; they would
never survive the voyage. Instead they have been parceled
out to various courtiers in London. Lord Jeffreys gives 'em

away like oysters in a pub. Their families in Taunton then
have no choice but to buy them back, at whatever price their
owners demand.

Abigail is now the property of an old college chum of
Lord Jeffreys: Louis Anglesey, the Earl of Upnor. Her father
has been hanged and her mother died years ago; of her
cousins, aunts, and uncles, many have been sent to Barbados, and the ones who remain do not have the money to buy
Abigail back. Upnor has amassed heavy gambling debts,
which drove his own father to bankruptcy and forced him to
sell his house years ago; now Upnor hopes to repay some of
those debts by selling Abigail.

It goes without saying that I want to kill Upnor. One day,
God willing, I shall. But this would not help Abigail—she'd
only be inherited by Upnor's heirs. Only money will buy her
freedom. I think that you are skilled where money is concerned. I ask you now to buy Abigail. In return, I give you
myself. I know you hate slavery and do not want a slave, but
if you do this for me I will be your slave in all but name.

As Bob Shaftoe had told his story, he had led Eliza
through a maze of paths through the lee woods, which he appeared to know quite well. Before long they had reached the
edge of a canal that ran from the city out to the shore at
Scheveningen. This canal was not lined with sharp edges of
stone, as in the city, but was soft and sloping at the edges,
and in some places lined with rushes. Cows stood chewing
on these, and watched Bob and Eliza walk by, interrupting
him from time to time with their weird, pointless lamenta-
tions. As they had drawn closer to the Hague, Bob had begun to show uncertainty at certain canal-intersections, and
Eliza had stepped into the lead. The scenery did not change
very much, except that houses and small feeder canals become more frequent. Woods appeared to their left side, and
continued for some distance. The Hague sneaked up on
them. For it was not a fortified city, and at no point did they
pass through anything like a wall or gate. But suddenly Eliza

turned to the right on the bank of another canal—a proper stone-edged one—and Bob realized that they had penetrated into something that could be called a neighborhood. And not just any neighborhood, but the Hofgebied. Another few minutes' walk would take them to the very foundations of the Binnenhof.

In the woods by the sea, it might have been foolhardy for Eliza to speak frankly; but here she could summon the St. George Guild from their clubhouse with a shout. "Your willingness to repay me is of no account," she told Bob.

This was a cold answer, but it was a cold day, and William of Orange had treated her coldly, and Bob Shaftoe had knocked her off her horse. Now Bob looked dismayed. He was not accustomed to being beholden to anyone save his master, John Churchill, and now he was in the power of two girls not yet twenty: Abigail, who owned his heart, and Eliza, who (or so he imagined) had it in her power to own Abigail. A man more accustomed to helplessness would have put up more of a struggle. But Bob Shaftoe had gone limp, like the Janissaries before Vienna when it had come clear to them that their Turkish masters were all dead. All he could do was look with watery eyes at Eliza and shake his head amazed. She kept walking. He had no choice but to follow.

"I was taken a slave just like your Abigail," Eliza said. "'Twas as if Mummy and I'd been plucked off the beach by a rogue wave and swallowed by the Deep. No man came forward to ransom *me*. Does that mean it was *just* that I was so taken?"

"Now you're talking *nonsense*. I don't—"

"If 'tis evil for Abigail to be a slave—as I believe—then your offer of service to me is neither here nor there. If *she* should be free, all the *others* should be as well. That you're willing to do me a *favor* or two should not advance her to the head of the queue."

"I see, now you're making it into a grand moral question. I am a soldier and we have good reasons to be suspicious of those."

They had entered into a broad square on the east side of the Binnenhof, called the Plein. Bob was looking about alertly. A stone's throw from here was a guard-house that served as a gaol; he might have been wondering whether Eliza was trying to lead him straight into it.

But instead she stopped in front of a house: a large place, grand after the Barock style, but a little odd in its decorations. For atop the chimneys, where one would normally expect to see crosses or statues of Greek gods, there were armillary spheres, weathercocks, and swivel-mounted telescopes. Eliza fished in the folds of her waistband, nudged the stiletto out of the way, found the key.

"What's this, a convent?"

"Don't be absurd, do I look like some French mademoiselle who stays at such places?"

"A rooming-house?"

"It is the house of a friend. A friend of a friend, really."

Eliza swung the key round on the end of the red ribbon to which she had tied it. "Come in," she finally said.

"Beg pardon?"

"Come inside this house with me that we may continue our conversation."

"The neighbors—"

"Nothing that could happen here could possibly faze this gentleman's neighbors."

"What of the gentleman himself?"

"He is asleep," Eliza said, unlocking the front door. "Be quiet."

"Asleep, at noon?"

"He stirs at night—to make observations of the stars," Eliza said, glancing upwards. Mounted to the roof of the house, four stories above their heads, was a wooden platform with a tubular device projecting over the edge—too frail to shoot cannonballs.

The first floor's main room might have been grand, for its generous windows looked out over the Plein and the Binnenhof. But it was cluttered with the debris of lens- and mirror-grinding—always messy, sometimes dangerous—and with thousands of books. Though Bob would not know this, these were not only about Natural Philosophy but history and literature as well, and nearly all of them were in French or Latin.

To Bob these artifacts were only moderately strange, and he learned to overlook them after a few moments' nervous glancing around the room. What really paralyzed him was the omnipresent noise—not because it was loud, but because it *wasn't*. The room contained at least two dozen clocks, or sub-assemblies of clocks, driven by weights or springs whose altitude or tension stored enough energy, summed, to raise a barn. That power was restrained and disciplined by toothy mechanisms of various designs: brass insects creeping implacably around the rims of barbed wheels, constellations of metal stars hung on dark stolid axle-trees, all marching or dancing to the beat of swinging plumb-bobs.

Now a man in Bob Shaftoe's trade owed his longevity, in part, to his alertness—his sensitivity to (among other things) significant noises. Even the dimmest recruits could be relied on to notice the *loud* noises. A senior man like Bob was supposed to scrutinize the *faint* ones. Eliza got the impression that Bob was the sort of bloke who was forever shushing every man in the room, demanding absolute stillness so that he could hold his breath and make out whether that faint sporadic itching was a mouse in the cupboard, or enemy miners tunnelling under the fortifications. Whether that distant rhythm was a cobbler next door or an infantry regiment marching into position outside of town.

Every gear and bearing in this room was making the sort of sound that normally made Bob Shaftoe freeze like a startled animal. Even after he'd gotten it through his head that they were all clocks, or studies for clocks, he was hushed and intimidated by a sense of being surrounded by patient mechanical life. He stood at attention in the middle of the big room, hands in his pockets, blowing steam from his mouth and darting his eyes to and fro. These clocks were made to tell time precisely and nothing else. There were no bells, no chimes, and certainly no cuckoos. If Bob was waiting for such entertainments, he'd wait until he was a dusty skeleton surrounded by cobweb-clogged gears.

Eliza noted that he had shaved before going out on this morning's strange errand, something that would never have entered Jack's mind, and she wondered how it all worked—what train of thoughts made a man say, "I had better scrape my face with a blade before undertaking this one." Perhaps it was some sort of a symbolic love-offering to his Abigail.

"It is all a question of pride, isn't it?" Eliza said, stuffing a cube of peat into the iron stove. "Or honor, as you'd probably style it."

Bob looked at her instead of answering; or maybe his look was his answer.

"Come on, you don't have to be *that* quiet," she said, setting a kettle on the stove to heat.

"What Jack and I have in common is an aversion to begging," he said finally.

"Just as I thought. So, rather than beg Abigail's ransom from me, you are proposing a sort of financial transaction— a loan, to be paid back in service."

"I don't know the words, the terms. Something like that is what I had in mind."

"Then why me? You're in the Dutch Republic. This is the financial capital of the world. You don't need to seek out one particular lender. You could propose this deal to anyone."

Bob had clutched a double handful of his cloak and was wringing it slowly. "The confusions of the financial markets are bewildering to me—I prefer not to treat with *strangers . . .*"

"What am I to you if not a stranger?" Eliza asked, laughing. "I am *worse* than a stranger, I threw a spear at your brother."

"Yes, and that is what makes you *not* a stranger to me, it is how I *know* you."

"It is proof that I hate slavery, you mean?"

"Proof of that and of other personal qualities—qualities that enter into this matter."

"I am no Person of Quality, or of qualities—do not speak to me of that. It is proof only that my hatred of slavery makes me do irrational things—which is what you are asking me to do now."

Bob lost his grip on his cloak-wad and sat down unsteadily on a stack of books.

Eliza continued, "She threw a harpoon at my brother— she'll throw some money at me—is that how it goes?"

Bob Shaftoe put his hands over his face and began to cry, so quietly that any sounds he made were drowned out by the whirring and ticking of the clocks.

Eliza retreated into the kitchen, and went back to a cool corner where some sausage-casings had been rolled up on a stick. She unrolled six inches—on second thought, twelve— and cut it off. Then she tied a knot in one end. She fit the little sock of sheep-gut over the handle of a meat-axe that was projecting firmly into the air above a chopping-block, then, with her fingertips, coaxed the open end of it to begin rolling up the handle. Once it was started, with a quick movement of her hand she rolled the whole length up to make a translucent torus with the knotted end stretched across the middle like a drum-head. Gathering her skirts up one leg, she tucked the object into the hem of her stocking, which came up to about mid-thigh, and finally went back into the great room where Bob Shaftoe was weeping.

There was not much point in subtlety, and so she forced her way in between his thighs and stuffed her bosom into his face.

After a few moment's hesitation he took his hands away from between his wet cheeks and her breasts. His face felt cold for a moment, but only a moment. Then she felt his hands locking together behind the small of her back, where her bodice was joined to her skirt.

He held her for a moment, not weeping anymore, but

thinking. Eliza found that a bit tedious and so she left off stroking his hair and began going to work on his ears in a way he would not tolerate for long. Then, finally, Bob knew what to do. She could see that for Bob, knowing what to do was always the hard part, and the doing was easy. All those years Vagabonding with Jack, Bob had been the older and wiser brother preaching sternly into Jack's one ear while the Imp of the Perverse whispered into the other, and it had made him a stolid and deliberate sort. But having made up his mind, he was a launched cannonball. Eliza wondered what the two of them had been like, partnered together, and pitied the world for not allowing it.

Bob cinched an arm around the narrowest part of her waist and hoisted her into the air with a thrust of rather good thigh-muscles. Her head grazed a dusty ceiling-beam and she ducked and hugged his head. He yanked a blanket from a couch; the books that had been scattered all over the blanket ended up differently scattered on the couch. Carrying Eliza and dragging the blanket, he trudged in a mighty floorboard-popping cadence to an elliptical dining-table scattered with the remains of a scholarly dinner: apple-peels and gouda-rinds. Making a slow orbit of this he flipped the corners of the tablecloth into the center. Gathering them together turned the tablecloth into a bag of scraps, which he let down gently onto the floor. Then he broadcast the blanket onto the table, slapped it once with his palm to stop it from skimming right off, and rolled Eliza's body out into the middle of the woolly oval.

Standing above her, he'd already begun fumbling with his breeches, which she deemed premature—so bringing a knee up smartly between his thighs and pulling down on a grabbed handful of his hair, she obliged him to get on top of her. They lay there for a while with thighs interlocked, like fingers of two hands clutching each other, and Eliza felt him get ready as she was getting ready. But long after that they ground away at each other, as if Bob could somehow force his way through all those layers of masculine and feminine clothing. They did this because it felt good, and they were together in a cold echoing house in the Hague and had no other demands on their time. Eliza learned that Bob was not a man who felt good very often and that it took him a long time to relax. His whole body was stiff at first, and it took a long time for that stiffness to drain out of his limbs and his neck, and concentrate in one particular Member, and for him to agree that this did not all have to happen in an instant. At the beginning his face was planted between her breasts, and his feet were square on the floor, but inch by inch she coaxed him upwards. At first he showed a fighting man's reluctance to sever his connection with the ground, but in time she made it understood that additional delights were to be found toward the head of the table, and so he kicked his boots off and got his knees, and eventually his toes, up on the tabletop.

For a long time then they were face-to-face, which Eliza thought was as pleasant as this was likely to get. But after a while she got Bob to raise his chin and entrust her with his throat. While she was exploring that terrain she was undoing the top few buttons of his shirt, pulling it down off his shoulders as she did so, pinning his arms to his sides and exposing his nipples.

She locked her right knee behind his left, then shoved her tongue through a protective nest of hair, found his right nipple, and carefully nipped it. He twisted up and away from her. Pulling down hard on his trapped knee she drew her left leg up, planted her foot on the raised blade of his pelvis, and shoved. Bob rolled over onto his back. She came up from under him and wound up sitting on his thighs. A hard yank down on his breeches freed his erect penis while binding his thighs together. She pulled the knotted sheepgut from her stocking, stripped it down over him, straddled him, and sat down hard. He was distracted with pretending to be angry, and the sudden pleasure ambushed him. The sudden pain astonished her, for this was the first time a man had ever been inside Eliza. She let out an angry yell and tears spurted from her eyes; she shoved clenched fists into her eye-sockets and tried to control her leg-muscles, which were convulsively trying to climb up and off of him. She felt that he was rocking her up and down, which made her angry, but her knees were grinding steadily into the hard wood of the table, and so the sensation of movement must arise from light-headedness: a swoon that needed to be fought off.

She did not want him looking up at her like this and so she fell forward and struck the table to either side of his head with the flats of both palms, then bowed her head so that her hair fell down in a curtain, hiding her face, and everything below his chest, from Bob's view. Not that he was doing a lot of sightseeing; he had apparently decided that there were worse situations he could be in.

She moved up and down on him for a while, very slowly, partly because she was in pain and partly because she did not know how close he might be to reaching his climax—all men were different, a particular man would be different according to the time of day, and the only way to judge it was by the rhythm of his breathing (which she could hear) and the slackness of his face (which she could monitor through a narrow embrasure between dangling locks of hair). By those measures, she was nowhere near finished, and a lengthy and painful grind awaited her. But finally he came complete, in a long ordeal of back-arching and head-thumping.

He took the first breath, the one that meant he was finished, and opened his eyes. She was staring directly back at him.

"I hurt like hell," she announced. "I have inflicted this on myself as a demonstration."

"Of *what*?" he asked, bewildered, stuporous, but pleased with himself.

"To show you what I think of honor, as you style it. Where was Abigail just now?"

Bob Shaftoe now tried to become angry, without much success. An Englishman of higher class would have huffed "Now see here!" but Bob set his jaw and tried to sit up. He had more success in that—at first—because Eliza was not a large girl. But then from behind the dazzling hair curtain

came a hand, and the hand was holding a small Turkish
dagger—very nice, a wriggling blade of watered steel—
which closed on his left eyeball and obliged him to lie flat
again.

"The demonstration is very important," Eliza said—or
growled, rather, for she really was very uncomfortable. "You
come with high talk of honor and expect me to swoon and
buy Abigail back for you. I have heard many men speak of
honor while ladies are in the room, and then seen them abandon all thought of it when the lusts and terrors of the body
overcame their noble pretensions. Like cavaliers throwing
down their polished armor and bright battle-flags to flee a
charging Vagabond-host. You are no worse—but no better. I
will not help you because I am touched by your love for Abigail or stirred by your prating about honor. I will help you
because I wish to be somewhat more than another wave
spreading and spending itself on a godforsaken beach. Monsieur Mansart may build kingly châteaux to prove that he
once existed, and you may marry your Abigail and raise up a
clan of Shaftoes. But if I am to make a mark on this world, it
will have something to do with slavery. I will help you only
insofar as it serves that end. And buying the freedom of one
maiden does not serve it. But Abigail may be of use to me in
other ways . . . I shall have to think on it. While I think,
she'll be a slave to this Upnor. If she remembers you at all, it
will be as a turncoat and a coward. You will be a miserable
wretch. In the fullness of melancholy time, perhaps you'll
come to see the wisdom of my position."

Now the conversation—if it could be called that—was interrupted by a mighty throat-clearing from the opposite end
of the room, gallons of air shifting dollops of phlegm out of
the main channel. "Speaking of Positions," said a husky
Dutch voice, "would you and your gentleman friend please
find a different one? For since you've made *sleep* quite impossible I should like to *eat*."

"With pleasure, *meinheer*, I would, but your lodger has a
poniard at my eye," said Bob.

"You are much cooler in dealing with men than with women," Eliza observed, *sotto voce*.

"A woman such as you has never seen a man in a cool condition, unless you were spying on him through a knot-hole," Bob returned.

More throat-clearing from the owner: a hearty, grizzled man in his middle fifties, with all that that implied in the way of eyebrows. He had hoisted one of them like a furry banner and was peering out from under it at Eliza; typically for an astronomer who did his best seeing through a single eye. "The Doctor warned me to expect odd callers . . . but not *business transactions.*"

"Some would call me a whore, and some *shall,*" Eliza admitted, giving Bob a sharp look, "but in this case you are assuming too much, Monsieur Huygens. The *transaction* we are discussing is not related to the *act* we have performed . . ."

"Then why do both at the same time? Are you in *such* a hurry? Is this how it is done in Amsterdam?"

"I am trying to clear this fellow's mind so that he can think straighter," said Eliza, straightening up herself as she said it, for her back was getting tired and her bodice was griping her stomach.

Bob knocked her dagger-hand aside and sat up violently, throwing her into a backward somersault. She'd have landed on her head except that he caught her upper arms in his hands and spun her over—or something rather complicated and dangerous—all she knew was that, when it was over, she was dizzy, and her heart had skipped a few beats, her hair was in her face and her dagger-hand was empty. Bob was behind her, using her as a screen while he pulled his breeches up with one hand. His other hand had a grip on her laces, which he was exploiting as a sort of bridle. "You should never have straightened your arm," he explained quietly, "It tells the opponent that you are unable to make a thrust."

Eliza thanked him for the fencing-lesson by pirouetting in a direction calculated to bend his fingers backwards. He cursed, let go of her laces, and yanked his breeches up finally.

"Mr. Huygens, Bob Shaftoe of the King's Own Black Torrent Guards. Bob, meet Christiaan Huygens, the world's foremost Natural Philosopher."

"Hooke would *bite* you for saying so . . . Leibniz is brighter than I . . . Newton, though *confused*, is said to be talented. So let us say only that I am the foremost Natural Philosopher *in this room*," Huygens said, taking a quick census of the occupants: himself, Bob, Eliza, and a skeleton hanging in the corner.

Bob had not noticed the skeleton before, and its sudden inclusion in the conversation made him uneasy. "I beg your pardon, sir, 'twas disgraceful—"

"Oh, stop!" Eliza hissed, "he is a Philosopher, he cares not."

"Descartes used to come up here when I was a young man, and sit at that very table, and drink too much and discourse of the Mind-Body Problem," Huygens mused.

"Problem? What's the problem? I don't see any problem," Bob muttered parenthetically, until Eliza crowded back against him and planted a heel on his instep.

"So Eliza's attempt to clarify your mental processes by purging you of imbalancing humours could not have been carried out in a more appropriate location," Huygens continued.

"Speaking of humours, what am I to do with this?" Bob muttered, dangling a narrow bulging sac from one finger.

"Put it in a box and post it to Upnor as a down payment," Eliza said.

The sun had broken through as they spoke, and golden light suddenly shone into the room from off the Plein. It was a sight to gladden most any Dutch heart; but Huygens reacted to it strangely, as if he had been put in mind of some tiresome obligation. He conducted a poll of his clocks and watches. "I have a quarter of an hour in which to break my fast," he remarked, "and then Eliza and I have work to do on the roof. You are welcome to stay, Sergeant Shaftoe, though—"

"You have already been more than hospitable enough," Bob said.

HUYGENS'S WORK CONSISTED OF STANDING very still on his roof as the clock-towers of the Hague bonged noon all around him, and squinting into an Instrument. Eliza was told to stay out of his way, and jot down notes in a waste-book, and hand him small necessaries from time to time.

"You wish to know where the sun is at noon—?"

"You have it precisely backwards. *Noon is* when the sun is in a particular place. Noon has no meaning otherwise."

"So, you wish to know when noon is."

"It is now!" Huygens said, and glanced quickly at his watch.

"Then all of the clocks in the Hague are wrong."

"Yes, including all of mine. Even a well-made clock drifts, and must be re-set from time to time. I do it here whenever the sun shines. Flamsteed will be doing it in a few minutes on top of a hill in Greenwich."

"It is unfortunate that a person may not be calibrated so easily," Eliza said.

Huygens looked at her, no less intensely than he had been peering at his instrument a moment earlier. "Obviously you have some specific person in mind," he said. "Of persons I will say this: it is difficult to tell when they are running *aright* but easy to see when something has gone *awry.*"

"Obviously *you* have someone in mind, Monsieur Huygens," Eliza said, "and I fear it is I."

"You were referred to me by Leibniz," Huygens said. "A shrewd judge of intellects. Perhaps a bit less shrewd about *character,* for he always wants to think the best of everyone. I made some inquiries around the Hague. I was assured by persons of the very best quality that you would not be a political liability. From this I presumed that you would know how to behave."

Suddenly feeling very high and exposed, she took a step back, and reached out with a hand to steady herself against a heavy telescope-tripod. "I am sorry," she said. "It was stupid, what I did down there. I *know* it was, for I *do* know how to behave. Yet I was not always a courtier. I came to this place in my life by a roundabout path, which shaped me in ways that are not always comely. Perhaps I should be ashamed. But I am more inclined to be defiant."

"I understand you better than you suppose," Huygens said. "I was raised and groomed to be a diplomat. But when I was thirteen years old, I built myself a lathe."

"Pardon me, a what?"

"A lathe. Down below, in this very house. Imagine my parents' consternation. They had taught me Latin, Greek, French, and other languages. They had taught me the lute, the viol, and the harpsichord. Of literature and history I had learned everything that was in their power to teach me. Mathematics and philosophy I learned from Descartes himself. But I built myself a lathe. Later I taught myself how to grind lenses. My parents feared that they had spawned a tradesman."

"No one is more pleased than I that matters turned out so well for you," Eliza said, "but I am too thick to understand how your story is applicable to my case."

"It is all right for a clock to run fast or slow at times, so long as it is calibrated against the sun, and set right. The sun may come out only once in a fortnight. It is enough. A few minutes' light around noon is all that you need to discover the error, and re-set the clock—provided that you bother to go up and make the observation. My parents somehow knew this, and did not become overly concerned at my strange enthusiasms. For they had confidence that they had taught me how to know when I was running awry, and to calibrate my behavior."

"Now I think I understand," Eliza said. "It remains only to apply this principle to *me,* I suppose."

"If I come down in the morning to find you copulating on

my table with a foreign deserter, as if you were some sort of Vagabond," Huygens said, "I am annoyed. I admit it. But that is not as important as what you do next. If you posture defiantly, it tells me that you have not learned the skill of recognizing when you are running awry, and correcting yourself. And you must leave my house in that case, for such people only go further and further astray until they find destruction. But if you take this opportunity to consider where you have gone wrong, and to adjust your course, it tells me that you shall do well enough in the end."

"It is good counsel and I thank you for it," Eliza said. "In principle. But in practice I do not know what to make of this Bob."

"There is something that you must settle with him, or so it would appear to me," Huygens said.

"There is something that I must settle with the world."

"Then by all means apply yourself to it. Then you are welcome to stay. But from now on please go to your bedchamber if you want to roger someone."

The Exchange
[Between Threadneedle and Cornhill]
SEPTEMBER 1686

I find that men (as high as trees) will write
Dialogue-wise; yet no man doth them slight
For writing so; indeed if they abuse
Truth, cursed be they, and the craft they use
To that intent; but yet let truth be free
To make her sallies upon thee, and me,
Which way it pleases God.
> —JOHN BUNYAN, *The Pilgrim's Progress*

DRAMATIS PERSONAE

DANIEL WATERHOUSE, a Puritan.
SIR RICHARD APTHORP, a former Goldsmith, proprietor of Apthorp's Bank.
A DUTCHMAN.
A JEW.
ROGER COMSTOCK, Marquis of Ravenscar, a courtier.
JACK KETCH, chief Executioner of England.
A HERALD.
A BAILIFF.
EDMUND PALLING, an old man.
TRADERS.
APTHORP'S MINIONS.

APTHORP'S HANGERS-ON AND FAVOR-SEEKERS.

JACK KETCH'S ASSISTANTS.

SOLDIERS.

MUSICIANS.

> *Scene: A court hemmed in by colonnades.*
>
> *Discover DANIEL WATERHOUSE, seated on a Chair amid scuffling and shouting TRADERS. Enter SIR RICHARD APTHORP, with Minions, Hangers-on, and Favor-seekers.*

APTHORP: It couldn't be—Dr. Daniel Waterhouse!

WATERHOUSE: Well met, Sir Richard!

APTHORP: Sitting in a chair, no less!

WATERHOUSE: The day is long, Sir Richard, my legs are tired.

APTHORP: It helps if you keep moving—which is the whole point of the 'Change, by the by. This is the Temple of Mercury—not of Saturn!

WATERHOUSE: Did you think I was being Saturnine? Saturn is Cronos, the God of Time. For your truly Saturnine character you had better look to Mr. Hooke, world's foremost clockmaker . . .

> *Enter Dutchman.*

DUTCHMAN: Sir! Our Mr. Huygens taught your Mr. Hooke everything he knows!

> *Exits.*

WATERHOUSE: Different countries revere the same gods under different names. The Greeks had Cronos, the Romans Saturn. The Dutch have Huygens and we have Hooke.

APTHORP: If you are not Saturn, what are you, then, to bide in a chair, so gloomy and pensive, in the middle of the 'Change?

WATERHOUSE: I am he who was born to be his family's designated participant in the Apocalypse; who was named after the strangest book in the Bible; who rode Pestilence out of London and Fire into it. I escorted Drake Waterhouse and King Charles from this world, and I put Cromwell's head back into its grave with these two hands.

APTHORP: My word! Sir!

WATERHOUSE: Of late I have been observed lurking round Whitehall, dressed in black, affrighting the courtiers.

APTHORP: What brings Lord Pluto to the Temple of Mercury?

Enter Jew.

JEW: By're leave, by're leave, Señor—pray—where stands the *tablero*?

Wanders off.

APTHORP: He sees that you have a Chair, and hopes you know where is the Table.

WATERHOUSE: That would be *mesa*. Perhaps he means *banca*, desk . . .

APTHORP: Every other man in this 'Change, who is seated upon a chair, is in front of such a *banca*. He wants to know where yours has got to!

WATERHOUSE: I meant that perhaps he is looking for the bank.

APTHORP: You mean, me?

WATERHOUSE: That is the new title you have given your goldsmith's shop now, is it not? A bank?

APTHORP: Why, yes; but why doesn't he just ask for me then?

WATERHOUSE: Señor! A moment, I beg you!

Jew returns with a paper.

JEW: Like this, like this!

APTHORP: What is he holding up there, I do not have my spectacles.

WATERHOUSE: He has drawn what a Natural Philosopher would identify as a Cartesian coordinate plane, and what you would style a ledger, and scrawled words in one column, and numerals in the next.

APTHORP: *Tablero*—he means the board where the

prices of something are billed. Commodities, most likely.

JEW: Commodities, yes!

WATERHOUSE: 'Sblood, it's right over there in the corner, is the man blind?

APTHORP: Rabbi, do not take offense at my friend's irritable tone, for he is the Lord of the Underworld, and known for his moods. Here in Mercury's temple all is movement, flux—which is why we name it the 'Change. Knowledge and intelligence flow like the running waters spoken of in the Psalms. But you have made the mistake of asking Pluto, the God of Secrets. Why is Pluto here? 'Tis something of a mystery—I myself was startled to see him just now, and supposed I was looking at a ghost.

WATERHOUSE: The tablero is over yonder.

JEW: That is all!?

APTHORP: You have come from Amsterdam?

JEW: Yes.

APTHORP: How many commodities are billed on the *tablero* in Amsterdam now?

JEW: This number . . .

Writes.

APTHORP: Daniel, what has he written there?

WATERHOUSE: Five hundred and fifty.

APTHORP: God save England, the Dutchmen have a *tablero* with near six hundred commodities, and we've a plank with a few dozen.

WATERHOUSE: No wonder he did not recognize it.

Exit Jew in the direction of said Plank, rolling his eyes and scoffing.

APTHORP (TO MINION): Follow that Kohan and learn what he is on about—he knows something.

Exit Minion.

WATERHOUSE: Now who is the God of Secrets?

APTHORP: You are, for you still have not told me why you are here.

WATERHOUSE: As Lord of the Underworld, I customarily sit enthroned in the Well of Souls, where departed spirits whirl about me like so many dry leaves. Arising this morning at my lodgings in Gresham's College and strolling down Bishopsgate, I chanced to look in 'tween the columns of the 'Change here. It was deserted. But a wind-vortex was picking up all the little scraps of paper dropped by traders yesterday and making 'em orbit round past all of the bancas like so many dry leaves . . . I became confused, thinking I had reached Hell, and took my accustomed seat.

APTHORP: Your discourse is annoying.

Enter Marquis of Ravenscar, magnificently attired.

RAVENSCAR: "The hypothesis of vortices is pressed with many difficulties!"

WATERHOUSE: God save the King, m'lord.

APTHORP: God save the King—and damn all riddlers—m'lord.

WATERHOUSE: 'Twere redundant to damn Pluto.

RAVENSCAR: He's damning me, Daniel, for prating about vortices.

APTHORP: The mystery is resolved. For now I perceive that the two of you have arranged to meet here. And since you are speaking of vortices, m'lord, I ween it has to do with Natural Philosophy.

RAVENSCAR: I beg leave to disagree, Sir Richard. For 'twas this fellow in the chair who chose the place of our meeting. Normally we meet in the Golden Grasshopper.

APTHORP: So the mystery endures. Why the 'Change today, then, Daniel?

WATERHOUSE: You will see soon enough.

RAVENSCAR: Perhaps it is because we are going to *exchange* some documents. Voilà!

APTHORP: What is that you have whipped out of your pocket m'lord, I do not have my spectacles.

RAVENSCAR: The latest from Hanover. Dr. Leibniz has

favored you, Daniel, with a personalized and auto-
graphed copy of the latest *Acta Eruditorum*. Lots of
mathematickal incantations are in here, chopped up
with great stretched-out S marks—extraordinary!

WATERHOUSE: Then the Doctor has finally dropped the
other shoe, for that could only be the Integral Calculus.

RAVENSCAR: Too, some letters addressed to you personally, Daniel, which means they've only been read by a
few dozen people so far.

WATERHOUSE: By your leave.

APTHORP: Good heavens, m'lord, if Mr. Waterhouse
had snatched 'em any quicker they'd've caught fire.
One who dwells in the Underworld ought to be more
cautious when handling Inflammable Objects.

WATERHOUSE: Here, m'lord, fresh from Cambridge, as
promised, I give you Books I and II of *Principia Mathematica* by Isaac Newton—have a care, some would
consider it a valuable document.

APTHORP: My word, is that the cornerstone of a building, or a manuscript?

RAVENSCAR: Err! To judge by weight, it is the former.

APTHORP: Whatever it is, it is too long, too long!

WATERHOUSE: It explains the System of the World.

APTHORP: Some sharp editor needs to step in and take
that wretch in hand!

RAVENSCAR: Will you just look at all of these damned illustrations . . . do you realize what this will cost, for
all of the woodcuts?

WATERHOUSE: Think of each one of them as saving a
thousand pages of tedious explanations full of great
stretched-out S marks.

RAVENSCAR: None the less, the cost of printing this is
going to *bankrupt* the Royal Society!

APTHORP: So that is why Mr. Waterhouse is seated at a
chair, with no *banca*—it is a symbolic posture, meant
to express the financial condition of the Royal Soci-

ety. I very much fear that I am to be asked for money at this point. Say, can either one of you hear a word I am saying?

Silence.

APTHORP: Go ahead and read. I don't mind being ignored. Are those documents terribly fascinating, then?

Silence.

APTHORP: Ah, like a salmon weaving a devious course up-torrent, slipping round boulders and leaping o'er logs, my assistant is making his way back to me.

Enter Minion.

MINION: You were right concerning the Jew, Sir Richard. He wants to purchase certain commodities in large amounts.

APTHORP: At this moment on a Board in Amsterdam, those commodities must be fetching a higher price than is scribbled on our humble English Plank. The Jew wants to buy low here, and sell high there. Pray tell, what sorts of commodities are in such high demand in Amsterdam?

MINION: He takes a particular interest in certain coarse, durable fabrics . . .

APTHORP: Sailcloth! Someone is building a navy!

MINION: He specifically does not want sailcloth, but cheaper stuff.

APTHORP: Tent cloth! Someone is building an army! Come, let us go and buy all the war-stuff we can find.

Exit Apthorp and entourage.

RAVENSCAR: So this is the thing Newton's been working on?

WATERHOUSE: How could he have produced that without working on it?

RAVENSCAR: When I work on things, Daniel, they come out in disjoint parts, a lump at a time; this is a unitary whole, like the garment of Our Saviour, seamless . . . what is he going to do in Book III? Raise the dead and ascend into Heaven?

WATERHOUSE: He is going to solve the orbit of the moon, provided Flamsteed will part with the requisite *data.*

RAVENSCAR: If Flamsteed doesn't, I'll see to it he parts with his fingernails. God! Here's a catchy bit: "To every action there is an equal and opposite reaction . . . if you press a stone with your finger, the finger is also pressed by the stone." The perfection of this work is obvious even to me, Daniel! How must it look to you?

WATERHOUSE: If you are going down that road, then ask rather how it looks to Leibniz, for he is as far beyond me as I am beyond you; if Newton is the finger, Leibniz is the stone, and they press against each other with equal and opposite force, a little bit harder every day.

RAVENSCAR: But Leibniz has not read it, and you have, so there would be little point in asking him.

WATERHOUSE: I have taken the liberty of conveying the essentials to Leibniz, which explains why he is writing so many of these damned letters.

RAVENSCAR: But certainly Leibniz would not dare to challenge a work of such radiance!

WATERHOUSE: Leibniz is at the disadvantage of not having seen it. Or perhaps we should count this as an advantage, for anyone who sees it is dumbfounded by the brilliance of the geometry, and it is difficult to criticize a man's work when you are down on your knees shielding your eyes.

RAVENSCAR: You believe that Leibniz has discovered an error in one of these proofs?

WATERHOUSE: No, proofs such as Newton's cannot have errors.

RAVENSCAR: Cannot?

WATERHOUSE: As a man looks at an apple on a table and says, "There is an apple on the table," you may look at these geometrical diagrams of Newton's and say, "Newton speaks the truth."

RAVENSCAR: Then I'll convey a copy to the Doctor forthwith, so that he may join us on his knees.

WATERHOUSE: Don't bother. Leibniz's objection lies not in what Newton has done but in what he has *not* done.

RAVENSCAR: Perhaps we can get Newton to do it in Book III, then, and remove the objection! You have influence with him . . .

WATERHOUSE: The ability to annoy Isaac is not to be confused with influence.

RAVENSCAR: We will convey Leibniz's objections to him directly, then.

WATERHOUSE: You do not grasp the nature of Leibniz's objections. It is not that Newton left some corollary unproved, or failed to follow up on some promising line of inquiry. Turn back, even before the Laws of Motion, and read what Isaac says in his introduction. I can quote it from memory: "For I here design only to give a mathematical notion of these forces, without considering their physical causes and seats."

RAVENSCAR: What is wrong with that?

WATERHOUSE: Some would argue that as Natural Philosophers we are *supposed* to consider their physical causes and seats! This morning, Roger, I sat in this empty courtyard, in the midst of a whirlwind. The whirlwind was invisible; how did I know 'twas here? Because of the motion it conferred on innumerable scraps of paper, which orbited round me. Had I thought to bring along my instruments I could have taken observations and measured the velocities and plotted the trajectories of those scraps, and if I were as brilliant as Isaac I could have drawn all of those data together into a single unifying picture of the whirlwind. But if I were Leibniz I'd have done none of those things. Instead I'd have asked, *Why is the whirlwind here?*

ENTR'ACTE

Noises off: A grave Procession ascending Fish Street Hill, coming from the TOWER OF LONDON.

Traders exhibit startlement and dismay as the Procession marches into the Exchange, disrupting Commerce.

Enter first two platoons of the King's Own Black Torrent Guards, armed with muskets, affixed to the muzzles whereof are long stabbing-weapons in the style recently adopted by the French Army, and nominated by them bayonets. Leveling these, the soldiers clear all traders from the center of the 'Change, and compel them to form up in concentric ranks, like spectators gathered round an impromptu Punchinello-show at a fair.

Enter now trumpeters and drummers, followed by a HERALD bellowing legal gibberish.

As drummers beat a slow and dolorous cadence, enter JACK KETCH in a black hood. The assembled traders are silent as the dead.

Jack Ketch walks slowly into the center of the empty space and stands with arms folded.

Enter now a wagon drawn by a black horse and loaded with faggots and jars, flanked by the ASSISTANTS of Jack Ketch. Assistants pile the wood on the ground and then soak it with oil poured from the jars.

Enter now BAILIFF carrying a BOOK bound up in chains and padlocks.

JACK KETCH: In the name of the King, stop and identify yourself!

BAILIFF: John Bull, a bailiff.

JACK KETCH: State your business.

BAILIFF: It is the King's business. I have here a prisoner to be bound over for execution.

JACK KETCH: What is the prisoner's name?

BAILIFF: *A History of the Late Massacres and Persecutions of the French Huguenots; to which is appended a brief relation of the bloody and atrocious crimes recently visited upon blameless Protestants dwelling in the realms of the Duke of Savoy, at the behest of King Louis XIV of France.*

JACK KETCH: Has this prisoner been accused of a crime?

BAILIFF: Not only accused, but justly convicted, of

spreading contumacious falsehoods, attempting to arouse civil discord, and leveling many base slanders against the good name of The Most Christian King Louis XIV, a true friend of our own King and a loyal ally of England.

JACK KETCH: Vile crimes, indeed! Has a sentence been pronounced?

BAILIFF: Indeed, as I mentioned before, it has been ordered by Lord Jeffreys that the prisoner is to be bound over to you for immediate execution.

JACK KETCH: Then I'll welcome him as I did the late Duke of Monmouth.

Jack Ketch advances toward the Bailiff and grips the end of the chain. The bailiff drops the Book and dusts off his hands. To a slow cadence of muffled drums, Jack Ketch marches to the wood-pile, dragging the book across the pavement behind him. He heaves the book onto the top of the pile, steps back, and accepts a torch from an assistant.

JACK KETCH: Any last words, villainous Book? No? Very well, then to hell with thee!

Lights the fire.

Traders, Soldiers, Musicians, Executioner's Staff, &c. watch silently as the Book is consumed by the flames.

Exeunt Bailiff, Herald, Executioners, Musicians, and Soldiers, leaving behind a smouldering heap of coals.

Traders resume commerce as if nothing had happened, save for EDMUND PALLING, an old man.

PALLING: Mr. Waterhouse! From the fact that you are the only one who brought something to sit on, may I assume you knew that this shameful poppet-show would disgrace the 'Change today?

WATERHOUSE: That would appear to be the unspoken message.

PALLING: *Unspoken* is an interesting word . . . what of the truths that were *spoken* in the late Book, concerning

the persecutions of our brethren in France and
Savoy? Have they now been *unspoken* because the
pages were burnt?

WATERHOUSE: I have heard many a sermon in my life,
Mr. Palling, and I know where this one is bound . . .
you're going to say that just as the immortal spirit de-
parts the body to be one with God, so the contents of
the late Book are now going to wherever its smoke is
distributed by the four winds . . . say, weren't you
Massachusetts-bound?

PALLING: I am only bating until I have raised money for
the passage, and would probably be finished by now
if Jack Ketch had not muddied and stirred the subtle
currents of the market.

Exits.
Enter Sir Richard Apthorp.

APTHORP: Burning books . . . is that not a favorite practice of the *Spanish Inquisition?*

WATERHOUSE: I have never been to Spain, Sir Richard,
and so the only way I know that they burn books is because of the vast number of books that have been
published on the subject.

APTHORP: Hmmm, yes . . . I take your meaning.

WATERHOUSE: I beg of you, do not say 'I take your
meaning' with such ponderous significance . . . I do
not wish to be Jack Ketch's next guest. You have
asked, sir, over and over, why I am sitting here in a
chair. Now you know the answer: I came to see justice
done.

APTHORP: But you knew 'twould happen—you had
aught to do with it. Why did you set it in the 'Change?
At Tyburn tree, during one of the regularly scheduled Friday hangings, 'twould've drawn a much more
appreciative crowd—why, you could burn a whole *library* there and the Mobb would be stomping their
feet for an encore.

WATERHOUSE: They don't read books. The point would've been lost on 'em.

APTHORP: If the point is to put the fear of God into *literate* men, why not burn it at Cambridge and Oxford?

WATERHOUSE: Jack Ketch hates to travel. The new carriages have so little leg-room, and his great Axe does not fit into the luggage bins . . .

APTHORP: Could it be because College men do not have the money and power to organize a rebellion?

WATERHOUSE: Why, yes, that's it. No point intimidating the weak. Threaten the dangerous.

APTHORP: To what end? To keep them in line? Or to put thoughts of rebellion into their minds?

WATERHOUSE: Your question, sir, amounts to asking whether I am a turncoat against the cause of my forebears—corrupted by the fœtid atmosphere of Whitehall—or a traitorous organizer of a secret rebellion.

APTHORP: Why, yes, I suppose it does.

WATERHOUSE: Then would you please ask easier questions or else go away and leave me alone? For whether I'm a back-stabber or a Phanatique, I am in either case no longer a scholar to be trifled with. If you must ply someone with such questions, ask them of yourself; if you insist on an answer, unburden your secrets to me before you ask me to trust you with mine. Assuming I have any.

APTHORP: I think that you do, sir.

Bows.

WATERHOUSE: Why do you doff your hat to me thus?

APTHORP: To honor you, sir, and to pay my respects to him who made you.

WATERHOUSE: What, Drake?

APTHORP: Why, no, I refer to your Mentor, the late John Wilkins, Lord Bishop of Chester—or as some would say, the living incarnation of Janus. For that good fellow penned the *Cryptonomicon* with one hand and the

Universal Character with the other; he was a good
friend of high and mighty Cavaliers at the same time
he was wooing and marrying Cromwell's own sister;
and, in sum, was Janus-like in diverse ways I'll not
bother enumerating to you. For you are truly his
pupil, his creation: one moment dispensing intelligence like a Mercury, the next keeping counsel like
Pluto.

WATERHOUSE: Mentor was a guise adopted by Minerva,
and her pupil was great Ulysses, and so by hewing to
a strict Classical interpretation of your words, sir, I'll
endeavour not to take offense.

APTHORP: Endeavour and succeed, my good man, for
no offense was meant. Good day.

Exits.

Enter Ravenscar, carrying Principia Mathematica.

RAVENSCAR: I'm taking this to the printer's straight-
away, but before I do, I was pondering this New-
ton/Leibniz thing . . .

WATERHOUSE: What!? Jack Ketch's performance made
no impression on you at all?

RAVENSCAR: Oh, that? I assume you arranged it that way
in order to buttress your position as the King's token
Puritan bootlick—whilst in fact stirring rebellious
spirits in the hearts and minds of the rich and powerful. Forgive me for not tossing out a compliment.
Twenty years ago I'd have admired it, but by my current standards it is only a modestly sophisticated ploy.
The matter of Newton and Leibniz is much more interesting.

WATERHOUSE: Go ahead, then.

RAVENSCAR: Descartes explained, years and years ago,
that the planets move round the sun like slips of paper caught up in a wind-vortex. So Leibniz's objection is groundless—there is no mystery, and
therefore Newton did not gloss over any problems.

WATERHOUSE: Leibniz has been trying to make sense of

Descartes' dynamics for years, and finally given up. Descartes was wrong. His theory of dynamics is beautiful in that it is purely geometrical and mathematical. But when you compare that theory to the world as it really is, it proves an unmitigated disaster. The whole notion of vortices does not work. There is no doubt that the inverse square law exists, and governs the motions of all heavenly bodies along conic sections. But it has nothing to do with vortices, or the cœlestial æther, or any of that other nonsense.

RAVENSCAR: What brings it about, then?

WATERHOUSE: Isaac says it is God, or God's presence in the physical world. Leibniz says it has to be some sort of interaction among particles too tiny to see . . .

RAVENSCAR: Atoms?

WATERHOUSE: Atoms—to make a long story short and leave out all the good bits—could not move and change fast enough. Instead Leibniz speaks of monads, which are more fundamental than atoms. If I try to explain we'll both get headaches. Suffice it to say, he is going at it hammer and tongs, and we will hear more from him in due course.

RAVENSCAR: That is very odd, for he avers in a personal letter to me that, having published the Integral Calculus, he'll now turn his attention to genealogical research.

WATERHOUSE: That sort of work entails much travel, and the Doctor does his best work when he's rattling round the Continent in his carriage. He can do both things, and more, at the same time.

RAVENSCAR: In the decision to study history, some will see an admission of defeat to Newton. I myself cannot understand why he should want to waste his time digging up ancient family trees.

WATERHOUSE: Perhaps I'm not the only Natural Philosopher who can put together a "moderately sophisticated ploy" when he needs to.

RAVENSCAR: What on earth are you talking about?

WATERHOUSE: Dig up some ancient family trees, stop assuming that Leibniz is a defeated ninehammer, and consider it. Put your *philosophick* acumen to use: know, for example, that the children of syphilitics are often syphilitic themselves, and unable to bear viable offspring.

RAVENSCAR: Now you are swimming out into the deep water, Daniel. Monsters are there—bear it in mind.

WATERHOUSE: 'Tis true, and when a man has got to a point in his life when he needs to slay a monster, like St. George, or be eaten by one, like Jonah, I think that is where he goes a-swimming.

RAVENSCAR: Is it your intention to slay, or be eaten?

WATERHOUSE: I have already been eaten. My choices are to slay, or else be vomited up on some bit of dry land somewhere—Massachusetts, perhaps.

RAVENSCAR: Right. Well, before you make me any more alarmed, I'm off to the printer's.

WATERHOUSE: It may be the finest errand you ever do, Roger.

Exit Marquis of Ravenscar.
Enter Sir Richard Apthorp solus.

APTHORP: Woe. Bad tidings and alarums! Fear for England . . . O miserable island!

WATERHOUSE: What can possibly have happened, in the Temple of Mercury, to alter your mood so? Did you lose a lot of money?

APTHORP: No, I made a lot, buying low and selling high.

WATERHOUSE: Buying what?

APTHORP: Tent-cloth, saltpeter, lead, and other martial commodities.

WATERHOUSE: From whom?

APTHORP: Men who knew less than I did.

WATERHOUSE: And you sold it to—?

APTHORP: Men who knew more.

WATERHOUSE: A typical commercial transaction, all in all.

APTHORP: Except that I acquired knowledge as part of the bargain. And the knowledge fills me with dread.

WATERHOUSE: Share it with Pluto, then, for he knows all secrets, and keeps most of 'em, and basks in Dread as an old dog lies in the sun.

APTHORP: The buyer is the King of England.

WATERHOUSE: Good news, then! Our King is bolstering our defences.

APTHORP: But why d'you suppose the Jew braved the North Sea to come and buy it here?

WATERHOUSE: Because 'tis cheaper here?

APTHORP: It *isn't*. But he saves money to buy it in England, because then there are no expenses for shipping. For these warlike commodities are supposed to be delivered, not to some foreign battle-ground, but *here*—to England—which is where the King intends to use 'em.

WATERHOUSE: That is extraordinary, since there are no foreigners here to practise war upon.

APTHORP: Only Englishmen, as far as the eye can see!

WATERHOUSE: Perhaps the King fears a foreign invasion.

APTHORP: Does it give you comfort to think so?

WATERHOUSE: To think of being invaded? No. To think of the Coldstream Guards, the Grenadiers, and the King's Own Black Torrent Guards fighting foreigners, 'stead of Englishmen, why yes.

APTHORP: Then it follows, does it not, that all good Englishmen should bend their efforts to bringing it about.

WATERHOUSE: Let us now choose our words carefully, for Jack Ketch is only just round the corner.

APTHORP: No man has been choosing his words more carefully than you, Daniel.

Waterhouse: *Lest native arms fraternal blood might shed,*
   For want of alien foes and righteous broil,
   We'd fain see foreign canvas off our shores,
   And English towns beset by armèd Boers.

Our soldiers, if they love by whom they're led,
May then let foreign blood on English soil.
And if they don't, and let their colors fall,
Their leader never was their King at all.

Versailles
1687

To d'Avaux, March 1687
Monseigneur,

Finally, a real spring day—my fingers have thawed out and I am able to write again. I would like to be out enjoying the flowers, but instead I am despatching letters to tulip-land.

You will be pleased to know that as of last week there are no beggars in France. The King has declared beggary illegal. The nobles who live at Versailles are of two minds concerning this. Of course they all agree that it is magnificent. But many of them are scarcely above beggars themselves, and so they are wondering whether the law applies to them.

Fortunately—for those who have daughters, anyway—Mme. de Maintenon has got her girls' school open at St.-Cyr, just a few minutes' ride from the château of Versailles. This has complicated my situation a little. The girl I have supposedly been tutoring—the daughter of the Marquise d'Ozoir—has begun attending the school, which makes my position redundant. So far, there has been no talk of letting me go. I have been putting my free time to good use, making two trips to Lyons to learn about how commerce works in that place. But apparently Édouard de Gex has been spreading tales of my great skills as a tutor to the Maintenon, who has begun making noises about bringing me to St.-Cyr as a teacher.

Did I mention that the teachers are all nuns?

De Maintenon and de Gex are so shrouded in outward Godliness that I cannot make out their motives. It is almost conceivable that they believe, sincerely, that I am a good candidate for the convent—in other words, that they are too detached from worldly matters to understand my true function here. Or perhaps they know full well that I am managing assets for twenty-one different French nobles, and they wish to neutralize me—or bring me under their control by threatening to do so.

To business: returns for the first quarter of 1687 have been satisfactory, as you know since you are a client. I pooled all of the money into a fund and invested it mostly through sub-brokers in Amsterdam, who specialize in particular commodities or species of V.O.C. derivatives. We are still making money on India cloth, thanks to King Louis who made it contraband and thereby drove up the price. But V.O.C. shares fell after William of Orange declared the League of Augsburg. William may be full of bluster about how the Protestant alliance is going to rein in the power of France, but his own stock market seems to take an extremely dim view of the project! As does the court here—*tout le monde* finds it tremendously amusing that William, and Sophie of Hanover, and a grab-bag of other frostbitten Lutherans believe they can stand up to *La France*. There is brave talk about how Father de Gex and Maréchal de Catinat, who suppressed the Protestants in Savoy with such force, ought now to ride North and give the same treatment to the Dutch and the Germans.

For now it is my rôle to set aside any personal feelings I may have concerning politics, and to think only of how this might affect markets. My footing here is soft—I am like a mare galloping down a mucky beach, afraid to falter, out of fear that she may be treading on quicksand. With markets in Amsterdam fluctuating hourly, I cannot really manage assets from Versailles—the day-to-day buying and selling is carried out by my associates in the north.

But French nobles will not be seen doing business with Dutch hereticks and Spanish Jews. So I am a sort of figurehead, like the pretty mermaid on the bow of a ship that is laden with other people's treasure and manned by swarthy corsairs. The only thing to be said in favor of being a figurehead is that the position gives one an excellent view ahead, and plenty of time to think. Help me, Monseigneur, to have as clear a view as possible of the seas we are about to plow up. I cannot help but think that in a year or two I shall be forced to gamble all of my clients' assets on the outcome of great events. Investing round the time of Monmouth's rebellion was not difficult because I knew Monmouth, and knew how it would come out. But I know William, too—not as well—but well enough to know I cannot gamble against him with certainty. Monmouth was a hobbyhorse and William is a stallion. Experience gained riding the first can only misinform me as to what it shall be like to ride the second.

So inform me, Monseigneur. Tell me things. You know your intelligence will be safe in transit, because of the excellence of this cypher, and you know it will be safe with me, for I have no friends here to whisper it to.

Only small minds want always to be right.

—Louis XIV

To d'Avaux, June 1687
Monseigneur,

When I complained that Fr. de Gex and Mme. de Maintenon were trying to make me over into a nun, I never imagined you would respond by making me out to be a whore! Mme. la duchesse d'Oyonnax has practically had to post Swiss guards at the entrance of her apartments to keep the young blades away from me. What sorts of rumors have you been spreading? That I am a nymphomaniac? That a thousand *louis d'or* will go to the first Frenchman who beds me?

At any rate, now I have some idea as to who belongs to the *cabinet noir*. One day, all of a sudden, Fr. de Gex was very cool to me, and Étienne d'Arcachon, the one-armed son of the Duke, called on me to say that he did not believe any of the rumors that were being spread about me. I think I was meant to be bowled over by his nobility—with him, it is difficult to tell. For on the one hand he is so excessively polite that some affirm he is not in his right mind, and on the other (though he has no other!) he saw me at the opera with Monmouth and knows some of my history. Otherwise why would a Duke's son even give the time of day to a common servant?

The only circumstance under which a man of his rank and a woman of mine could ever be seen conversing with each other is a fancy-dress ball, when ranks are of no account and all the normal rules of precedence are suspended for a few hours. The other evening, Étienne d'Arcachon escorted me to one at Dampierre, the château of the duc de Chevreuse. He dressed as Pan and I as a Nymph. Here any proper Court lady would devote several pages to describing the costumes, and the intrigues and machinations that went into their making, but since I am not a proper Court lady and you are a busy man, I will leave it at that—pausing only to mention that Étienne had a special prosthetic hand carved out of boxwood and strapped to his stump. The hand was gripping a silver Pan-pipe all twined about with ivy (emerald leaves, of course, and ruby berries) and from time to time he would raise this to his lips and pipe a little melody that he had Lully compose for him.

As we rode in the carriage to Dampierre, Étienne mentioned to me, "You know, our host the duc de Chevreuse is the son-in-law of a commoner: Colbert, the late Contrôleur-Général, who built Versailles among other accomplishments."

As you know, this is not the first such veiled remark that has been directed my way by a Frenchman of high rank. The first time it happened I became ever so excited, thinking I was about to be ennobled at any minute. Then for a time I affected a cynical view, supposing that this was like a snatch of meat dangled high above a dog's nose to make it do tricks. But on this evening, riding to the splendid château of Dampierre on the arm of a future Duke, the burden of my low rank lifted for a few hours by a mask and costume, I phant'sied that Étienne's remark really meant something, and that if I could use my skills to achieve some great accomplishment, I might be rewarded as Colbert had been.

Pretend now that I have dutifully described all of the costumes, the table-settings, the food, and the entertainments that the duc de Chevreuse had brought together at Dampierre. This will spare enough pages to make a small book. At first the mood was somewhat gloomy, for Mansart—the King's architect—was there, and he had just received news that the Parthenon in Athens has been blown up. Apparently the Turks had been using it as a powder-magazine and the Venetians, who are trying to bring that city back into Christendom, bombarded it with mortars and touched off a great explosion. Mansart—who had always harbored an ambition of making a pilgrimage to Athens to see that building with his own eyes—was inconsolable. There was some blustery talk from Étienne to the effect that he would personally lead a squadron of his father's Mediterranean fleet to Athens to take that city back into Christendom. This was a *faux pas* of sorts because Athens is not actually located on the water. Therefore it led to a few moments' awkward silence.

I decided to strike. No one knew who I was, and even if they found out, my status and my reputation (thanks to you!) could scarcely sink lower. "So gloomy are we because of this news from abroad," I exclaimed, "and yet what is news but words, and what are words but air?"

Now this produced only a few titters because everyone was assuming that I was just another empty-headed Duchess who had read too much Pascal. But I had their attention (if you could see my gown, Monseigneur, you would know I had their attention; my face was hidden, everything else was getting a good airing-out).

I continued, "Why should we not conjure up some news more to our liking, and throw our enemies the Dutchmen into a gloomy mood, so that we may be infused with gaiety and joy?"

Now most of them were nonplussed, but several took an interest—including one chap who was dressed up as Orion after he had been blinded by Oenopion, so that his mask had blood running out of the eye-sockets. Orion asked me to say more, and so I did: "Here, we are susceptible to emotion, because we are people of great feeling and passion, and accordingly we are saddened by the destruction of the Parthenon, for we value beauty. In Amsterdam, they have investments instead of emotions, and all they value is their precious V.O.C. stock. We could destroy all the treasures of the Classical world and they would not care; but if they hear bad news that touches the V.O.C., they are plunged into despair—or rather the price of the stock falls, which amounts to the same thing."

"Since you appear to know so much about it, tell us

what would be the worst news they could hear," said blind Orion.

"Why, the fall of Batavia—for that is the linch-pin of their overseas empire."

By now Orion had come face-to-face with me and we were in the middle of a ring of costumed nobles who were all leaning forward to listen. For it was obvious to everyone that the man dressed as Orion was none other than the King himself. He said, "The doings of the cheese-mongers are a vulgar muddle to us—trying to understand them is like watching muddy English peasants at one of their shin-kicking contests. If it is so easy to bring about a crash in the Amsterdam market, why doesn't it crash all the time? For anyone could spread such a rumor."

"And many do—it is very common for a few investors to get together and form a cabal, which is a sort of secret society that manipulates the market for profit. The machinations of these cabals have grown exceedingly complex, with as many moves and variations as dance steps. But at some point they all rely upon spreading false news into the ears of credulous investors. Now these cabals form and join, split and vanish like clouds in the summer sky, and so the market has become resistant to news, especially bad news; for most investors now assume that any bad news from abroad is false information put out by a cabal."

"Then what hope have we of convincing these skeptical hereticks that Batavia has fallen?" asked Orion.

"My answering your question is complicated somewhat by the fact that everyone here is wearing a disguise," I said, "but it would not be unreasonable to suppose that the Grand Admiral of the French Navy (the duc d'Arcachon) and the *Contrôleur* of the French East India Company (the Marquis d'Ozoir) are present, and able to hear my words. For men of such eminence, it would be no great thing to make it believed and understood, from the top to the bottom of the French naval and merchant fleets, and in every port from Spain to Flanders, that a French expeditionary force had rounded the Cape of Good Hope and fallen suddenly upon Batavia and seized it from the V.O.C. The news would spread north up the coast like fire along a powder-trail, and when it reached the Damplatz—"

"The Damplatz is the powder-keg," Orion concluded. "This plan has beauty, for it would require little risk or expenditure from us, yet would cause more damage to William of Orange than an invasion by fifty thousand of our dragoons."

"While at the same time bringing profit to anyone who knew in advance, and who took the right positions in the market," I added.

Now, Monseigneur, I know for a fact that on the next morning Louis XIV went on a trip to his lodge at Marly, and invited the Marquis d'Ozoir and the duc d'Arcachon to join him.

Speaking for myself, I have spent all the time since talking to French nobles who are desperate to know what "the right position" is. I have lost track of the number of times I have had to explain the concept of selling short, and that when V.O.C. stock falls it tends to bring about a rise in commodity prices as capital flies from one to the other. Above all, I've had to make it clear that if a lot of Frenchmen, new to the markets, suddenly sell the V.O.C. short while investing in commodities futures, it will make it obvious to the Dutch that a cabal has formed at the court of the Sun King. That (in other words) the ground-work must be laid with great care and subtlety—which amounts to saying that I must do it.

In any event, a lot of French gold is going to be making its way north in the next week. I will send details in another letter.

The diligent *Dutch* seeing the Easiness of the
managing and curing the Berry, and how that
Part had no Dependence, either upon the
Earth, the Air, the Water, or anything else
more there, than in another Place, took the
Hint, and planted the Coffee Tree in the Island of *Java,* near their City of *Batavia,* there
it thrives, bears, and ripens every jot as well as
at *Mocha;* and now they begin to leave off the
Red Sea, and bring 20 to 30 Tons of Coffee,
at a time, from *Batavia,* in the Latitude of 5
Deg. S.

—DANIEL DEFOE,
A Plan of the English Commerce

To Leibniz, August 1687
Doctor,
   Increase is the order of the day here;* the gardens,
orchards, and vineyards are buried in their own produce and the country roads crowded with wagons
bringing it to market. France is at peace, her soldiers at
home, mending and building *and getting maidens pregnant out of wedlock so that there will be a next generation of soldiers.* New construction is going on all over
Versailles, and many here have become modestly
wealthy *or at least paid off part of their gambling debts*
in the wake of the stock market crash in Amsterdam.
   *I am sorry not to have written in so many weeks.
This cypher is extremely time-consuming and I have
been too busy with all of the machinations surrounding the "fall of Batavia."*
   Mme. la duchesse d'Oyonnax threw a garden party
the other evening; the highlight was a re-enactment of

* ☰ Increase: Hexagram 42 of the *I Ching*, or 110001.

the Fall of Batavia—which, as everyone knows by now, never really happened—played out on the Canal. A fleet of French "frigates," no bigger than rowboats, and trimmed and decorated phantastically, like dream-ships, besieged a model "Batavia" built on the brink of the canal. The Dutchmen in the town were drinking beer and counting gold until they fell asleep. Then the dream-fleet made its attack. The Dutchmen were alarmed at first, until they woke up and understood it had all been a dream . . . but when they returned to their counting-tables, they found that their gold was really gone! The vanishing of the gold was accomplished through some sleight-of-hand so that everyone in the party was completely surprised. Then the dream-fleet cruised up and down the canal for the better part of an hour, and everyone crowded along the banks to admire it. Each vessel represented some virtue that is representative of *la France,* e.g., Fertility, Martial Prowess, Piety, *et cetera, et cetera,* and the captain of each one was a Duke or Prince, dressed up in costumes to match. As they drifted up and down the Canal they threw the captured coins in showers of gold into the ranks of the party-goers.

The Dauphin wore a golden frock embroidered with . . . *I have seen this man Upnor now. He enjoys a high rank in the court of James II and has many friends in France, for he was a boy here during the time of Cromwell. Everyone wants to hear about his Protestant slave-girl and he is not slow to talk about her. He is too well-bred to gloat openly, but it is obvious that he takes great pleasure in owning her. Here, the enslavement of rebels in England is likened to the French practice of sending Huguenots to the galleys, and rated as more humane than simply killing them all as was done in Savoy. I had not been sure whether to credit Bob Shaftoe's tale and so I was quite startled to see Upnor in the flesh, and to hear him talking about this. It seems shameful to me—a scandal that the guilty would wish to hide from the world. But to them it is nothing. While sympathizing with poor Abigail Frome, I rejoice that this has come to pass. If the slavers had shown more discretion and continued to take their victims only from black Africa, no one would notice or care—why, I am as guilty as the next person of putting sugar in my coffee without considering the faraway Negroes who made it for me. For James and his ilk to take slaves from Ireland entails more risk, even when they are criminals. But to take English girls from farm-towns is repugnant to almost everyone (the population of Versailles excepted) and an invitation to rebellion. After listening to Upnor I am more certain than ever that England will soon rise up in arms—and James apparently agrees with me, for word has it that he's built great military camps on the edge of London and lavished money on his prize regiments. I fear only that in the chaos and excitement of rebellion, the people of that country will forget about the Taunton schoolgirls and what they signify about slavery in general* . . . the tiller and rudder of which were all overgrown with living grape-vines.

Forgive me this endless description of the various Dukes and their dream-boats, I look back over the preceding several pages and see I quite forgot myself.

To Leibniz, October 1687
Doctor,

Family, family, family* is all anyone wants to talk about. Who is talking to me, you might ask, given that I am a commoner? The answer is that in certain recesses of this immense château there are large salons that are given over entirely to gambling, which is the

---

* ☰☰ Family: Hexagram 37 of the *I Ching,* or 110101.

only thing these nobles can do to make their lives interesting. In these places the usual etiquette is suspended and everyone talks to everyone. Of course the trick is gaining admission to such a salon in the first place—but after my success with the "Fall of Batavia" some of these doors were opened to me (back doors, anyway—I must come in through the servants' entrances) and so it is not unusual for me now to exchange words with a Duchess or even a Princess. But I don't go to these places as often as you might think, for when you are there you have no choice but to gamble, and I don't enjoy it *I loathe it and the people who do it is more accurate. But some of the men who will read this letter are heavy gamblers and so I will be demure.*

More and more frequently people ask me about my family. Someone has been spreading rumors that I have noble blood in my veins! I hope that during your genealogical research you can turn up some supporting evidence . . . turning me into a Countess should be easy compared to making Sophie an Electress. *Enough people here now depend on me that my status as a commoner is awkward and inconvenient. They need a pretext to give me a title so that they can have routine conversations with me without having to set up elaborate shams, such as fancy-dress balls, to circumvent the etiquette.*

Just the other day I was playing basset with M. le duc de Berwick, who is the bastard of James II by Arabella Churchill, sister of John. This places him in excellent company since as you know this means his paternal grandmother was Henrietta Maria of France, the sister of Louis XIII . . . *again, forgive the genealogical prattle. Will you please sort out everything to do with sorcerers, alchemists, Templars, and Satanworshippers? I know that you got your start in life by bamboozling some rich alchemists into thinking you actually believed their nonsense. And yet you appear to be a sincere friend of the man called Enoch the Red, who is apparently an alchemist of note. From time to time, his name comes up around a gambling table. Most are nonplussed but certain men will cock an eyebrow or cough into a hand, exchange tremendously significant looks, et cetera, conspicuously trying not to be conspicuous. I have observed the same behaviors in connection with other subjects that are of an esoteric or occult nature. Everyone knows that Versailles was infested with Satan-worshippers, poisoners, abortionists, et cetera, in the late 1670s and that most but not all of them were purged; but this only makes it seem murkier and more provocative now. The father of the Earl of Upnor—the Duke of Gunfleet—died suddenly in those days, after drinking a glass of water at a garden party thrown by Mme. la duchesse d'Oyonnax, whose own husband died in similar fashion a fortnight later, leaving all his titles and possessions to her. There is not a man or woman here who does not suspect poisoning in these and other cases. Upnor and Oyonnax would probably come in for closer scrutiny if there weren't so many other poisonings to distract people's attention. Anyway, Upnor is obviously one of those gentlemen who takes an interest in occult matters, and keeps making dark comments about his contacts at Trinity College in Cambridge. I am tempted to dismiss all of this as a faintly pathetic hobby for noble toffs bored out of their minds by the ingenious tedium, the humiliating inconsequence, of Versailles. But since I have picked out Upnor as an enemy I would like to know if it amounts to anything . . . can he cast spells on me? Does he have secret brethren in every city? What is Enoch Root?*

I am going to spend much of the winter in Holland and will write to you from there.

Eliza

Bank of Het Kanaal, *Between Scheveningen and the Hague*

DECEMBER 1687

No man goes so high as he who knows not where he is going.

—CROMWELL

"WELL MET, BROTHER WILLIAM," said Daniel, getting a boot up on the running-board of the carriage, vaulting in through the door, and surprising the hell out of a dumpling-faced Englishman with long stringy dark hair. The passenger snatched the hem of his long black frock coat and drew it up; Daniel could not tell whether he was trying to make room, or to avoid being brushed against by Daniel. Both hypotheses were reasonable. This man had spent a lot more time in ghastly English prisons than Daniel had, and learned to get out of other men's way. And Daniel was mud-spattered from riding, whereas this fellow's clothes, though severe and dowdy, were immaculate. Brother William had a tiny mouth that was pursed sphincter-tight at the moment.

"Recognized your arms on the door," Daniel explained, slamming it to and reaching out the window to give it a familiar slap. "Flagged your coachman down, reckoning we must be going to the same lodge to see the same gentleman."

"When Adam delved and Eve span, who *then* was the Gentleman?"

"Forgive me, I should have said chap, bloke . . . how are things in your Overseas Possession, Mr. Penn? Did you ever settle that dispute with Maryland?"

William Penn rolled his eyes and looked out the window. "It will take a hundred years and a regiment of Surveyors to settle it! At least those damned Swedes have been brought to heel. Everyone imagines that, simply because I own the Biggest Pencil in the World, that my ticket is punched, my affairs settled once and for all . . . but I tell you, Brother Daniel, that it has been nothing but troubles . . . if it is a sin to lust after worldly goods, *videlicet* a horse or a door-knocker, then what have I got myself into *now?* It is a whole new universe of sinfulness."

"'Twas either accept Pennsylvania, or let the King continue owing you sixteen thousand pounds, yes?"

Penn did not take his gaze away from the window, but squinted as if trying to hold back a mighty volume of flatulence, and shifted his focal point to a thousand miles in the distance. But this was coastal Holland and there was nothing out that window save the Curvature of the World. Even pebbles cast giant shadows in the low winter sun. Daniel could not be ignored.

"I am chagrined, appalled, mortified that you are here! You are *not welcome,* Brother Daniel, you are a problem, and obstacle, and if I were not a pacifist I would beat you to death with a rock."

"Brother William, meeting as we so often do at Whitehall, in the King's Presence, to have our lovely chats about Religious Toleration, it is most difficult for us to hold frank exchanges of views, and so I am pleased you've at last found this opportunity to hose me down with those splenetic humours that have been so long pent up."

"I am a plain-spoken fellow, as you can see. Perhaps *you* should say what you mean more frequently, Brother Daniel—it would make everything so much simpler."

"It is easy for you to be that way, when you have an estate the size of Italy to go hiding in, on the far side of an ocean."

"That was unworthy of you, Brother Daniel. But there is some truth in what you say . . . it is . . . distracting . . . at the oddest times . . . my mind drifts, and I find myself wondering what is happening on the banks of the Susquehanna . . ."

"Right! And if England becomes completely unlivable, you have someplace to go. Whereas *I* . . ."

Finally Penn looked at him. "Don't tell me you haven't considered moving to Massachusetts."

"I consider it every day. Nonetheless, most of my constituency does not have that luxury available and so I'd like to see if we can avoid letting Olde Englande get any more fouled up than 'tis."

Penn had disembarked from a ship out at Scheveningen less than an hour ago. That port-town was connected to the Hague by several roads and a canal. The route that Penn's driver had chosen ran along a canal-edge, through stretches of Dutch polder-scape and fields where troops drilled, which extended to within a few hundred yards of the spires of the Binnenhof.

The carriage now made a left turn onto a gravel track that bordered an especially broad open park, called the Malieveld, where those who could afford it went riding when the weather was pleasant. No one was there today. At its eastern end the Malieveld gave way to the Haagse Bos, a carefully managed forest laced through with riding-paths. The carriage followed one of these through the woods for a mile, until it seemed that they had gone far out into the wild. But then suddenly cobblestones, instead of gravel, were beneath the wheel-rims, and they were passing through guarded gates and across counterweighted canal-bridges. The formal gardens of a small estate spread around them. They rolled to a stop before a gate-house. Daniel glimpsed a hedge and the corner of a fine house before his view out the carriage-window was blocked by the head, and more so by the hat, of a captain of the Blue Guards. "William Penn," said William Penn. Then, reluctantly, he added: "And Dr. Daniel Waterhouse."

* * *

THE PLACE WAS BUT A small lodge, close enough to the Hague to be easily reached, but far enough away that the air was clean. William of Orange's asthma did not trouble him when he was here, and so, during those times of the year when he had no choice but to stick at the Hague, this was where he abided.

Penn and Waterhouse were ushered to a parlor. It was a raw day outside, and even though a new fire was burning violently on the hearth, making occasional lunges into the room, neither Penn nor Waterhouse made any move to remove his coat.

There was a girl there, a petite girl with large blue eyes, and Daniel assumed she was Dutch at first. But after she'd heard the two visitors conversing in English she addressed them in French, and explained something about the Prince of Orange. Penn's French was much better than Daniel's because he had spent a few years exiled to a Protestant college (now extirpated) in Saumur, so he exchanged a few sentences with the girl and then said to Daniel: "The sand-sailing is excellent today."

"Could've guessed as much from the wind, I suppose."

"We'll not be seeing the Prince for another hour."

The two Englishmen stood before the fire until well browned on both sides, then settled into chairs. The girl, who was dressed in a rather bleak Dutch frock, set a pan of milk there to heat, then busied herself with some kitchen-fuss. It was now Daniel's turn to be distracted, for there was something in the girl's appearance that was vaguely disturbing or annoying to him, and the only remedy was to look at her some more, trying to figure it out; which made the feeling worse. Or perhaps better. So they sat there for a while, Penn brooding about the Alleghenies and Waterhouse trying to piece together what it was that provoked him about this girl. The feeling was akin to the nagging sense that he had met a person somewhere before but could not recall the particulars. But that was not it; he was certain that this was the first time. And yet he had that same unscratchable itch.

She said something that broke Penn out of his reverie. Penn fixed his gaze upon Daniel. "The girl is offended," he said. "She says that there may be women, of an unspeakable nature, in Amsterdam, who do not object to being looked at as you are looking at *her;* but how dare you, a visitor on Dutch soil, take such liberties?"

"She said a lot then, in five words of French."

"She was pithy, for she credits me with wit. I am discursive, for I can extend you no such consideration."

"You know, merely knuckling under to the King, simply because he waves a Declaration of Indulgence in front of your eyes, is no proof of wit—some would say it proves the opposite."

"Do you really want another Civil War, Daniel? You and I both grew up during such a war—*some* of us have elected to move on—*others* want to re-live their childhoods, it seems."

Daniel closed his eyes and saw the image that had been branded onto his retinas thirty-five years ago: Drake hurling a stone saint's head through a stained-glass window, the gaudy image replaced with green English hillside, silvery drizzle reaching in through the aperture like the Holy Spirit, bathing his face.

"I do not think you see what we can make of England now if we only try. I was brought up to believe that an Apocalypse was coming. I have not believed that for many years. But the people who believe in that Apocalypse are my people, and their way of thinking is my way. I have only just come round to a new way of looking at this, a new viewpoint, as Leibniz would have it. Namely that there is something to the *idea* of an Apocalypse—a sudden changing of all, an overthrow of old ways—and that Drake and the others merely got the *particulars* wrong, they fixed on a date certain, they, in a word, *idolized.* If idolatry is to mistake the symbol for the thing symbolized, then that is what they did with the symbols that are set down in the Book of Revelation. Drake and the others were like a flock of birds who all sense that something is nigh, and take flight as one: a majestic sight and a miracle of Creation. But they were confused, and flew into a trap, and their revolution came to naught. Does that mean that they were mistaken to have spread their wings at all? No, their senses did not deceive them . . . their higher minds did. Should we spurn them forever because they erred? Is their legacy to be laughed at only? On the contrary, I would say that we might bring about the Apocalypse now with a little effort . . . not precisely the one they phant'sied but the same, or better, in its effects."

"You really should move to Pennsylvania," Penn mused. "You are a man of parts, Daniel, and certain of those parts, which will only get you half-hanged, drawn, and quartered in London, would make you a great man in Philadelphia—or at least get you invited to a lot of parties."

"I've not given up on England just yet, thank you."

"England may prefer that you give up, rather than suffer another Civil War, or another Bloody Assizes."

"Much of England sees it otherwise."

"And you may number me in that party, Daniel, but a scattering of Nonconformists does not suffice to bring about the changes you seek."

"True . . . but what of the men whose signatures are on these letters?" said Daniel, producing a sheaf of folded parchments, each one be-ribboned and wax-sealed.

Penn's mouth shrank to the size of a navel and his mind worked for a minute. The girl came round and served chocolate.

"For you to surprise me in this way was not the act of a gentleman."

"When Adam delved and Eve span . . ."

"Shut up! Do not trifle with me. Owning Pennsylvania does not make me any better than a Vagabond in the eyes of God, Daniel, but it serves as a reminder that I'm not to be trifled and toyed with."

"And that, Brother William, is why I nearly killed myself to cross the North Sea on the front of a wind-storm, and galloped through frost and muck to intercept you—*before* you

met with your next King." Daniel drew out a Hooke-watch
and turned its ivory face toward the fire-light. "There is still
time for you to write a letter of your own, and put it on the
top of this stack, if you please."

"I WAS GOING TO ASK, do you have any idea how many people in Amsterdam want to kill you . . . but by coming up
here, you seem to've answered the question: no," said
William, Prince of Orange.

"You had fair warning in my letter to d'Avaux, did you
not?"

"It barely reached me in time . . . the brunt of the blow
was absorbed by some big shareholders there, whom I held
off from warning."

"Francophiles."

"No, the bottom has quite fallen out of *that* market, very
few Dutchmen are selling themselves to the French nowadays. My chief enemies nowadays are what you would call
Dutchmen of limited vision. At any rate, your Batavia cha-
rade caused no end of headaches for me."

"Establishing a first-rate intelligence source at the Court
of Louis XIV cannot come cheaply."

"That insipid truism can be turned around easily: when it
comes so dear, then I demand first-rate intelligence. What
did you learn from the two Englishmen, by the way?"
William glanced at a dirty spoon and flared his nostrils. A
Dutch houseboy, fairer and more beautiful than Eliza, bus-
tled over and began to clear away the gleaming, crusted evidence of a long chocolate binge. The clattering of the cups
and spoons seemed to irritate William more than gunfire on
a battlefield. He leaned back deep into his armchair, closed
his eyes, and turned his face toward the fire. To him the
world was a dark close cellar with a net-work of covert
channels strung through it, frail and irregular as cobwebs,
transmitting faint cyphers of intelligence from time to time,
and so a fire broadcasting clear strong radiance all directions
was a sort of miracle, a pagan god manifesting itself in a spi-

dery Gothick chapel. Eliza did not speak until the boy was finished and the room had gone quiet again and the folds and creases in the prince's face had softened. He was a couple of years shy of forty, but time spent in sun and spray had given him the skin, and battles had given him the mentality, of an older man.

"Both believe the same things, and believe them sincerely," Eliza said, referring to the two Englishmen. "Both have been tested by suffering. At first I thought the fat one had been corrupted. But the slender one did not think so."

"Maybe the slender one is naïve."

"He is not naïve in *that* way. No, those two belong to a common sect, or something—they knew and recognized each other. They dislike each other and work at cross-purposes but betrayal, corruption, any straying from whatever common path they have chosen, these are inconceivable. Is it the same sect as Gomer Bolstrood?"

"No and yes. The Puritans are like Hindoos—impossibly various, and yet all of a type."

Eliza nodded.

"Why are you so fascinated by the Puritans?" William asked.

It was not asked in a friendly way. He suspected her of some weakness, some occult motive. She looked at him like a little girl who had just been run over by a cart-wheel. It was a look that would cause most men to fall apart like stewed chickens. It didn't work. Eliza had noticed that William of Orange had a lot of gorgeous boys around him. But he also had a mistress, an Englishwoman named Elizabeth Villiers, who was only moderately beautiful, but famously intelligent and witty. The Prince of Orange would never make himself vulnerable by relying on one sex or the other; any lust he might feel for Eliza he could easily channel towards that houseboy, as Dutch farmers manipulated their sluice-gates to water one field instead of another. Or at least that was the message he wanted to convey, by keeping the company he did.

Eliza sensed that she had quite inadvertently gotten into danger. William had found an inconsistency in her, and if it weren't explained to his satisfaction, he'd brand her as Enemy. And while Louis XIV kept his enemies in the gilded cage of Versailles, William probably had more forthright ways of dealing with his.

The truth wasn't so bad after all. "I think they are interesting," she said, finally. "They are so different from anyone else. So peculiar. But they are not ninehammers, they are formidable in the extreme; Cromwell was only a prelude, a practice. This Penn controls an estate that is stupefyingly vast. New Jersey is a place of Quakers, too, and different sorts of Puritans are all over Massachusetts. Gomer Bolstrood used to say the most startling things . . . overthrowing monarchy was the *least* of it. He said that Negroes and white men are equal before God and that all slavery everywhere must be done away with, and that his people would never let up until everyone saw it their way. 'First we'll get the Quakers on our side, for they are rich,' he said, 'then the other Nonconformists, then the Anglicans, then the Catholics, then all of Christendom.'"

William had turned his gaze back to the fire as she spoke, signalling that he believed her. "Your fascination with Negroes is very odd. But I have observed that the best people are frequently odd in one way or another. I have got in the habit of seeking them out, and declining to trust anyone who has no oddities. Your queer ideas concerning slavery are of no interest to me whatever. But the fact that you harbor queer ideas makes me inclined to place some small amount of trust in you."

"If you trust my judgment, the slender Puritan is the one to watch," Eliza said.

"But he has no vast territories in America, no money, no followers!"

"That is *why*. I would wager he had a father who was very strong, probably older brothers, too. That he has been checked and baffled many times, never married, never enjoyed even the small homely success of having a child, and has come to that time in his life when he must make his mark, or fail. This has become all confused, in his thinking, with the coming rebellion against the English King. He has decided to gamble his life on it—not in the sense of living or dying, but in the sense of making something of his life, or not."

William winced. "I pray you never see that deep into *me*."

"Why? Perhaps 'twould do you good."

"Nay, nay, you are like some Fellow of the Royal Society, dissecting a living dog—there is a placid cruelty about you."

"About *me*? What of *you*? To fight wars is *kindness*?"

"Most men would rather be shot through with a broad-headed arrow than be *described* by you."

Eliza could not help laughing. "I do not think my description of the slender one is at all cruel. On the contrary, I believe he will succeed. To judge from that pile of letters, he has many powerful Englishmen behind him. To rally that many supporters while remaining close to the King is very difficult." Eliza was hoping, now, that the Prince would let slip some bit of information about *who* those letter-writers were. But William perceived the gambit almost before she uttered the words, and looked away from her.

"It is very dangerous," he said. "Rash. Insane. I wonder if I should trust a man who conceives such a desperate plan."

A bit of a silence now. Then one of the logs in the fireplace gave way in a cascading series of pops and hisses.

"Are you asking me to do something about it?"

More silence, but this time the burden of response was on William. Eliza could relax, and watch his face. His face showed that he did not like being put in this position.

"I have something important for you to do at Versailles," he admitted, "and cannot afford to send you to London to tend to Daniel Waterhouse. But, where he is concerned, you might be more useful in Versailles anyway."

"I don't understand."

William opened his eyes wide, took a deep breath, and sighed it out, listening clinically to his own lungs. He sat up straighter, though his small hunched body was still overwhelmed by the chair, and looked alertly into the fire. "I can tell Waterhouse to be careful and he will say, 'yes, sire,' but it is all meaningless. He will not really be careful until he has something to live for." William looked Eliza straight in the eye.

"You want me to give him that?"

"I cannot afford to lose him, and the men who put their signatures on these letters, because he suddenly decides he cares not whether he lives or dies. I want him to have some reason to care."

"It is easily done."

"Is it? I cannot think of a pretext for getting the two of you in the same room together."

"I have another oddity, sire: I am interested in Natural Philosophy."

"Ah yes, you stay with Huygens."

"And Huygens has another friend in town just now, a Swiss mathematician named Fatio. He is young and ambitious and *desperate* to make contacts with the Royal Society. Daniel Waterhouse is the Secretary. I'll set up a dinner."

"That name Fatio is familiar," William said distantly. "He has been pestering me, trying to set up an audience."

"I'll find out what he wants."

"Good."

"What of the other thing?"

"I beg your pardon?"

"You said you had something important for me to do at Versailles."

"Yes. Come to me again before you leave and I'll explain it. Now I am tired, tired of talking. The thing you must do

there for me is pivotal, everything revolves around it, and I
want to have my wits about me when I explain it to you."

> M. Descartes had found the way to have his
> conjectures and fictions taken for truths. And
> to those who read his *Principles of Philosophy*
> something happened like that which happens
> to those who read novels which please and
> make the same impression as true stories. The
> novelty of the images of his little particles and
> vortices are most agreeable. When I read the
> book . . . the first time, it seemed to me that
> everything proceeded perfectly; and when I
> found some difficulty, I believe it was my fault
> in not fully understanding his thought. . . . But
> since then, having discovered in it from time
> to time things that are obviously false and oth-
> ers that are very improbable, I have rid myself
> entirely of the prepossession I had conceived,
> and I now find almost nothing in all his physics
> that I can accept as true. . . .
> —HUYGENS, TRANSLATED BY R.S. WESTFALL IN
> *The Concept of Force in Newton's Physics:*
> *The Science of Dynamics in*
> *the Seventeenth Century*

CHRISTIAAN HUYGENS SAT at the head of the table, the peri-
helion of the ellipse, and Daniel Waterhouse sat at the opposite end, the aphelion. Nicolas Fatio de Duilliers and Eliza
sat across from each other in between. A dinner of roast
goose, ham, and winter vegetables was served up by various
members of a family that had long been servants in this
house. Eliza was the author of the seating plan. Huygens and
Waterhouse must not sit next to each other or they'd fuse to-

gether and never say a word to the others. This way was better: Fatio would only want to talk to Waterhouse, who would
only want to talk to Eliza, who would pretend she had ears
only for Huygens, and so the guests would pursue each other
round the table clockwise, and with a bit of luck, an actual
conversation might eventuate.

It was near the time of the solstice, the sun had gone down
in the middle of the afternoon, and their faces, lit up by a
still-life of candles thrust into wax-crusted bottles, hung in
the darkness like Moons of Jupiter. The ticking of Huygens's clock-work at the other end of the room was distracting at first, but later became part of the fabric of space; like
the beating of their hearts, they could hear it if they wanted
to, its steady process reassured them that all was well while
reminding them that time was moving onwards. It was difficult to be uncivilized in the company of so many clocks.

Daniel Waterhouse had arrived first and had immediately
apologized to Eliza for having taken her for a house-servant
earlier. But he had not dropped the other shoe and asked
what she *really* was. She'd accepted his apology with tart
amusement and then declined to offer any explanation. This
was light flirtation of the most routine sort—at Versailles it
would have elicited a roll of the eyes from anyone who had
bothered to notice it. But it had been more than enough to
plunge Waterhouse into utter consternation. Eliza found this
slightly alarming.

He had tried again: "Mademoiselle, I would be less
than . . ."

"Oh, speak English!" she'd said, in English. This had
practically left him senseless: first, with surprise that she
could speak English at all, then with alarm that she'd overheard his entire conversation with William Penn. "Now,
what was it you were saying?"

He scrambled to remember what he had been saying. In a
man half his age, to've been so flustered would have been
adorable. As it stood, she was dismayed, wondering what
would happen to this man the first time some French-trained

countess got her talons into him. William had been right. Daniel Waterhouse was a Hazard to Navigation.

"Err . . . I'd be less than honest if, er . . ." he winced. "It sounded gallant in French. Pompous in English. I was wondering . . . the state of international relations being so troublous and relations 'tween the sexes more so, and etiquette being an area in which I am weak . . . whether there was any pretext at all under which I might converse with you, or send letters, without giving offense."

"Isn't this dinner good enough?" she'd asked, flirtatiously mock-offended, and just then Fatio had arrived. In truth, she'd seen him coming across the Plein, and adjusted her timing accordingly. Waterhouse was obliged to stand off to one side and stew and draw up a great mental accompt of his failures and shortcomings while Eliza and Fatio enacted a greeting-ritual straight out of the Salon of Apollo at Versailles. This had much in common with a courtly dance, but with overtones of a duel; Eliza and Fatio were probing each other, emanating signals coded in dress, gesture, inflection, and emphasis, and watching with the brilliant alertness of sword-fighters to see whether the other had noticed, and how they'd respond. As one who'd lately come from the Court of the Sun King, Eliza held the high ground; the question was, what level of esteem should she accord Fatio? If he'd been Catholic, and French, and titled, this would have been settled before he came in the door. But he was Protestant, Swiss, and came from a gentle family of no particular rank. He was in his early twenties, Eliza guessed, though he tried to make himself older by wearing very good French clothes. He was not a handsome man: he had giant blue eyes below a high domelike forehead, but the lower half of his face was too small, his nose stuck out like a beak, and in general he had the exhausting intensity of a trapped bird.

At some point Fatio had to tear those eyes away from Eliza and begin the same sort of dance-*cum*-duel with Waterhouse. Again, if Fatio had been a Fellow of the Royal Society, or a Doctor at some university, Waterhouse would have had some idea what to make of him; as it was, Fatio had to conjure his credentials and *bona fides* out of thin air, as it were, by dropping names and scattering references to books he'd read, problems he'd solved, inflated reputations he had punctured, experiments he had performed, creatures he had seen. "I had half expected to see Mr. Enoch Root here," he said at one point, looking about, "for a (ahem) gentleman of my acquaintance here, an *amateur* of (ahem) chymical studies, has shared with me a rumor—only a rumor, mind you—that a man owning Root's description was observed, the other day, debarking from a canal-ship from Brussels." As Fatio stretched this patch of news thinner and thinner, he flinched his huge eyes several times at Waterhouse. Certain French nobles would have winked or stroked their moustaches interestedly; Waterhouse offered up nothing but a basilisk-stare.

That was the last time Fatio had anything to say concerning Alchemy; from that point onwards it was strictly mathematics, and the new work by Newton. Eliza had heard from both Leibniz and Huygens that this Newton had written some sort of discourse that had left all of the other Natural Philosophers holding their heads between their knees, and quite dried up the ink in their quills, and so she was able to follow Fatio's drift here. Though from time to time he would turn his attention to Eliza and revert to courtly posturing for a few moments. Fatio prosecuted all of these uphill strugglings with little apparent effort, which spoke well of his training, and of the overall balance of his humours. At the same time it made her tired just to watch him. From the moment he came in the door he controlled the conversation; everyone spent the rest of the evening reacting to Fatio. That suited Eliza's purposes well enough; it kept Daniel Waterhouse frustrated, which was how she liked him, and gave her leisure to observe. All the same, she wondered what supplied the energy to keep a Fatio going; he was the loudest and fastest clock in the room, and must have an internal spring keyed up very tight. He had no sexual interest whatever in Eliza, and that was a relief, for she could tell that he would be relentless and probably tiresome in wooing.

Why didn't they just eject Fatio and have a peaceful dinner? Because he had genuine merit. Confronted by a nobody so desperate to establish his reputation, Eliza's first impulse (and Waterhouse's, too, she inferred) was to assume he was a *poseur*. But he was not. Once he figured out that Eliza wasn't Catholic he had interesting things to say concerning religion and the state of French society. Once he figured out that Waterhouse was no alchemist, he began to discourse of mathematical functions in a way that snapped the Englishman awake. And Huygens, when he finally woke up and came downstairs, made it obvious by his treatment of Fatio that he rated him as an equal—or as close to equal as a man like Huygens could ever have.

"A man of my tender age and meager accomplishments cannot give sufficient honor to the gentleman who once dined at this table—"

"Actually Descartes dined here *many* times—not just *once!*" Huygens put in gruffly.

"—and set out his proposal to explain physical reality with mathematics," Fatio finished.

"You would not speak of him that way unless you were about to say something against him," Eliza said.

"Not against him, but some of his latter-day followers. The project that Descartes started is finished. Vortices will never do! I am surprised that Leibniz still holds out any hope for them."

Everyone sat up straighter. "Perhaps you have heard from Leibniz more recently than I have, sir," Waterhouse said.

"You give me more credit than I deserve, Doctor Waterhouse, to suggest that Doctor Leibniz would communicate his freshest insights to *me,* before despatching them to the *Royal Society*! Please correct me."

"It is not that Leibniz has any particular attachment to vortices, but that he cannot bring himself to believe in any sort of mysterious action at a distance." Hearing this, Huygens raised a hand momentarily, as if seconding a motion. Fatio did not fail to notice. Waterhouse continued, "Action at a distance is a sort of occult notion—which may appeal to a certain sort of mentality—"

"But not to those of us who have adopted the Mechanical Philosophy that Monsieur Descartes propounded at this very table!"

"In that very chair, sir!" said Huygens, pointing at Fatio with a drumstick.

"I have my own Theory of Gravitation that should account for the inverse square relation," Fatio said. "As a stone dropped into water makes spreading ripples, so a planet makes concentric disturbances in the cœlestial æther, which press upon its satellites . . ."

"Write it down," Waterhouse said, "and send it to me, and we will print it alongside Leibniz's account, and may the better one prevail."

"Your offer is gratefully accepted!" Fatio said, and glanced at Huygens to make sure he had a witness. "But I fear we are boring Mademoiselle Eliza."

"Not at all, Monsieur, any conversation that bears on the Doctor is of interest to me."

"Is there any topic that does not relate to Leibniz in some way?"

"Alchemy," Waterhouse suggested darkly.

Fatio, whose chief object at the moment was to draw Eliza into the conversation, ignored this. "I can't but wonder whether we may discern the Doctor's hand in the formation of the League of Augsburg."

"I would guess not," Eliza said. "It has long been Leibniz's dream to re-unite the Catholic and Lutheran churches, and prevent another Thirty Years' War. But the League looks to me like a *preparation* for war. It is not the conception of the Doctor, but of the Prince of Orange."

"The Protestant Defender," Fatio said. Eliza was accustomed to hearing that phrase drenched in French sarcasm, but Fatio uttered it carefully, like a Natural Philosopher weighing an unproven hypothesis. "Our neighbors in Savoy could have used some defending when de Catinat came through with his dragoons. Yes, in this matter I must disagree with the Doctor, as well-meaning as he is . . . we do need a Defender, and William of Orange will make a good one, provided he stays out of the clutches of the French." Fatio was staring at Eliza while he said this.

Huygens chuckled. "That should not be difficult, since he never leaves Dutch soil."

"But the coast is long, and mostly empty, and the French could put a force ashore anywhere they pleased."

"French fleets do not sail up and down the Dutch coast without drawing attention," Huygens said, still amused by the idea.

Continuing to watch Eliza, Fatio replied, "I said nothing about a *fleet*. A single *jacht* would suffice to put a boat-load of dragoons on the beach."

"And what would those dragoons do against the might of the Dutch army?"

"Be destroyed, if they were stupid enough to encamp on the beach and wait for that army to mobilize," Fatio answered. "But if they happened to light on the particular stretch of beach where William goes sand-sailing, at the right time of the morning, why, they could redraw the map, and rewrite the future history, of Europe in a few minutes' work."

Now nothing could be heard for a minute or so except the clocks. Fatio still held Eliza fast with his vast eyes, giant blue lenses that seemed to take all the light in the room. What might they not have noticed, and what might the mind in back of them not know?

On the other hand, what tricks could the mind not conjure up, and with those eyes, whom couldn't he draw into his snares?

"It is a clever conceit, like a chapter from a picaroon-romance," Eliza said. Fatio's high brow shriveled, and the eyes that had seemed so penetrating a moment ago now looked pleading. Eliza glanced toward the stairs. "Now that Fatio has provided us with entertainment, will you elevate us, Monsieur Huygens?"

"How should I translate that word?" Huygens returned. "The last time one of your guests became elevated in my house, I had to look the other way."

"Elevate us to the roof, where we may see the stars and planets, and then elevate our minds by showing us some new phenomenon through your telescope," Eliza answered patiently.

"In company such as this we must all elevate one another, for I carry no advantage on these men," Huygens said. This triggered a long tedious volley of self-deprecations from Fatio and Waterhouse. But soon enough they all got their winter coats on and labored up a staircase devious and strait, and emerged into starlight. The only clouds in this sky were those that condensed in front of their lips as they breathed. Huygens lit up a clay pipe. Fatio, who had assisted Huygens before, took the wraps off the big Newtonian reflector with the tense precision of a hummingbird, keeping an ear cocked toward Huygens and Waterhouse, who were talking about optics, and an eye on Eliza, who was strolling around the parapet enjoying the view: to the east, the Haagse Bos, woolly and black with trees. To the south, the smoking chimneys and glowing windows of the Hofgebied. To the west, the windy expanse of the Plein, stretching to the Grenadier's Gate on the far side, which controlled access to the Binnenhof. A lot of wax and whale-oil was being burnt there tonight, to illuminate a soiree in the palace's Ballroom. To the young ladies who had been invited, it must have seemed never so glamorous. To Huygens it was a damnable nuisance, for the humid air snared the radiance of all those tapers and lamps, and glowed faintly, in a way that most people would never notice. But it ruined the seeing of his telescope.

Within a few minutes the two older men had gotten embroiled in the work of aiming the telescope at Saturn: a body that would show up distinctly no matter how many candles were burning at the Binnenhof. Fatio glided over to keep Eliza company.

"Now let us set aside formalities and speak directly," she said.

"As you wish, Mademoiselle."

"Is this notion of the *jacht* and the dragoons a phant'sy of yours or—"

"Say if I am wrong: on mornings when the weather is not perfectly abominable, and the wind is off the sea, the Prince of Orange goes to his boat-house on the beach at Scheveningen at ten o'clock, chooses a sand-sailer, and pilots it northwards up the beach to the dunes near Katwijk—though on a clear day he'll venture as far as Noordwijk—then turns round and is back in Scheveningen by midday."

Not wanting to give Fatio the satisfaction of telling him he was right, Eliza answered, "You have made a study of the Prince's habits?"

"No, but Count Fenil has."

"Fenil—I have heard his name in the salon of the Duchess of Oyonnax—he originates in that place where Switzerland and Savoy, Burgundy, and the Piedmont are all convolved, yes?"

"Yes."

"And he is Catholic, and a Francophile."

"He is Savoyard in name, but he saw very early that Louis XIV would eclipse the Duke of Savoy, and swallow up his dominions, and so he became more French than the French, and served in the army of Louvois. That alone should prove his *bona fides* to the King of France. But after the recent show of force by the French Army next door to his lands, Fenil evidently feels some further demonstration of his loyalty is needed. So he has devised the plan I mentioned, of abducting William from the beach and carrying him back to France in chains."

They had now paused at a corner where they could look out over the Plein toward the Binnenhof. To Eliza this had seemed grand (at least by European standards) when d'Avaux had taken her skating there. Now that she'd grown accustomed to Versailles, it looked like a woodshed. Lit up for this evening's fête, it was as grand as it would ever be. William Penn would be there, and various members of the diplomatic corps—including d'Avaux, who had invited her to attend it on his arm. She had accepted, then changed her mind so that she could organize the present dinner. D'Avaux had not been happy about it and had asked questions that were difficult to answer. Once d'Avaux had recruited her, and sent her down to Versailles, their relationship had changed to that of lord and vassal. He had allowed her to see his hard, cruel, vengeful aspects, mostly as an implicit warning of what would come if she disappointed him. Eliza supposed it must have been d'Avaux who had supplied intelligence to Fenil concerning William's routine.

It had been a mild winter so far, and the Hofvijver, in front of the Binnenhof, was a black rectangle, not yet frozen, reflecting gleams of candlelight from the party as gusts of wind wrinkled its surface. Eliza recalled her own abduction from a beach, and felt like crying. Fatio's yarn might or might not be true, but in combination with some cutting remarks that d'Avaux had made to her earlier, it had put real melancholy into her heart. Not connected with any one particular man, or plan, or outcome, but melancholy like the black water that ate up the light.

"How do you know the mind of M. le comte de Fenil?"

"I was visiting my father at Duillier—our seat in Switzerland—a few weeks ago. Fenil came on a visit. I went for a stroll with him and he told me what I have told you."

"He must be an imbecile to talk about it openly."

"Perhaps. Inasmuch as the purpose is to enhance his prestige, the more he talks about it, the better."

"'Tis an outlandish plan. Has he suggested it to anyone who could realize it?"

"Indeed, he proposed it to the Maréchal Louvois, who wrote back to him and directed him to make preparations."

"How long ago?"

"Long enough, mademoiselle, for the preparations to have been made by now."

"So you have come here to warn William?"

"I have been striving to warn him," Fatio said, "but he will not grant me an audience."

"It is very strange, then, that you should approach *me*. What makes you believe that *I* have the ear of the Prince of Orange? I live at Versailles and I invest money for members of the Court of the King of France. I journey up this way from time to time to consult with my brokers, and to meet with my dear friend and client the comte d'Avaux. What on earth makes you believe that I should have any connection to William?"

"Suffice it to say, I know that you do," Fatio returned placidly.

"Who else knows?"

"Who knows that bodies in an inverse square field move on conic sections? Who knows that there is a division between the Rings of Saturn?"

"Anyone who reads *Principia Mathematica,* or looks through a telescope, respectively."

"And who has the wit to understand what he has read, or seen."

"Yes. Anyone can possess Newton's book, few can understand it."

"Just so, mademoiselle. And likewise anyone may observe you, or listen to gossip about you, but to interpret those *data* and know the truth requires gifts that God hoards jealously and gives out to very few."

"Have you learned much of me, then, from talking to your brethren? For I know that they are to be found in every Court, Church, and College, and that they know each other by signs and code-words. Please do not be coy with me, Fatio, it is ever so tedious."

"Coy? I would not dream of so insulting a woman of your sophistication. Yes, I tell you without reserve that I belong to

an esoteric brotherhood that numbers many of the high and
the mighty among its members; that the very *raison d'être*
of that brotherhood is to exchange information that should
not be spread about promiscuously; and that I have learned
of you from that source."

"Are you saying that my lord Upnor, and every other gentleman who pisses in the corridors of Versailles, knows of
my connexion to William of Orange?"

"Most of them are *poseurs* with very limited powers of understanding. Do not change your plans out of some phant'sy
that they will penetrate what I have penetrated," Fatio said.

Eliza, who did not find this a very satisfying answer, said
nothing. Her silence caused Fatio to get that pleading look
again. She turned away from him—the only alternative being to scoff and roll her eyes—and gazed down into the
Plein. There something caught her eye: a long figure darkly
cloaked, silver hair spilling out onto his shoulders. He had
lately emerged from the Grenadiers' Gate, as if he had just
excused himself from the party. A gust of steam flourished
from his mouth as he shouted, "How is the seeing tonight?"

"Much better than I should like," returned Eliza.

"Bad, very bad, Mr. Root, because of our troublesome
neighbor!"

"Do not be disheartened," said Enoch the Red, "I believe
that Pegasus, to-night, shall be adorned by a *meteor;* turn
your telescope thither."

Eliza and Fatio both turned and looked towards the telescope, which was situated cater-corner from them, meaning
that Huygens and Waterhouse could neither hear nor see
Enoch Root. When they turned back around, Root had
turned his back on them, and was vanishing into one of the
many narrow side-streets of the Hofgebied.

"Most disappointing! I was going to invite him up here . . .
he must have come from the fête at the Binnenhof," Fatio said.

Eliza finished the thought herself: *Where he was hobnob-*
bing with my brethren of the Dutch court—the same ones
who cannot keep their mouths shut concerning you, Eliza.

Fatio looked toward Polaris. "It is half past midnight, never mind what the church-bells say . . ."

"How can you tell?"

"By reading the positions of the stars. Pegasus is far to the west, there. It shall descend beneath the western horizon within two hours. A miserable place to make observations! And in any case, meteors come and go too quickly for one to aim a telescope at 'em . . . what did he mean?"

"Is this a fair sample of the esoteric brotherhood's discourse? No wonder that Alchemists are famed mostly for blowing up their own dwellings," Eliza said, feeling somewhat relieved to get this glimpse into the mystery, and to find nothing but bafflement there.

They spent the better part of an hour looking at, and arguing about, the gap in Saturn's rings, which was named after Cassini, the French royal astronomer, and which Fatio could explain mathematically. Which was to say that Eliza was cold, bored, and ignored. Only one person could peer into the telescope's eyepiece at a time, and these men quite forgot their manners, and never offered her a turn.

Then Fatio persuaded the others to point the telescope into Pegasus, or those few stars of it that had not yet been drowned in the North Sea. The search of Pegasus was not nearly so interesting to them as Saturn had been, and so they let Eliza look all she wanted, sweeping the instrument back and forth, hoping to catch the predicted meteor.

"Have you found something, Mademoiselle?" Fatio asked at one point, when he noticed Eliza's stiff fingers pawing at the focusing-screw.

"A cloud, just peeking over the horizon."

"Weather as fine as today's could never last," said Huygens, in a fair sample of Dutch pessimism; for the weather had been wretched.

"Does it have the appearance of a rain-cloud or . . ."

"That is what I am trying to establish," Eliza said, trying to bring it into focus.

"Enoch was having you on a bit," Huygens said, for the

others had by now told him the story of Enoch's enigmatic
turn in the Plein. "He felt his joints aching and knew a
change in the weather was in the offing! And he knew it
would come out of Pegasus since that is in the west, and that
is where the wind is from. Very clever."

"A few wisps of cloud, indeed . . . but what I first mistook
for heavy rain-clouds, is actually a ship under sail . . . taking
advantage of the moon-light to raise her sails, and make a
run up the coast," Eliza said.

"Cloth-smugglers," Waterhouse predicted, "coming in
from round Ipswich." Eliza stepped back and he took a turn
at the eyepiece. "No, I'm wrong, 'tis the wrong sail-plan for
a smuggler."

"She is rigged for speed, but proceeding cautiously just
now," Huygens pronounced. Then it was Fatio's turn: "I
would wager she is bringing contraband from France—
salt, wine, or both." And so they continued, more and more
tediously, until Eliza announced that she was going down
to bed.

SHE WAS AWAKENED BY THE tolling of a church-bell. For
some reason she felt it was terribly important to count the
strokes, but she woke up too late to be sure. She had left her
long winter coat across the foot of her bed to make her toes
a little warmer and she now sat up and snatched it and drew
it round her shoulders in one quick movement, before the
chill could rush through the porous linen of her nightgown.
She swung her feet out of bed, poked at the pair of rabbit-
pelt slippers on the floor to chase away any mice that might
be using them as beds, and then pushed her feet into them.

For in somewhat the same way as rodents may quietly set
up house-keeping in one's clothing during the hours of darkness, an idea had established itself in Eliza's mind while she
had been asleep. She did not become fully conscious of this
idea until a few minutes later when she went into the great
room to stoke up the fire, and saw all of Huygens's clocks

reading the same time: a few minutes past nine o'clock in the morning.

She looked out a window over the Plein and saw high white clouds. From the myriad chimneys of the Binnenhof, plumes of smoke trailed eastwards before a steady onshore breeze. Perfect day for sand-sailing.

She went to the door of Huygens's bedchamber and raised a fist, then held off. If she were wrong, it were foolish to disturb him. If she were right, it were foolish to spend a quarter of an hour waking him up and trying to convince him.

Huygens kept only a few horses here. The riding-fields of the Malieveld and the Koekamp lay only a musket-shot from the house, and so when he or any of his guests felt like going riding, they need only stroll to one of the many livery-stables that surrounded those places.

Eliza ran out a back door of the house, nearly knocking down a Dutch woman out sweeping the pavement, and took off round the corner running in her rabbit-slippers.

Then she faltered, remembering she'd not brought any money.

"Eliza!" someone shouted.

She turned around to see Nicolas Fatio de Duilliers running up the street after her.

"Do you have money?" she called.

"Yes!"

Eliza ran away from him and did not stop until she reached the nearest livery stable, a couple of hundred long strides away, far enough to get her heart pounding and her face flushed. By the time Fatio caught up with her she had wrapped up a negotiation with the owner; the Swiss mathematician came in the gate just in time to see Eliza thrusting a finger at him and shouting, "and *he* pays!"

Saddling the horses would take several minutes. Eliza felt on the verge of throwing up. Fatio was agitated, too, but breeding was at war with common sense in him, and breeding prevailed; he attempted to make conversation.

"I infer, Mademoiselle, that you too have received some communication from Enoch the Red on this morning?"

"Only if he came and whispered in my ear while I was sleeping!"

Fatio didn't know what to make of that. "I encountered him a few minutes ago at my usual coffee-house . . . he elaborated on his cryptic statement of last night . . ."

"What we saw last night was enough for me," Eliza answered. A sleepy stable-boy dropped a saddle, and instead of bending to pick it up, tried to make some witty comment. The owner was doing sums with a quill-pen that wouldn't hold its ink. Tears of frustration came to Eliza's eyes. "Damn it!"

"RIDING BARE-BACK IS LIKE RIDING, only more so," Jack Shaftoe had said to her once. She preferred to remember Jack as little and as infrequently as possible, but now this memory came to her. Until the day they had met underneath Vienna, Eliza had never ridden a horse. Jack had taken obvious pleasure in teaching her the rudiments, more so when she seemed uncertain, or fell off, or let Turk run away with her. But after she had become expert, Jack had turned peevish and haughty, and lost no opportunity to remind her that riding well in a saddle was no accomplishment, and that until one learned to ride bare-back, one didn't know how to ride at all. Jack knew all about it, of course, because it was how Vagabonds stole horses.

Choosing the proper mount was of the utmost importance (he had explained). Given a string or stable of horses to choose from, one wanted to pick a mount with a flat back, and yet not too wide-bodied or else it wouldn't be possible to get a good grip with the knees. The wither, or bony hump at the base of the neck, should not be too large (which would make it impossible to lie flat while galloping) nor too small (which gave no purchase for the hands), but somewhere in between. And the horse should be of a compliant disposition, for at some point it was bound to happen that the horse-thief would become disarranged on the horse's back, as the outcome of some bump or swerve, and then it would be entirely up to the horse whether the Vagabond would be flung off into space or coaxed back into balance.

Now it might have been pure chance that Eliza's favorite horse in this stable—the mare she asked for by name whenever she called—possessed a flat but not overly broad back, a medium-sized wither, and a sweet disposition. Or perhaps Jack Shaftoe's advice on the finer points of horse-thievery had subtly informed her choice. At any rate, the mare's name was Vla ("cream"), and Eliza rated it as unlikely she would ever try to pitch Eliza off her bare back. The stable-boy was attempting to saddle up a different mare, but Vla was in a stall only a few paces away.

Eliza walked over and opened the gate to that stall, greeting Vla by name, and then stepped forward until her nose was caressing the mare's, and breathed very gently into Vla's nostrils. This prompted Vla to raise her enormous head slightly, trying to draw closer to that warmth. Eliza cupped the mare's chin in her hand and exhaled into those nostrils again, and Vla responded with a little shudder of gratitude. Giant overlapping slabs of muscle twitched here and there, coming awake. Eliza now stepped into the stall, trailing a hand along the mare's side, and then used the stall's side-planks as a ladder, climbing to a level from which she was able to dive across Vla's back. Then, by gripping that convenient medium-sized wither with one hand, she was able to spin herself round on her belly and get her legs wrapped around Vla's body—this required pulling the narrow skirts of her nightgown up round her hips, but her coat hung down to either side and covered her legs. Her bare buttocks, thighs, and calves were pressed directly against the mare's body, which was exquisitely warm. Vla took this all calmly enough. She did not respond the first time Eliza pinched her bottom, but on the second pinch she walked out into the stable-yard, and when Eliza told her what a good girl she was and pinched her a third time she broke into a trot that

nearly bounced Eliza straight off. Eliza flung herself full-
length onto the mare's back and neck, and buried her face in
the mane, and clenched a hank of the coarse hair in her
teeth. All her attention was concentrated for those few moments on not falling off. The next time she looked around,
they had trotted out into the street, pursued none too effectively by a few grooms and stable-hands who still could not
make out whether they were witnessing a bizarre mishap or
a criminal act.

They were headed northwards along the edge of the
riding-ground called Koekamp, which was limned on this
side by the big canal that ran straight to Scheveningen. Vla
wanted to turn her nose out of the stinging sea-wind and
stray off into the Koekamp, which was what she did for a living. Every time her nose bent that way, Eliza gave her a
sharp reprimand, and a dig on that side with her foot. So
progress was balky, and relations between horse and rider
were tense, as long as the Koekamp and then the Malieveld
beckoned to their right. But once they had ridden clear of
such temptations, Vla seemed to understand that they were
riding up the canal to Scheveningen, and settled down no-
ticeably. Another pinch caused Vla to break into a canter,
which was both smoother and faster. Very soon after that
Eliza was galloping down the canal-side hollering "Make
way in the name of the Stadholder!" whenever she saw anyone in the way. But this was rarely, for by now they were out
in open country, and cows were more common than people.

Jack had been right, she decided—remaining on the back
of a galloping horse without benefit of saddle was a question
of balance, and of anticipating the horse's movements, while
also relying on some cooperation from the horse! Soon Vla
began to sweat, which made her slippery, and then Eliza had
to abandon all pretense of holding on by brute force and rely
entirely on a very complicated and ever-changing sort of
sympathy between her and the mare.

Fatio did not catch up with her until she was most of the
way to Scheveningen. They were being pursued, at a dis-

tance, by two men who were presumably members of the St. George Guild. As long as these did not draw close enough to loose any pistol-balls in their direction, they did not especially care. It could all be explained later.

"The ship . . . we saw . . ." Eliza shouted, forcing out the occasional word when not gasping for breath or being jolted by the mare. "'Twas the *jacht*?"

"The same. . . . It is . . . *Météore*, the flagship . . . of the Duc . . . d'Arcachon! We may . . . assume it . . . to be full . . . of dragoons!" Fatio returned.

Behind them, someone had begun blowing a horn from the top of a watch-tower in the Hague. It was a signal to the sheriff in Scheveningen, who was answerable to the town council of the Hague; very soon Fatio and Eliza would find out how diligent this sheriff was, and how well he had organized his watchmen.

They reached the boat-house at Scheveningen at ten minutes past ten o'clock. As they approached, Eliza saw a sand-sailer out on the beach, being worked on by a ship-wright, and cried "Aha!" thinking they'd arrived in time. But then she noticed wheel-tracks in the sand, and followed them north up the beach until she saw another sailer, already a mile away, heeled over by the sea-breeze.

The boat-house was not really a single house, but a horse-shoe-shaped compound of diverse sheds, shacks, and workshops scabbed on to one another, crammed with distracting detail: tools, forges, lathes, lofts. . . . Eliza got lost in that detail for a few moments, then turned around to look behind them, and discovered a landscape of pandemonium in their wake: breathless Guildsmen from the Hague, Blue Guards, marines from ships in the harbor, enraged members of Scheveningen's Watch, all seemingly contending with one another to lay hands first on Fatio—who was trying to explain everything in French. He was throwing unreadable looks at Eliza, half pleading for assistance, half wanting to defend her from the mob.

"Fire guns!" Eliza shouted in Dutch. "The Prince is in

danger." Then she explained what she could, in what little
Dutch she had. Nodding his head the whole time was the
Captain of the Blue Guards, who, she collected, had always
taken a dim view of the Prince's beach-sailing anyway. At
some point he decided he had heard plenty. He fired a pistol
in the air to silence the crowd and tossed the empty, smoking
weapon to a guardsman, who tossed him a loaded one back.
Then he uttered a few words in Dutch and everyone scattered.

"What did he say, mademoiselle?" Fatio asked.

"He said, 'Guards, ride! Watchmen, fire! Sailors, launch!
Others, get out of the way!'"

Fatio watched in fascination: a squadron of mounted Blue
Guards took off hell-for-leather up the beach, galloping in
pursuit of the Prince. Sailors were sprinting down towards
the waterfront, the gunners on the harbor batteries were
loading their cannons. Anyone with a loaded firearm was
shooting in the air; but the Prince, far away in a cosmos of
wind and surf, could not hear them. "I suppose we belong in
the category of 'others,'" Fatio said, a bit dejectedly. "It will
be all right, I suppose . . . those cavalrymen will catch up to
him anon."

The sun had found a rift in the high clouds and illumi-
nated veils of steam rising from the sweaty coats of their
horses. "They'll never catch him," Eliza demurred, "in this
wind he can out-sail them with ease."

"Perhaps the Prince will take notice of *that*!" Fatio said,
startled by a ragged volley of cannon-fire.

"He'll only assume it is a salute, for some ship approaching the harbor."

"What can we do, then?"

"Follow orders. Leave," Eliza said.

"Then pray tell why are you dismounting?"

"Fatio, you are a gentleman," Eliza called over her shoulder, kicking off the rabbit-pelts and stepping barefoot across
the sand towards the other sailer. "You grew up near Lake
Geneva. Do you know how to sail?"

"Mademoiselle," said Fatio, dismounting, "on a rig of this plan I can out-sail a *Dutchman.* I want only one thing."

"Name it."

"The craft will heel over. The sail will spill wind and I will lose speed. Unless I had someone small, nimble, tenacious, and very brave, to lean out of the vehicle on the windward side, and act as a counterweight."

"Let us go and defend the Defender then," Eliza said, climbing aboard.

THEY COULD NOT POSSIBLY BE moving as fast as it *seemed,* or so Eliza told herself until they caught up with the squadron of Blue Guards. With a twitch of the tiller Fatio could have veered round them as if they were standing still. Instead he let out the main-sheet and spilled a huge dollop of air, causing the sailer to drop to what felt like a slow walking pace—and yet they were staying abreast of the galloping Guards. The sailer dropped back onto all three wheels and Eliza, leaning way out on what had been the high side, nearly planted her head in the sand. Fortunately she was gripping with both hands a line that Fatio had hitched round the mast, and by pulling hard on this she was able to draw herself up faster than the zooming sand could lunge at her. And now she had a few moments to wipe spray and grit out of her face, and to tie her hair into a sodden knot that lay cold and rough against her neck. Fatio had got the attention of some of the Blue Guards by gesticulating and shouting in a hotchpotch of languages. Something came flying towards them, tumbling end-over-end, plopped into the mainsail, and slid down the curved canvas into Fatio's lap: a musket. Then another, flung by a different Guard, whirled just over their heads and embedded itself barrel-first in the sand, surf swirling around its stock, and fell away aft. Now a pistol came flying toward them and Eliza, finally ready, was able to reach up and slap it out of the air with one hand.

Instantly Fatio hauled in on the sheet and the sailer hurled itself forward. He got in front of the foremost of the Guards and then veered up away from the surf onto drier and firmer sand. Eliza had had time to shove the pistol into her coat-sash now, and to get that rope wrapped securely round her hands; Fatio hauled the sheet in recklessly, and the sailer bit so fiercely into the wind that it nearly capsized. One of its wheels was spinning in the air, flinging sand and water at Eliza, who clambered over its rim, planted both of her bare feet on the end of the axle, and let the rope slither through her numb hands until she was leaning back almost horizontally and gazing (when she could see anything) at the under-carriage of the sand-sailer.

It occurred to her to wonder whether they were now traveling faster than any human beings had ever gone. For a minute she fancied it was so—then the Natural Philosopher in her weighed in with the observation that ice-boats had less friction to contend with and probably went even faster.

Then why was she so exhilarated? Because despite the cold and the danger and the uncertainty of what they might find at the end of the journey, she had a kind of freedom here, a wildness she had not known since her Vagabond days with Jack. All the cares and intrigues of Versailles were forgotten.

Craning her neck around, she was able to look out to sea. There was the normal clutter of coastal traffic, but mostly these vessels had triangular sails. The square-rigged *jacht* of the duc d'Arcachon should be conspicuous. Indeed, she thought she could see a square-rigger standing off several leagues from shore, a short distance to the north—that must be *Météore*! The longboat would have come in at dawn and been hauled up on the beach so that the Prince would not notice it until too late.

Fatio had been raving for some minutes about the Bernoullis—Swiss mathematicians, therefore friends and colleagues of his. "Sail-makers of a hundred years ago phant'sied that sails worked as literal wind-bags, which is why ships in old pictures all have a big-bellied appearance that is very odd to our modern eyes, as if they need to be

taken in . . . now we have learned that sails develop force by
virtue of air-currents to either side, shaping, and shaped by,
the curve of the canvas . . . but we understand not the *particulars* . . . the Bernoullis are making this their field of spe-
cialization . . . soon we'll be able to use my calculus to loft
sails according to *rational* principles. . . ."

"*Your* calculus!?"

"Yes . . . and it will enable us to attain speeds even . . .
better . . . than . . . *this*!"

"I see him!" Eliza shouted.

Fatio's view ahead was blocked by sail and rigging, but
Eliza was in the clear, and she could see the top of William's
mast protruding above a low hummock of sand and beach-
scrub. The Prince's sailer was heeled over, but not so much
as theirs, since he lacked a human counter-weight. He was
perhaps half a mile ahead. Halfway between them, but coming up on them rapidly, was the said hummock, which (Eliza
realized) was just the sort of visual obstacle behind which
the dragoons would want to set up their ambuscade. And indeed she could see the mast of William's sailer swinging up
to vertical as he faltered and lost speed . . .

"It is happening now," she shouted.

"Would you like me to stop and let you off, mademoiselle, or—"

"Don't be foolish."

"Very well!" Fatio now steered the sailer in a slashing arc
around the end of the hummock. In that moment a mile of
open beach was revealed to them.

Straight ahead and alarmingly close was a longboat, still
cluttered with branches that had been laid over it as camou-
flage. This had just been dragged out of a hiding place on the
north face of the hummock and was now being hauled and
shoved down toward the water by half a dozen hefty French
dragoons. At the moment its keel was slicing directly across
the tracks that had been laid in the sand by William's sailer a
few seconds ago. It was cutting off the Prince's line of retreat—and it barred Eliza and Fatio's advance. Fatio jerked

on the tiller and steered up-slope, round behind the boat. Eliza could only hold her rope. She clenched her teeth so that she would not bite off her tongue, and kept her eyes closed through a series of jolts. The wheels that were on the ground plunged across the furrow that had been cut by the longboat's keel, and the one that was in the air smashed into the head of a startled dragoon and felled him like a statue.

The trim of the sails and balance of the vehicle were now all awry, and there was some veering and bouncing as Fatio brought matters in hand again. Sheer speed was not as important as it had been, and so Eliza put her whole weight on the hand-rope, raised her knees, and swung inwards far enough to plant her feet near the mast of the sailer. Fatio settled into a slower pace. They both looked up the beach.

A bow-shot ahead of them, another contingent of half a dozen dragoons were running in pursuit of the Prince of Orange's sand-sailer. This had come to a stop before a barrier consisting of a chain stretched along a row of pilings that the Frenchmen had apparently pounded into the sand. The ambushers all had their backs to Eliza and Fatio, and their attention fixed upon the Prince, who had clambered out of his sailer and turned round to face the attackers.

William strode free of his sailer, shrugged his cape off into the sand, reached round himself, and drew his sword.

Fatio sailed into the line of dragoons, taking two of them, including their captain, from behind. But this was the end of his and Eliza's sand-sailing career, for the vehicle planted its nose in the sand and tumbled over smartly. Eliza landed face-first in wet sand and sensed wreckage slamming down near her, but nothing touched her save a few snarled wet ropes. Still, these were an impediment to getting up. When she struggled to her feet, all water-logged, sand-covered, cold, and battered, she discovered that she'd lost the pistol; and by the time she'd pulled it up out of the sand, the action at this end of the beach was over—William's sword, which had been bright a moment ago, was red now, and two dragoons were lying on sand clutching at their vitals. Another was being held at bay by Fatio with his musket, and the sixth member of the squad was running toward the longboat, waving his arms over his head and shouting.

The longboat was in the surf now, ready to convey the dragoons and their prisoner back out to *Météore*. After a short discussion, four of the men who'd dragged it down the beach detached themselves and took off running towards the stopped sand-sailers while another stayed behind to mind the boat's bow-rope. The sixth member of that contingent was still face-down in the sand with a wheel-track running over his back.

Eliza had not been noticed yet.

She crouched down behind the broken frame of the sand-sailer and devoted a few moments to examining the firing-mechanism of the pistol, trying to brush out the sand while leaving some powder in the pan.

Hearing a scream, she looked up to see that William had simply walked up to the captured dragoon and run him through with his sword. Then the prince took the musket from Fatio, dropped to one knee, took careful aim, and fired toward the five dragoons now running toward them.

Not a one of them seemed to take any notice.

Eliza lay down on her belly and began crawling south down the beach. In a moment the dragoons ran past her, about ten paces off to her left. As she'd hoped, none of them noticed her. They had eyes only for the two men, William and Fatio, who now stood, swords drawn, back to back, waiting.

Eliza clambered to her feet and shed her long heavy coat. Before boarding the sand-sailer at Scheveningen, she'd borrowed Fatio's dagger and used it to slit the skirt of her nightgown and cut off the bottom few inches, freeing her legs. She sprinted toward the longboat. She was dreading the sound of pistols or muskets, which would mean that the dragoons had decided to drop William and Fatio on the spot. But she heard nothing except surf. The Frenchmen must have orders to bring the Prince back alive. Fatio was unknown to them and wholly expendable, but they could not shoot at him without hitting William of Orange.

The solitary dragoon holding the longboat's bow-rope watched, dumbfounded, as Eliza ran towards him. Even if he hadn't been dumbfounded there was nothing he could have done save stand there; if he dropped the rope, the boat would be lost, and he lacked the strength to beach it unaided. As Eliza drew closer she observed that this fellow had a pistol stuck in his waistband. But since the troughs of the waves were around his hips, and the crests wrapped themselves around his chest, the weapon was no cause for concern.

Eliza planted herself on the shore, took out the pistol, cocked the hammer, and took dead aim at the dragoon from perhaps ten paces. "This may fire or it may not," she said in French. "You have until I count to ten to decide whether you'll gamble your life and your immortal soul on it. One . . . two . . . three . . . did I mention I'm on the rag? Four . . ."

He lasted until seven. It was not the pistol that concerned him so much as her overall jaggedness, the look in her eye. He dropped the rope in the sea, raised his hands, and sidled up onto the beach, keeping well clear of Eliza, then turned and took off running toward the other group. 'Twas not a bad play. If he'd stayed, the pistol might have fired, and he'd be dead and they'd lose the boat for certain. But there was a good chance that they could get it back from Eliza if he got help from the others.

Eliza let the hammer down gently, tossed the pistol into the longboat, waded out a few steps, reached up over her head to grip the boat's transom, and hauled herself up. After a few kicks she was able to get an ankle hooked over the top of the transom, and then she brought herself up out of the water and rolled sideways over the stern and dropped into the bottom of the boat.

Her first view was of a caulked sea-chest. Pulling herself up on it, she saw that it was one of several massive lockers that rested on the deck. Presumably they contained weapons. But if it came to gunplay they were all lost.

The weapons she *needed* were oars, and these were lying out in plain sight on the boat's simple plank benches. She tried to snatch one up and was dismayed to find it was twice as long as she was tall, too heavy and unwieldy to be snatched; but at any rate she heaved it up off the benches and rotated its blade down into the water. Standing in the stern, where the water under the keel was shallowest, she stabbed down through the surf and into the firm sand. The longboat was reluctant to move, and one who had not recently familiarized herself with the contents of Isaac Newton's *Principia Mathematica* might have given up. But the elemental precepts of that work were certain laws of motion that stated that, if she pushed on the oar, the boat *had* to move; at first it might move too slowly to be perceived, but it *had* to be moving. Eliza ignored the unreliable evidence of her senses, which were telling her that the boat was not moving at all, and pushed steadily with all her might. Finally she felt the oar's angle change as the boat moved out from shore.

The moment she pulled the oar out, wind and surf began pushing her back, sapping the *vis inertiae* she had imparted to the longboat. She planted the oar a second time. The water seemed very little deeper than the first time around.

She wanted in the worst way to look up the beach, but looking would not do any good. Only getting the boat clear of the beach would serve their purposes. And so she waited until she had planted the oar half a dozen times, and doubled her distance from the surf-line, before she dared to look up.

Fatio was down. A dragoon was sitting on him, holding something near his head. William was at bay, sword still drawn, but surrounded by four dragoons who were leveling guns at him. One of these seemed, from his stance and his gestures, to be talking to the Prince—negotiating terms of surrender, Eliza guessed. The dragoon who had been left behind to hold the longboat's bow-rope had finally reached the others and was gesticulating, trying to get their attention. The ones who surrounded William ignored him, but the one who was sitting on Fatio took notice, and looked at Eliza.

Eliza glanced toward shore and perceived that the surf had pushed her back in a few yards; the water below the longboat was only waist-deep. In a hurry now, she planted the oars in their locks, sat down, and began to row. Her first several strokes were useless, as the seas, summing and subtracting chaotically, exposed the blades of one or both oars so that they flailed and skittered across the surface. But the dragoons were re-deploying themselves with admirable coolness and she decided she'd better learn from their example. She half-stood and raised the oar-handles high, driving the blades deep, and fell back, thrusting with her legs and arching her body backwards, and felt the boat move. Then she did it again.

Fatio was unguarded and unmoving. William was bracketed between two dragoons who were leveling muskets at his head. The remaining four Frenchmen had run down the beach and were now staring at Eliza across perhaps fifty feet of rough water. One of them had already stripped off most of his clothes, and as Eliza stood up for another oar-stroke she saw him race out into the surf several paces and dive in. The remaining three knelt in the sand, aimed their muskets at the boat, and waited for Eliza to show herself again.

By crouching in the bilge she could remain out of their line of fire—but she couldn't row the longboat.

A hand gripped the gunwale. Eliza smashed it with the butt of the pistol and it went away. But a minute later it reappeared, bleeding, somewhere else—followed by another hand, then elbows, then a head. Eliza aimed the pistol between the blinking eyes and pulled the trigger; the flint whipped around and cast off a feeble spark but nothing further happened. She turned the weapon around, thinking to smash him on the head, but he raised a hand to parry the blow, and she thought better of it. Instead she stood up, gripped the handles of a gun-chest, heaved it up off the deck, and, just as he was whipping one leg over the gunwale, launched it into his face with a thrust of her hips. He fell off the boat. The dragoons on the shore opened fire and splintered a bench, but they missed Eliza. Still, the sight of those craters of fresh clean wood that had been torn into the benches crushed any sense of relief she might have felt over getting rid of the swimmer.

She had an opportunity now to pull on the oars several times while the dragoons re-loaded. As she stood up for an oar-stroke, movement caught her eye off to the south. She turned that way to see a dozen of the Prince's Blue Guards cresting the hummock, or circumventing it along the beach, all riding at a dead gallop on foaming and exhausted chargers. As they took in the scene ahead they stood up in their stirrups, raised sabers high, and erupted in shouts of mixed indignation and triumph. Disgustedly, the French dragoons all flung their weapons down into the sand.

"You must not come near me now for a good long while," said William of Orange. "I shall make arrangements to spirit you out of this place, and my agents shall spread some story or other that shall account for your whereabouts this morning."

The Prince paused, distracted by shouts from the far side of a dune. One of the Blue Guards ran up onto its crest and announced he had found fresh horse-tracks. A rider had tarried for some time recently there (the manure of his horse was still warm) and smoked some tobacco, and then galloped away only moments ago (the sand disturbed by his horse's hooves was still dry). On hearing this news three of the Blue Guards spurred their horses into movement and took off in pursuit. But those mounts were exhausted, whereas the spy's had been well rested—everyone knew the pursuit would be bootless.

"'Twas d'Avaux," William said. "He would be here, so that he could come out of hiding and taunt me after I had been put in chains."

"Then he knows about me!"

"Perhaps, and perhaps not," said the Prince, showing a lack of concern that did nothing for Eliza's peace of mind. He glanced curiously at Fatio, who was sitting up now, having a bloody head-wound bandaged. "Your friend is a Natural Philosopher? I shall endow a chair for him at the university here. You, I will proclaim a Duchess, when the time is right. But now you must return to Versailles, and make love to Liselotte."

"What!?"

"Do not put on this show of outrage, it is very tedious. You know what I am, I think, and so you must know what *she* is."

"But *why*?"

"That is a more intelligent question. What you have just witnessed here, Eliza, is the spark that ignites the pan, that fires the musket, that ejects the ball, that fells the king. If you do nothing else today, fix that clearly in your mind. Now I have no choice but to make Britain mine. But I shall require troops, and I dare not pull so many of them from my southern marches while Louis menaces me there. But if, as I expect, Louis decides to enlarge his realms at the expense of the Germans, he'll draw off his forces on his Dutch flank, and free me to send mine across the North Sea."

"But what has this to do with Liselotte?"

"Liselotte is the grand-daughter of the Winter Queen—who, some say, sparked the Thirty Years' War by accepting the crown of Bohemia. At any rate the said Queen spent most of those Thirty Years just yonder, in the Hague—my people sheltered her, for Bohemia was by then a shambles, and the Palatinate, which was rightfully hers, had fallen to the Papists as a spoil of that war. But when the Peace of Westphalia was finally signed, some forty years ago now, the Palatinate was returned to that family; the Winter Queen's eldest son, Charles Louis, became Elector Palatinate. Various of his siblings, including Sophie, moved there, and set up housekeeping in Heidelberg Castle. Liselotte is the daughter of that same Charles Louis, and grew up in that household. Charles Louis died a few years ago and passed the crown to the brother of Liselotte, who was demented—he died not long ago conducting a mock-battle at one of his Rhine-castles. Now the succession is in dispute. The King of France has very chivalrously decided to take the side of Liselotte, who, after all, is his sister-in-law now."

"It is very adroit," Eliza said. "By extending a brotherly hand to Madame, *Le Roi* can add the Palatinate to France."

"Indeed, it would be a pleasure to watch Louis XIV go about his work, if he were not the Antichrist," William said. "I cannot help Liselotte and I can do nothing for the poor people of the Palatinate. But I can make France pay for the Rhine with the British Isles."

"You need to know if *Le Roi* intends to move his regiments away from your borders, towards the Rhine."

"Yes. And no one is in a better position to know that than Liselotte—if not precisely a *pawn,* she is a sort of captured *queen,* on France's side of the board."

"If the stakes are that high, then I suppose the least I can do is contrive some way to get close to Liselotte."

"I don't want you to get close to her, I want you to *seduce* her, I want you to make her your *slave.*"

"I was trying to be delicate."

"My apologies!" William said with a courtly bow, looking her up and down. Covered in salt and sand, and wrapped up in a bloody dragoon-coat, Eliza couldn't have looked delicate at all. William looked as if he were on the verge of saying as much. But he thought better of it, and looked away.

"You have ennobled me, my prince. It was done some years ago. You have grown used to thinking of me as a noblewoman, even if that is only a secret between you and me. To Versailles I am still a commoner, and a foreigner to boot. As long as this remains true you may be assured that Liselotte will have nothing to do with me."

"*In public.*"

"Even in private! Not everyone there is as much of a hypocrite as you seem to think."

"I did not say it would be easy. This is why I am asking *you* to do it."

"As I said, I am willing to give it a try. But if d'Avaux has seen me here today, going back to Versailles would seem unwise."

"D'Avaux prides himself on playing a deep and subtle game, and that is his weakness," William announced. "Besides, he depends on your financial advice. He will not crush you *immediately.*"

"*Later,* then?"

"He'll *try* to," William corrected her.

"And he will succeed."

"No. For by that point you will be the mistress of Madame—Liselotte—the King's sister-in-law. Who has her rivals and her weaknesses, true—but who is of infinitely higher rank than d'Avaux."

Versailles

To Leibniz, February 3, 1688
Doctor,

Madame has graciously offered to send this letter to Hanover along with some others that her friend is carrying personally to Sophie, and so I'll dispense with the cypher.

You may wonder why Madame is offering such courtesies to me now, since in the past she has always viewed me as a mouse turd in the pepper.

It seems that as the King of France was rising one day recently, he remarked, to the nobles who were attending his getting-out-of-bed ceremony, that he had heard that "the woman from Qwghlm" was secretly of noble blood.

It was a secret even to me until an hour or so later, when I heard someone calling for "Mademoiselle la comtesse de la Zeur," which (as I slowly figured out) is their way of trying to pronounce Sghr. As you may know, my island is a well-known Hazard to Navigation, recognizable, to terrified sailors, by its three towers of rock, which we denote by that name. Evidently some courtier, who had been so reckless as to sail within view of Qwghlm at some point, remembered this detail and concocted a title for me. To the Court ladies here, especially those of ancient families, it has a savage ring to it. Fortunately there are many foreign princesses here who do not have such exacting standards, and they have already sent minions around to invite me to parties.

Of course Kings may ennoble commoners whenever they please, and so it isn't clear to me why someone has gone to the trouble of making me out to be a *hereditary* noble. Here is a clue, though: Father Édouard de Gex has been asking me questions about the Qwghlmian Church, which is not technically Protestant in that it was founded before the Roman Catholic Church was established (or at least before anyone notified the Qwghlmians). The Father speaks of going to visit Qwghlm to seek out proofs that our faith is really no different from his and that the two should be merged.

Meanwhile I keep hearing expressions of sympathy from various French nobles, who cluck their tongues over the barbaric occupation of my homeland by England. In fact, every Qwghlmian would be pleased if Englishmen *did* come and occupy our Island, for presumably they would bring some food and warm clothes. I suspect that Louis knows he may soon see a sworn enemy sitting on the throne of England, and is making ready to out-flank that foe by shoring up relations with places such as Ireland, Scotland, and that flyspeck of rock where I was born. It has been ages since Qwghlm had hereditary nobles (nine hundred years ago the Scots rounded them all up and sealed them into a cave with some bears), but now they have decided I am one. Mother would have been so proud!

According to the date at the top of your last letter, you penned it while you were paying a visit to Sophie's daughter at the Court of Brandenburg around the time of Christmas. Please tell me what Berlin is like! I know that many Huguenots have ended up there. It is strange to consider that only a few years ago Sophie and Ernst August were offering their daughter's hand in marriage to Louis XIV. Yet now Sophie Charlotte is Electress of Brandenburg instead, and (if the rumors are to be believed) presiding over a salon of religious dissidents and free-thinkers in Berlin. If the marriage had gone the other way she would bear a measure of responsibility for putting the very same men to death or slavery. I can't help but suppose she is happier where she is.

They say that Sophie Charlotte participates in the discussions of those savants with ever so much poise and confidence. I can't help but suppose that this is because she grew up around you, Doctor, and listened to the conversations you had with her mother. Now that I am reckoned a Countess, and am considered fit to exchange chit-chat with Madame, I have begged her to tell me what you and Sophie talk about at Hanover. But she only rolls her eyes and claims that erudite talk makes no sense to her. I believe that she has spent too much time around self-styled Alchemists, and suspects that all such talk is rubbish.

The Star Chamber, Westminster Palace

APRIL 1688

🜍

For to accuse, requires less eloquence, such is
man's nature, than to excuse; and condemna-
tion, than absolution more resembles justice.
—HOBBES, *Leviathan*

"HOW DOES THE SAYING GO? 'All work and no play . . . a dull
boy,'" said a disembodied voice. It was the only perception
that Daniel's brain was receiving at the moment. Vision,
taste, and the other senses were dormant, and memory did
not exist. This made it possible for him to listen with more-
than-normal acuteness to the voice, and to appreciate its fine
qualities—of which there were many. It was a delicious
voice, belonging to an upper-class man who was used to being listened to, and who liked it that way.

"This boy's lucubrations have made him very dull indeed,
he is a very sluggard!" the voice continued.

A few men chuckled, and shifted bodies sheathed in silk.
The sounds echoed from a high and hard ceiling.

Daniel's mind now recollected that it was attached to a
body. But like a regiment that has lost contact with its colonel, the body had not received any orders in a long time. It
had gone all loose and discomposed, and had stopped sending signals back to headquarters.

"Give him more water!" commanded the beautiful voice.

Daniel heard boots moving on a hard floor to his left, felt blunt pressure against numbed lips, heard the rim of a bottle crack against one of his front teeth. His lungs began to fill up with some sort of beverage. He tried to move his head back but it responded sluggishly, and something cold hit him on the back of the neck hard enough to stop him. The fluid was flooding down his chin now and trickling under his clothes. His whole thorax clenched up trying to cough the fluid out of his lungs, and he tried to move his head forward—but now something cold caught him across the throat. He coughed and vomited at the same moment and sprayed hot humours all over his lap.

"These Puritans cannot hold their drink—really one cannot take them anywhere."

"Save, perhaps, to Barbados, my Lord!" offered up another voice.

Daniel's eyes were bleary and crusted. He tried raising his hands to his face, but halfway there each one of them collided with a bar of iron that was projecting across space. Daniel groped at these, but dire things happened to his neck when he did, and so he ended up feeling around them to paw at his eyes and wipe grit and moisture away from his face. He could make out now that he was sitting on a chair in the middle of a large room; it was night, and the place was lit up by only a modest number of candles. The light gleamed from white lace cravats round the throats of several gentlemen who were arranged round Daniel in a horseshoe.

The light wasn't bright enough, and his vision wasn't clear enough, to make sense of this ironmongery that was about his neck, so he had to explore that with his hands. It seemed to be a band of iron bent into a neck-ring. From four locations equally spaced around its circumference rods of iron projected outwards like spokes from a wheel-hub, to a radius of perhaps half a yard, where each split into a pair of back-curved barbs, like the flukes of grappling-hooks.

"While you were sleeping off the effects of M. LeFebure's draught, I took the liberty of having you fitted out with new neckwear," said the voice, "but as you are a Puritan, and have no use for vanity, I called upon a *blacksmith* instead of a *tailor*. You'll find that this is all the mode in the sugar plantations of the Caribbean."

The barbs sticking out behind had gotten lodged in the back of the chair when Daniel had unwisely tried to sit forward. Now he gripped the ones in front and pushed himself back hard, knocking the rear ones free. Momentum carried him and the collar back; his spine slammed into the chair and the collar kept moving and tried to shear his head off. He ended up with his head tilted back, gazing almost straight up at the ceiling. His first thought was that candles had somehow been planted up there, or burning arrows shot at random into the ceiling by bored soldiery, but then his eyes focused and he saw that the vault had been decorated with painted stars that gleamed in the candle-light from beneath. Then he knew where he was.

"The Court of Star Chamber is in session—Lord Chancellor Jeffreys presiding," said another excellent voice, husky with some kind of precious emotion. And what sort of man got choked up over *this*?

Now just as Daniel's senses had recovered one at a time, beginning with his ears, so his mind was awakening piecemeal. The part of it that warehoused ancient facts was, at the moment, getting along much better than the part that did clever things. "Nonsense . . . the Court of Star Chamber was abolished by the Long Parliament in 1641 . . . five years before I was *born*, or *you* were, Jeffreys."

"I do not recognize the self-serving decrees of that rebel Parliament," Jeffreys said squeamishly. "The Court of Star Chamber was ancient—Henry VII convened it, but its procedures were rooted in Roman jurisprudence—consequently, 'twas a model of clarity, of effiency, unlike the time-encrusted monstrosity of Common Law, that staggering, cobwebbed Beast, that senile compendium of folklore and wives' tales, a scabrous Colander seiving all the chunky bits

out of the evanescent flux of Society and compacting 'em
into legal head-cheese."

"Hear, hear!" said one of the other Judges, who apparently felt that Jeffreys had now encompassed everything
there was to be said about English Common Law. Daniel assumed they must all be judges, at any rate, and that they'd
been hand-picked by Jeffreys. Or, more like it, they'd simply
gravitated to him during his career, they were the men that
he always saw, whenever he troubled to glance around him.

Another one of them said, "The late Archbishop Laud
found this Chamber to be a convenient facility for the sup-
pression of Low Church dissidents, such as your father,
Drake Waterhouse."

"But the entire point of my father's story is *that he was not
suppressed*—Star Chamber cut his nose and his ears off and
it only made him more formidable."

"Drake was a man of exceptional strength and resilience,"
Jeffreys said. "Why, he haunted my very nightmares when I
was a boy. My father told me tales of him as if he were a
bogey-man. I know that you are no Drake. Why, you stood
by and watched one of your own kind be murdered, under
your window, at Trinity, by my lord Upnor, twenty-some
years ago, and you did *nothing*—nothing! I remember it
well, and I know that you do as well, Waterhouse."

"Does this sham have a purpose, other than to reminisce
about College days?" Daniel inquired.

"Give him a *revolution*," Jeffreys said.

The fellow who had poured water into Daniel's mouth
earlier—some sort of armed bailiff—stepped up, grabbed
one of the four grappling-hooks projecting from Daniel's
collar, and gave it a wrench. The whole apparatus spun
round, using Daniel's neck as an axle, until he could get his
arms up to stop it. A simpler man would have guessed—
from the sheer amount of pain involved—that his head had
been half sawed away. But Daniel had dissected enough
necks to know where all the important bits were. He ran a

few quick experiments and concluded that, as he could swallow, breathe, and wiggle his toes, none of the main cables had been severed.

"You are charged with perverting the English language," Jeffreys proclaimed. "To wit: that on numerous occasions during idle talk in coffee-houses, and in private correspondence, you have employed the word 'revolution,' heretofore a perfectly innocent and useful English word, in an altogether new sense, conceived and propagated by you, meaning radical and violent overthrow of a government."

"Oh, I don't think violence need have anything to do with it."

"You admit you are guilty then!"

"I know how the *genuine* Star Chamber worked . . . I don't imagine this *sham* one is any different . . . why should I dignify it by pretending to put up a defense?"

"The defendant is guilty as charged!" Jeffreys announced, as if, by superhuman effort, he'd just brought an exhausting trial to a close. "I shan't pretend to be surprised by the outcome—while you were asleep, we interrogated several witnesses—all agreed you have been using 'revolution' in a sense that is not to be found in any treatise of Astronomy. We even asked your old chum from Trinity . . ."

"Monmouth? But didn't you chop his head off?"

"No, no, the other one. The Natural Philosopher who has been so impertinent as to quarrel with the King in the matter of Father Francis . . ."

"Newton!?"

"Yes, that one! I asked him, 'You have written all of these fat books on the subject of Revolutions, what does the word signify to you?' He said it meant one body moving about another—he uttered *not a word* about politics."

"I cannot believe you have brought Newton into this matter."

Jeffreys abruptly stopped playing the rôle of Grand Inquisitor, and answered in the polite, distracted voice of the busy man-about-town: "Well, I had to grant him an audience

anyway, on the Father Francis matter. He does not know you
are here. . . . just as you, evidently, did not know he was in
London."

In the same sort of tone, Daniel replied, "Can't blame you
for finding it all just a bit bewildering. Of course! You'd assume that Newton, on a visit to London, would renew his acquaintance with me, and other Fellows of the Royal
Society."

"I have it on good authority he has been spending time
with that damned Swiss traitor instead."

"Swiss traitor?"

"The one who warned William of Orange of the French
dragoons."

"Fatio?"

"Yes, Fatio de Duilliers."

Jeffreys was absent-mindedly patting his wig, puzzling
over this fragment re Newton. The sudden change in the
Lord Chancellor's affect had engendered, in Daniel, a giddi-
ness that was probably dangerous. He had been trying to sti-
fle it. But now Daniel's stomach began to shake with
suppressed laughter.

"Jeffreys! Fatio is a *Swiss* Protestant who warned the
Dutch of a *French* plot, on *Dutch* soil . . . and for this you
call him a traitor?"

"He betrayed Monsieur le comte de Fenil. And now this
traitor has moved to London, for he knows that his life is for-
feit anywhere on the Continent . . . anywhere Persons of
Quality observe a decent respect for justice. But here! London, England! Oh, in other times his presence would not
have been tolerated. But in these parlous times, when such a
man comes and takes up residence in our city, no one bats an
eye . . . and when he is seen buying alchemical supplies, and
talking in coffee-houses with our foremost Natural Philosopher, no one thinks of it as scandalous."

Daniel perceived that Jeffreys was beginning to work
himself up into another frenzy. So before the Lord Chancellor completely lost his mind, Daniel reminded him: "The

real Star Chamber was known for pronouncing stern sentences, and executing them quickly."

"True! And if this assembly had such powers, your nose would be lying in the gutter, and the rest of you would be on a ship to the West Indies, where you would chop sugar cane on my plantation for the rest of your life. As it stands, I cannot punish you until I've convicted you of something in the common-law court. Shouldn't be all that difficult, really."

"How do you suppose?"

"Tilt the defendant back!"

The Star Chamber's bailiffs, or executioners or whatever they were, converged on Daniel from behind, gripped the back of his chair, and yanked, raising its front legs up off the floor and leaving Daniel's feet a-dangle. His weight shifted from his buttocks to his back, and the iron collar went into motion and tried to fall to the floor. But it was stopped by Daniel's throat. He tried to raise his hands to take the weight of the iron off his wind-pipe, but Jeffreys' henchmen had anticipated that: each of them had a spare hand that he used to pin one of Daniel's hands down to the chair. Daniel could see nothing but stars now: stars painted on the ceiling when his eyes were open, and other stars that zoomed across his vision when his eyes were closed. The face of the Lord Chancellor now swam into the center of this firmament like the Man in the Moon.

Now Jeffreys had been an astonishingly beautiful young man, even by the standards of the generation of young Cavaliers that had included such Adonises as the Duke of Monmouth and John Churchill. His eyes, in particular, had been of remarkable beauty—perhaps this accounted for his ability to seize and hold the young Daniel Waterhouse with his gaze. Unlike Churchill, he had not aged well. Years in London, serving as solicitor general to the Duke of York, then as a prosecutor of supposed conspirators, then Lord Chief Justice, and now Lord Chancellor, had put leaves of lard on him, as on a kidney in a butcher-stall. His eyebrows had grown out into great gnarled wings, or horns. The eyes were

beautiful as ever, but instead of gazing out from the fair un-
blemished face of a youth, they peered out through a sort of
embrasure, between folds of chub below and snarled brows
above. It had probably been fifteen years since Jeffreys
could list, from memory, all the men he had murdered
through the judicial system; if he hadn't lost count while ex-
tirpating the Popish Plot, he certainly had during the Bloody
Assizes.

At any rate Daniel could not now tear his eyes away from
those of Jeffreys. In a sense Jeffreys had planned this spectacle poorly. The drug must have been slipped into Daniel's
drink at the coffee-house and Jeffreys's minions must have
abducted him after he'd fallen asleep in a water-taxi. But the
elixir had made him so groggy that he had failed to be afraid
until this moment.

Now, *Drake* wouldn't have been afraid, even fully awake;
he'd sat in this room and defied Archbishop Laud to his face,
knowing what they would do to him. Daniel had been brave,
until now, only insofar as the drug had made him stupid. But
now, looking up into the eyes of Jeffreys, he recalled all of
the horror-stories that had emanated from the Tower as this
man's career had flourished: Dissidents who "committed
suicide" by cutting their own throats to the vertebrae; great
trees in Taunton decorated with hanged men, dying slowly;
the Duke of Monmouth having his head gradually hacked
off by Jack Ketch, five or six strokes of the axe, as Jeffreys
looked on with those eyes.

The colors were draining out of the world. Something
white and fluffy came into view near Jeffreys's face: a hand
surrounded by a lace cuff. Jeffreys had grasped one of the
hooks projecting up from Daniel's collar. "You say that your
revolution does not have to involve any violence," he said. "I
say you must think harder about the nature of revolution. For
as you can see, this hook is on top now. A different one is on
the bottom. True, we can raise the low one up by a simple
revolution—" Jeffreys wrenched the collar around, its entire
weight bearing on Daniel's adam's apple—giving Daniel

every reason to scream. But he made no sound other than a pitiable attempt to suck in some air. "Ah, but observe! The one that was *high* is now *low*! Let us raise it up then, for it does not love to be low." Jeffreys wrenched it back up. "Alas, we are back to where we started; the high is high, the low is low, and what's the point of having a revolution at all?" Jeffreys now repeated the demonstration, laughing at Daniel's struggle for air. "Who could ask for a better career!" he exclaimed. "Slowly decapitating the men I went to college with! We made Monmouth last as long as 'twas possible, but the axe is imprecise, Jack Ketch is a butcher, and it ended all too soon. But this collar is an excellent device for a gradual sawing-off, I could make *him* last for *days*!" Jeffreys sighed with delight. Daniel could not see any more, other than a few pale violet blotches swimming in turbulent gray. But Jeffreys must have signalled the bailiffs to right the chair, for suddenly the weight of the collar was on his collarbones and his efforts to breathe were working. "I trust I have disabused you of any ludicrous ideas concerning the true nature of revolutions. If the low are to be made high, Daniel, then the high must be made low—but the high *like* to be high—and they have an army and a navy. 'Twill never occur without violence. And 'twill fail given enough time, as your father's failed. Have you quite learnt the lesson? Or shall I repeat the demonstration?"

Daniel tried to say something: namely to beg that the demonstration *not* be repeated. He had to because it hurt too much and might kill him. To beg for mercy was utterly reasonable—and the act of a coward. The only thing that prevented him from doing it was that his voice-box was not working.

"It is customary for a judge to give a bit of a scolding to a guilty man, to help him mend his ways," Jeffreys reflected. "That part of the proceedings is now finished—we move on to Sentencing. Concerning this, I have Bad News, and Good News. 'Tis an ancient custom to give the *recipient* of Bad and Good News, the choice of which to hear first. But as

Good News for me is Bad for you, and vice versa, allowing you to make the choice will only lead to confusion. So: the Bad News, for me, is that you are correct, the Star Chamber has not been formally re-constituted. 'Tis just a pastime for a few of us Senior Jurists and has no legal authority to carry out sentences. The Good News, for me, is that I can pronounce a most severe sentence upon *you* even without legal authority: I sentence you, Daniel Waterhouse, to be Daniel Waterhouse for the remainder of your days, and to live, for that time, every day with the knowledge of your own disgusting cravenness. Go! You disgrace this Chamber! Your father was a vile man who deserved what he got here. But you are a disfigurement of his memory! Yes, that's right, on your feet, about face, march! Get out! Just because *you* must live with yourself does not mean *we* must be subjected to the same degradation! Out, out! Bailiffs, throw this quivering mound of shite out into the gutter, and pray that the piss running down his legs will wash him down into the Thames!"

THEY DUMPED HIM like a corpse in the open fields upriver from Westminster, between the Abbey and the town of Chelsea. When they rolled him out the back of the cart, he came very close to losing his head, as one of the collar-hooks caught in a slat on the wagon's edge and gave him a jerk at the neck so mighty it was like to rip his soul out of his living body. But the wood gave way before his bones did, and he fell down into the dirt, or at least that was what he inferred from evidence near to hand when he came to his senses.

His desire at this point was to lie full-length on the ground and weep until he died of dehydration. But the collar did not permit lying down. Having it round his neck was a bit like having Drake stand over him and berate him for not getting up. So up he got, and stumbled round and wept for a while. He reckoned he must be in Hogs-den, or Pimlico as men in the real estate trade liked to name it: not the country and not the city, but a blend of the most vile features of both. Stray dogs chased feral chickens across a landscape that had been churned up by rooting swine and scraped bald by scavenging goats. Nocturnal fires of bakeries and breweries shot rays of ghastly red light through gaps in their jumble-built walls, spearing whores and drunks in their gleam.

It could have been worse: they could have dumped him in a place with vegetation. The collar was designed to prevent slaves from running away by turning every twig, reed, vine, and stalk into a constable that would grab the escapee by the nape as he ran by. As Daniel roamed about, he explored the hasp with his fingers and found it had been wedged shut with a carven peg of soft wood which had been hammered through the loops. By worrying this back and forth he was able to draw it out. Then the collar came loose on his neck and he got it off easily. He had a dramatical impulse to carry it over to the river-bank and fling it into the Thames, but then coming to his senses he recollected that there was a mile of dodgy ground to be traversed before he reached the edge of Westminster, and any number of dogs and Vagabonds who might need to be beaten back in that interval. So he kept a grip on it, swinging it back and forth in the darkness occasionally, to make himself feel better. But no assailant came for him. His foes were not of the sort that could be struck down with a rod of iron.

ON THE SOUTHERN EDGE of the settled and civilized part of Westminster, a soon-to-be-fashionable street was under construction. It was the latest project of Sterling Waterhouse, who was now Earl of Willesden, and spent most of his days on his modest country estate just to the northwest of London, trying to elevate the self-esteem of his investors.

One of the people who'd put money into this Westminster street was the woman Eliza, who was now Countess of Zeur. Eliza occupied something like fifty percent of all Daniel's waking thoughts now. Obviously this was a disproportionate figure. If it'd been the case that Daniel continually come up with *new and original* thoughts on the subject of Eliza, then he might have been able to justify thinking about her ten or even twenty percent of the time. But all he did was think the same things over and over again. During the hour or so he'd spent in the Star Chamber, he'd scarcely thought of her at all, and so now he had to make up for that by thinking about nothing else for an hour or so.

Eliza had come to London in February, and on the strength of personal recommendations from Leibniz and Huygens, she had talked her way into a Royal Society meeting—one of the few women ever to attend one, unless you counted Freaks of Nature brought in to display their multiple vaginas or nurse their two-headed babies. Daniel had escorted the Countess of Zeur into Gresham's College a bit nervously, fearing that she'd make a spectacle of herself, or that the Fellows would get the wrong idea and use her as a subject for vivisection. But she had dressed and behaved modestly and all had gone well. Later Daniel had taken her out to Willesden to meet Sterling, with whom she had gotten along famously. Daniel had known they would; six months earlier both had been commoners, and now they strolled in what was to become Sterling's French garden, deciding where the urns and statues ought to go, and compared notes as to which shops were the best places to buy old family heirlooms.

At any rate, both of them now had money invested in this attempt to bring civilization to Hogs-den. Even Daniel had put a few pounds into it (not that he considered himself much of an investor; but British coinage had only gotten worse in the last twenty years, if that was imaginable, and there was no point in keeping your money that way). To prevent the site from being ravaged every night by the former inhabitants (human and non-), a porter was stationed there, in a makeshift lodge, with a large number of more or less demented dogs. Daniel managed to wake all of them up by stumbling over the fence at 3:00 A.M. with his neck half sawn through. Of course the porter woke up last, and didn't call the dogs off until half of Daniel's remaining clothes had been torn away. But by that point in the evening, those clothes could not be accounted any great loss.

Daniel was happy just to be recognized by someone, and made up the customary story about having been set upon by blackguards. To this, the porter responded with the obligatory wink. He gave Daniel ale, an act of pure kindness that brought fresh tears to Daniel's eyes, and sent his boy a-running into Westminster to summon a hackney-chair. This was a sort of vertical coffin suspended on a couple of staves whose ends were held up by great big taciturn men. Daniel climbed into it and fell asleep.

When he woke up it was dawn, and he was in front of Gresham's College, on the other end of London. A letter was waiting for him from France.

THE LETTER BEGAN,
   Is the weather in London still quite dismal? From
   the vantage point of Versailles, I can assure you that
   spring approaches London. Soon, I will be approaching, too.

Daniel (who was reading this in the College's entrance hall) stopped there, stuffed the letter into his belt, and stumbled into the penetralia of the Pile. Not even Sir Thomas Gresham his own self would be able to find his way around the place now, if he should come back to haunt it. The R.S. had been having its way with the building for almost three decades and it was just about spent. Daniel scoffed at all talk of building a new Wren-designed structure and moving the Society into it. The Royal Society was not reducible to an inventory of strange objects, and could not be re-located by transporting that inventory to a new building, any more than a man could travel to France by having his internal organs cut out and packed in barrels and shipped across the Channel. As a geometric proof contained, in its terms and its references, the whole history of geometry, so the piles of stuff in the larger Pile that was Gresham's College encoded the development of Natural Philosophy from the first meetings of Boyle, Wren, Hooke, and Wilkins up until to-day. Their arrangement, the order of stratifications, reflected what was going on in the minds of the Fellows (predominantly Hooke) in any given epoch, and to move it, or to tidy it up, would have been akin to burning a library. Anyone who could not find what he needed there, didn't deserve to be let in. Daniel felt about the place as a Frenchman felt about the French language, which was to say that it all made perfect sense once you understood it, and if you didn't understand it, then to hell with you.

He found a copy of the *I Ching* in about a minute, in the dark, and carrying it over to where rosy-fingered Dawn was clawing desperately at a grime-caked window, found the hexagram 19, *Lin,* Approach. The book went on at length concerning the bottomless significance of this symbol, but the only meaning that mattered to Daniel was 000011, which was how the pattern of broken and unbroken lines translated to binary notation. In decimal notation this was 3.

It would have been perfectly all right for Daniel to have crawled up to his garret atop the College and fallen asleep, but he felt that having been stupefied with opium for a night and a day ought to have enabled him to catch up on his sleep, and events in the Star Chamber and later in Hogs-den had got him rather keyed up. Any one of these three things sufficed to prevent sleep: the raw wounds around his neck, the commotion of the City coming awake, and his beastly, uncontrollable lust for Eliza. He went up-stairs to a room that was optimistically called the Library, not because it had books (every room did) but because it had windows. Here he spread out Eliza's letter on a table all streaked and splotched with disturbing stains. Next to it he set down a rectangle of scrap paper (actually a proof of a woodcut intended for Volume III of Newton's *Principia Mathematica*). Examining the characters in Eliza's letter one by one, he assigned each to either the 0 alphabet or the 1 alphabet and wrote a corresponding digit on the scrap paper, arranging them in groups of five. Thus

D O C T O   R W A T E   R H O U S   E
0 I I 0 0   0 0 I 0 0   I 0 0 0 0   0

The first group of binary digits made the number 12, the
second 4, the next 16, and the one after that 6. So writing
these out on a new line, and subtracting a 3 from each, he got

```
12  4   16  6
 3  3    3  3
_____

 9  I   13  3
```

Which made the letters

I A M C

The light got better as he worked.

Leibniz was building a splendid library in Wolfenbüttel,
with a high rotunda that would shed light down onto the
table below . . .

His forehead was on the table. Not a good way to work. Not
a good way to sleep either, unless your neck was so torn up as
to make lying down impossible, in which case it was the *only*
way to sleep. And Daniel *had* been sleeping. The pages under
his face were a sea of awful light, the unfair light of noon.

"Truly you are an inspiration to all Natural Philosophers,
Daniel Waterhouse."

Daniel sat up. He was stiff as a grotesque. He could feel
and hear the scab-work on his neck cracking. Seated two tables away, quill in hand, was Nicolas Fatio de Duilliers.

"Sir!"

Fatio held up a hand. "I do not mean to disturb you, there
is no need for—"

"Ah, but there is a need for me to express my gratitude. I
have not seen you since you saved the life of the Prince of
Orange."

Fatio closed his eyes for a moment. "'Twas like a conjunction of planets, purely fortuitous, reflecting no distinction on me, and let us say no more of it."

"I learned only recently that you were in town—that your life was in danger so long as you remained on the Continent. Had I known as much earlier, I'd have offered you whatever hospitality I could—"

"And if I were worthy of the title of gentleman, I'd have waited for that offer before making myself at home here," Fatio returned.

"Isaac of course has given you the run of the place and that is splendid."

Daniel now noticed Fatio gazing at him with a penetrating, analytical look that reminded him of Hooke peering through a lens. From Hooke it was not objectionable, somehow. From Fatio it was mildly offensive. Of course Fatio was wondering how Daniel knew that he'd been hobnobbing with Isaac. Daniel could have told him the story about Jeffreys and the Star Chamber, but it would only have confused matters more.

Fatio now appeared to notice, for the first time, the damage to Daniel's neck. His eyes saw all, but they were so big and luminous that it was impossible for him to conceal what he was gazing at; unlike the eyes of Jeffreys, which could secretly peer this way and that in the shadow of their deep embrasures, Fatio's eyes could never be used discreetly.

"Don't ask," Daniel said. "You, sir, suffered an honorable wound on the beach. I've suffered one, not so honorable, but in the same cause, in London."

"Are you quite all right, Doctor Waterhouse?"

"Splendid of you to inquire. I am fine. A cup of coffee and I'll be as good as new."

Whereupon Daniel snatched up his papers and repaired to the coffee-house, which was full of people and yet where he felt more privacy than under the eyes of Fatio.

The binary digits hidden in the subtleties of Eliza's handwriting became, in decimal notation,

4   16   6   18   16   12   17   10

which when he subtracted 3 from each (that being the key
hidden in the *I Ching* reference) became

9   1   13   3   15   13   9   14   7 . . .

which said,

I AM COMING . . .

THE FULL DECIPHERMENT took a while, because Eliza provided details concerning her travel plans, and wrote of all
she wanted to do while she was in London. When he was finished writing out the message he came alive to the fact that
he had sat for a long time, and consumed much coffee, and
needed to urinate in the worst way. He could not recall the
last time he had made water. And so he went back to a sort of
piss-hole in the corner of the tiny court in back of the coffee-
house.

Nothing happened, and so after about half a minute he
bent forward as if bowing, and braced his forehead against
the stone wall. He had learned that this helped to relax some
of the muscles in his lower abdomen and make the urine
come out more freely. That stratagem, combined with some
artful shifting of the hips and deep breathing, elicited a few
spurts of rust-colored urine. When it ceased to work, he
turned round, pulled his garments up around his waist, and
squatted to piss in the Arab style. By shifting his center of
gravity just so, he was able to start up a kind of gradual
warm seepage that would provide relief if he kept it up for a
while.

This gave him lots of time to think of Eliza, if spinning
phant'sies could be named thinking. It was plain from her
letter that she expected to visit Whitehall Palace. Which signified little, since any person who was wearing clothes and
not carrying a lighted granadoe could go in and wander

about the place. But since Eliza was a Countess who dwelt at Versailles, and Daniel (in spite of Jeffreys) a sort of courtier, when she said she wanted to visit Whitehall it meant that she expected to stroll and sup with Persons of Quality. Which could easily be arranged, since the Catholic Francophiles who made up most of the King's court would fall all over themselves making way for Eliza, if only to get a look at the spring fashions.

But to arrange it would require planning—again, if the dreaming of fatuous dreams could be named planning. Like an astronomer plotting his tide-tables, Daniel had to project the slow wheeling of the seasons, the liturgical calendar, the sessions of Parliament and the progress of various important people's engagements, terminal diseases, and pregnancies into the time of the year when Eliza was expected to show up.

His first thought had been that Eliza would be here at just the right time: for in another fortnight the King was going to issue a new Declaration of Indulgence that would make Daniel a hero, at least among Nonconformists. But as he squatted there he began to count off the weeks, tick, tick, tick, like the drops of urine detaching themselves one by one from the tip of his yard, and came aware that it would be much longer before Eliza actually got here—she'd be arriving no sooner than mid-May. By that time, the High Church priests would have had several Sundays to denounce Indulgence from their pulpits; they'd say it wasn't an act of Christian toleration at all, but a stalking-horse for Popery, and Daniel Waterhouse a dupe at best and a traitor at worst. Daniel might have to go *live* at Whitehall around then, just to be safe.

It was while imagining *that*—living like a hostage in a dingy chamber at Whitehall, protected by John Churchill's Guards—that Daniel recalled another datum from his mental ephemeris, one that stopped up his pissing altogether.

The Queen was pregnant. To date she'd produced no children at all. The pregnancy seemed to have come on more suddenly than human pregnancies customarily did. Perhaps they'd been slow to announce it because they'd expected it would only end in yet another miscarriage. But it seemed to have taken, and the size of her abdomen was now a matter of high controversy around Whitehall. She was expected to deliver in late May or early June—just the same time that Eliza would be visiting.

Eliza was using Daniel to get inside the Palace so that she, Eliza, could know as early as possible whether King James II had a legitimate heir, and adjust her investments accordingly. This should have been as obvious as that Daniel had a big stone in his bladder, but somehow Daniel managed to finish what he was doing and go back into the coffee-house without becoming aware of either.

The only person who seemed to understand matters was Robert Hooke, who was in the same coffee-house. He was *talking,* as usual, to Sir Christopher Wren. But he had been *observing* Daniel, this whole time, through an open window. He had the look on his face of a man who was determined to speak plainly of unpleasant facts, and Daniel managed to avoid him.

Versailles

JULY 1688

✣

To d'Avaux
Monsieur,

As you requested, I have changed over to the new cypher. To me it seems preposterous to imagine that the Dutch had broken the old one and read all of your letters! But, as always, you are the soul of discretion, and I will follow whatever precautions you demand of me.

It was good that you wrote me that lovely, if vaguely sarcastic, letter of congratulations on the occasion of my being accorded my rightful hereditary title (since we are now of equal rank—whatever doubts you may harbor as to the legitimacy of my title—I hope you are not offended that I address you as Monsieur instead of Monseigneur now). Until your letter arrived, I had not heard from you in many months. At first, I assumed that the Prince of Orange's vulgar over-reaction to the so-called abduction attempt had left you isolated in the Hague, and unable to send letters out. As months went by, I began to worry that your affection for your most humble and obedient servant had cooled. Now I can see that this was all just idle phant'sy—the sort of aimless fretting to which my sex is so prone. You and I are as close as ever. So I will try to write a good letter and entice you to write me back.

Business first: I have not tallied the numbers for the

second quarter of 1688, and so please keep what follows in confidence from the other investors, but I am confident that we have made out better than anyone suspects. True, V.O.C. stock has been performing miserably, and yet the market has been too volatile to make a winning proposition out of selling it short or playing derivatives. Yet a few things—all in London, strangely enough—have saved our investments from disaster. One is traffic in commodities, particularly silver. England's coinage is becoming more debased every day, counterfeiters are a plague on the land, and, not to bore you with details, this entails flows of gold and silver in and out of that island from which we can profit if we make the right bets.

You may wonder how I can possibly know which bets to make, living as I do in Versailles. Let me ease your concerns by explaining to you that I have made two visits to London since I last saw you, one in February and one in May, around the time that the son of King James II was born. The second visit was mandatory, of course, for everyone knew that the Queen of England was pregnant, and that the future of Britain and of Europe hinged upon her producing a legitimate male heir. The markets in Amsterdam were bound to react strongly to any news from Whitehall and so I had to be there. I have seduced an Englishman who is close to the King—so close that he was able to get me into Whitehall during the time that the Queen went into labor. Since this is a business report, Monsieur, I'll say no more here; but allow me to mention that there are certain peculiarities surrounding the delivery of this infant with which I'll entertain you some other time.

The Englishman is a figure of some note in the Royal Society. He has an older half-brother who makes money in more ways than I can enumerate. The family has old connections to the goldsmith's shops that used to be situated around Cornhill and Thread-needle, and newer connections to the *banca* that was set up by Sir Richard Apthorp after Charles II put many of the goldsmiths out of business. If you are not familiar with a *banca,* it means something akin to a goldsmith, except that they have dropped any pretense of goldsmithing *per se;* they are financiers dealing in metal and paper. Odd as it might sound, this type of business actually makes sense, at least in the context of London, and Apthorp is doing well by it. It was through this connexion that I became aware of the trends in silver and gold mentioned earlier, and was able to make the right bets, as it were.

Lacking the refinement of the French, the English have no equivalent of Versailles, so the high and mighty, the adherents of diverse religions, *commerçants,* and Vagabonds are all commingled in London. You've spent time in Amsterdam, which may give you some idea of what London is like, except that London is not nearly as well organized. Much of the mixing takes place in coffee-houses. Surrounding the 'Change are diverse coffee- and chocolate-houses that, over time, have come to serve specific clientele. Birds of a feather flock together and so those who trade in East India Company stocks go to one place and so forth. Now as the overseas trade of England has waxed, the business of under-writing ships and other risky ventures has become a trade of some significance in and of itself. Those who are in the market for insurance have recently begun going to Lloyd's Coffeehouse, which has, for whatever reason, become the favorite haunt of the underwriters. This arrangement works well for buyer and seller alike: the buyer can solicit bids from diverse underwriters simply by strolling from table to table, the sellers can distribute the risks by spontaneously forming associations. I hope I am not boring you to death, Monsieur, but it is a fascinating thing to watch, and you yourself have now made a bit of money from this quarter, which you can use to buy yourself a picaroon-romance if my discourse is too tedious. *Tout le monde* at Versailles agree that *L'Emmerdeur in Barbary* is a good read, and I have it on high authority that a copy was spied in the King's bedchamber.

Enough of business; now, gossip.

Madame deigns to recognize me now that I am known to be a Countess. For the longest time, she regarded me as a parasite, a strangling vine, and so I expected she would be the last person at Court to accept me as a noblewoman. But she astonished me with a welcome that was courteous and almost warm, and begrudged me a few moments' polite conversation, when I encountered her in the gardens the other day. I believe her previous coldness toward me came from two reasons. One is that like all the other foreign royals, *la Palatine* (as Liselotte is sometimes referred to here) is insecure about her rank, and tends to exalt herself by belittling those whose bloodlines are even more questionable than hers. This is not an attractive feature but it is all too human! The second reason is that her chief rival at Court is de Maintenon, who came up from a wretched state to become the unofficial Queen of France. And so whenever Madame sees a woman at Court who has aspirations, it reminds her of the one she hates.

Many nobles of ancient families sneer at me because I handle money. Liselotte is not, however, one of these. On the contrary, I believe it explains why she has accepted me.

Now that I have spent two years in the household of Mme. la duchesse d'Oyonnax, surrounded by the very type of ambitious young woman Madame despises so much, I can understand why she takes such care to avoid them. Those girls have very few assets: their

names, their bodies, and (if they are lucky enough to
have been born with any) their wits. The first of
these—their names, and the pedigrees attached—suffice to get them in the gates. They are like an invitation
to the ball. But most of those families have more lia-
bilities than assets. Once one of those girls has found a
position in some household at Versailles, she has only
a few years to make arrangements for the remainder of
her life. She is like a plucked rose in a vase. Every day
at dawn she looks out the window to see a gardener
driving a wagon loaded with wilted flowers that are
taken out to the countryside to be used for mulch, and
the similitude to her own future is clear. In a few years
she will be outshined, at all the parties, by younger
girls. Her brothers will inherit any assets the family
might have. If she can marry well, as Sophie did, she
may have a life to look forward to; if not, she will be
shipped off to some convent, as two of Sophie's beautiful and brilliant sisters were. When that desperation
is combined with the heedless irresponsible nature of
young persons generally, cruelty becomes mundane.

It's only reasonable for Madame to want to avoid
young women of that type. She has always assumed
that I was one of them—having no way to distinguish
me from the others. But lately, as I mentioned, she has
become aware that I handle investments. This sets me
apart—it tells her that I have interests and assets outside of the intrigues of Court and so am not as dangerous as the others. In effect, she is treating me as if I
had just married a rich handsome Duke, and gotten all
my affairs in order. Instead of a cut rose in a vase, I am
a rose-bush with living roots in rich soil.

Or perhaps I'm reading too much into a brief conversation!

She asked me if the hunting was good on Qwghlm.
Knowing how much she loves to hunt, I told her it was
miserable, unless throwing stones at rats qualified—

and how, pray tell, was the hunting here at Versailles? Of course I meant the vast game parks that the King has constructed around the château, but Liselotte shot back, "Indoors or out?"

"I have seen game taken indoors," I allowed, "but only through trapping or poisoning, which are common *peasant* vices."

"Qwghlmians are more accustomed to the *outdoor* life?"

"If only because our dwellings keep getting blown down, madame."

"Can you ride, mademoiselle?" she asked.

"After a fashion—for I learned *bareback* style," I answered.

"There are no saddles where you come from?"

"In olden days there were, for we would suspend them from tree-branches overnight, to prevent them from being eaten by small creatures in the night-time. But then the English cut down the trees, and so now it is our custom to ride bareback."

"I should like to see that," she returned, "but it is hardly proper."

"We are guests in the King's house and must abide by his standards of propriety," I said dutifully.

"If you can ride well in a saddle *here,* I shall invite you to St. Cloud—that is *my* estate, and you may abide by *my* rules there."

"Do you think Monsieur would object?"

"My husband objects to *everything* I do," she said, "and so he objects to *nothing.*"

In my next letter, I'll let you know whether I passed the riding-test, and got the invitation to St. Cloud.

And I will send the quarterly figures as well!

Eliza de la Zeur

Tower of London

SUMMER AND AUTUMN 1688

❧

> Therefore it happeneth commonly, that such
> as value themselves by the greatness of their
> wealth, adventure on crimes, upon hope of es-
> caping punishment, by corrupting public jus-
> tice, or obtaining pardon by money, or other
> rewards.
>
> —HOBBES, *Leviathan*

NOW AS ENGLAND WAS A country of fixed ways, they imprisoned him in the same chamber where they had put Oldenburg twenty years before.

But some things changed even in England; James II was
peevish and fitful where his older brother had been merry,
and so Daniel was kept closer than Oldenburg had been, and
allowed to leave the chamber to stroll upon the walls only
rarely. He spent all his time in that round room, encircled by
the eldritch glyphs that had been scratched into the stone by
condemned alchemists and sorcerers of yore, and pathetic
Latin plaints graven by Papists under Elizabeth.

Twenty years ago he and Oldenburg had made idle jests
about carving new graffiti in the Universal Character of John
Wilkins. The words he had exchanged with Oldenburg still
seemed to echo around the room, as if the stone were a telescope mirror that forever recurved all information towards

the center. The idea of the Universal Character now seemed queer and naïve to Daniel, and so it didn't enter his mind to begin scratching at the stone for the first fortnight or so of his imprisonment. He reckoned that it would take a long time to make any lasting mark, and he assumed he would not live long enough. Jeffreys could only have put him in here to kill him, and when Jeffreys set his mind to killing someone there was no stopping him, he did it the way a farmer's wife plucked a chicken. But no specific judicial proceedings were underway—a sign that this was not to be a *judicial* murder (meaning a stately and more or less predictable one), but the *other* kind.

It was marvelously *quiet* at the Tower of London, the Mint being shut down at the moment, and people never came to visit him, and this was good—rarely was a murder victim afforded such an opportunity to get his spiritual house in order. Puritans did not go to confession or have a special sacrament before dying, as Papists did, but even so, Daniel supposed there must be a bit of tidying-up he could do, in the dusty corners of his soul, before the men with the daggers came.

So he spent a while searching his soul, and found nothing there. It was as sparse and void as a sacked cathedral. He did not have a wife or children. He lusted after Eliza, Countess de la Zeur, but something about being locked up in this round room made him realize that she neither lusted after nor particularly liked him. He did not have a career to speak of, because he was a contemporary of Hooke, Newton, and Leibniz, and therefore predestined for rôles such as scribe, amanuensis, sounding-board, errand-boy. His thorough training for the Apocalypse had proved a waste, and he had gamely tried to redirect his skills and his energies towards the shaping of a secular Apocalypse, which he styled Revolution. But prospects for such a thing looked unfavorable at the moment. Scratching something on the wall might enable him to make a permanent mark on the world, but he would not have time.

All in all, his epitaph would be: DANIEL WATERHOUSE 1646–1688 SON OF DRAKE. It might have made an ordinary man just a bit melancholy, this, but something about its very bleakness appealed to the spirit of a Puritan and the mind of a Natural Philosopher. Suppose he'd had twelve children, written a hundred books, and taken towns and cities from the Turks, and had statues of himself all over, and *then* been clapped in the Tower to have his throat cut? Would matters then stand differently? Or would these be meaningless distractions, a clutter of vanity, empty glamour, false consolation?

Souls were created somehow, and placed in bodies, which lived for more or fewer years, and after that all was faith and speculation. Perhaps after death was nothing. But if there was *something,* then Daniel couldn't believe it had anything to do with the earthly things that the body had done—the children it had spawned, the gold it had hoarded—except insofar as those things altered one's soul, one's state of consciousness.

Thus he convinced himself that having lived a bleak spare life had left his soul no worse off than anyone else's. Having children, for example, might have changed him, but only by providing insights that would have made it easier, or more likely, to have accomplished some *internal* change, some transfiguration of the spirit. Whatever growth or change occurred in one's soul *had* to be internal, like the metamorphoses that went on inside of cocoons, seeds, and eggs. External conditions might help or hinder those changes, but could not be strictly *necessary.* Otherwise it simply was not *fair,* did not make *sense.* Because in the end every soul, be it never so engaged in the world, was like Daniel Waterhouse, alone in a round room in a stone tower, and receiving impressions from the world through a few narrow embrasures.

Or so he told himself; either he would be murdered soon, and learn whether he was right or wrong, or be spared and left to wonder about it.

On the twentieth day of his imprisonment, which Daniel

reckoned to be August 17th, 1688, the perceptions coming in through his embrasures were of furious argument and wholesale change. The soldiers he'd been glimpsing out in the yard were gone, replaced by others, in different uniforms. They looked like the King's Own Black Torrent Guards, but that couldn't be, for they were a household regiment, stationed at Whitehall Palace, and Daniel couldn't imagine why they would be uprooted from their quarters there and moved miles down-river to the Tower of London.

Unfamiliar men came to empty his chamber-pot and bring him food—better food than he'd become accustomed to. Daniel asked them questions. Speaking in Dorsetshire accents, they said that they were indeed the King's Own Black Torrent Guards, and that the food they were bringing him had been piling up for quite some time in a porter's lodge. Daniel's friends had been bringing it. But the men who'd been running the Tower until yesterday—a distinctly inferior foot regiment—had not been delivering it.

Daniel then moved on to questions of a more challenging nature and the men stopped supplying answers, even after he shared a few oysters with them. When he became insistent, they allowed as how they would relay his questions to their sergeant, who (as they warned him) was very busy just now, taking an inventory of the prisoners and of the Tower's defenses.

It was two days before the sergeant came to call on Daniel. They were trying days. For just when Daniel had convinced himself that his soul was a disembodied consciousness in a stone tower, perceiving the world through narrow slits, he had been given oysters. They were of the best: Roger Comstock had sent them. They made his body happy when he ate them, and affected his soul much more than seemed proper, for a disembodied consciousness. Either his theory was wrong, or the seductions of the world were more powerful than he'd remembered. When Tess had got the smallpox she'd got it bad, and the pustules had all joined together and her whole skin had fallen off, and her guts had shot out of her anus into a bloody pile on the bed. After that she had somehow remained alive for a full ten and a half hours. Considering the carnal pleasures she had brought him during the years she'd been his mistress, Daniel had taken this the same way Drake would've: as a cautionary parable about fleshly delights. Better to perceive the world as Tess had during those ten and a half hours than as Daniel had while he'd been fucking her. But the oysters were extraordinarily good, their flavor intense and vaguely dangerous, their consistency clearly sexual.

Daniel shared some with the sergeant, who agreed that they were extraordinary but had little else to say—most of Daniel's questions caused him to go shifty-eyed, and some even made him cringe. Finally he agreed to take the matter up with *his* sergeant, giving Daniel a nightmare vision of some endless regression of sergeants, each more senior and harder to reach than the last.

Robert Hooke showed up with a firkin of ale. Daniel assaulted it in much the same way as the murderers would him. "I was apprehensive that you would spurn my gift, and pour it into the Thames," Hooke said irritably, "but I see that the privations of the Tower have turned you into a veritable *satyr.*"

"I am developing a new theory of bodily perceptions, and their intercourse with the soul, and this is *research,*" said Daniel, quaffing vigorously. He huffed ale-foam out of his whiskers (he'd not shaved in weeks) and tried to adopt a searching look. "Being condemned to die is a mighty stimulus to philosophick ratiocination, all of which is however wasted at the instant the sentence is carried out—fortunately I've been spared—"

"So that you may pass on your insights to *me,*" Hooke finished dourly. Then, with ponderous tact: "My memory has become faulty, pray just write it all down."

"They won't allow me pen and paper."

"Have you asked again recently? They would not allow me, or anyone, to visit you until today. But with the new regiment, a new regimen."

"I've been scratching on yonder wall instead," Daniel announced, waving at the beginnings of a geometric diagram.

Hooke's gray eyes regarded it bleakly. "I spied it when I came in," he confessed, "and supposed 'twas something very *ancient* and *time-worn*. Very *recent* and *in progress* would never have crossed my mind."

Daniel was flummoxed for a few moments—just long enough for his pulse to rouse, his face to flush, and his vocal cords to constrict. "It is difficult not to take that as a *rebuke*," he said. "I am merely trying to see if I can reconstruct one of Newton's proofs from memory."

Hooke looked away. The sun had gone down a few minutes ago. A westerly embrasure reflected in his eyes as an identical pair of vertical red slits. "It is a perfectly defensible practice," he admitted. "If I'd spent more of my youth learning geometers' tricks and less of it looking at things, and learning how to see, perhaps I'd have written the *Principia* instead of him."

This was an appalling thing to say. Envy was common as pipe-smoke at Royal Society meetings, but to voice it so baldly was rare. But then Hooke had never cared, or even noticed, what people thought of him.

It took a few moments for Daniel to collect himself, and to give Hooke's utterance the ceremonial silence it demanded. Then he said, "Leibniz has much to say on the subject of *perceptions* which I have but little understood until recently. And you may love Leibniz or not. But consider: Newton has thought things that no man before has ever thought. A great accomplishment, to be sure. Perhaps the greatest achievement any human mind has ever made. Very well—what does that say of Newton, and of us? Why, that his mind is framed in such a way that it can out-think anyone else's. So, all hail Isaac Newton! Let us give him his due, and glorify and worship whatever generative force can frame such a mind. Now, consider Hooke. Hooke has perceived things that no man before has ever perceived. What

does that say of Hooke, and of us? That Hooke was framed
in some special way? No, for just look at you, Robert—by
your leave, you are stooped, asthmatic, fitful, beset by aches
and ills, your eyes and ears are no better than those of men
who've not perceived a thousandth part of what you have.
Newton makes his discoveries in geometrickal realms where
our minds cannot go, he strolls in a walled garden filled with
wonders, to which he has the only key. But you, Hooke, are
cheek-by-jowl with all of humanity in the streets of London.
Anyone can look at the things you have looked at. But in
those things *you* see what no one else has. You are the millionth human to look at a spark, a flea, a raindrop, the moon,
and the first to see it. For anyone to say that this is less remarkable than what Newton has done, is to understand
things in but a hollow and jejune way, 'tis like going to a
Shakespeare play and remembering only the sword-fights."

Hooke was silent for a time. The room had gone darker,
and he'd faded to a gray ghost, that vivid pair of red sparks
still marking his eyes. After a while, he sighed, and the
sparks winked out for a few moments.

"I shall *have* to fetch you quill and paper, if this is to be
the nature of your discourse, sir," he said finally.

"I am certain that in the fullness of time, the opinion I
have just voiced will be wide spread among learned persons," Daniel said. "This may not however elevate your
stature during the years you have remaining; for fame's a
weed, but repute is a slow-growing oak, and all we can do
during our lifetimes is hop around like squirrels and plant
acorns. There is no reason why I should conceal my opinions. But I warn you that I may express them all I like without bringing you fame or fortune."

"It is enough you've expressed them to *me* in the aweful
privacy of this chamber, sir," Hooke returned. "I declare that
I am indebted to you, and will repay that debt one day, by
giving you something of incalculable value when you least
expect it. A pearl of great price."

* * *

LOOKING AT THE MASTER SERGEANT made Daniel feel old. From the way that lower ranks had alluded to this man, Daniel had expected some sort of graybearded multiple amputee. But under the scars and weathering was a man probably no more than thirty years of age. He entered Daniel's chamber without knocking or introducing himself, and inspected it as if he owned the place, taking particular care to learn the field of fire commanded by each of its embrasures. Moving sideways past each of those slits, he seemed to envision a fan-shaped territory of dead enemies spread across the ground beyond.

"Are you expecting to fight a war, sergeant?" said Daniel, who'd been scratching at some paper with a quill and casting only furtive dart-like glances at the sergeant.

"Are you expecting to start one?" the sergeant answered a minute later, as if in no especial hurry to respond.

"Why do you ask me such an odd question?"

"I am trying to conjure up some understanding of how a Puritan gets himself clapped in Tower just *now,* at a time when the only friends the King *has* are Puritans."

"You have forgotten the Catholics."

"No, sir, the *King* has forgotten 'em. Much has changed since you were locked up. *First* he locked up the Anglican bishops for refusing to preach toleration of Catholics and Dissenters."

"I know that much—I was a free man at the time," Daniel said.

"But the whole country was like to rise up in rebellion, Catholic churches were being put to the torch just for sport, and so he let 'em go, just to quiet things down."

"But that is very different from forgetting the Catholics, sergeant."

"Ah but *since*—since you've been immured here—why, the King has begun to fall apart."

"So far I've learned nothing remarkable, sergeant, other

than that there is a sergeant in the King's service who actually knows how to use the word 'immured.'"

"You see, no one believes his son is really his son—that's
what has him resting so uneasy."

"What on earth do you mean?"

"Why, the story's gotten out that the Queen was never
pregnant at all—just parading around with pillows stuffed
under her dress—and that the so-called Prince is just a common babe snatched from an orphanage somewhere, and
smuggled into the birth-chamber inside a warming-pan."

Daniel contemplated this, dumbfounded. "I saw the baby
emerge from the Queen's vagina with my own eyes," he
said.

"Hold on to that memory, Professor, for it may keep you
alive. No one in England thinks the child is anything but a
base smuggled-in changeling. And so the King is retreating
on every front now. Consequently the Anglicans no longer
fear him, while the Papists cry that he has abandoned the
only true faith."

Daniel pondered. "The King wanted Cambridge to grant a
degree to a Benedictine monk named Father Francis, who
was viewed, around Cambridge, as a sort of stalking-horse
for the Pope of Rome," he said. "Any news of him?"

"The King tried to insinuate Jesuits and such-like *everywhere*," said the sergeant, "but has withdrawn a good many of
'em in the last fortnight. I'd wager Cambridge can stand down,
for the King's power is ebbing—ebbing halfway to France."

Daniel now went silent for a while. Finally the sergeant
resumed speaking, in a lower, more sociable tone: "I am not
learned, but I've been to many plays, which is where I
picked up words like 'immured,' and it oftimes happens—
especially in your newer plays—that a player will forget his
next line, and you'll hear a spear-carrier or lutenist muttering 'im a prompt. And in that spirit, I'll now supply you with
your next line, sir: something like 'My word, these are disas-
trous tidings, my King, a true friend to all Nonconformists,

is in trouble, what shall become of us, how can I be of service to his Majesty?'"

Daniel said nothing. The sergeant seemed to have become provoked, and could not now contain himself from prowling and pacing around the room, as if Daniel were a specimen about whom more could be learned by peering at it from diverse angles. "On the other hand, perhaps you are not a run-of-the-mill Nonconformist, for you are in the Tower, sir."

"As are you, sergeant."

"I have a key."

"Poh! Do you have permission to leave?"

This shut him up for a while. "Our commander is John Churchill," he said finally, trying a new tack. "The King no longer entirely trusts him."

"I was wondering when the King would begin to doubt Churchill's loyalty."

"He needs us close, as we are his best men—yet not so close as the Horse Guards, hard by Whitehall Palace, within musket-shot of his apartments."

"And so you have been moved to the Tower for safe-keeping."

"You've got mail," said the sergeant, and flung a letter onto the table in front of Daniel. It bore the address: GRUBENDOL LONDON.

It was from Leibniz.

"It *is* for you, isn't it? Don't bother denying it, I can see it from the look on your face," the sergeant continued. "We had a devil of a time working out who it was supposed to be given to."

"It is intended for whichever officer of the Royal Society is currently charged with handling foreign correspondence," Daniel said indignantly, "and at the moment, that is my honor."

"You're the one, aren't you? You're the one who conveyed certain letters to William of Orange."

"There is no incentive for me to supply an answer to that

question," said Daniel after a brief interval of being too appalled to speak.

"Answer this then: do you have friends named Bob Carver and Dick Gripp?"

"Never heard of them."

"That's funny, for we have come upon a page of written instructions, left with the warder, saying that you're to be allowed no visitors at all, except for Bob Carver and Dick Gripp, who may show up at the oddest hours."

"I do not know them," Daniel insisted, "and I beg you not to let them into this chamber under any circumstances."

"That's begging a lot, Professor, for the instructions are written out in my lord Jeffreys's own hand, and signed by the same."

"Then you must know as well as I do that Bob Carver and Dick Gripp are just murderers."

"What I *know* is that my lord Jeffreys is Lord Chancellor, and to disobey his command is an act of rebellion."

"Then I ask you to rebel."

"You first," said the sergeant.

Hanover, August 1688
Dear Daniel,

I haven't the faintest idea where you are, so I will send this to good old GRUBENDOL and pray that it finds you in good health.

Soon I depart on a long journey to Italy, where I expect to gather evidence that will sweep away any remaining cobwebs of doubt that may cling to Sophie's family tree. You must think me a fool to devote so much effort to genealogy, but be patient and you'll see there are good reasons for it. I'll pass through Vienna along the way, and, God willing, obtain an audience with the Emperor and tell him of my plans for the Universal Library (the silver-mining project in the Harz has failed—not because there was anything wrong with my inventions, but because the miners feared that they would be thrown out of work, and resisted me in every imaginable way—and so if the Library is to be funded, it will not be from silver mines, but from the coffers of some great Prince).

There is danger in any journey and so I wanted to write down some things and send them to you before leaving Hanover. These are fresh ideas—green apples that would give a stomach-ache to any erudite person who consumed them. On my journey I shall have many hours to recast them in phrasings more pious (to placate the Jesuits), pompous (to impress the scholastics), or simple (to flatter the salons), but I trust you will forgive me for writing in a way that is informal and plain-spoken. If I should meet with some misfortune along the way, perhaps you or some future Fellow of the Royal Society may pick up the thread where I've dropped it.

Looking about us we can easily perceive diverse Truths, viz. that the sky is blue, the moon round, that humans walk on two legs and dogs on four, and so on. Some of those truths are brute and geometrickal in nature, there is no imaginable way to avoid them, for example that the shortest distance between any two points is a straight line. Until Descartes, everyone supposed that such truths were few in number, and that Euclid and the other ancients had found almost all of them. But when Descartes began his project, we all got into the habit of mapping things into a space that could be described by numbers. We now cross two of Descartes' number-lines at right angles to define a co-ordinate plane, to which we have given the name Cartesian coordinates, and this conceit appears to be catching on, for one can hardly step into a lecture-room anywhere without seeing some professor drawing a great + on the slate. At any rate, when we all got into the habit of describing the size and position and speed of everything in the world using numbers, lines, curves, and other constructions that are familiar, to erudite men, from Euclid, I say, then it became a sort of vogue to try to explain all of the truths in the universe by geometry. I myself can remember the very moment that I was seduced by this way of thinking: I was fourteen years old, and was wandering around in the Rosenthal outside of Leipzig, ostensibly to smell the blooms but really to prosecute a sort of internal debate in my own mind, between the old ways of the Scholastics and the Mechanical Philosophy of Descartes. As you know I decided in favor of the latter! And I have not ceased to study mathematics since.

Descartes himself studied the way balls move and collide, how they gather speed as they go down ramps, *et cetera,* and tried to explain all of his data in terms of a theory that was purely geometrical in nature. The result of his lucubrations was classically French in that it did not square with reality but it was very beautiful, and logically coherent. Since then our friends Huygens and Wren have expended more toil towards the same end. But I need hardly tell you that it is Newton, far beyond all others, who has vastly expanded the realm of truths that are geometrickal in nature. I truly believe that if Euclid and Eratosthenes could be brought back to life they would prostrate themselves at his feet and (pagans that they were) worship him as a god. For their geometry treated mostly simple abstract shapes, lines in the sand, while Newton's lays down the laws that govern the very planets.

I have read the copy of *Principia Mathematica* that you so kindly sent me, and I know better than to imagine I will find any faults in the author's proofs, or extend his work into any realm he has not already conquered. It has the feel of something finished and complete. It is like a dome—if it were not whole, it would not stand, and because it is whole, and does stand, there's no point trying to add things on to it.

And yet its very completeness signals that there is more work to be done. I believe that the great edifice of the *Principia Mathematica* encloses nearly all of the geometrickal truths that can possibly be written down about the world. But every dome, be it never so large, has an inside and an outside, and while Newton's dome encloses all of the geometrickal truths, it excludes the other kind: truths that have their sources in fitness and in final causes. When Newton encounters such a truth—such as the inverse square law of gravity—he does not even consider trying to understand it, but instead says that the world simply *is* this way, because that is how God made it. To his way of thinking, any truths of this nature lie outside the realm of Natural Philosophy and belong instead to a realm he thinks is best approached through the study of alchemy.

Let me tell you why Newton is wrong.

I have been trying to salvage something of value from Descartes' geometrickal theory of collisions and have found it utterly devoid of worth.

Descartes holds that when two bodies collide, they should have the same quantity of motion after the collision as they had before. Why does he believe this? Because of empirical observations? No, for apparently he did not make any. Or if he did, he saw only what he wanted to see. He believes it because he has made up his mind in advance that his theory must be *geometrickal,* and geometry is an austere discipline—there are only certain quantities a geometer is allowed to measure and to write down in his equations. Chief among these is extension, a pompous term for "anything that can be measured with a ruler." Descartes and most others allow time, too, because you can measure time with a pendulum, and you can measure the pendulum with a ruler. The distance a body travels (which can be measured with a ruler) divided by the time it took covering it (which can be measured with a pendulum, which can be measured with a ruler) gives speed. Speed figures into Descartes' calculation of Quantity of Motion—the more speed, the more motion.

Well enough so far, but then he got it all wrong by treating Quantity of Motion as if it were a scalar, a simple directionless number, when in fact is is a vector. But that is a minor lapse. There is plenty of room for vectors in a system with two orthogonal axes, we simply plot them as arrows on what I call the Cartesian plane, and lo, we have geometrickal constructs that obey geometrickal rules. We can add their components geometrickally, reckon their magnitudes with the Pythagorean Theorem, &c.

But there are two problems with this approach. One is relativity. Rulers move. There is no fixed frame of reference for measuring extension. A geometer on a moving canal-boat who tries to measure the speed of a flying bird will get a different number from a geometer on the shore; and a geometer riding on the bird's back would measure no speed at all!

Secondly: the Cartesian Quantity of Motion, mass multiplied by velocity (mv), is not conserved by falling bodies. And yet by doing, or even imagining, a very simple experiment, you can demonstrate that mass multiplied by the *square* of velocity (mv^2) *is* conserved by such bodies.

This quantity mv^2 has certain properties of interest. For one, it measures the amount of work that a moving body is capable of doing. Work is something that has an absolute meaning, it is free from the problem of relativity that I mentioned a moment ago, a problem unavoidably shared by all theories that are founded upon the use of rulers. In the expression mv^2 the velocity is squared, which means that it has lost its direction, and no longer has a geometrickal meaning.

While mv may be plotted on the Cartesian plane and
subjected to all the tricks and techniques of Euclid,
mv^2 may not be, because in being squared the velocity
v has lost its directionality and, if I may wax metaphysical, transcended the geometrickal plane and
gone into a new realm, the realm of Algebra. This
quantity mv^2 is scrupulously conserved by Nature, and
its conservation may in fact be considered a law of the
universe—but it is outside Geometry, and excluded
from the dome that Newton has built, it is another contingent, non-geometrickal truth, one of many that have
been discovered, or will be, by Natural Philosophers.
Shall we then say, like Newton, that all such truths are
made arbitrarily by God? Shall we seek such truths in
the occult? For if God has laid these rules down arbitrarily, then they are occult by nature.

To me this notion is offensive; it seems to cast God
in the rôle of a capricious despot who desires to hide
the truth from us. In some things, such as the
Pythagorean Theorem, God may not have had any
choice when He created the world. In others, such as
the inverse square law of gravity, He may have had
choices; but in such cases, I like to believe he would
have chosen wisely and according to some coherent
plan that our minds—insofar as they are in God's image—are capable of understanding.

Unlike the Alchemists, who see angels, demons,
miracles, and divine essences everywhere, I recognize
nothing in the world but bodies and minds. And nothing in bodies but certain observable quantities such as
magnitude, figure, situation, and changes in these.
Everything else is merely said, not understood; it is
sounds without meaning. Nor can anything in the
world be understood clearly unless it is reduced to
these. Unless physical things can be explained by mechanical laws, God cannot, even if He chooses, reveal
and explain nature to us.

I am likely to spend the rest of my life explaining these ideas to those who will listen, and defending them from those who won't, and anything you hear from me henceforth should probably be viewed in that light, Daniel. If the Royal Society seems inclined to burn me in effigy, please try to explain to them that I am trying to extend the work that Newton has done, not to tear it down.

Leibniz

P.S. I know the woman Eliza (de la Zeur, now) whom you mentioned in your most recent letter. She seems to be attracted to Natural Philosophers. It is a strange trait in a woman, but who are we to complain?

"Dr. Waterhouse."

"Sergeant Shaftoe."

"Your visitors have arrived—Mr. Bob Carver and Mr. Dick Gripp."

Daniel rose from his bed; he had never come awake so fast. "Please, I beg you, Sergeant, do not—" he began, but he stopped there, for it had occurred to him that perhaps Sergeant Shaftoe's mind was already made up, the deed was all but done, and that Daniel was merely groveling. He got to his feet and shuffled over the wooden floor towards Bob Shaftoe's face and his candle, which hung in darkness like a poorly resolved binary star: the face a dim reddish blob, the flame a burning white point. The blood dropped from Daniel's head and he tottered, but did not hesitate. He'd be nothing more than a bleating voice in the darkness until he entered the globe of light balanced on that flame; if Bob Shaftoe had thoughts of letting the murderers into this room, let him look full on Daniel's face first. The brilliance of the light was governed by an inverse square law, just like gravity.

Shaftoe's face finally came into focus. He looked a little sea-sick. "I'm not such a black-hearted bastard as'd admit a pair of hired killers to spit a helpless professor. There is only one man alive whom I hate enough to wish such an end on him."

"Thank you," Daniel said, drawing close enough now that he could feel the candle's faint warmth on his face.

Shaftoe noticed something, turned sideways to Daniel, and cleared his throat. This was not your delicate pretentious upper-class 'hem but an honest and legitimate bid to dislodge an actual phlegm-ball that had sprung into his gorge.

"You've noticed me pissing myself, haven't you?" Daniel said. "You imagine that it's your fault—that you put such a terror into me, just now, that I could not hold my urine. Well, you did have me going, it is true, but that's not why piss is running down my leg. I have the stone, Sergeant, and cannot make water at times of my own choosing, but rather I leak and seep like a keg that wants caulking."

Bob Shaftoe nodded and looked to have been somewhat relieved of his burden of guilt. "How long d'you have then?"

He asked the question so offhandedly that Daniel did not get it for a few moments. "Oh—you mean, *to live*?" The Sergeant nodded. "Pardon me, Sergeant Shaftoe, I forget that your profession has put you on such intimate terms with death that you speak of it as sea-captains speak of wind. How long have I? Perhaps a year."

"You could have it cut out."

"I have seen men cut for the stone, Sergeant, and I'll take death, thank you very much. I'll wager it is worse than anything you may have witnessed on a battlefield. No, I shall follow the example of my mentor, John Wilkins."

"Men have been cut for the stone, and lived, have they not?"

"Mr. Pepys was cut nigh on thirty years ago, and lives still."

"He walks? Talks? Makes water?"

"Indeed, Sergeant Shaftoe."

"Then, by your leave, Dr. Waterhouse, being cut for the stone is *not* worse than anything I have seen on battlefields."

"Do you know how the operation is performed, Sergeant? The incision is made through the perineum, which is that tender place between your scrotum and your anus—"

"If it comes down to swapping blood-curdling tales, Dr. Waterhouse, we shall be here until this candle has burnt down, and all to no purpose; and if you really intend to die of the stone, you oughtn't to be wasting that much time."

"There is nothing to do, here, *but* waste time."

"That is where you are wrong, Dr. Waterhouse, for I have a lively sort of proposition to make you. We are going to help each other, you and I."

"You want money in exchange for keeping Jeffreys's murderers out of my chamber?"

"That's what I should want, were I a base, craven toad," Bob Shaftoe said. "And if you keep mistaking me for that sort, why, perhaps I *shall* let Bob and Dick in here."

"Please forgive me, Sergeant. You are right in being angry with me. It is only that I cannot imagine what sort of transaction you and I could . . ."

"Did you see that fellow being whipped, just before sundown? He would've been visible to you out in the dry-moat, through yonder arrow-slit."

Daniel remembered it well enough. Three soldiers had gone out, carrying their pikes, and lashed them together close to their points, and spread their butts apart to form a tripod. A man had been led out shirtless, his hands tied together in front of him, and the rope had then been thrown over the lashing where the pikes were joined, and drawn tight so that his arms were stretched out above his head. Finally his ankles had been spread apart and lashed fast to the pikes to either side of him, rendering him perfectly immobile, and then a large man had come out with a whip, and used it. All in all it was a common rite around military camps, and went a long way towards explaining why people of means tried to live as far away from barracks as possible.

"I did not observe it closely," Daniel said, "I am familiar with the general procedure."

"You might've watched more carefully had you known that the man being whipped calls himself Mr. Dick Gripp."

Daniel was at a loss for words.

"They came for you last night," said Bob Shaftoe. "I had them clapped into separate cells while I decided what to do with 'em. Talked to 'em separately, and all they gave me was a deal of hot talk. Now. Some men are entitled to talk that way, they have been ennobled, in a sense, by their deeds and the things they have lived through. I did not think that Bob Carver and Dick Gripp were men of that kind. Others may be suffered to talk that way simply because they entertain the rest of us. I once had a brother who was like that. But not Bob and Dick. Unfortunately I am not a magistrate and have no power to throw men in prison, compel them to answer questions, *et cetera*. On the other hand, I am a sergeant, and have the power to recruit men into the King's service. As Bob and Dick were clearly idle fellows, I recruited them into the King's Own Black Torrent Guards on the spot. In the next instant, I perceived that I'd made a mistake, for these two were discipline problems, and wanted chastisement. Using the oldest trick in the book, I had Dick—who struck me as the better man—whipped directly in front of Bob Carver's cell window. Now Dick is a strong bloke, he is unbowed, and I may keep him in the regiment. But Bob feels about *his* chastisement—which is scheduled for dawn—the same way you feel about being cut for the stone. So an hour ago he woke up his guards, and they woke me, and I went and had a chat with Mr. Carver."

"Sergeant, you are so industrious that I almost cannot follow everything you are about."

"He told me that Jeffreys personally ordered him and Mr. Gripp to cut your throat. That they were to do it slow-like, and that they were to explain to you, while you lay dying, that it had been done by Jeffreys."

"It is what I expected," Daniel said, "and yet to hear it set out in plain words leaves me dizzy."

"Then I shall wait for you to get your wits back. More to

the point, I shall wait for you to become angry. Forgive me for presuming to instruct a fellow of your erudition, but at a moment like this, you are supposed to be angry."

"It is a very odd thing about Jeffreys that he can treat people abominably and never make them angry. He influences his victims' minds strangely, like a glass rod bending a stream of water, so that we feel we deserve it."

"You have known him a long time."

"I have."

"Let's kill him."

"I beg your pardon?"

"Slay, murder. Let us bring about his death, so he won't plague you any more."

Daniel was shocked. "It is an extremely fanciful idea—"

"Not in the least. And there is something in your tone of voice that tells me you like it."

"Why do you say 'we'? You have no part in my problems."

"You are high up in the Royal Society."

"Yes."

"You know many Alchemists."

"I wish I could deny it."

"You know my lord Upnor."

"I do. I've known him as long as I've known Jeffreys."

"Upnor owns my lady love."

"I beg your pardon—did you say he *owns* her?"

"Yes—Jeffreys sold her to him during the Bloody Assizes."

"Taunton—your love is one of the Taunton schoolgirls!"

"Just so."

Daniel was fascinated. "You are proposing some sort of pact."

"You and I'll rid the world of Jeffreys and Upnor. I'll have my Abigail and you'll live your last year, or whatever time God affords you, in peace."

"I do not mean to quail and fret, Sergeant—"

"Go ahead! My men do it all the time."

"—but may I remind you that Jeffreys is the Lord Chancellor of the Realm?"

"Not for long," Shaftoe answered.

"How do you know?"

"He's as much as admitted it, by his actions! You were thrown in Tower why?"

"For acting as go-between to William of Orange."

"Why, that is treason—you should've been half-hanged, drawn, and quartered for it! But you were kept alive why?"

"Because I am a witness to the birth of the Prince, and as such, may be useful in attesting to the legitimacy of the next King."

"If Jeffreys has now decided to kill you, what does that signify then?"

"That he is giving up on the King—my God, on the entire *dynasty*—and getting ready to flee. Yes, I understand your reasoning now, thank you for being so patient with me."

"Mind you, I'm not asking you to take up arms, or do anything else that ill suits you."

"Some would take offense at that, Sergeant, but—"

"E'en though my chief grievance may lie with Upnor, the first cause of it was Jeffreys, and I would not hesitate to swing my spadroon, if he should chance to show me his neck."

"Save it for Upnor," Daniel said, after a brief pause to make up his mind. In truth, he'd long since made it up; but he wanted to put on a show of thinking about it, so that Bob Shaftoe would not view him as a man who took such things lightly.

"You're with me, then."

"Not so much that *I* am with *you* as that *we* are with most of *England,* and England with us. You speak of putting Jeffreys to death with the strength of your right arm. Yet I tell you that if we must rely on your arm, strong as it is, we would fail. But if, as I believe, England is with us, why, then we need do no more than find him and say in a clear voice,

'This fellow here is my lord Jeffreys,' and his death will follow as if by natural law, like a ball rolling down a ramp. This is what I mean when I speak of revolution."

"Is that a French way of saying 'rebellion'?"

"No, rebellion is what the Duke of Monmouth did, it is a petty disturbance, an aberration, predestined to fail. Revolution is like the wheeling of stars round the pole. It is driven by unseen powers, it is inexorable, it moves all things at once, and men of discrimination may understand it, predict it, benefit from it."

"Then I'd best go find a man of discrimination," muttered Bob Shaftoe, "and stop wasting the night with a hapless wretch."

"I simply have not understood, until now, how *I* might benefit from the revolution. I have done all for England, naught for myself, and I have lacked any organizing principle by which to shape my plans. Never would I have dared to imagine I might strike Jeffreys down!"

"As a mudlark, Vagabond soldier, I am always at your service, to be a bringer of base, murderous thoughts," said Bob Shaftoe.

Daniel had receded to the outer fringes of the light and worried a candle out of a bottle on his writing-table. He hustled back and lit it from Bob's candle.

Bob remarked, "I've seen lords die on battlefields—not as often as I'd prefer, mind you—but enough to know it's not like in paintings."

"Paintings?"

"You know, where Victory comes down on a sunbeam with her tits hanging out of her frock, waving a laurel for said dying lord's brow, and the Virgin Mary slides down on another to—"

"Oh, yes. *Those* paintings. Yes, I believe what you say." Daniel had been working his way along the curving wall of the Tower, holding the candle close to the stone, so that its glancing light would deepen the scratchings made there by prisoners over the centuries. He stopped before a new one, a half-finished complex of arcs and rays that cut through older graffiti.

"I do not think I shall finish this proof," he announced, after gazing at it for a few moments.

"We'll not leave tonight. You shall likely have a week—maybe more. So there's no cause for breaking off work on whatever that is."

"It is an ancient thing that used to make sense, but now it has been turned upside-down, and seems only a queer, jumbled bag of notions. Let it bide here with the other old things," Daniel said.

Château Juvisy
NOVEMBER 1688

From Monsieur Bonaventure Rossignol,
Château Juvisy
To His Majesty Louis XIV, Versailles
21 November 1688

Sire,

It was my father's honor to serve your majesty and your majesty's father as cryptanalyst to the Court. Of the art of decipherment, he endeavoured to teach me all that he knew. Moved by a son's love for his father as well as by a subject's ardent desire to be of service to his King, I strove to learn as much as my lesser faculties would permit; and if, when my father died six years ago, he had imparted to me a tenth part of what he knew, why then it sufficed to make me more nearly fit to serve as your majesty's cryptanalyst than any man in Christendom; a measure, not of *my* eminence (for I cannot claim to possess any) but of my father's, and of the degraded condition of cryptography in the uncouth nations that surround France as barbarian hordes once hemmed in mighty Rome.

Along with some moiety of his knowledge, I have inherited the salary your beneficent majesty bestowed upon him, and the château that Le Nôtre built for him at Juvisy, which your majesty knows well, as you have more than once honored it with your presence, and

ANGLIA
Cambridge
Ipswich

NORT
ZEE

Sheerness
Chatham

TEXEL
Groningen

Haarlem
Scheveningen
The Hague
Rotterdam

UNITED
NETHERLANDS
Amsterdam
Waal

Bremen

Münster

Meuse
Nijmegen

Duisburg

ZEELAND
Brugge
Dunkirk
Gent
Antwerpen
Maastricht
Köln

Harz Mts.

Lille
Bruxelles
Liège
Bonn

Arras
BELGICA
GERMANIA
Frankfurt

ARTOIS
Amiens
Ardennes
Bastogne
LUXEMBURG
Luxemburg
Mainz

Mannheim
Heidelberg

Rouen
PICARDY

Meuse
Verdun
SAAR
LAND
Saarbrücken
PALATINATE

Seine
St. Cloud
Paris
Reims
Marne
Versailles
Meaux
Orcois
St. Dizier

ARGONNE
FOREST
Nancy

LORRAINE
Metz

Haguenau
ALSACE
Stuttgart
Tübingen

Rhine
Strasbourg

Orleans
Auxerre

CHAMPAGNE

Dijon
FRANCHE
Besançon
COMTÉ

Bazel
Zurich

GALLIA
Riom

HELVETIÆ

Bern

Oyonnax
Lyon
Geneva

SAVOY
Aosta
ITALIA

Valence
Grenoble
PIEDMONT
Milano
MILAN

RHINE
VALLEY

graced it with your wit, as you journeyed to and from Fontainebleau. Many affairs of state have been discussed in the *petit salon* and the garden; for your father of blessed memory, and Cardinal Richelieu, also were known to ennoble this poor house with their presences during the days when my father, by deciphering the communications passing into and out of the fortifications of the Huguenots, was helping to suppress the rebellions of those heretics.

Than your majesty no monarch has been more keenly alive to the importance of cryptography. It is only to this acuity on your majesty's part, and not to any intrinsic merit of mine, that I attribute the honors and wealth that you have showered upon me. And it is only because of your majesty's oft-demonstrated interest in these affairs that I presume to pick up my quill and to write down a tale of cryptanalysis that is not without certain extraordinary features.

As your majesty knows, the incomparable château at Versailles is adorned by several ladies who are indefatigable writers of letters, notably my friend Madame de Sévigné; *la Palatine;* and Eliza, the Countess de la Zeur. There are many others, too; but we who have the honor of serving in your majesty's *cabinet noir* spend as much time reading the correspondence of these three as of all the other ladies of Versailles combined.

My narrative chiefly concerns the Countess de la Zeur. She writes frequently to M. le comte d'Avaux in the Hague, using the approved cypher to shield her correspondence from my Dutch counterparts. As well she carries on a steady flow of correspondence to certain Jews of Amsterdam, consisting predominantly of numbers and financial argot that, read, cannot be deciphered, and decyphered, cannot be understood, unless one is familiar with the workings of that city's commodities markets, as vulgar as they are complex. These letters are exceptionally pithy, and of no inter-

est to anyone save Jews, Dutchmen, and other persons
who are motivated by money. Her most voluminous
letters by far go to the Hanoverian savant Leibniz,
whose name is known to your majesty—he made a
computing machine for Colbert some years ago, and
now toils as an advisor to the Duke and Duchess of
Hanover, whose exertions on behalf of united Protes-
tantism have been the cause of so much displeasure to
your majesty. Ostensibly the letters of the Countess de
la Zeur to this Leibniz consist of interminable descriptions of the magnificence of Versailles and its inhabitants. The sheer volume and consistency of this
correspondence have caused me to wonder whether it
was not a channel of encrypted communications; but
my poor efforts at finding any hidden patterns in her
flowery words have been unavailing. Indeed, my suspicion of this woman is grounded, not on any flaw in
her cypher—which, assuming it exists at all, is a very
good one—but on what little understanding I may
claim to possess of human nature. For during my occasional visits to Versailles I have sought this woman
out, and engaged her in conversation, and found her to
be highly intelligent, and conversant with the latest
work of mathematicians and Natural Philosophers
both foreign and domestic. And of course the brilliance and erudition of Leibniz is acknowledged by
all. It is implausible to me that such a woman could
devote so much time to writing, and such a man so
much time to reading, about hair.

Perhaps two years ago, M. le comte d'Avaux, on
one of his visits to your majesty's court, sought me
out, and, knowing of my position in the *cabinet noir,*
asked many pointed questions about the Countess's
epistolary habits. From this it was plain enough that he
shared some of my suspicions. Later he told me that
he had witnessed with his own eyes an incident in

which it was made obvious that this woman was an agent of the Prince of Orange. D'Avaux at this time mentioned a Swiss gentleman of the name of Fatio de Duilliers, and intimated that he and the Countess de la Zeur were in some way linked.

D'Avaux seemed confident that he knew enough to crush this woman. Instead of doing so outright, he had decided that he could better serve your majesty by pursuing a more complex and, by your majesty's leave, risky strategy. As is well known, she makes money for many of your majesty's vassals, including d'Avaux, by managing their investments. The price of liquidating her outright would be high; not a consideration that would ever confound your majesty's judgment, but telling among men of weak minds and light purses. Moreover, d'Avaux shared my suspicion that she was communicating over some encrypted channel with Sophie and, through Sophie, with William, and hoped that if I were to achieve a cryptological break of this channel the *cabinet noir* might thereafter read her despatches without her being aware of it; which would be altogether more beneficial to France and pleasing to your majesty than locking the woman up in a nunnery and keeping her incommunicado to the end of her days, as she deserves.

There had been during the first part of this year a sort of flirtation between the Countess de la Zeur and *la Palatine,* which appeared to culminate in August when the Countess accepted an invitation from Madame to join her (and your majesty's brother) at St. Cloud. Everyone who knew of this assumed that it was a common, albeit Sapphic, love affair: an interpretation so obvious that it ought by its nature to have engendered more skepticism among those who pride themselves on their sophistication. But it was summer, the weather was warm, and no one paid it any heed. Not long after her arrival at St. Cloud, the Countess sent a letter to d'Avaux in the Hague, which has subsequently found its way back to my writing desk. Here it is.

St. Cloud

AUGUST 1688

Eliza, Countess de la Zeur, to d'Avaux
16 August 1688
Monsieur,

Summer has reached its pinnacle here and for those, such as Madame, who like to hunt wild animals, the best months lie in the future. But for those, such as Monsieur, who prefer to hunt (or be hunted by) highly cultivated humans, this is the very best time of the year. So Madame endures the heat, and sits with her lap-dogs and writes letters, while Monsieur's only complaint is that the torrid weather causes his makeup to run. St. Cloud is infested with young men, aficionados of fencing, who would give anything to sheathe their blades in his scabbard. To judge from the noises emanating from his bedchamber, his chief lover is the Chevalier de Lorraine. But when the Chevalier is spent, the Marquis d'Effiat is never far behind; and behind him (as it were) is a whole queue of handsome cavaliers. In other words, here as at Versailles, there is a strict pecking-order (though one must imagine a different sort of pecking), and so most of these young blades can never hope to be anything more than ornaments. Yet they are continually lustful like any other men. Since they cannot satiate themselves on Monsieur inside the château, they practice on one another in the gardens. One cannot go for a stroll or a ride without breaking into the middle of a tryst. And when these young men are interrupted, they do not slink away meekly, but (emboldened by the favor shown them by Monsieur) upbraid one in the most abusive way imaginable. Wherever I go, my nose detects the humour of lust wafted on every draught and breeze, for it is spilled about the place like wine-slops in a tavern.

Liselotte has been putting up with this for seventeen years now, ever since the day when she crossed over the Rhine, never to cross back. And so it's no wonder that she ventures out into society only rarely, and prefers the company of her dogs and her ink-well. Madame has been known to grow very attached to members of her household—she used to have a lady-in-waiting named Théobon who was a great comfort to her. But the lovers of Monsieur—who are supported by him, and who have nothing to do all day long but hatch plots—began to whisper vile rumors into Monsieur's ear, and caused him to send this Théobon away. Madame was so angry that she complained to the King himself. The King reprimanded Monsieur's lovers but balked at intervening in the household affairs of his own brother, and so Théobon has presumably ended up in a convent somewhere, and will never return.

From time to time they entertain guests here, and then, as you know, protocol dictates that everyone dress up in the sort of costume known as *en manteau*, which is even stiffer and less comfortable (if you can imagine it) than dressing *en grand habit* as is done at Versailles. As an ambassador, you see women dressed in that manner all the time, but as a man, you never see machinations that go on in ladies' private chambers for hours ahead of time, to make them look that way. Dressing *en manteau* is an engineering project at least as complicated as rigging a ship. Neither can even be contemplated without a large and well-trained crew. But Madame's household has been reduced to a skeleton crew by the ceaseless petty intrigues of the lovers of Monsieur. And in any case she has no patience with female vanities. She is old enough, and foreign enough, and intelligent enough, to understand that Fashion (which lesser women view as if it were Gravity) was merely an invention, a device. It was devised by Colbert as a way to neutralize those Frenchmen and Frenchwomen who, because of their wealth and independence, posed the greatest threat to the King. But Liselotte, who might have been formidable, has already been neutralized by marrying Monsieur and joining the royal family. The only thing that prevents her country from being annexed to France is a dispute as to whether she, or another descendant of the Winter Queen, should succeed her late brother.

At any rate, Liselotte refuses to play the game that Colbert devised. She has a wardrobe, of course, and it includes several costumes that are worthy of the names *grand habit* and *manteau*. But she has had them made up in a way that is unique. In Madame's wardrobe, all the layers of lingerie, corsetry, petticoats, and outer garments that normally go on one at a time are sewn together into a single construct, so heavy and stiff that it stands by itself, and slit up the back. When Monsieur throws a grand party, Liselotte plods naked into her closet and walks into one of these and stands for a few moments as a lady-in-waiting fastens it in the back with diverse buttons, hooks, and ties. From there she goes straight to the party, without so much as a glance in the mirror.

I will complete this little portrait of life at St. Cloud with a story about dogs. As I mentioned, *la Palatine,* like Artemis, is never far from her pack of dogs. Of course these are not swift hounds, but tiny lap-dogs that curl up on her feet in the winter to keep her toes warm. She has named them after people and places she remembers from her childhood in the Palatinate. They scurry about her apartments all day long, getting into absurd feuds and controversies, just like so many courtiers. Sometimes she herds them out onto the lawn and they run around in the sunshine interrupting the *amours* of Monsieur's hangers-on, and then the peace of these exquisite gardens is broken by the angry shouts of the lovers and the yelps of the dogs; the cavaliers, with their breeches down around their ankles, chase them out from their trysting-places, and Monsieur comes out onto his balcony in his dressing-gown and damns them all to hell and wonders aloud why God cursed him to marry Liselotte.

The King has a pair of hunting-dogs named Phobos and Deimos who are very aptly named, for they have been fed on the King's own table-scraps and have grown enormous. The King has indulged them terribly and so they want discipline, and feel they are entitled to attack whatever strikes their fancy. Knowing how much Liselotte loves hunting and dogs, and knowing how lonely and isolated she is, the King has tried to interest her in these beasts—he wants Liselotte to think of Phobos and Deimos as her own pets and to look upon them with affection, as the King does, so that they can go hunting for large game in the east when the season comes around. So far this is nothing more than a proposal. Madame is more than a little ambivalent. Phobos and Deimos are too big and unruly to be kept at Versailles any more, and so the King prevailed upon his brother to keep them at St. Cloud, in a paddock where they can run around loose. The beasts have long since killed and eaten all of the rabbits who used to dwell in that enclosure, and now they devote all their energies to searching for weak places in the fence where they might tunnel out or jump over and go marauding in the territory beyond. Recently they broke through the southeast corner and got loose in the yard beyond and killed all the chickens. That hole has been repaired. As I write this I can see Phobos patrolling the northern fence-line, looking for a way to jump over into the neighboring property, which is owned by another nobleman who has never had good relations with my hosts. Meanwhile Deimos is working on an excavation under the eastern wall, hoping to tunnel through and run amok in the yard where Madame exercises her lap-dogs. I have no idea which of them will succeed first.

Now I must lay down my pen, for some months ago I promised Madame that I would one day give her a demonstration of bareback riding, Qwghlmian-style, and now the time is finally at hand. I hope that my little description of life at St. Cloud has not struck you as overly vulgar, but since you, like any sophisticated man, are a student of the human condition, I thought you might be fascinated to learn what peasant-like noise and rancor prevail behind the supremely elegant façade of St. Cloud.

Eliza, Countess de la Zeur

Rossignol to Louis XIV Continued

NOVEMBER 1688

Your majesty will already have perceived that Phobos and Deimos are metaphors for the armed might of France; their chicken-killing escapade is the recent campaign in which your majesty brought the rebellious Protestants of Savoy to heel; and the question of where they might attack next, a way of saying that the Countess could not guess whether your majesty intended to strike north into the Dutch Republic or east into the Palatinate. Just as obviously, these sentences were written as much for William of Orange—whose servants would read the letter before it reached d'Avaux—as for the recipient.

Perhaps less transparent is the reference to bareback riding. I would have assumed it signified some erotic practice, except that the Countess is never so vulgar in her letters. In time I came to understand that it was meant literally. As hard as it might be for your majesty to believe, I have it on the authority of several of Monsieur's friends that Madame and the Countess de la Zeur did indeed go riding that day, and moreover that the latter requested that no saddle be placed on her horse. They rode off into the park thus, escorted by two of Madame's young male cousins from Hanover. But when they returned, the Countess's horse was bare, not only of saddle, but of rider, too;

for, as the story went, she had fallen off after the horse had been startled, and suffered an injury that made it impossible for her to ride back. This had occurred near the banks of the river. Fortunately they had been able to summon a passing boat, which had taken the injured Countess upriver to a nearby convent that is generously supported by Madame. There, or so the story went, the Countess would be tended to by the nuns until her bones had mended.

Needless to say, no one but the smallest child would believe such a story; everyone assumed the obvious, which is that the Countess had become pregnant and that her period of recuperation in the nunnery was to last only long enough for her to arrange an abortion, or to deliver the baby. I myself gave it no further thought until I received a communication from d'Avaux several weeks later. This was, of course, encyphered. I enclose the plaintext, shorn of pleasantries, formalities, and other impedimenta.

French Embassy, the Hague
17 SEPTEMBER 1688

From Jean Antoine de Mesmes, comte d'Avaux
French Embassy, the Hague
To Monsieur Bonaventure Rossignol
Château Juvisy, France
Monsieur Rossignol,

You and I have had occasion to speak of the Countess de la Zeur. I have known for some time that her true allegiance lay with the Prince of Orange. Until today she has been at pains to conceal this. Now she has at last run her true colors up the mast. Everyone believes she is in a nunnery near St. Cloud having a baby. But today, below the very battlements of the Binnenhof, she disembarked from a canal-boat that had just come down from Nijmegen. Most of the heretics who came pouring out of it had originated from much farther upstream, for they are people of the Palatinate who, knowing that an invasion was imminent, have lately fled from that place as rats are said to do from a house in the moments before an earthquake. To give you an idea of their quality, among them were at least two Princesses (Eleanor of Saxe-Eisenach and her daughter Wilhelmina Caroline of Brandenburg-Ansbach), as well as any number of other persons of rank; though as much could never have been guessed from their degraded and bedraggled appearance. Con-

sequently the Countess de le Zeur—who was even
more dishevelled than most—attracted less notice
than is her wont. But I know that she was there, for my
sources in the Binnenhof inform me that the Prince of
Orange ordered a suite to be made available to her, for
a stay of indefinite duration. Previously she has been
coy about her dealings with the said Prince; today she
lives in his house.

I shall have more to say on this later, but for now I
should like to ask the rhetorical question of how this
woman was able to get from St. Cloud to the Hague,
via the Rhine, in one month, during the preparations
for a war, without anyone's having noticed? That she
was working as a spy for the Prince of Orange is too
obvious to mention; but where did she go, and what is
she now telling William in the Binnenhof?

Yours in haste,
d'Avaux

Rossignol to Louis XIV Continued

NOVEMBER 1688

Your majesty will already have understood how fascinated I was by this news from d'Avaux. The letter had reached me after a considerable delay, as, owing to the war, d'Avaux had been forced to show some ingenuity in finding a way to have it delivered to Juvisy. I knew that I could not expect to receive any more, and to attempt to respond in kind would have been a waste of paper. Accordingly, I resolved to travel in person, and *incognito*, to the Hague. For to be of service to your majesty is my last thought as I go to bed in the night-time and my first upon waking in the morning; and it was plain that where this matter was concerned I was useless so long as I remained at home.

Of my journey to the Hague, much could be written in a vulgar and sensational vein, if I felt that I could better serve your majesty by producing an entertainment. But it is all beside the point of this report. And as better men than I have sacrificed their lives in your service with no thought of fame, or of reward beyond a small share in the glory of *la France*, I do not think it is meet for me to relate my tale here; after all, what an Englishman (for example) might fancy to be a stirring and glorious adventure is, to a gentleman of France, altogether routine and unremarkable.

I arrived in the Hague on the 18th of October and

reported to the French embassy, where M. le comte d'Avaux saw to it that what remained of my clothing was burned in the street; that the body of my manservant was given a Christian burial; that my horse was destroyed so that he would not infect the others; and that my pitchfork-wounds and torch-burns were tended to by a French barber-surgeon who dwells in that city. On the following day I began my investigation, which naturally was erected upon the solid foundation that had been laid by d'Avaux during the weeks since his letter to me. As it happened, it was on this very day—the 19th of October, *anno domini* 1688— that an unfortunate change in the wind made it possible for the Prince of Orange to set sail for England at the head of five hundred Dutch ships. As distressing as this event was for the small colony of French in the Hague, it militated to our advantage in that the heretics who engulfed us were so beside themselves (for to them, invading other countries is a new thing, and a tremendous adventure) that they paid me little heed as I went about my work.

My first task, as I have suggested, was to familiarize myself with all that d'Avaux had learned of the matter during the previous weeks. The Hofgebied, or diplomatic quarter of the Hague, may not contain as many servants and courtiers as its counterpart in France, but there are more than enough; those who are *venal,* d'Avaux has bought, and those who are *venereal,* he has compromised in one way or another, so that he may know practically anything he wishes to of what goes on in that neighborhood, provided only that he has the diligence to interview his sources, and the wit to combine their fragmentary accounts into a coherent story. Your majesty will in no way be surprised to learn that he had done so by the time of my arrival. D'Avaux imparted to me the following:

First, that the Countess de la Zeur, unlike all of the

other refugees on the canal-ship, had not taken it all the way from Heidelberg. Rather, she had embarked at Nijmegen, filthy and exhausted, and accompanied by two young gentlemen, also much the worse for wear, whose accents marked them as men of the Rhineland.

This in itself told me much. It had already been obvious that on that August day at St. Cloud, Madame had made some arrangement to spirit the Countess aboard a boat on the Seine. By working its way upstream to Paris, such a vessel could take the left fork at Charenton and go up the Marne deep into the northeastern reaches of your majesty's realm, within a few days' overland journey of Madame's homeland. It is not the purpose of this letter to cast aspersions on the loyalty of your sister-in-law; I suspect that the Countess de la Zeur, so notorious for her cunning, had preyed upon Madame's natural and humane concern for her subjects across the Rhine, and somehow induced her to believe that it would be beneficial to despatch the Countess on a sight-seeing expedition to that part of the world. Of course this would take the Countess into just that part of France where preparations for war would be most obvious to a foreign spy.

Your majesty during his innumerable glorious campaigns has devoted many hours to studying maps, and contemplating all matters of logistics, from grand strategy down to the smallest detail, and will recollect that there is no direct connection by water from the Marne to any of the rivers that flow down into the Low Countries. The Argonne Forest, however, nurses the headwaters, not only of the Marne, but also of the Meuse, which indeed passes to within a few miles of Nijmegen. And so, just as d'Avaux had already done before me, I settled upon the working hypothesis that after taking a boat from St. Cloud up the Marne, the Countess had disembarked in the vicinity of the Argonne—which as your majesty well knows was an active theatre of military operations during these weeks—and made some sort of overland journey that had eventually taken her to the Meuse, and via the Meuse to Nijmegen where we have our first report of her from d'Avaux's informants.

Second, all who saw her on the Nijmegen-Hague route agree that she had practically nothing with her. She had no luggage. Her personal effects, such as they were, were stored in the saddlebag of one of her German companions. Everything was soaked through, for in the days before her appearance at Nijmegen the weather had been rainy. During the voyage on the canal-ship, she and the two Germans emptied the saddlebags and spread out their contents on the deck to dry. At no time were any books, papers, or documents of any kind observed, and no quills or ink. In her hands she carried a small bag and an embroidery frame with a piece of crewel-work mounted on it. There was nothing else. All of this is confirmed by d'Avaux's informants in the Binnenhof. The servants who furnished the Countess's suite there insist that nothing came off the canal-boat save:

(Item) The dress on the Countess's back. Mildewed and creased from (one assumes) a lengthy journey in the bottom of a saddlebag, this was torn up for rags as soon as she peeled it off. Nothing was hidden beneath.

(Item) A set of boy's clothing approximately the Countess's size, badly worn and filthy.

(Item) The embroidery frame and crewel-work, which had been ruined by repeated soakings and dryings (the colors of the thread had run into the fabric).

(Item) Her handbag, which turned out to contain nothing but a scrap of soap, a comb, an assortment of rags, a sewing-kit, and a nearly empty coin-purse.

Of the items mentioned, all were removed or destroyed save the coins, the sewing-kit, and the embroidery project. The Countess showed a curiously strong attachment to the latter, mentioning to the servants that they were not to touch it, be it never so badly damaged, and even keeping it under her pillow when she slept, for fear that it might be taken away by mistake and used as a rag.

Third, after she had recuperated for a day, and been supplied with presentable clothing, she went to the forest-hut of the Prince of Orange that is out in the wilderness nearby, and met with him and his advisors on three consecutive days. Immediately thereafter the Prince withdrew his regiments from the south and set in motion his invasion of England. It is said that the Countess produced, as if by sorcery, a voluminous report filled with names, facts, figures, maps, and other details difficult to retain in the memory.

So much for d'Avaux's work. He had given me all that I could have asked for as a cryptologist. It remained only for me to apply Occam's Razor to the facts that d'Avaux had amassed. My conclusion was that the Countess had made her notes, not with ink on paper, but with needle and thread on a work of embroidery. The technique, though extraordinary, had certain advantages. A woman who is forever writing things down on paper makes herself extremely conspicuous, but no one pays any notice to a woman doing needle-work. If a person is suspected of being a spy, and their possessions searched, paper is the first thing an investigator looks for. Crewel-work will be ignored. Finally, paper-and-ink documents fare poorly in damp conditions, but a textile document would have to be unraveled thread by thread before its information was destroyed.

By the time of my arrival in the Hague, the Countess had vacated her chambers in the Binnenhof and moved across the Plein to the house of the heretic "philosopher" Christiaan Huygens, who is her friend. On the day of my arrival she departed for Amsterdam

to pay a call on her business associates there. I paid a
cat-burglar, who has done many such jobs for d'Avaux
in the past, to enter the house of Huygens, find the embroidery, and bring it to me without disturbing anything else in the room. Three days later, after I had
conducted an analysis detailed below, I arranged for
the same thief to put the embroidery back just where
he had found it. The Countess did not return from her
sojourn to Amsterdam until several days afterwards.

It is a piece of coarsely woven linen, square, one
Flemish ell on a side. She has left a margin all round
the edges of about a hand's breadth. The area in the
center, then, is a square perhaps eighteen inches on a
side: suitable for an *opus pulvinarium* or cushion-
cover. This area has been almost entirely covered in
crewel-work. The style is called gros-point, a technique that is popular among English peasants, overseas colonists, and other rustics who amuse
themselves sewing naïve designs upon the crude tex-
tiles they know how to produce. As it has been super-
seded, in France, by petit-point, it may be unfamiliar
to your majesty, and so I will permit myself the indulgence of a brief description. The fabric or matrix is always of a coarse weave, so that the warp and weft may
be seen by the naked eye, forming a regular square
grid à la Descartes. Each of the tiny squares in this
grid is covered, during the course of the work, by a
stitch in the shape of a letter *x,* forming a square of
color that, seen from a distance, becomes one tiny element of the picture being fashioned. Pictures formed
in this manner necessarily have a jagged-edged appearance, particularly where an effort has been made
to approximate a curve; which explains why such
pieces have been all but banished from Versailles and
other places where taste and discrimination have van-
quished sentimentality. In spite of which your majesty
may easily envision the appearance of one of these

minute x-shaped stitches when viewed closely: one leg
running from northwest to southeast, as it were, and
the other southwest to northeast. The two legs cross in
the center. One must lie over the other. Which lies on
top is a simple matter of the order in which they were
laid down. Some embroiderers are creatures of habit,
always performing the stitches in the same sequence,
so that one of the legs invariably lies atop the other.
Others are not so regular. As I examined the Countess's work through a magnifying lens, I saw that she
was one of the latter—which I found noteworthy, as
she is in other respects a person of the most regular
and disciplined habits. It occurred to me to wonder
whether the orientations of the overlying legs might
be a hidden vector of information.

The pitch of the canvas's weave was about twenty
threads per inch. A quick calculation showed that the
total number of threads along each side would be
around 360, forming nearly 130,000 squares.

A single square by itself could only convey a scin-
tilla of information, as it can only possess one of two
possible states: either the northwest-southeast leg is on
top, or the southwest-northeast. This might seem useless; as how can one write a message in an alphabet of
only two letters?

Mirabile dictu, there is a way to do just that, which I
had recently heard about because of the loose tongue
of a gentleman who has already been mentioned: Fatio
de Duilliers. This Fatio fled to England after the Continent became a hostile place for him, and befriended a
prominent English Alchemist by the name of Newton.
He has become a sort of Ganymede to Newton's Zeus,
and follows him wherever he can; when they are perforce separated, he prates to anyone who will listen
about his close relationship to the great man. I know
this from Signore Vigani, an Alchemist who is at the
same college with Newton and so is often forced to

break bread with Fatio. Fatio is prone to irrational jealousy, and he endlessly schemes to damage the reputation of anyone he imagines may be a rival for Newton's affections. One such is a Dr. Waterhouse, who shared a room with Newton when they were boys, and for all I know buggered him; but the facts do not matter, only Fatio's imaginings. In the library of the Royal Society, Fatio recently happened upon Dr. Waterhouse sleeping over some papers on which he had been working out a calculation consisting entirely of ones and zeroes—a mathematical curiosity much studied by Leibniz. Dr. Waterhouse woke up before Fatio could get a closer look at what he had been doing; but as the document in question appeared to be a letter from abroad, he inferred that it might be some sort of cryptographic scheme. Not long after, he went to Cambridge with Newton and let this story drop at High Table so that all could know how clever he was, and that Waterhouse was certainly a dolt and probably a spy.

From my records of the *cabinet noir* I knew that the Countess de la Zeur had sent a letter to the Royal Society at the same time, and that she has had business contacts with the brother of Dr. Waterhouse. And I have already mentioned her suspiciously voluminous and inane correspondence with Leibniz. And so once again applying Occam's Razor I formulated the hypothesis that the Countess uses a cypher, probably invented by Leibniz, based upon binary arithmetic, which is to say consisting of ones and zeroes: an alphabet of two letters, perfectly suited to representation in cross-stitch embroidery, as I have explained.

I enlisted a clerk from the Embassy, who had keen eyesight, to go over the embroidery stitch by stitch, marking down a numeral 1 for each square in which the northwest-to-southeast leg lay on top, and a 0 otherwise. I then applied myself to the problem of breaking the cypher.

A series of binary digits can represent a number; for example, 01001 is equal to 9. Five binary digits can represent up to 32 different numbers, sufficient to encypher the entire Roman alphabet. My early efforts assumed that the Countess's cypher was of that sort; but alas, I found no intelligible message, and no patterns tending to give me hope that my fortunes would ever change.

Presently I departed from the Hague, taking the transcript of ones and zeroes with me, and bought passage on a small ship down the coast to Dunquerque. Most of the crew on this vessel were Flemish, but there were a few who looked different from the rest and who spoke to one another in a pithy, guttural tongue unlike any I had ever heard. I asked where they were from—for they were redoubtable seamen all— and they answered with no little pride that they were men of Qwghlm. At this moment I knew that Divine Providence had led me to this boat. I asked them many questions concerning their extraordinary language and their way of writing: a system of runes that is as primitive as an alphabet can possibly be and yet be worthy of the name. It contains no vowels, and sixteen consonants, several of which cannot be pronounced by anyone who was not born on that rock.

As it happens, an alphabet of sixteen letters is perfectly suited to translation into a binary cypher, for only four binary digits—or four stitches of embroidery—are required to represent a single letter. The Qwghlmian language is almost unbelievably pithy— one of these people can say with a few grunts, gags, and stutters what would take a Frenchman several sentences—and little known outside of that God-cursed place. Both of which made it perfectly suited to the purposes of the Countess, who need communicate, in this case, only with herself. In sum, the Qwghlmian language need not be encyphered, for it is already a nearly perfect cypher to begin with.

I tried the experiment of breaking down the tran-
scribed 1s and 0s into groups of four and translating
each group into a number between 1 and 16, and
shortly began to see patterns of the sort that give a
cryptographer great confidence that he is progressing
rapidly to a solution. Upon my return to Paris I was
able to find in the *Bibliothèque du Roi* a scholarly work
about Qwghlmian runes, and thereby to translate the
list of numbers into that alphabet—some 30,000 runes
in all. A cursory comparison of the results against the
word-list in the back of this tome suggested that I was
on the correct path to a full solution; but to translate it
was beyond my powers. I consulted with Father
Édouard de Gex, who has lately taken an interest in
Qwghlm, hoping to convert it to the True Faith and
make it a thorn in the side of the heretics. He referred
me to Father Mxnghr of the Society of Jesus in Dublin,
who is a Qwghlmian born and bred, and known to be
absolutely loyal to your majesty as he travels frequently to Qwghlm, at great risk, to baptize the people
there. I sent him the transcript and he replied, some
weeks later, with a translation of the text into Latin that
ran to almost forty thousand words; which is to say that
it requires more than one word in Latin to convey what
is signified by a single rune in Qwghlmian.

This text is so pithy and fragmentary as to be nearly
unreadable, and makes use of many curious word sub-
stitutions—"gun" written as "England stick" and so
on. Much of its bulk consists of tedious lists of names,
regiments, places, *et cetera,* which are of course sta-
ples of espionage, but of little interest now that the war
has begun and everything become fluid. Some of it,
however, is personal narrative that she apparently set
down in crewel when she was bored. This material
solves the riddle of how she got from St. Cloud to Nijmegen. I have taken the liberty of translating it into a
more elevated style and redacting it into a coherent, if

episodic narrative, which is copied out below for your majesty's pleasure. From place to place I have inserted a note supplying additional information about the Countess's activities which I have gleaned from other sources in the meantime. At the end, I have attached a postscript as well as a note from d'Avaux.

> If I had to read romances for long stretches at a time, I should find them tiresome; but I only read three or four pages in the mornings and evenings when I sit (by your leave) on my close-stool, and then it is neither fatiguing nor dull.
> —Liselotte in a letter to Sophie,
> 1 May 1704

Journal entry
17 August 1688

Dear reader,

There is no way for me to guess whether this scrap of linen will, on purpose or through some calamity, be destroyed; or be made into a cushion; or, by some turn of events, fall under the scrutiny of some clever person and be decyphered, years or centuries from now. Though the fabric is new, clean, and dry as I sew these words into it, I cannot but expect that by the time anyone reads them, it will have become streaked with rain or tears, mottled and mildewed from age and damp, perhaps stained with smoke or blood. In any event I congratulate you, whoever you may be and in whatever era you may live, for having been clever enough to read this.

Some would argue that a spy should not keep a written account of her actions lest it fall into the wrong hands. I would answer that it is my duty to find out detailed information, and supply it to my lord, and if I do not learn more than I can recite from memory, then I have not been very industrious.

On 16 August 1688, I met Liselotte von der Pfalz, Elisabeth Charlotte, duchesse d'Orleans, who is known to the French Court as Madame or La Palatine, and to her loved ones in Germany as the Knight of the Rustling Leaves, at the gate of a stable on her estate at St. Cloud on the Seine, just downstream of Paris. She ordered her favorite hunting-horse brought out and saddled, while I went from stall to stall and selected a mount that would be suitable for riding bareback; that being the outward purpose of the expedition. Together we rode off into the woods that line the bank of the Seine for some miles in the neighborhood of the château. We were accompanied by two young men from Hanover. Liselotte maintains close relations with her family in that part of the world, and from time to time some nephew or cousin will be sent out to join her household for a time, and be "finished" in the society of Versailles. The personal stories of these boys are not devoid of interest, but, reader, they do not pertain to my narration, and so I will tell you only that they were German Protestant heterosexuals, which meant that they could be trusted within the environment of St. Cloud, if only because they were utterly isolated.

In a quiet backwater of the Seine, shielded from view by overhanging trees, a small flat-bottomed boat was waiting. I climbed aboard and burrowed under a tangle of fishing-

nets. The boatman shoved off and poled the craft out into
the main stream of the river, where we shortly made rendezvous with a larger vessel making its way upstream. I
have been on it ever since. We have already passed up
through the middle of Paris, keeping to the north side of
the Île de la Cité. Just outside the city, at the confluence of
the rivers Seine and Marne, we took the left fork, and began
to travel up the latter.

JOURNAL ENTRY
20 AUGUST 1688

For several days we have been working our languid way up
the Marne. Yesterday we passed through Meaux, and [as I
believed] left it many miles behind us, but today we came
again close enough to hear its church-bells. This is because
of the preposterous looping of the river, which turns in on
itself like the arguments of Father Édouard de Gex. This
vessel is what they call a *chaland*, a long, narrow, cheaply
made box with but a single square sail that is hoisted whenever the wind happens to come from astern. But most of
the time the mast is used only as a hitching-place for tow-
ropes by which the *chaland* is pulled against the current by
animals on the banks.

My captain and protector is Monsieur LeBrun, who
must live in mortal terror of Madame, for whenever I venture near the gunwale or do anything else the least bit dangerous he begins to sweat, and holds his head in his hands as
if it were in danger of falling off. Mostly I sit on a keg of salt
near the stern and watch France go by, and observe traffic

on the river. I wear the clothes of a boy and keep my hair under my hat, which is sufficient to hide my sex from men on other boats and on the riverbank. If anyone hails me, I smile and say nothing, and after a few moments they falter and take me for an imbecile, perhaps a son of M. LeBrun who has been hit on the head. The lack of activity suits me, for I have been menstruating most of the time I've been on the chaland, and am in fact sitting on a pile of rags.

It is obvious that this countryside produces abundant fodder. In a few weeks' time the barley will be ripe and then it will be easy to march an army through here. If an invasion of the Palatinate is being planned, the armies will come from the north [for they are stationed along the Dutch border] and the food will come from here; so there is nothing for a spy to look for, except, perhaps, shipments of certain military stocks. The armies would carry many of their own supplies with them, but it would not be unreasonable to expect that certain items, such as gunpowder, and especially lead, might be shipped up the river from arsenals in the vicinity of Paris. For to move a ton of lead in wagons requires teams of oxen, and many more wagon-loads of fodder, but to move the same cargo in the bilge of a *chaland* is easy. So I peer at the *chalands* making their way upriver and wonder what is stored down in their holds. To outward appearances they are all carrying the same sort of cargo as the *chaland* of M. LeBrun, viz. salted fish, salt, wine, apples, and other goods that originated closer to where the Seine empties into the sea.

Journal entry
25 August 1688

Sitting still day after day has its advantages. I am trying to view my surroundings through the eye of a Natural Philosopher. A few days ago I was gazing at another *chaland* making its way up-stream about a quarter of a mile ahead of us. One of the boatmen needed to reach a lashing on the mast that was too high for him. So he gripped the rim of a large barrel that was standing upright on the deck, tipped it back towards himself, and rolled it over to where he wanted it, then climbed up onto its end. From the way he managed this huge object and from the sound that it made under his feet, I could tell that it must be empty. Nothing terribly unusual in and of itself, since empty barrels are commonly shipped from place to place. But it made me wonder whether there was any outward sign by which I could distinguish between a *chaland* loaded as M. LeBrun's is, and one that had a few tons of musket-balls in the bilge with empty barrels above to disguise the true nature of its cargo from spies?

Even from a distance it is possible to observe the sideways rocking of one of these *chalands* by watching the top of its mast——for being long, the mast magnifies the small movements of the hull, and being high, it can be seen from far off.

I borrowed a pair of wooden shoes from M. LeBrun and set both of them afloat in the stagnant water that has accumulated in the bilge. Into one of these, I placed an iron bar, which rested directly upon the sole of the shoe. Into the other, I packed an equal weight of salt, which had spilled out of a fractured barrel. Though the weights of the shoes' cargoes were equal, the distributions of those weights were not, for the salt was evenly distributed through the whole volume of the shoe, whereas the iron bar was concentrated in its "bilge." When I set the two shoes to rocking, I could easily observe that the one laden with iron rocked with a slower, more ponderous motion, because all of its weight was far from the axis of the movement.

After re-uniting M. LeBrun with his shoes I returned to my position on the deck of the *chaland*, this time carrying a watch that had been given to me by Monsieur Huygens. First I timed one hundred rockings of the *chaland* I was on, and then I began to make the same observation of other *chalands* on the river. Most of them rocked at approximately the same frequency as the one of M. LeBrun. But I noticed one or two that rocked very slowly. Naturally I then began to scrutinize these *chalands* more carefully, whensoever they came into view, and familiarized myself with their general appearance and their crews. Somewhat to my disappointment, the first one turned out to be laden with quarried stones. Of course, no effort had been made to conceal the nature of its cargo. But later I saw one that had been filled up with barrels.

M. LeBrun really does think I am an imbecile now, but it is of no concern as I shall not be with him for very much longer.

JOURNAL ENTRY
28 AUGUST 1688

I have now passed all the way across Champagne and arrived at St.-Dizier, where the Marne comes very near the frontier of Lorraine and then turns southwards. I need to go east and north, so here is where I disembark. The journey has been slow, but I have seen things I would have overlooked if it had been more stimulating, and to sit in the sun on a slow boat in quiet country has hardly been a bad thing. No matter how strongly I hold to my convictions, I feel my resolve weakening after a few weeks at Court. For the people there are so wealthy, powerful, attractive, and cocksure that after a while it is impossible not to feel their influence. At first it induces a deviation too subtle to detect, but eventually one falls into orbit around the Sun King.

The territory I have passed through is flat, and unlike western France, it is open, rather than being divided up into hedgerows and fences. Even without a map one can sense that a vast realm lies beyond to the north and east. The term "fat of the land" is almost literal here, for the grain-fields are ripening before my eyes, like heavy cream rising up out of the very soil. As one born in a cold stony place, I think it looks like Paradise. But if I view it through the eyes of a man, a man of power, I see that it demands to be invaded. It is spread thick with the fodder and fuel of war, and war is bound to come across it in one direction or the other; so best have it go away from you at a time of your choosing than wait for it to darken the horizon and come sweeping towards you. Anyone can see that France will ever be invaded across these fields until she extends her border to the natural barrier of the Rhine. No border embedded in such a landscape will endure.

Fortune has presented Louis with a choice: he can try to maintain his influence over England, which is a very uncertain endeavour and does not really add to the security of France, or he can march on the Rhine, take the Palatinate, and secure France against Germany forever. It seems obvious that this is the wiser course. But as a spy it is not my charge to advise Kings how they *ought* to rule, but to observe how they *do*.

St.-Dizier, where I am about to disembark, is a river-port of modest size, with some very ancient churches and Roman ruins. The dark forest Argonne rises up behind it, and somewhere through those woods runs the border separating France from Lorraine. A few leagues farther to the east lies the vale of the river Meuse, which runs north into the Spanish Netherlands, and then becomes convolved with the shifting frontiers that separate Spanish, Dutch, and German states.

Another ten leagues east of the Meuse lies the city of Nancy, which is on the river Moselle. That river likewise flows north, but it sweeps eastwards after skirting the Duchy of Luxembourg, and empties into the Rhine between Mainz and Cologne. Or at least that is what I recollect from gazing at the maps in the library at St. Cloud. I did not think it politic to take any of them with me!

Continuing east beyond Nancy toward the Rhine, then, the maps depicted twenty or thirty leagues of jumbled and confused territory: an archipelago of small isolated counties and bishoprics, crumbs of land that belonged to the Holy Roman Empire until the Thirty Years' War. Eventu-

ally one reaches Strasbourg, which is on the Rhine. Louis
XIV seized it some years ago. In some sense this event created me, for the plague and chaos of Strasbourg drew Jack
there, and later the prospects of a fine barley-harvest and its
inevitable result——war——drew him to Vienna where he
met me. I wonder if I will complete the circle by journeying
as far as Strasbourg now. If so, I shall complete another circle at the same time, for it was from that city that Liselotte
crossed into France seventeen years ago to marry Monsieur, never to return to her homeland.

JOURNAL ENTRY
30 AUGUST 1688

At St.-Dizier I changed back into the clothes of a gentle-
woman and lodged at a convent. It is one of those convents
where women of quality go to live out their lives after
they've failed, or declined, to get married. In its ambience it
is closer to a bordello than a nunnery. Many of the inmates
are not even thirty years old, and never so lusty; when they
cannot sneak men inside, they sneak out, and when they
cannot sneak out, they practice on one another. Liselotte
knew some of these girls when they were at Versailles and
has continued to correspond with them. She sent letters
ahead telling them that I was a sort of shirt-tail relative of
hers, a member of her household, and that I was traveling
to the Palatinate to pick up certain art-objects and family
curios that Liselotte was supposed to have inherited upon
the death of her brother, but which had been the subject of
lengthy haggling and disputation with her half-siblings.

Since it is inconceivable for a woman to undertake such a journey herself, I was to bide at the convent in St.-Dizier until my escort arrived: some minor nobleman of the Palatinate who would journey to this place with horses and a carriage to collect me, then convey me northeastwards across Lorraine, and the incomprehensible tangle of borders east of it, to Heidelberg. My identity and mission are false, but the escort is real——for needless to say, the people of the Palatinate are as eager to know their fate as their captive Queen, Liselotte.

As of this writing my escort has not arrived, and no word has been heard of him. I am anxious that they have been detained or even killed, but for now there is nothing for me to do but go to Mass in the morning, sleep in the afternoon, and carouse with the nuns in the night-time.

I was making polite conversation with the Mother Superior, a lovely woman of about threescore who turns a blind eye to the young women's comings and goings. She mentioned in passing that there are iron works nearby, and this caused me to doubt my own judgment concerning those slow-rolling *chalands*. Perhaps they were only carrying iron, and not lead. But later I went out on the town with some of the younger girls, and we passed within view of the riverfront, where a *chaland* was being unloaded. Barrels were being rolled off and stacked along the quay, and heavy ox-carts were standing by waiting. I asked these girls if this was typical, but they affect complete ignorance of practical matters and were of no use at all.

Later I claimed I was tired, and went to my allotted cell as if to sleep. But instead I changed into my boy-clothes and sneaked out of the convent using one of the well-worn

escape-routes used by nuns going to trysts in the town. This
time I was able to get much closer to the quay, and to observe the *chaland* from between two of the barrels that had
been taken from it earlier. And indeed I saw small but massive objects being lifted up out of its bilge and loaded onto
those ox-carts. Overseeing the work was a man whose face I
could not see, but of whom much could be guessed from his
clothing. About his boots were certain nuances that I had
begun to notice in the boots of Monsieur's lovers shortly
before my departure from St. Cloud. His breeches——

No. By the time anyone reads these words, fashions will
have changed, and so it would be a waste of time for me to
enumerate the details——suffice it to say that everything
he wore had to have been sewn in Paris within the last
month.

My observations were cut short by the clumsiness of a
few Vagabonds who had crept down to the quay hoping to
pilfer something. One of them leaned against a barrel, assuming it was full and would support his weight, but being
empty it tilted away from him and then, when he sprang
back, came down with a hollow boom. Instantly the
courtier whipped out his sword and pointed it at me, for he
had spied me peering at him between barrels, and several
men came running towards me. The Vagabonds took off at
a run and I followed them, reasoning that they would know
better than I how to disappear into this town. And indeed
by vaulting over certain walls and crawling down certain
gutters they very nearly disappeared from me, who was but
a few paces behind them.

Eventually I followed them as far as a church-yard,
where they had set up a little squat in a tangle of vines grow-

ing up the side of an ancient mausoleum. They made no effort either to welcome me or to chase me away, and so I
hunkered down in the darkness a few paces off, and listened
to them mutter. Much of their zargon was incomprehensible, but I could discern that there were four of them. Three
seemed to be making excuses, as if resigned to whatever fate
awaited them. But the fourth was frustrated, he had the energy to be critical of the others, and to desire some improvement in their situation. When this one got up and
stepped aside for a piss, I rose and drew a little closer to him
and said, "Meet me alone at the corner of the convent
where the ivy grows," and then I darted away, not knowing
whether he might try to seize me.

An hour later I was able to observe him from the parapet
of the convent. I threw him a coin and told him that he
would receive ten more of the same if he would follow the
ox-carts, observe their movements, and report back to me
in three days. He receded into the darkness without saying a
word.

The next morning the Mother Superior delivered a letter to one of the girls, explaining that it had been left at the
gate the night before. The recipient took one look at the
seal and exclaimed, "Oh, it is from my dear cousin!" She
opened it with a jerk and read it then and there, pronouncing half the words aloud, as she was barely literate. The import seemed to be that her cousin had passed through
St.-Dizier the night before but very much regretted he'd
not been able to stop in for a visit, as his errand was very
pressing; however, he expected to be in the area for some
time, and hoped that he would have the opportunity to see
her soon.

When she pulled the letter open, the disc of wax sealing
it shut popped off and rolled across the floor under a chair.
As she was reading the letter I went over and picked it up.
The coat of arms pressed into that seal was one I did not
fully recognize, but certain elements were familiar to me
from my time at Versailles——I could guess that he was
related to a certain noble family of Gascony, well known for
its military exploits. It seemed safe to assume he was the
gentleman I'd spied on the quay the night before.

JOURNAL ENTRY
2 SEPTEMBER 1688

CRYPTANALYST'S NOTE: *In the original, the section below
contains considerable detail about the cargoes being unloaded
from the* chalands *at St.-Dizier, and the coats of arms and
insignias of persons that the Countess observed there, all of
which were no doubt of greater interest to the Prince of
Orange than they can be to your majesty. I have elided them.
——B.R.*

A slow three days at the convent of St.-Dizier have given me
more than enough time to catch up on my embroidery!
With any luck my Vagabond will come back tonight with
news. If I have received no word from the Palatinate by tomorrow I shall have little choice but to strike out on my
own, though I have no idea how to manage it.

I have tried to make what use I could of this fallow time,
as I did on the *chaland*. During the days I have tried to
make conversation with Eloise, the girl who received the

letter. This has been difficult because she is not very intelligent and we have few interests in common. I let it be known that I have been at Versailles and St. Cloud recently. In time, word reached her of this, and she began to sit near me at meals, and to ask if I knew this or that person there, and what had become of so-and-so. So at last I have learned who she is, and who her well-dressed cousin is: the Chevalier d'Adour, who has devoted his last several years to currying favor with Maréchal Louvois, the King's commander-in-chief. He distinguished himself in the recent massacres of Protestants in the Piedmont and, in sum, is the sort who might be entrusted with a mission of some importance.

In the evenings I have tried to keep an eye on the river-front. Several more *chalands* have been unloaded there, in the same style as the first.

JOURNAL ENTRY
5 SEPTEMBER 1688

Suddenly so much happened I could not tend to my embroidery for a few days. I am catching up on it now, in a carriage on a bumpy road in the Argonne. This type of writing has more advantages to a peripatetic spy than I appreciated at first. It would be impossible for me to write with pen and ink here. But needlework I can just manage.

To say it quickly, my young Vagabond came back and earned his ten silver pieces by informing me that the heavy ox-carts carrying the cargo from the *chalands* were being driven east, out of France and into Lorraine, circumventing Toul and Nancy on forest tracks, and then continuing east to Alsace, which is France again [the Duchy of Lorraine being flanked by France to both east and west]. My Vagabond had been forced, for lack of time, to turn round and come back before he could follow the carts all the way to their destination, but it is obvious enough that they are bound towards the Rhine. He heard from a wanderer he met on the road that such carts were converging from more than one direction on the fortress of Haguenau, which lately had been a loud and smoky place. This man had fled the area because the troops had been press-ganging any idlers they could find, putting them to work chopping down trees——little ones for firewood and big ones for lumber. Even the shacks of the Vagabonds were being chopped up and burnt.

After hearing this news I did not sleep for the rest of the night. If my recollection of the maps was right, Haguenau is on a tributary of the Rhine, and is part of the *barrière de fer* that Vauban built to protect France from the Germans, Dutch, Spanish, and other foes. Supposing that I was right in thinking that the cargo was lead; then the meaning of what I'd just been told was that it was being melted down at Haguenau and made into musket- and cannon-balls. This would explain the demand for firewood. But why did they also require lumber? I guessed it was to build barges that could carry the ammunition down to the Rhine. The current would then take them downstream into the Palatinate in a day or two.

Certain things I had noticed at Court now became imbued with new meanings. The Chevalier de Lorraine—— lord of the lands over which the ox-carts passed en route to Haguenau——has long been the most senior of Mon-

sieur's lovers, and the most cruel and implacable of
Madame's tormentors. In theory he is a vassal of the Holy
Roman Emperor, of which Lorraine is still a tributary
state, but in practice he has become completely surrounded
by France——one cannot enter or leave Lorraine without
traveling over territory that is ruled from Versailles. This
explains why he spends all his time in the French Court instead of Vienna.

Conventional wisdom has it that the duc d'Orleans was
raised to be effeminate and passive so that he would never
pose a threat to his older brother's kingship. One might
suppose that the Chevalier de Lorraine, who routinely penetrates Monsieur, and who rules his affections, has thereby
exploited a vulnerability in the ruling dynasty of France.
That, again, is the conventional wisdom at Court. But now
I was seeing it in a different light. One cannot penetrate
without being encompassed, and the Chevalier de Lorraine
is encompassed by Monsieur just as his territory has been
encompassed by France. Louis invades and penetrates, his
brother seduces and surrounds, they share a common will,
they complement each other as brothers should. I see a homosexual who makes a sham marriage and spurns his wife
for the love of a man. But Louis sees a brother who will
fight a sham war in the Palatinate, supposedly to defend his
wife's claim on that territory, while using his lover's fief-
dom as a highway to transport matériel to the front.

When these three——Monsieur, Madame, and the
Chevalier——were packed off to St. Cloud on short notice
a few weeks ago, I assumed it was because the King had
grown sick of their squabbling. But now I perceive that the
King thinks in metaphors, and that he had to put them all

together, like animals in a baiting-ring, to bring their conflict to a head, before undertaking his military campaign. Just as the domestic squabbles of Jupiter and Juno were thought by the Romans to be manifested in thunderstorms, so the squalid triangle of St. Cloud will be manifested as war in the Palatinate. Louis' empire, which now is interrupted in the Argonne, will be extended across and down the Rhine, as far as Mannheim and Heidelberg, and when domestic tranquillity is finally restored to St. Cloud, France will be two hundred miles wider, and the *barrière de fer* will run across burnt territory where German-speaking Protestants used to dwell.

All of this came together in my head in an instant, but then I lay awake until dawn fretting over what I should do. Weeks before, I had made up a little metaphor of my own, concerning two dogs named Phobos and Deimos, and put it in a letter to d'Avaux in the hopes that the Prince of Orange's spies would read it, and understand its message. At the time I'd thought myself very clever. But now my metaphor seemed childish and inane compared to that of Louis. Worse, its message was ambiguous——for its entire point was that I could not be sure, yet, whether Louvois intended to attack northwards into the Dutch Republic, or draw back, wheel round to the east, and launch himself across the Rhine. Now I felt sure I knew the answer, and needed to get word to the Prince of Orange. But I was stuck in a convent in St.-Dizier and had nothing to base my report on, save Vagabond hearsay, as well as a conviction in my own mind that I had understood the mentality of the King. And even this might evaporate like dew in a few hours, as the fears of the night-time so often do in the morning.

I was on the verge of becoming a Vagabond myself, and striking out on the eastern road, when a spattered and dusty carriage pulled up in front of the convent, just before morning Mass, and a gentleman knocked on the door and asked for me under the false name I'd adopted.

That gentleman and I were on our way as soon as his team could be fed and watered. He is Dr. Ernst von Pfung, a long-suffering gentleman scholar of Heidelberg. When he was a boy, his homeland was occupied and ravaged by the Emperor's armies; at the end of the Thirty Years' War, when the Palatinate was handed over to the Winter Queen in the peace settlement, his family helped them establish their royal household in what remained of Heidelberg Castle. So he has known Sophie and her siblings for a long time. He got all of his education, including a doctorate of jurisprudence, at Heidelberg. He served as an advisor to Charles Louis [the brother of Sophie, and father of Liselotte] when he was Elector Palatinate, and later tried to exert some sort of steadying influence on Liselotte's elder brother Charles when he succeeded to the Electoral throne. But this Charles was daft, and only wanted to conduct mock-sieges at his Rhine castles, using rabble like Jack as his "soldiers." At one of these, he caught a fever and died, precipitating the succession dispute on which the King of France now hopes to capitalize.

Dr. von Pfung, whose earliest and worst memories are of Catholic armies burning, raping, and pillaging his homeland, is beside himself with worry that the same thing is about to happen all over again, this time with French instead of Imperial troops. The events of the last few days have done nothing to reassure him.

Between Heidelberg and the Duchy of Luxembourg, the Holy Roman Empire forms a hundred-mile-wide salient that protrudes southwards into France, almost as far as the River Moselle. It is called the Saarland and Dr. von Pfung, as a petty noble of the Empire, is accustomed to being able to travel across it freely and safely. As it gets closer to Lorraine, this territory becomes fragmented into tiny principalities. By threading his way between them Dr. von Pfung had intended to make safe passage to Lorraine, which is technically part of the Empire. A brief transit across Lorraine would have brought him across the French border very close to St.-Dizier.

Fortunately Dr. von Pfung has the wisdom and foresight one would expect in a man of his maturity and erudition. He had not simply assumed that his plan would work out, but had sent riders out a few days in advance to scout the territory. When they had not returned, he had set out anyway, hoping for the best; but very shortly he had met one of them on the road, returning with gloomy tidings. Certain obstacles had been discovered, of a complicated nature that Dr. von Pfung declined to explain. He had ordered a volte-face and ridden south down the east bank of the Rhine as far as the city of Strasbourg, where he had crossed over into Alsace, and from there he made his way as fast as he could. As a gentleman he is entitled to bear arms, and he has not been slow to take advantage of that right, for in addition to the rapier on his hip he has a pair of pistols and a musket inside the carriage. We are accompanied by two out-riders: young gentlemen similarly armed. At every inn and river-crossing they have had to force their way through by bluff and bluster, and the strain is showing on Dr. von Pfung's face; after we left the precincts of St.-Dizier he very courteously excused himself, removed his wig to reveal a bald pate fringed with gray, leaned back next to an open window, and rested his eyes for a quarter of an hour.

The journey has left him *suspecting* much but *knowing* nothing, which puts him in the same predicament as I. When he had revived, I put a suggestion to him: "I hope you will not think me forward, Doctor, but it seems to me that vast consequences balance on the intelligence that we collect, or fail to, in the next days. You and I have each used all the craft and wit that we could muster, and only skirted the matter. Could it be that we must now relax our grip on Subtlety, and fling our arms around Courage, and strike for the heart of this thing?"

Contrary to what I had expected, these words eased and softened the face of Dr. von Pfung. He smiled, revealing a finely carven set of teeth, and nodded once, in a sort of bow. "I had already resolved to gamble my life on it," he admitted. "If I have seemed nervous or distracted to you, it is because I could not see my way clear to risking *yours* as well. And it makes me uneasy still, for you have much more life ahead of you than I do. But——"

"Say no more, we must not waste our energies on this sort of idle talk," I said. "It is decided——we'll roll the dice. What of your escorts?"

"Those young men are officers of a cavalry regiment——probably the first to be cut down when Louvois invades. They are men of honor."

"Your driver?"

"He has been in the service of my family his whole life and would never permit me to journey, or to die, alone."

"Then I propose we strike out for the Meuse, which ought to lie two or three days' hard riding east of here, on the far side of the forest Argonne."

As quickly as that, Dr. von Pfung rapped on the ceiling and instructed the driver to keep the sun on his right hand through most of the coming day. The driver naturally fell onto those eastward roads that seemed most heavily traveled, and so we ended up following the deep wheel-ruts that had been scored across the ground by the heavy ox-carts in preceding days.

We'd not been on the road for more than a few hours before we overtook a whole train of them, laboring up a long grade between the valleys of the Marne and the Ornain. By taking advantage of occasional wide places in the road, our driver was able to pass these carts one at a time. Peering out through the carriage windows, Dr. von Pfung and I could now plainly see that the carts were laden with pigs of a gray metal that might have been iron——but as there was not a speck of rust on any of them, they must have been lead. Reader, I hope you will not think me silly and girlish if I confess that I was pleased and excited to see my suspicions borne out and my cleverness proven at last. But a glance at the face of Dr. von Pfung crushed any such emotions, for he looked like a man who has returned home in the night-time to discover flames and smoke billowing from the windows of his own house.

At the head of the train rode a French cavalry officer, looking as if he had just been condemned to serve a hundred-year stint in Purgatory. He made no effort to hail us and so we quickly left him and his column far to the rear. But our hopes of making up for lost time were quashed by the nature of the terrain. The Argonne is a broad ridge running from north to south, directly across our path, and in many places the ground drops away into deep river-courses. Where the terrain is level, it is densely forested. So one has no choice but to follow the roads and to make use of the fords and bridges provided, be they never so congested and tumbledown.

But the sight of that miserable young officer had given me an idea. I asked Dr. von Pfung to close his eyes, and made him promise not to peek. This intimidated him to such a degree that he simply climbed down out of the carriage and walked alongside it for a while. I changed out of the drab habit of the nunnery and into a dress I had brought along. At Versailles this garment would scarce have been fit to mop the floor with. Here in the Argonne Forest, though, it rated as a significant Fire Hazard.

A few hours later, as we descended into the valley of a smaller river called the Ornain, we overtook another train of lead-bearing ox-carts, which was picking its way down the grade with an infinity of cursing, collisions, and splintering wood. Just as before, there was a young officer riding at the head. He looked every bit as miserable as the first one——until I popped out of the carriage window, and almost out of my dress. Once he got over his astonishment, he almost wept with gratitude. It made me happy to give this poor man such pleasure, and by nothing more than putting on a dress and opening a window. His mouth fell open in a way that reminded me of a fish; so I resolved to go fishing. "Excuse me, Monsieur, but can you tell me where I might find my uncle?"

At this his mouth opened a little wider, and his face reddened. "Mademoiselle, I am ever so sorry, but I do not know him."

"That is impossible! Every officer knows him!" I tried.

"Pardon me, Mademoiselle, but you have mistaken my meaning. No doubt, your uncle is a great man whose name I would recognize, and honor, if I heard it——but I am too foolish and ignorant to know who *you* are, and consequently I do not know *which* great man has the privilege of being your uncle."

"I thought you would know who I was!" I pouted. The officer looked extremely dismayed. "I am——" Then I turned around and slapped Dr. von Pfung lightly on the arm. "Stop it!" Then, to the officer: "My chaperone is an old fart who will not allow me to introduce myself."

"Indeed, Mademoiselle, for a young lady to introduce herself to a young man would be unpardonable."

"Then we shall have to conduct our conversation *incognito*, and say it never happened——as if it were a lovers' tryst," I said, leaning a bit farther out the window, and beckoning him to ride a little closer. I was afraid he would swoon and get himself wrapped around the axle of our carriage. He maintained his balance with some effort, though, and drew so close that I was able to reach out and steady myself by putting my hand on the pommel of his saber. In a lower voice I continued: "You have probably guessed that my uncle is a man of very high rank who has been sent out to these parts to execute the will of the King, in coming days."

The officer nodded.

"I was on my way up from Oyonnax, returning to Paris, when I learned he was in these parts, and I have decided to

find his camp and pay him a surprise visit, and neither you
nor my chaperone nor anyone else can prevent it! I just
need to know where to find his headquarters."

"Mademoiselle, is your uncle the Chevalier d'Adour?"

I adopted the look of one who has been gagged with the
handle of a spoon.

"Of course not, I didn't really think so . . . neither are
you of the House of Lorraine, I gather, or you would not
need directions . . . is it Étienne d'Arcachon? No, forgive
me, he has no siblings and could not have a niece. But I see
from the softening of your beautiful face, Mademoiselle,
that I am drawing nearer the truth. The only one in these
parts who is above the young Arcachon in rank is the
Maréchal de Louvois himself. And I do not know whether
he has yet come south from the Dutch front . . . but when
he does, you may look for him along the banks of the
Meuse. Provided, that if you ask for him there, and learn
that he has already disembarked, you will have to follow his
track eastwards into the Saarland."

That conversation occurred the day before yesterday, and
we have done nothing since then but toil eastwards through
the woods. It has had the air of a funeral procession, for as
soon as Dr. von Pfung heard the name of Louvois, all doubt
vanished that the Palatinate was to be invaded. But the officer who uttered that name might have been guessing, or
passing on a baseless rumor, or telling me what he thought I
wanted to hear. We must see this thing through and view in-
controvertible evidence with our own eyes.

As I write this we are descending another long tedious
grade into what must be the valley of the Meuse. From here

that river flows up through the Ardennes and across the Spanish Netherlands into the territory along the Dutch border where the best regiments of the French Army have long been encamped to menace William's flank and pin down the Dutch Army.

> CRYPTANALYST'S NOTE: *At this point the account becomes badly disjointed. The countess blundered into the midst of your majesty's army and had an adventure, which she did not have the leisure to write down. Later, as she was fleeing north in the direction of Nijmegen, she made a few cryptic notes as to what had happened. These are intermingled with more lengthy espionage reports listing the regiments and officers she observed moving south to join your majesty's forces along the Rhine. I have been able to reconstruct the Countess's actions, and thereby to make some sense of her notes, by interviewing several of the persons who saw her in the French camp. The narrative that follows is incomparably more discursive than what appears in her needlework but I believe that it is accurate, and I hope that it will be more informative, and therefore more pleasing, to your majesty than the original. At the same time, I have removed all of the Countess's tedious lists of battalions, et cetera. ——B.R.*

JOURNAL ENTRY
7 SEPTEMBER 1688

I am riding north post-haste and can only jot down a few words during pauses to change horses. The carriage is lost. The driver and Dr. von Pfung are dead. I am traveling with

the two cavalrymen from Heidelberg. As I write these
words we are in a village beside the Meuse, near Verdun I
believe. Now I'm told we must ride again.

It is later, and I think we are near where France, the
Duchy of Luxembourg, and the Spanish Netherlands come
together. We have had to strike up away from the Meuse
and into the forest. Between here and Liège, which lies
some hundred miles to the north, the river does not run in
a direct line, but makes a lengthy excursion to westward,
running for much of the way through French lands. This
makes it perfectly suited to serve as a conduit for French
military traffic from the north, but bad for us. Instead we
shall attempt to traverse the Ardennes [as these woods are
called] northwards.

JOURNAL ENTRY
8 SEPTEMBER 1688

Catching our breath and rubbing our saddle-sores along a
riverbank while Hans looks for a ford. Will try to explain as
I go along.

When we at last reached the Meuse, three days ago [had
to count on my fingers, as it seems nearer three weeks!], we
immediately saw the evidence we had been looking for.
Thousands of ancient trees felled, valley full of smoke,
landing-stages improvised on the riverbank. Vanguards of
the regiments from the Dutch front had come upriver,
made rendezvous with officers sent out from Versailles, and
begun preparations to receive the regiments themselves.

For many hours Dr. von Pfung did not say a word. When he did, only slurred meaningless sounds came from his mouth, and I understood that he had suffered a stroke.

I asked him if he wanted to turn back and he only shook his head no, pointed to me, and then pointed north.

Everything had fallen apart. Until that moment I had presumed that we were operating according to some coherent plan of Dr. von Pfung's, but now in retrospect I understood that we had been plunging into danger heedlessly, like a man carried into a battlefield by a wild horse. I could not think at all for a while. I am ashamed to report that because of this failure we blundered into the camp of a cavalry regiment. A captain rapped on the door of the carriage and demanded that we explain ourselves.

It was already obvious to them that most of our party were German-speaking, and it would not take long for them to understand that Dr. von Pfung and the others were of the Palatinate; this would mark us as enemy spies and lead to the worst imaginable consequences.

During my long journey up the Marne on the *chaland* I had had plenty of time to imagine bad outcomes, and had concocted and rehearsed several false stories to tell my captors in the event I should be caught spying. But looking into the face of that captain, I was no more able to tell tales than the stricken Dr. von Pfung. The problem lay in that this operation was on a much vaster scale than either Liselotte or I had imagined, and many more people of Court rank were involved; for all I knew, some Count or Marquis might be nearby, with whom I had dined or danced at Versailles, and who would recognize me the moment I got out of the carriage. To adopt some made-up name and elaborate some tale would amount to confessing that I was a spy.

So I told the truth. "Do not look to this man to make introductions, for he has suffered a stroke, and lost the faculty of speech," I said to the astonished captain. "I am Eliza, Countess de la Zeur, and I am here in the service of Elisabeth Charlotte, the Duchess of Orleans and rightful inheritor of the Palatinate. It is in her name you are about to invade that land. It is she whom my escorts serve, for they are Court officials of Heidelberg. And it is she who has sent me here, as her personal representative, to look into your operations and ensure that the right thing is done."

This bit of nonsense, "that the right thing is done," was a list of dead words I tacked on to the end of the sentence because I did not know what to say, and was losing my nerve. For even when I stood beneath the Emperor's palace in Vienna, waiting to feel the blade of a Janissary's scimitar biting into my neck, I had not felt so uncertain as I did there. But I think the very vagueness of my words had a great effect on this captain, for he stepped back from the window and bowed deeply, and proclaimed that he would send word of my arrival to his superiors without delay.

Hans has come back saying he has found a place where we may attempt to ford this river and so I will only narrate that in due course, word of our arrival was passed up the chain of command until it reached a man whose rank at Court was high enough that he could entertain me without violating any rules of precedence. That man turned out to be Étienne d'Arcachon.

JOURNAL ENTRY
10 SEPTEMBER 1688

They think we are somewhere around Bastogne. Have been
unable to do needlework for some while as our day-to-day
affairs have pressed in on us sorely. The Ardennes Forest is
crowded with Vagabonds and highwaymen [and, some say,
witches and goblins] at the best of times. To these have now
been added a large number of deserters from the French
regiments that are being moved southwards. They jump off
the slow-moving barges and wade to the bank and infiltrate
the forest. We have had to move carefully and to post
watches all night long. I am making these notes on my
watch. To sit by a crackling fire would be folly and so I am
perched up in the fork of a tree, wrapped up in blankets,
sewing by moonlight.

Men who have weathered terrible trials are wont to have
dull and useless children to demonstrate their power, as
rich Arabs grow their fingernails long. So with the duc d'Arcachon and his only legitimate son, Étienne. The Duke survived the bad dream of the Fronde Rebellion and built a
navy for the King. Étienne has chosen a career in the Army;
this is his notion of youthful rebellion.

It is said of some men that "he would cut off his right
arm before doing thus-and-such." Of Étienne, it used to be
said that he would sacrifice a limb before violating the
smallest rule of etiquette. But now people say, rather, that
he actually *did* cut off his right arm out of politeness, for
several years ago something happened at a party to that
general effect——accounts vary, for I get the impression it
was in some way disgraceful to his family. At any rate the

details are unknown to me, but the tale rings true. He has become a great patron of woodcarvers and silversmiths, whom he pays to make artificial hands for him. Some of them are shockingly lifelike. The hand he extended to help me down out of the carriage was carved of ivory with finger-nails fashioned from mother-of-pearl. When we dined on roast grouse in his quarters, he had switched to a hand of carven ebony, permanently gripping a serrated knife, which he used to cut his meat, though it looked as if it would have made an excellent weapon, too! And after dinner, when he undertook to seduce me, he wore a special hand carved out of jade, with an extremely oversized middle finger. That digit was, in fact, a perfect reproduction of a man's erect phallus. As such it was nothing I had not already seen in various private "art" collections in and around Versailles, for lords, and even ladies, love to have such things in their private chambers, as proof of their sophistication, and many of their rooms are veritable Shrines to the god Pria-pus. But I was caught unawares by a hidden feature of this hand: it must have been hollow, and stuffed with clockwork, for when Étienne d'Arcachon tripped a hidden lever, it sud-denly came alive, and began to hum and buzz like a hornet in a bottle. Inside, it seemed, was a coil spring that had been tightly wound in advance.

I need hardly tell you, reader, that events of the past few days had left me rather tightly wound myself, and I can as-sure you that the tension was gone from my body long be-fore it was gone from the spring.

You may despise me for having reveled in fleshly plea-sure while Dr. von Pfung was laid out with a stroke, but to have been pent up in a stifling carriage with a dying man for all that time had left me with a ravening to partake of life. I closed my eyes at the moment of climax and fell back onto the bed, exhausting my lungs in a long cry, and feeling all tension drain from my body. Étienne executed some deft maneuver of which I was scarcely aware. When I opened my eyes, I found that the jade phallus had been withdrawn and replaced by a real one, that of Étienne d'Arcachon. Again, you may well doubt my judgment in allowing myself to be taken in this way. That is your prerogative. Indeed, to marry such a man would be a grievous error. But in looking for a lover, one could do worse than a man who is clean, extremely polite, and has a madly vibrating jade phallus for a right forefinger. The warmth of his trunk felt good against my thighs; it did not occur to me to object; before I could really consider my situation, I realized that he was already climaxing inside of me.

JOURNAL ENTRY
12 SEPTEMBER 1688

Still in the damnable Ardennes, creeping northwards, pausing from time to time to observe the movements of the French battalions. These woods cannot possibly go on much farther. At least we have grown accustomed to the territory now, and know how to make our way. But at times we seem to move no faster than mice chewing their way through wood.

When I woke up in the bed of Étienne d'Arcachon the next morning, he had, in typical fashion, already left; but somewhat less typically, he had written me a love-poem and left it on the bedside table.

Some ladies boast of ancient pedigrees
And prate about their ancestors a lot
But cankers flourish on old family trees
Whose mossy trunks do oft conceal rot.

My lady's blood runs pure as mountain streams
So I don't care if her high rank was bought
Her beauty lends fresh vigor to my dreams
Of children free of blemish and of blot.

His quarters was a little château on the east bank of the Meuse. Out the window I could see Belgian river-boats——variously leased, borrowed, bought, or comman-deered——coming upstream, their decks crowded with French soldiers. I dressed and went downstairs to find Dr. von Pfung's carriage-driver waiting for me.

The night before, I had explained my friend's plight to Étienne d'Arcachon, who had made arrangements for his own personal physician to administer treatment. Having personally witnessed the violence inflicted upon no less a personage than the King of France himself by the Royal Physician, I had assented to this with some ambivalence. Indeed, Dr. von Pfung's driver now informed me that the poor man had been bled twice during the night and was now very weak. He had signalled his desire to return to the Palatinate without delay, in hopes that he might look upon Heidelberg Castle one last time before he went to his long home.

The driver and I both understood that this would be im-possible. According to the tale I had told my host, we were there as forward observers representing Liselotte. If that

were true, we should either stay with the main body, or re-
tire westwards towards St. Cloud——never run ahead of
the invasion force. Yet Dr. von Pfung wanted to do just
that, whereas I needed to strike out for the north and inform the Prince of Orange that his southern flank was soon
to be free of French troops. And so we devised a plan, which
was that our little group would leave that day on the pretext
of taking Dr. von Pfung back to the west, but that when conditions were right, the carriage would break eastwards towards Heidelberg while I would go north accompanied by
the two cavalrymen [who have imposing names and titles
but whom I now call by their Christian names, Hans and
Joachim]. When eyebrows were raised about this later, as
seemed more than likely, I would claim that the others had
turned out to be Protestant spies, working for William of
Orange, and that I had been borne along against my will.

The plan unfolded correctly at first; we crossed the
Meuse again as if going back into the west, but then began
to make our way northwards up the bank, fighting against
an increasing stream of south-bound military traffic. For
since the boats were coming up against the river's current,
most of them were drawn by teams of animals on the banks.

After we had traveled north for about half a day we came
to a ferry, where we resolved to part ways. I went into the
carriage and kissed Dr. von Pfung and said some words to
him——though all words, especially ones improvised in
haste, seemed inadequate, and the doctor managed to say
more with his eyes and his one good hand than I did with
my entire faculties. I changed once again into a man's
clothes, hoping to pass myself off as a page to Hans and
Joachim, and mounted a pony we'd borrowed from the sta-

bles of Étienne d'Arcachon. After some haggling with the
ferryman——who was loath to venture across through the
regimental traffic——the carriage was driven onto the
ferry, its wheels were chocked, the horses hobbled, and the
short voyage across the Meuse began.

They had almost reached the eastern bank when they
were hailed by a French officer on one of the south-bound
vessels. He had perceived, through his spyglass, Dr. von
Pfung's coat of arms painted on the door of the carriage,
and recognized him as coming from the Palatinate.

Now, the driver had a letter from Étienne d'Arcachon
giving him permission to travel *west*——but he had now
been observed crossing the Meuse *eastwards*. His only hope
was therefore to make a run for it. That is what he attempted to do when the ferry reached the east bank. The
only available road ran parallel to the bank for some distance before turning away from the river into a village. He
therefore had to drive along in full view of all the boats
crowding the river, whose decks were thronged with French
musketeers. Some of the boats were armed with swivel-guns
as well. By this time a hue and cry had gone up among the
boats, and there was plenty of time for them to load their
guns as the carriage disembarked from the ferry. The officer had traded his spyglass for a saber, which he raised high,
then brought down as a signal. Instantly, the French boats
were completely obscured in clouds of powder-smoke. The
valley of the Meuse was filled with flocks of birds that
erupted from the trees, startled by the sound of the guns.
The carriage was reduced to splinters, the horses torn
apart, and the fates of the brave driver and his stricken passenger perfectly obvious.

I could have tarried on the spot and wept for a long time, but on this bank were several locals who had seen us arrive in the company of the carriage, and it would not be long before one of them sold that intelligence to the Frenchmen on the river. So we struck out for the north, beginning the journey that continues even as I write these words.

JOURNAL ENTRY
13 SEPTEMBER 1688

The peasants around here say that the lord of the manor is a Bishop. This gives me hope that we are now in the Bishopric of Liège, not terribly far from one of the outlying tendrils of the Dutch Republic. Hans and Joachim have been having a long discussion in German, which I understand but meagerly. One thinks he ought to strike out alone to the East, go to the Rhine, and then double back to the South and warn the Palatinate. The other fears it is too late; there is nothing they can do now for their homeland; it is better to seek revenge by throwing all of their energies behind the Protestant Defender.

Later. The dispute was resolved as follows: we shall ride north past French lines to Maestricht and take passage on a canal-boat down the river to Nijmegen, where the Meuse and the Rhine almost kiss each other. That is some hundred miles north of here, yet it may be a quicker way to reach the Rhine than to cut east cross-country through God knows what perils and complications. In Nijmegen, Hans and Joachim can get the latest news from passengers and boatmen who have lately come down the Rhine from Heidelberg and Mannheim.

It did not take long, once we left our camp near Liège, to pass out of the zone of French military control. We rode over an area of torn-up ground that, until a few days ago, was the permanent camp of a French regiment. Ahead of us are a few French companies left along the border as a façade. They stop and interrogate travelers trying to come in, but ignore those like us who are only trying to pass out towards Maestricht.

JOURNAL ENTRY
15 SEPTEMBER 1688

On a canal-boat bound from Maestricht to Nijmegen. Conditions not very comfortable, but at least we do not have to ride or walk any more. Am renewing my acquaintance with soap.

JOURNAL ENTRY
16 SEPTEMBER 1688

I am in a cabin of a canal-ship making its way west across the Dutch Republic.

I am surrounded by slumbering Princesses.

The Germans have a fondness for faery-tales, or *Märchen* as they call them, that is strangely at odds with their orderly dispositions. Ranged in parallel with their tidy Christian world is the *Märchenwelt*, a pagan realm of ro-

mance, wonders, and magical beings. *Why* they believe in
the *Märchenwelt* has ever been a mystery to me; but I am
closer to understanding it today than I was yesterday. For
yesterday we reached Nijmegen. We went direct to the bank
of the Rhine and I began looking for a canal-boat bound in
the direction of Rotterdam and the Hague. Hans and
Joachim meanwhile canvassed travelers debarking from
boats lately come from upstream. I had no sooner settled
myself in a comfortable cabin on a Hague-bound canal-ship
when Joachim found me; and he had in tow a pair of characters straight out of the *Märchenwelt*. They were not
gnomes, dwarves, or witches, but Princesses: one full-grown
[I believe she is not yet thirty] and one pint-sized [she has
told me three different times that she is five years old].
True to form, the little one carries a doll that she insists is
also a princess.

They do not look like princesses. The mother, whose
name is Eleanor, has something of a regal bearing. But this
was not obvious to me at first, for when they joined me, and
Eleanor noticed a clean bed [mine] and saw that Caroline——for that is the daughter's name——was under my
watch, she fell immediately into [my] bed, went to sleep,
and did not awaken for some hours, by which time the boat
was well underway. I spent much of that time chatting with
little Caroline, who was at pains to let me know she was a
princess; but as she made the same claim of the dirty lump
of stuffed rags she bore around in her arms, I did not pay it
much mind.

But Joachim insisted that the disheveled woman snoring
under my blankets was genuine royalty. I was about to chide
him for having been deluded by mountebanks, when I be-

gan to recollect the tales I had been told of the Winter Queen, who after being driven out of Bohemia by the Pope's legions, wandered about Europe as a Vagabond before finding safe haven at the Hague. And my time at Versailles taught me more than I wished to know about the desperate financial straits in which many nobles and royals live their whole lives. Was it really so unthinkable that three Princesses——mother, daughter, and doll—— should be wandering about lost and hungry on the Nijmegen riverfront? For war had come to this part of the world, and war rends the veil that separates the everyday world from the *Märchenwelt*.

By the time Eleanor woke up, I had mended the doll, and I had been looking after little Caroline for long enough that I felt responsible for her, and would have been willing to snatch her away from Eleanor if the latter had proved, upon awakening, to be some sort of madwoman [this is by no means my usual response to small children, for at Versailles, playing my role as governess, I had been put in charge of many a little snot-nose whose names I have long since forgotten. But Caroline was bright, and interesting to talk to, and a welcome relief from the sorts of people I had been spending time with for the last several weeks].

When Eleanor had arisen, and washed, and eaten some of my provisions, she told a story that was wild but, by modern standards, plausible. She claims to be the daughter of the Duke of Saxe-Eisenach. She married the Margrave of Brandenburg-Ansbach. The daughter is properly called Princess Wilhelmina Caroline of Ansbach. But this Margrave died of smallpox a few years ago and his title passed to a son by an earlier wife, who had always considered Eleanor

to be a sort of wicked stepmother [this being a *Märchen*, after all] and so cast her and little Caroline out of the *Schloß*.
They drifted back to Eisenach, Eleanor's place of birth.
This is a place on the edge of the Thüringer Wald, perhaps
two hundred miles east of where we are now. Her position
in the world at that time, a few years ago, was the reverse of
mine: she had a lofty title, but no property at all. Whereas I
had no titles other than Slave and Vagabond, but I did have
some money. At any rate, she and Caroline were suffered to
dwell in what sounds like a family hunting-lodge in the
Thüringer Wald. But she does not seem to have been much
more welcome in Eisenach than she had been at Ansbach
following the death of her husband. And so, while spending
part of each year at Eisenach, it has been her practice to
roam about and pay extended visits to shirttail relatives all
over northern Europe, moving from time to time lest she
wear out her welcome in any one place.

Recently she paid a brief visit to Ansbach in an effort to
patch things up with her hostile stepson. Ansbach is within
striking distance of Mannheim on the Rhine, and so she
and Caroline next went there to look in on some cousins
who had shown them charity in the past. They arrived, naturally, at the worst possible moment, a few days ago, just as
the French regiments were swarming over the Rhine on
the barges built at Haguenau, and bombarding the defen-
sive works. Someone there had the presence of mind to
pack them on a boat full of well-heeled refugees, bound
down the river. And so they passed quickly out of the area
of danger, though they continued to hear cannon-fire for a
day or more, echoing up the valley of the Rhine. They
reached Nijmegen without incident, though the boat was

so crowded with refugees——some of them with suppurating wounds——that she was unable to take more than the
occasional catnap. When they debarked, Joachim——who
is a Person of Quality in the Palatinate——recognized
them as they stumbled down the gangplank, and brought
them to me.

Now the current of the Rhine slowly flushes us, and a lot
of other war-flotsam, downstream towards the sea. I have
oft heard French and Germans alike speak disparagingly of
the Netherlands, likening the country to a gutter that col-
lects all the refuse and fœces of Christendom, but lacks the
vigor to force it out to sea, so that it piles up in a bar around
Rotterdam. It is a cruel and absurd way to talk about a noble and brave little country. Yet as I look on my condition,
and on that of the Princesses, and review our recent travels
[blundering about in dark and dangerous parts until we
stumbled upon running water, then drifting downstream],
I can recognize a kind of cruel truth in that slander.

We shall not, however, let ourselves be flushed out to
sea. At Rotterdam we divert from the river's natural course
and follow a canal to the Hague. There the Princesses can
find refuge, just as did the Winter Queen at the end of her
wanderings. And there I shall try to deliver a coherent report to the Prince of Orange. This bit of embroidery is ruined before it was finished, but it contains the information
that William has been waiting for. When I have finished my
report I may make it into a pillow. Everyone who sees it will
wonder at my foolishness for keeping such a dirty, stained,
faded thing around the house. But I will keep it in spite of
them. It is an important thing to me now. When I started
it, I only intended to use it to record details of French

troop movements and the like. But as the weeks went on and I frequently found myself with plenty of time on my hands to tend to my needlework, I began to record some of my thoughts and feelings about what was going on around me. Perhaps I did this out of boredom; but perhaps it was so that some part of me might live on, if I were killed or made a captive along the way. This might sound like a foolish thing to have done, but a woman who has no family and few friends is forever skirting the edges of a profound despair, which derives from the fear that she could vanish from the world and leave no trace she had ever existed; that the things she has done shall be of no account and the perceptions she has formed [as of Dr. von Pfung for example] shall be swallowed up like a cry in a dark woods. To write out a full confession and revelation of my doings, as I've done here, is not without danger; but if I did not do so I would be so drowned in melancholy that I would do nothing at all, in which event my life truly would be of no account. This way, at least, I am part of a story, like the ones Mummy used to tell me in the *banyolar* in Algiers, and like the ones that were told by Shahrazad, who prolonged her own life for a thousand and one nights by the telling of tales.

But given the nature of the cypher that I am using, chances are that you, reader, will never exist, and so I cannot see why I should continue running this needle through the dirty old cloth when I am so tired, and the rocking of the boat invites me to close my eyes.

Rossignol to Louis XIV Continued

NOVEMBER 1688

Your majesty will have been dismayed by the foregoing tale of treason and perfidy. If it were generally
known, I fear it would do grave damage to the reputation of your majesty's sister-in-law the duchesse d'Orléans. She is said to be prostrate with grief, and
ungrateful for all that your majesty's legions have
done in order to secure her rights in the Palatinate. Out
of a gentleman's respect for her rank, and humane
compassion for her feelings, I have been as discreet as
possible with this intelligence which could only bring
her further suffering if it were known. I have shared
the foregoing account only with your majesty.
D'Avaux has importuned me for a copy, but I have deflected his many requests and will continue to do so
unless your majesty instructs me to send the document
to him.

In the weeks that I have spent in the decypherment
of this document, Phobos and Deimos have been un-
leashed on the east bank of the Rhine. The lead that
the Countess so assiduously followed to the banks of
the Meuse has been conveyed in bulk to the Palatinate,
and ended its long journey traveling at inconceivable
velocities through the bodies and the buildings of
heretics. Half the young blades of Court have quit Versailles to go hunting in Germany, and many of them

write letters, which it is my duty to read. I am told that
Heidelberg Castle burnt brilliantly for days, and that
everyone is looking forward to repeating the experiment in Mannheim. Philippsburg, Mainz, Speier,
Trier, Worms, and Oppenheim are scheduled for later
in the year. As winter draws on, your majesty will be
troubled to learn of all the brutality. You will draw
your forces back, and give Louvois a firm scolding for
having acted so excessively. Historians will record
that the Sun King cannot be held responsible for all of
the unpleasantness.

From your majesty's many excellent sources in England, your majesty will know that the Prince of Orange is now there, commanding an army made up not
only of Dutchmen, but of the English and Scottish regiments that were stationed on Dutch soil by treaty;
Huguenot scum who filtered up from France; mercenaries and freebooters from Scandinavia; and Prus-
sians who've been lent to the cause by Sophie
Charlotte—the daughter of the cursed Hanoverian
bitch Sophie.

All of which only seems to prove that Europe is a
chessboard. Even your majesty cannot gain (say) the
Rhine without sacrificing (say) England. Likewise,
whatever Sophie and William may gain from their
ceaseless machinations they'll have to pay for in the
end. And as for the Countess de la Zeur, why, the new
King of England might make her Duchess of
Qwghlm, but in return your majesty will no doubt see
to it that her sacrifices are commensurate.

M. le comte d'Avaux has redoubled his surveillance
of the Countess in the Hague. He has received assur-
ances from the laundresses who work in the house of
Huygens that she has not bled a single drop of men-
strual blood in the nearly two months she's been there.
She is pregnant with a bastard of Arcachon. She is
therefore now a part of the family of France, of which

your majesty is the patriarch. As it is become a family matter, I will refrain from any further meddling unless your majesty instructs me otherwise.

> I have the honour to be, your majesty's
> humble and obedient servant,
> Bonaventure Rossignol

Sheerness, England
11 DECEMBER 1688

⚜

> Then the Kings countenance was changed,
> and his thoghts troubled him, so that the
> joyntes of his loines were loosed, and his knees
> smote one against the other.
>
> —DANIEL 5:6

ON ANY OTHER DAY, Daniel did not have a thing in common with anyone else at the Court of St. James. Indeed, that was the very reason he was allowed to bide there. Today, though, he had two things in common with them. One, that he had spent most of the preceding night, and most of this day, traipsing all over Kent trying to figure out where the King had got to. And two, that he stood in utmost need of a pint.

Finding himself alone on a boat-flecked mudflat, and happening on a tavern, he entered it. The only thing he sought in that place was that pint and maybe a banger. In additition to which, he found James (by the Grace of God King of England, Scotland, Ireland, and the occasional odd bit of France) Stuart being beaten up by a couple of drunken English fishermen. It was just the sort of grave indignity absolute monarchs tried at all costs to avoid. In normal times, procedures and safeguards were in place to prevent it. One could imagine one of the ancient Kings of England, say, your Sven Forkbeard, or your Ealhmund the Under-King of Kent, wandering into an inn somewhere and throwing a few punches. But barroom brawling had been pushed off the bottom of the list of Things Princes Should Know How to Do during the great Chivalry vogue of five centuries back. And it showed: King James II had a bloody nose. To be fair, though, he'd been having an epic one for weeks. As past generations sang of Richard Lion-heart's duels against Saladin before Jerusalem, future ones would sing of James Stuart's nosebleed.

It was, in sum, not a scenario that had ever been contem-plated by the authors of the etiquette-books that Daniel had perused when he'd gone into the Courtier line of work. He'd have known just how to address the King during a masque at the Banqueting House or a hunt in a royal game-park. But when it came to breaking up a royal bar-fight in a waterfront dive at the mouth of the Medway, he was at a loss, and could only order himself that pint, and consider his next move.

His Majesty was standing up to the treatment surprisingly well. Of course, he'd fought in battles on land and at sea; no one had ever accused him of being a ninehammer. And this altercation was really more of a cuffing and slapping about: not so much fight as improvised entertainment by and for men who got out to Punchinello shows only infrequently. This was a very old tavern, half sunk into the riverside muck, and the ceiling was so close to the floor that the fishermen scarcely had room to draw their fists back properly. There were flurries of jabs that failed to connect with any part of the King's body. The blows that did land were open-handed, roundhouse slaps. Daniel sensed that if the King would only stop flinching, say something funny, and buy a round for the house, everything would change. But if he were that sort of King he wouldn't have ended up here in the first place.

At any rate Daniel was immensely relieved that it was not a serious beating. Otherwise he would've been obliged to draw the sword hanging from his belt, which he had no idea how to use. King James II most certainly *would* know what to do with it, of course. As Daniel plunged his upper lip through the curtain of foam on his pint, he had a moment's phant'sy of unbelting the weapon and tossing it across the room to the sovereign, who'd snatch it from the air, whip it out, and commence slaying subjects. Then Daniel could perhaps embroider 'pon his deed by smashing a bit of crockery over someone's head—better yet, sustain an honorable wound or two. This would guarantee him a free, all-expenses paid, but strictly one-way trip to France, where he'd probably be rewarded with an English earldom that he'd never be able to visit, and get to lounge around in James's exile court all day.

This phant'sy did not last for very long. One of the King's attackers had felt something in His Majesty's coat-pocket and yanked it out: a crucifix. A moment of silence. Those here who were conscious enough to see the object, felt obliged to give it due reverence; either because it was an emblem of Our Lord's passion, or because it was made predominantly out of gold. Through the tavern's atmosphere, which had approximately the mass and consistency of aspic, the artifact gleamed attractively, and even cast off a halo. Descartes had abhorred the idea of a vacuum, and held that what we took to be empty space was really a plenum, a solidly packed ocean of particles, swirling and colliding, trading and trafficking in a fixed stock of movement that had been imparted to the universe at its creation by the Almighty. He must have come up with that idea in a tavern like this one; Daniel wasn't sure a pistol-ball would be able to dig a tunnel through this air from one side of the room to the other.

"What's this, then!?" the fellow holding up the crucifix wanted to know.

James II looked suddenly exasperated. "Why, it is a crucifix!"

Another blank moment passed. Daniel had completely let go of the idea of being an exiled earl at Versailles, and was now feeling uncomfortably rabble-like himself, and strongly tempted to go and take a poke at His Majesty—if only for the sake of Drake, who'd never have hesitated.

"Well, if you're *not* a bleeding Jesuit spy, then why're you bearing this bit o' idolatry about!?" demanded the fellow with the quick hands, shaking the crucifix just out of the King's reach. "Didjer *loot* it? Didjer steal this holy object from a burnin' church, didjer?"

They had no idea who he was. At this the scene made sense for the first time. Until then Daniel had wondered just *who* was suffering from syphilitic hallucinations around here!

James had surprised all London by galloping away from Whitehall Palace after midnight. Someone had caught sight of him hurling the Great Seal of the Realm into the Thames, which was not a wholly usual thing for the Sovereign to do, and with that he'd pelted off into the night, east-bound, and no person of gentle or noble rank had seen him since, until the moment Daniel had blundered into this tavern in search of refreshment.

Mercifully, the urge to sprint over and take a swing at the royal gob had passed. A semi-comatose man, slumped on a bench against the wall, was eyeing Daniel in a way that was not entirely propitious. Daniel reflected that if it was considered meet and proper for a well-heeled stranger to be beaten up and robbed on the mere suspicion that he was a Jesuit, things might not go all that well for Daniel Waterhouse the Puritan.

He drained about half the pint and turned round in the middle of the tavern so that his cloak fell open, revealing the sword. The weapon's existence was noted, with professional interest, by the tavernkeeper, who didn't look directly at it; he was one of those blokes who used peripheral vision for everything. Give him a spyglass, he'd raise it to his ear, and see as much as Galileo. His nose had been broken at least twice and he'd endured a blowout fracture of the left eye-socket, which made it seem as if his face were a clay effigy squirting out between the fingers of a clenching fist. Daniel said to him, "Let your friends understand that if serious harm comes to that gentleman, there lives a witness who'll tell a tale to make a judge's wig uncurl."

And then Daniel stepped out onto a deal boardwalk that might've answered to the name of *verandah* or *pier,* depend-

ing on whence you looked at it. In theory boats of shallow
draught might be poled up to it and made fast, in practice
they'd been drawn up on the muck about a horseshoe-throw
away from the crusty ankles of its pilings. The tracks of the
boatmen were swollen wounds in the mudflat, and spatterings
across the planks. Half a mile out, diverse ships were riding
at anchor in the wide spot where the Medway exhausted into
the Thames. It was low tide! James, the sea-hero, the Admiral
who'd fought the Dutch, and occasionally beaten 'em, who'd
made Isaac Newton's ears ring with the distant roar of his
cannons, had galloped out from London at exactly the wrong
moment. Like King Canute, he would have to wait for the
tide. It was simply too awful. Exhausted from the ride, left
with no choice but to kill a few hours, the King must've wandered into this tavern—and why not? Every place he'd ever
entered into, people had served him on bended knee. But
James, who did not drink and did not curse, who stuttered,
who couldn't speak the English of fishermen, might as well
have been in a Hindoo temple. He'd switched to a dark wig
from the usual blond one, and it had been knocked from his
head early in the scuffle, revealing a half-bald head, thin
yellow-white hair in a Caesar cut, shellacked to his pocked
pate by sweat and grease. Wigs enabled one to avert one's attention from the fact of the wearer's age. Daniel had seen an
odd-looking chap, fifty-five years old, lost.

   Daniel was beginning to feel he had more in common
with this syphilitic Papist despot than with the people of
Sheerness. He did not like where his feelings were taking
him. So he had his feet take him elsewhere—to what passed
for the high street of Sheerness, to an inn, where an uncom-
mon number of well-dressed gentlemen were milling about,
wringing their hands and kicking at the chickens. These
men, Daniel included, had come out from London post-
haste, only a few hours behind their fleeing King, on the pre-
sumption that if the Sovereign had left London, then they
must all be missing something important by tarrying in the
city. Wrong!

* * *

HE WENT IN AND TOLD the tale to Allesbury, the Gentleman
of the Bedchamber, then turned to leave; but practically
ended up with spur-marks in his back, as every courtier
wanted to be first on the spot. In the stable-yard a horse was
brought out for Daniel. Climbing into the saddle, and ascending to the same plane as all the other equestrians, he
noted diverse faces turned his way, none of them looking
very patient. So without sharing in any of the sense of romantic drama that animated all of the others, he rode out
into the street, and led them on a merry gallop back down to
the river. To uninformed bystanders, it must have looked like
a Cavalier hunting-party pursuing a Roundhead, which
Daniel hoped was no prefiguring of events to follow.

When they reached the tavern, an astounding number of
Persons of Quality packed themselves inside, and commenced making stentorian announcements. One might've
expected drunks and ne'er-do-wells to flood out through
windows and trap-doors, like mice fleeing when the lantern
is lit, but not a soul left the building, even after it was made
known that they were all in the Presence. There seemed, in
other words, to be a general failure, among the waterfront
lowlives of Sheerness, to really take the notion of monarchy
seriously.

Daniel lingered outside for a minute or two. The sun was
setting behind a gapped cloud-front and shoving fat rays of
gaudy light across the estuary of the Medway: a big brackish
sump a few miles across, with a coastline as involuted as a
brain, congested with merchant and naval traffic. Most of
the latter huddled sheepishly down at the far end, behind the
chain that was stretched across the river, below the shelter-
ing guns of Upnor Castle. James had for some reason expected William of Orange's fleet to attack there, in the worst
possible place. Instead the Protestant Wind had driven the
Dutchman all the way to Tor Bay, hundreds of miles to the
west—almost Cornwall. Since then the Prince had been
marching steadily eastwards. English regiments marched

forth to stand in his path, only to defect and about-face. If William was not in London yet, he would be soon.

The waterfront people were already reverting to a highly exaggerated Englishness: womenfolk were scurrying toward the tavern, hitching up their skirts to keep 'em out of the muck, so that they glissaded across the tidelands like bales on rails. They were bringing victuals to the King! They hated him and wanted him gone. But that was no reason to be inhospitable. Daniel had reasons to tarry—he felt he should go in and say good-bye to the King. And, to be pragmatic, he was fairly certain he could be charged with horse-thievery if he turned this mount towards London.

On the other hand, he had another hour of twilight, and the low tide could cut a few hours off the time it would take him to work his way round the estuary, cross the river, and find the high road to London. He had the strongest feeling that important things were happening there; and as for the King, and his improvised Court here at Sheerness: if the local pub scum couldn't bring themselves to take him seriously, why should the Secretary of the Royal Society? Daniel aimed his horse's backside at the King of England and then spurred the animal forward into the light.

Since the time of the Babylonian astronomers, solar eclipses had from time to time caused ominous shadows to fall upon the land. But England in winter sometimes afforded its long-suffering populace a contrary phenomenon, which was that after weeks of dim colorless skies, suddenly the sun would scythe in under the clouds after it had seemed to set, and wash the landscape with pink, orange, and green illumination, clear and pure as gems. Empiricist though he was, Daniel felt free to ascribe meaning to this when it went his way. Ahead all was clear light, as if he were riding into stained glass. Behind (and he only bothered to look back once) the sky was a bruise-colored void, the land a long scrape of mud. The tavern rose up from the middle of the waste on a sheaf of pilings that leaned into each other like a crowd of drunks. Its plank walls pawed a bit of light out of the sky, its one window glowed like a carbuncle. It was the sort of grotesque sky-scape that Dutchmen would come over to paint. But come to think of it, a Dutchman *had* come over and painted it.

MOST TRAVELERS WOULD TAKE LITTLE note of Castle Up-nor. It was but a stone fort, built by Elizabeth a hundred years ago, but looking much older—its vertical stone walls obsolete already. But since the Restoration it had been the nominal seat of Louis Anglesey, the Earl of Upnor, and own-er of the fair Abigail Frome (or at least Daniel presumed she was fair). As such it gave Daniel the shudders; he felt like a little boy riding past a haunted house. He'd have gone wide of it if he could, but the ferry next to it was by far the most expeditious way of crossing the Medway, and this was no time to let superstition take him out of his way. The alterna-tive would've been to ride a few miles up the east bank to the huge naval shipyard of Chatham, where there were several ways of getting across. But passing through a naval base did not seem the most efficient way of getting around, during a foreign invasion.

He pretended to give his horse a few minutes' rest at the ferry landing, and did what half-hearted spying he could. The sun was positively down now and everything was dark blue on a backdrop of even darker blue. The Castle fronted on the west bank of the river and was buried in its own shadow. However, lights were burning in some of the win-dows, and particularly in the outbuildings. A sharp two-masted vessel was anchored in the dredged channel nearby.

When the Dutch had sailed up here in '67 and, over the course of a leisurely three-day rampage, stolen some of Charles II's warships and burned diverse others, Castle Upnor had acquitted itself reasonably well, declining to surrender and taking pot-shots at any Dutchmen who'd come anywhere near close enough. The Earl of Upnor, whose travails with gambling debts and Popish Plot hysteria still lay in the future, had picked up some reflected luster. But to have one's chief Navy Yard infested with Dutchmen was embarrassing even to a foreign-policy slut like Charles II. So modern defenses with proper earthworks had since been put up in the neighborhood, and Upnor had been demoted to the status of a giant powder-magazine, sort of an outlying gunpowder depot for the Tower of London—the unspoken message being that no one cared if it blew up. Powder-barges came hither frequently from the Tower and moored in the place claimed, tonight, by that two-master. Daniel knew only a little of ships, but even a farmer could see that this one had several cabins astern, well-appointed with windows, and lights burning behind their drawn curtains and closed shutters. Louis Anglesey hardly ever came to this place, as why should any Earl in his right mind go to a dank stone pit to sit upon powder-kegs? And yet in times of trouble there were worse places to bolt. Those stone walls might not stop Dutch cannonballs, but they would keep Protestant mobs at bay for weeks, and the river was only a few steps away; once he stepped off the quay and boarded his boat, Upnor was as good as in France.

There were a few watchmen posted about the place, hugging their pikes to their chests so they could keep their hands stuffed into their armpits, shooting the breeze, mostly gazing outwards towards the Roman road, occasionally turning round to enjoy some snatch of domestic comedy playing itself out within the walls. Potato peels and chicken feathers were bobbing in the river's back-waters, and he caught whiffs of yeast on the breeze. There was, in other words, a functioning household there. Daniel decided that Upnor was not here at the moment, but that he was expected. Perhaps not tonight, but soon.

He left Castle Upnor behind him and went back to riding around England by himself in the dark, which seemed to be how he had spent half of his life. Now that he'd crossed over the Medway there were no real barriers between him and London, which was something like twenty-five miles away. Even if there hadn't been a Roman road to follow, he probably would have been able to find the route by riding from one fire to the next. The only hazard was that some mob might

take him for an Irishman. That Daniel bore no resemblance to
an Irishman was of no account—rumors had spread that
James had shipped in a whole legion of Celtic avengers. No
doubt many an Englishman would agree, tonight, that strange
riders should be burnt first and identified on the basis of their
dental peculiarities after the ashes had cooled.

So it was boredom and terror, boredom and terror, all the
way. The boring bits gave Daniel some leisure to ponder the
quite peculiar family curse he seemed to be living under,
namely, this marked tendency to be present at the demise of
English Kings. He'd literally seen Charles I's head roll, and
he'd watched Charles II being done in by his physicians, and
now this. If the next Sovereign knew what was good for him,
he'd make sure Daniel was assigned, by the Royal Society,
to spend the rest of his life taking daily measurements of the
baroscopic pressure in Barbados.

The last bit of his route ran within view of the river, which
was a pleasant sight, a snaking constellation of ships'
lanterns. By contrast the flat countryside was studded with
pylons of streaming fire that warmed Daniel's face from half
a mile away, like the first uncontrollable flush of shame.
Mostly these were simply bonfires, which were the only way
Englishmen had of showing emotion. But in one town that
he rode through, the Catholic church was being not merely
burnt but pulled down, its very bricks prised apart by men
with sharpened bars—men made orange by the fire-light,
not people he recognized, any more, as countrymen.

The river attracted him. At first he told himself that it did
so because it was cool and serene. When he got finally to
Greenwich he turned aside from the road and rode onto the
lumpy pasture of the Park. He couldn't see a damned thing,
which was funny because the place was supposed to be an
Observatory. But he kept to a policy of insisting that his
horse go the way it *didn't* want to—which meant uphill. This
had more than a little in common with trying to get a large
and basically prosperous country to revolt.

A saltbox of a building perched on the edge of a precipice

in the midst of this little range of hills out in the middle of nowhere: a house, queer-looking and haunted. Haunted by philosophers. Its pedestal—a brick of living-space—was surrounded by trees in a way that obscured the view out its windows. Any other tenant would have chopped them down. But Flamsteed had let them grow; they made no difference to him, as he slept all day, and his nights were devoted to looking not out but up.

Daniel reached a place where he could see the light of London shining through gaps among trees. The lambent sky was dissected by the spidery black X of the sixty-foot refracting telescope, supported by a mast scavenged from a tall ship. As he neared the crest he diverted to the right, instinctively avoiding Flamsteed, who exerted a mysterious repulsive force all his own. He was likely to be awake, but unable to make observations because of the light in the sky, therefore more irritable than usual, perhaps scared. His apartment's windows had solid wooden shutters that he had clapped shut for safety. He was holed up in one of the tiny rooms, probably unable to hear anything save the ticking of diverse clocks. Upstairs, in the octagonal saltbox, were two Hooke-designed, Tompion-built clocks with thirteen-foot pendulums that ticked, or rather clunked, every two seconds, slower than the human heartbeat, a hypnotic rhythm that could be felt everywhere in the building.

Daniel led his horse on a slow traverse round the top of the hill. Below, along the riverbank, the brick ruins of Placentia, the Tudor palace, swung gradually into view. Then the new stone buildings that Charles II had begun to put up there. Then the Thames: first the Greenwich bend, then a view straight upriver all the way into the east end. Then all of London was suddenly unrolled before him. Its light shone from the wizened surface of the river, interrupted only by the silhouettes of the anchored ships. If he had not long ago seen the Fire of London with his own eyes, he might have supposed that the whole city was ablaze.

He had entered into the upper reaches of a little wood of

oak and apple trees that gripped the steepest part of the hill. Flamsteed's apartments were only a few yards above and behind him along the Prime Meridian. The fragrance of fermenting apples was heady, for Flamsteed had not bothered to collect them as they dropped from the trees during the autumn. Daniel did not bother to tie his horse, but let it forage there, getting fed and drunk on the apples. Daniel moved to a place where he could see London between trees, dropped his breeches, squatted down on his haunches, and began experimenting with various pelvic settings in hopes of allowing some urine to part with his body. He could feel the boulder in his bladder, shifting from side to side like a cannonball in a poke.

London had never been so bright since it had burned to the ground twenty-two years ago. And it had never *sounded* thus in all its ages. As Daniel's ears adjusted themselves to this quiet hill-top he could hear a clamor rising up from the city, not of guns or of cart-wheels but of human voices. Sometimes they were just babbling, each to his own, but many times they came together in dim choruses that swelled, clashed, merged, and collapsed, like waves of a tide probing and seeking its way through the mazy back-waters of an estuary. They were singing a song, *Lilliburlero,* that had become universal in the last few weeks. It was a sort of nonsense-song but its meaning was understood by all: down with the King, down with Popery, out with the Irish.

If the scene in the tavern hadn't made it clear enough, the very appearance of the city tonight told him that the thing had happened—the thing that Daniel had been calling the Revolution. The Revolution was done, it had been Glorious, and what made it glorious was that it had been an anticlimax. There'd been no Civil War this time, no massacres, no trees bent under the weight of hanged men, no slave-ships. Was Daniel flattering himself to suppose that this could be put down to his good work?

All his upbringing had taught him to expect a single dramatic moment of apocalypse. Instead this had been slow evolution spread all round and working silently, like manure on a field. If anything important had happened, it had done so in places where Daniel *wasn't*. Buried in it somewhere was an inflection point that later they'd point to as the Moment It All Happened.

He was not such an old tired Puritan that he didn't get joy out of it. But its very anticlimactitude, if that was a word, its diffuseness, was a sort of omen to him. It was like being an astronomer, up in that tower behind him, at the moment that the letter arrived from the Continent in which Kepler mentioned that the earth was not, in fact, at the center of the universe. Like that astronomer, Daniel had much knowledge, and only *some* of it was wrong—but *all* of it had to be gone over now, and re-understood. This realization settled him down a bit. As when a queer wind-gust comes down chimney and fills a room of merry-makers with smoke, and covers the pudding with a black taste. He was not quite ready for life in this England.

Now he understood why he'd felt so attracted to the river earlier: not because it was serene, but because it had the power to take him somewhere else.

He left the horse there, with an explanatory note for Flamsteed, who'd be apoplectic. He walked down to the Thames and woke up a waterman he knew there, a Mr. Bhnh, the patriarch of a tiny Qwghlmian settlement lodged in the south bank. Mr. Bhnh had grown so accustomed to the nocturnal crossings of Natural Philosophers that someone had nominated him, in jest, as a Fellow of the Royal Society. He agreed to convey Daniel across to the Isle of Dogs on the north bank.

Of late, reductions in the cost of window-glass, and improvements in the science of architecture, had made it possible to build whole blocks of shops with large windows facing the street, so that fine goods could be set out in view of passers-by. Shrewd builders such as Sterling (the Earl of Willesden) Waterhouse and Roger (the Marquis of Ravenscar) Comstock had built neighborhoods where courtiers went to do just that. The noun "shop" had been verbed; people went "shopping" now. Daniel of course never lowered himself to this newfangled vice—except that as he crossed the river he seemed to be doing it with ships. And he was a discriminating shopper. The watermen's boats, the smacks and barges of the estuary were beneath his notice altogether, and the coasting vessels—anything with a fore-and-aft rig— were scarcely more than impediments. He raised his eyes up out of the clutter to scan for the great ships thrusting their yards up, like High Church priests exalting the sacraments above the rabble, into the sky where the wind blew straight and brave. The sails hung from those yards like vestments. There were not many such ships in the Pool tonight, but Daniel sought them all out and appraised each one shrewdly. He was shopping for something to take him away; he wanted to voyage out of sight of land for once in his life, to die and be buried on another continent.

One in particular caught his eye: trim, clean-lined, and sharply managed. She was taking advantage of the in-coming tide to make her way up-stream, ushered forward by a faint southerly breeze. The movement of the air was too faint for Daniel to feel it, but the crew of this ship, *Hare,* had seen flickers of life in the streamers dangling from her mast-heads, and spread out her topsails. These stopped a bit of air. They stopped some of the fire-light from the city, too, pro-jecting long prismatic shadows off into the void. The sails of *Hare* hovered above the black river, glowing like curtained windows. Mr. Bhnh tracked them for half a mile or so, tak-ing advantage of the lead that the great ship forced among the smaller vessels. "She's fitted out for a long voyage," he mused, "probably sailing for America on the next tide."

"Would I had a grapnel," Daniel said, "I'd climb aboard like a pirate, and stow away on her."

This startled Mr. Bhnh, who was not used to hearing such flights of fancy from his clientele. "Are you going to Amer-ica, Mr. Waterhouse?"

"Someday," Daniel allowed, "there is tidying-up to do in this country yet."

Mr. Bhnh was loath to discharge Daniel in the fiery wilds of East London, which tonight was thronged with drunken mud-larks lighting out in torrid pursuit of real or imaginary Jesuits. Daniel gave no heed to this good man's worries. He had made it all the way from Sheerness without any trouble. Even in the tavern there, he had been left alone. Those who took any no-tice of him at all, soon lost their interest, or (strange to relate) lost their nerve and looked away. For Daniel carried now the unstudied nonchalance of a man who knew he'd be dead in a year no matter what; people seemed to smell the grave about him, and were happy to leave him alone.

On the other hand, a man with little time to live, and no heirs, need not be so miserly. "I shall give you a pound if you take me direct to the Tower," Daniel said. Then, observing a wary look on Mr. Bhnh's face, he teased his purse open and tossed a handful of coins beside the boat's lantern until he found one that shone a little, and was nearly round. In the center was a battered and scratched plop of silver that with careful tilting and squinting and use of the imagination could be construed as a portrait of the first King James, who had died sixty-some odd years ago, but who was held to have managed the Mint competently. The waterman's hand closed over this artifact and almost as quickly Daniel's eye-lids came to with an almost palpable slamming noise. He was remotely aware of massive wool blankets being thrown over his body by the solicitous Mr. Bhnh, and then he was aware of nothing.

> For the King of the North shal returne, and
> shal set forthe a greater multitude then afore,
> and shal come forthe (after certeine yeres)
> with a mightie armie, & great riches.
>
> And at the same time there shal manie stand
> up against the King of the South: also the rebel-
> lious children of thy people shal exalte them
> selves to establish the vision, but they shal fall.

> So the King of the North shal come, and cast
> up a mounte, & take the strong citie: and the
> armes of the South shal not resist, neither his
> chosen people, neither shal there be anie
> strength to withstand.
>
> —DANIEL 11:13–15

HAVING GONE TO SLEEP in that boat on that night he should on
no account have been surprised to wake up in the same boat on
the same night; but when it happened he was perfectly a-
mazed, and had to see and understand everything afresh. His
body was hot on the top and cold on the bottom, and on the
whole, not happy with its management. He tried closing and
opening his eyes a few times to see if he could conjure up a
warm bed, but a mightier conjuration had been wrought on
him, and condemned him to this place and time. To call it
nightmarish was too easy, for it had all the detail, the lively
perversity that nightmares wanted. London—burning, smoking, singing—was still all around. However, he was confronted
by a sheer wall of stone that rose up out of the Thames, and
was thickly jacketed in all of the unspeakables that flowed in it.
Atop that wall was a congeries of small buildings, hoists, large
guns, a few relatively small and disciplined bonfires, armed
men, but snarls of running boys, too. There was the smell of
coal, iron, and sulfur, reminding Daniel of Isaac's laboratory.
And because the sense of smell is plumbed into the mind down
in the cellar, where dark half-formed notions lurk and breed,
Daniel entertained a momentary phant'sy that Isaac had come
to London and set his mind to the acquisition of temporal
power, and constructed a laboratory the size of Jerusalem.

Then he perceived stone walls and towers rising up behind
this wharf, and taller ones rising up behind them, and an
even higher fort of pale stone above and behind those, and
he understood that he lay before the Tower of London. The
roar of the artificial cataracts between the starlings of London Bridge, off to his left, confirmed it.

The wharf-wall was pierced by an arch whose floor was a noisome back-water of the Thames. The boat of Mr. Bhnh was more or less keeping station before that arch, though the current was flowing one way and the tide striving against it, so they were being ill-used by marauding vortices and pounced upon by rogue waves. The waterman, in other words, was using every drowning-avoidance skill he'd practised in the rocky flows off Qwghlm, and more than earning his pound. For in addition to duelling those currents he had been prosecuting a negotiation with a figure who stood on the top of the wharf, just above the arch. That man in turn was exchanging shouts through a speaking trumpet with a periwigged gentleman up on the parapet of the wall behind: a crenellated medieval sort of affair with a modern cannon poking out through each slot, and each cannon conspicuously manned.

Some of the men on the wharf were standing near enough to bonfires that Daniel could make out the colors of their garments. These were the Black Torrent Guards.

Daniel rose up against the gravity of many stout damp blankets, his body reminding him of every injustice he had dealt it since he had been awakened, twenty-four hours ago, with news that the King had gone on the lam. "Sergeant!" he hollered to the man on the wharf, "please inform yonder officer that the escaped prisoner has returned."

THE KING'S OWN BLACK TORRENT Guards had gone into the west country with King James just long enough for their commander, John Churchill, to sneak away from camp and ride to join up with William of Orange. This might have surprised some of the Guards, but it had not surprised Daniel, for almost a year ago he had personally conveyed letters from John Churchill, among others, to the Prince of Orange in the Hague; and though he hadn't read those letters, he could guess what they had said.

Within a few days, Churchill and his regiment had been back in London. But if they'd hoped to be stationed back at their old haunt of Whitehall, they'd been disappointed. William, still trying to sort out his newly acquired Kingdom, was posting his own Dutch Blue Guards at the royal palaces of Whitehall and St. James, and was happy to keep Churchill and the Black Torrent Guards at arm's length in the Tower—which needed defending in any case, as it housed the Royal Mint, and controlled the river with its guns, and was the chief arsenal of the Realm.

Now Daniel was known, to the men of that regiment, as a wretch who'd been imprisoned there by King James II; one cheer for Daniel! Jeffreys had sent murderers to slay him—two cheers! And he had arrived at some untalked-about agreement with Sergeant Bob: three cheers! So in the last weeks before his "escape" Daniel had become a sort of regimental mascot—as Irish regiments kept giant wolf-hounds, this one had a Puritan.

And so the long and the short of it was that Mr. Bhnh was suffered to bring his boat through that tunnel under the wharf. After they passed under the arch, the sky appeared again briefly, but a good half of it was occulted by that outthrust bulwark: St. Thomas's Tower, a fortress unto itself, grafted to the outer wall of the Tower complex, straddling another stone arch-way paved with fœtid moat-water. Their progress was barred by a water-gate filling that arch. But as they approached, the gates were drawn open, each vertical bar leaving an arc of oily vortices in its wake. Mr. Bhnh hesitated, as any sane man would, and tilted his head back for a moment, in case he never got a chance to see the sky again. Then he probed for the bottom with his pole.

"This is my family coat of arms, such as it is," Daniel remarked, "a stone castle bestriding a river."

"Don't say that!" Mr. Bhnh hissed.

"Why ever not?"

"We are entering into Traitor's Gate!"

PAST THE NARROW APERTURE OF THE Gate lay a pool vaulted over with a vast, fair stone arch. Some engineer had lately

constructed a tide-driven engine there for raising water to a
cistern in some higher building back in the penetralia of the
citadel, and its fearsome grinding—like a troll gnashing its
teeth in a cave—appalled Mr. Bhnh more than anything he'd
seen all night. He took his leave gladly. Daniel had disembarked onto some ancient slime-covered stairs. He ascended, carefully, to the level of the Water Lane, which ran
between the inner and outer fortifications. This had become
the scene of a makeshift camp: several hundred Irish people
at least were here, taking their ease on blankets or thin scat-
terings of straw, smoking pipes if they were lucky, playing
hair-raising plaints on penny-whistles. No celebratory bonfires here: just a few brooding cook-fires setting kettle-
bottoms aglow, and begrudging faint red warmth on the
hands and faces of the squatters. There had to be a rational
explanation for their being here, but Daniel could not conjure one up. But that was what made city life interesting.

Bob Shaftoe approached, harried by a couple of boys who
were running around barefoot even though this was December. He ordered them away gruffly, even a bit cruelly, and as
they turned to run off, Daniel got a look at one of their faces.
He thought he saw a familial resemblance to Bob.

Sergeant Shaftoe was headed down the lane in the direction of the Byward Tower, which was the way out to London.
Daniel fell into step beside him and in a few paces they'd left
the water-engine far enough behind that they could talk
without shouting.

"I was ready to set off without you," Bob said somewhat
bitterly.

"For where?"

"I don't know. Castle Upnor."

"He's not there yet. I'd wager he's still in London."

"Let's to Charing Cross, then," Bob said, "as I think he
has a house near there."

"Can we get horses?"

"You mean, is the Lieutenant of the Tower going to supply
you, an escaped prisoner, with a free horse—?"

"Never mind, there are other ways of getting down the Strand. Any news concerning Jeffreys?"

"I have impressed 'pon Bob Carver the grave importance of his providing useful information to us concerning that man's whereabouts," Bob said. "I do not think his fear was affected; on the other hand, he has a short memory, and London contains many diversions to-night, most appealing to a man of his character."

Passing through the Byward Tower they came out into the open and began to traverse the causeway over the moat: first a plank bridge that could be moved out of the way, then a stone ramp onto the permanent causeway. Here they encountered John Churchill, smoking a pipe in the company of two armed gentlemen whom Daniel recognized well enough that he could have recalled their names, had it been worth the effort. Churchill broke away from them when his eyes fell on Daniel, and pursued for a few steps, glaring at Bob Shaftoe in a way that meant "keep walking." So Daniel ended up isolated in mid-causeway, face to face with Churchill.

"In truth I have no idea whether you're about to embrace and thank me, or stab me and shove me into the moat," Daniel blurted, because he was nervous, and too exhausted to govern his tongue.

Churchill appeared to take Daniel's words with utmost gravity—Daniel reckoned he must've said something terribly meaningful, out of blind luck. Daniel had encountered Churchill many times at Whitehall, where he had always been surrounded by a sort of aura or nimbus of Import, of which his wig was only the innermost core. You could feel the man coming. He had never been more important than he was to-night—yet here on this causeway all that remained of his aura was his wig, which stood sore in need of maintenance. It was easy to see him as Sir Winston's lad, a Royal Society whelp who had gone to sojourn in the world of affairs.

"So it'll be for everyone, from now on," Churchill said. "The old schemes by which we reckoned a man's virtue have now been o'erthrown along with Absolute Monarchy.

Your Revolution is pervasive. It is tricky, too. I don't know whether you will run afoul of its tricks in the end. But if you do, it shall not be by my hand . . ."

"Your face seems to say, '*provided* . . .'"

"Provided you continue to be the enemy of my enemies—"

"Alas, I've little choice."

"So you say. But when you walk through yonder gate," Churchill said, pointing toward the Middle Tower at the end of the causeway, which was visible only as a crenellated cutout in the orange sky, "you'll find yourself in a London you no longer know. The changes wrought by the Fire were nothing. In *that* London, loyalty and allegiance are subtle and fluxional. 'Tis a chessboard with not only black and white pieces, but others as well, in diverse shades. You're a Bishop, and I'm a Knight, I can tell that much by our shapes, and the changes we have wrought on the board; but by fire-light 'tis difficult to make out your true shade."

"I have been awake for twenty-four hours and cannot follow your meaning when you speak in figures."

"It is not that you are tired, but that you are a Puritan and a Natural Philosopher; neither group is admired for its grasp of the subtle and the ambiguous."

"I am defenseless against your japes. But as we are not within earshot of anyone, please avail yourself of this opportunity to speak plainly."

"Very well. I know many things, Mr. Waterhouse, because I make it my business to converse with fellows like those— we trade news as fervidly as traders swapping stocks on the 'Change. And one thing I know is that Isaac Newton is in London to-night."

It struck Daniel as bizarre that John Churchill should even know who Isaac was. Until Churchill continued, "Another thing I know is that Enoch turned up in our city a few days ago."

"Enoch the Red?"

"Don't act like an imbecile. It makes me distrustful, as I know you are not one."

"I take such a dim view of the Art that my heart denies what my mind knows."

"That is just the sort of thing you would say if you were one of them, and wished to hide it."

"Ah. Now I perceive what you meant with your talk of chess-pieces and colors—you think I am hiding the red robes of an Alchemist beneath these weeds?! What a thought!"

"You'd have me just *know* that the notion is absurd? Pray tell, sir, how should I *know* it? I'm not learned as you are, I'll admit it; but no one has yet accused me of being stupid. And I say to you that I do not know whether you are mixed up in Alchemy or no."

"It is vexing to you," Daniel thought aloud, "not to follow it."

"More than that, it is *alarming*. In a given circumstance, I know what a soldier will do, what a Puritan will do, what a French cardinal or a Vagabond will do—certain ones excepted—but the motives of the esoteric brotherhood are occult to me, and I do not love that. And as I look forward to being a man of moment in the new order—"

"Yes, I know, I know." Daniel sighed and tried to gather himself. "Really, I think you make too much of them. For never have you seen such a gaggle of frauds, fops, ninehammers, and mountebanks."

"Which of these is Isaac Newton?"

The question was like a bung hammered into Daniel's gob.

"What of King Charles II? Which was His Majesty, ninehammer or mountebank?"

"I have to go and talk to them anyway," Daniel finally said.

"If you can penetrate that cloud, Mr. Waterhouse, I shall consider myself obliged to you."

"*How* obliged?"

"What is on your mind?"

"If an earl dies on a night such as this, might it be overlooked?"

"Depends on the earl," Churchill said evenly. "There will

be someone, somewhere, who'll not be of a mind to overlook it. You must never forget that."

"I entered from the river tonight," Daniel said.

"This is an oblique way of saying, you came in through the Traitor's Gate—?"

Daniel nodded.

"I arrived from the land, as you can see, but there shall be many who shall say that I passed through the same portal as you."

"Which puts us in the same boat," Daniel proclaimed. "Now they say that there's no honor among thieves—I wouldn't know—but perhaps there may be a kind of honor among traitors. If I'm a traitor, I'm an honorable one; my conscience is clear, if not my reputation. So now I am holding my hand out to you, John Churchill, and you may stand there eyeing it all night long if you please. But if you would care to stand behind me and shore me up as I look into this question of Alchemy, I should like it very much if you took that hand in yours and shook it, as a gentleman; for as you have noticed the esoteric brotherhood is powerful, and I cannot work against it without a brotherhood of sorts to stand with me."

"You have entered into contracts before, Mr. Waterhouse?" asked Churchill, still appraising Daniel's outstretched hand. Daniel could sense Bob Shaftoe looking at them from one end of the causeway.

"Yes, as when working as an architect, *et cetera.*"

"Then you know every contract involves obligations *reciprocal.* I might agree to 'shore you up' when you are undermined—but in return I may call upon you from time to time."

Daniel's hand did not move.

"Very well, then," said Churchill, reaching out across smoke, damp, and dark.

CHARING CROSS was strewn with bonfires. But it was the green one that caught Daniel's eye.

"M'Lord Upnor's town-house lies *this* way," shouted Bob Shaftoe, pointing insistently in the direction of Piccadilly.

"Work with me, Sergeant," Daniel said, "as if I were a guide taking you on a hunt for strange game of which you know nothing." They began to push their way across the vast cosmos of the square, which was crowded with dark matter: huge mobs pressing in round bonfires, singing *Lilliburlero,* and diverse knaves who'd come up out of Hogs-den to prey upon 'em, and patchwork mutts fighting over anything that escaped the attention of the knaves. Daniel lost sight of the green flames for a while and was about to give up when he saw red flames shooting up in the same place—not the usual orange-red but an unnatural scarlet. "If we should become separated, I shall meet you at the northern end of the Tilt Yard where King Street loses itself in the Cross."

"Right you are, Guv."

"Who was that boy I saw you talking to before the Bulwark, as we were leaving the Tower?"

"A messenger from Bob Carver."

"Ah, what news from him?"

"The house of Jeffreys is boarded up, and dark."

"If he went to the trouble of having it boarded up, then he's done a proper job."

"It's as we reckoned it, these many weeks ago, Guv," Bob answered, "Jeffreys planned his departure well."

"Well for *us.* If he fled in a panic, how would we find him? Has Mr. Carver any other news?"

"The intent was not to supply us with news, so much as to impress on us what a hard-working and diligent bloke he is."

"That's what I was afraid of," Daniel said, distracted by a rage of blue flame up ahead.

"Fireworks?" Bob guessed.

"Some plan their departures better than others," Daniel answered.

Finally they reached the southwestern margin of the square, where King Street bent round into Pall Mall, and the view of the park and the Spring Garden was screened by an arc of town-houses that seemed to bulge out into Charing Cross, like a dam holding back pressure behind. The bonfire that kept changing its color was planted before those houses, a bow-shot away. This one was not surrounded by any crowd. This might've been because the true center of drinking, singing, and sociability lay elsewhere, up towards Haymarket, or perhaps it could be laid to the fact that this fire sputtered evilly and let off vile smells. Daniel fell into orbit round it, and saw books, maps, and wooden boxes being dismantled and dissolved in the flames. A chest was being devoured, and small glass phials spilled out of it a few at a time, bursting in the heat to release jets of vapor that sometimes exploded in brilliant-colored flames.

Bob Shaftoe nudged him and pointed toward one of the town-houses. The front door was being held open by a servant. Two younger servants were lugging a portmanteau out and down the front steps. The lid was half open and papers and books were spilling out. The servant who had held the door open let it fall to and then scurried after the others, picking up what they'd let drop, and stuffing it all together in a great wad, a double armload, which rested comfortably on his belly as he waddled across the dirt towards the fire. It looked as if he were planning to fling himself headlong into the particolored inferno, but he stopped just short and with a final grand belly-thrust projected the load of goods into the flames. A moment later the other two caught up with him and heaved the portmanteau right into perdition. The fire dimmed for a minute, seeming taken aback, but then the flames began to get their teeth into the new load of fuel, and to whiten as they built heat.

Still circling round, Daniel stopped to stare at a map, drawn with inks of many colors upon excellent vellum. The hottest part of the fire was behind it, so the light shone through the empty places on the map—which were many, as it was a map of some mostly uncharted sea, the voids decorated with leviathans and dreadlocked cannibals. There was a scattering of islands literally gilded onto the page with some sort of golden ink, labelled "Ye Islands of King Solomon." As Daniel gazed at them, the ink finally burst into flames and burnt like trails of gunpowder; the words vanished from the world but were committed to his memory in letters of fire.

"It is the house of M. LeFebure," Daniel explained, walking towards it with Bob in tow. "Mark those three great windows above the entrance, glowering blood-red as the light shines through their curtains. Once I spied on Isaac Newton through those windows, using his own telescope."

"What was he doing?"

"Making the acquaintance of the Earl of Upnor—who wanted to meet him so badly that he'd made arrangements for him to be followed."

"What is that house, then? A den of sodomites?"

"No. It has been the chief nest of Alchemists in the city ever since the Restoration. I've never set foot in it, but I go there now; if I fail to come out, go to the Tower and tell your master the time has come to make good on his end of our contract."

The big-bellied servant had seen Daniel approaching and was standing warily at the door. "I am here to join them," Daniel snapped, brushing past into the entrance hall.

The place had been decorated in the Versailles way, all magnificent, as expensive as possible, and calculated to overawe the Persons of Quality who came here to buy powders and philtres from M. LeFebure. He was not here, having fled the country already. This went a long way toward explaining the fact that the house, tonight, was about as elegant as a fish-market. Servants, and two gentlemen, were bringing goods down from the upper floors, and up from the cellar, dumping them out on tables or floors, and messing through them. After a few moments Daniel realized that one of the gentleman was Robert Boyle and the other Sir Elias Ashmole. Nine things out of ten were tossed in the general direction of the entrance to be hauled out to the fire. The rest were packed in bags and boxes for transport. Transport *where,* was the question. In the kitchen, a cooper was at work, sealing ancient books up inside of barrels, which suggested a sea-voyage was contemplated by someone.

Daniel ascended the stairs, moving purposefully, as if he actually knew his way around the place. In fact, all he had to go on was vague memories of what he'd spied through the telescope twenty years ago. If they served, the room where Upnor and Newton had met was dark-paneled, with many books. Daniel had been having odd dreams about that room for two decades. Now he was finally about to enter it. But he was dead on his feet, so exhausted that everything was little different from a dream anyway.

At least a gross of candles were burning in the stairs and the upstairs hall: little point in conserving them now. Cobwebby candelabras had been dragged out of storage, and burdened with mismatched candles, and beeswax tapers had been thrust into frozen wax-splats on expensive polished banisters. A painting of Hermes Trismegistus had been pulled down from its hook and used to prop open the door of a little chamber, a sort of butler's pantry at the top of the stairs, which was mostly dark; but enough light spilled in from the hall that Daniel could see a gaunt man with a prominent nose, and large dark eyes that gave him a sad preoccupied look. He was conversing with someone farther back in the room, whom Daniel could not see. He had crossed his arms, hugging an old book to himself with an index finger thrust into it to save his place. The big eyes turned Daniel's way and regarded him without surprise.

"Good morning, Dr. Waterhouse."

"Good morning, Mr. Locke. And welcome back from Dutch exile."

"What news?"

"The King is run to ground at Sheerness. And what of you, Mr. Locke, shouldn't you be writing us a new Constitution or something?"

"I await the pleasure of the Prince of Orange," said John Locke patiently. "In the meantime, this house is no worse a place to wait than any other."

"It is certainly better than where I have been living."

"We are all in your debt, Dr. Waterhouse."

Daniel turned round and walked five paces down the hall, moving now towards the front of the house, and paused before the large door at the end.

He could hear Isaac Newton saying, "What do we know, truly, of this Viceroy? Supposing he *does* succeed in conveying it to Spain—will he understand its true value?"

Daniel was tempted to stand there for a while listening, but he knew that Locke's eyes were on his back and so he opened the door.

Opposite were the three large windows that looked over Charing Cross, covered with scarlet curtains as big as mainsails, lit up by many tapers in sconces and candelabras curiously wrought, like vine-strangled tree-branches turned to solid silver. Daniel had a dizzy sensation of falling into a sea of red light, but his eyes adjusted, and with a slow blink his balance recovered.

In the center of the room was a table with a top of black marble shot through with red veins. Two men were seated there, looking up at him: on Daniel's left, the Earl of Upnor, and on his right, Isaac Newton. Posed nonchalantly in the corner of the room, pretending to read a book, was Nicolas Fatio de Duilliers.

Daniel immediately, for some reason, saw this through the suspicious eyes of a John Churchill. Here sat a Catholic nobleman who was more at home in Versailles than in London; an Englishman of Puritan upbringing and habits, lately fallen into heresy, the smartest man in the world; and a Swiss Protestant famous for having saved William of Orange from a French plot. Just now they'd been interrupted by a Nonconformist traitor. These differences, which elsewhere sparked duels and wars, counted for naught here; their Brotherhood was somehow above such petty squabbles as the Protestant Reformation and the coming war with France. No wonder Churchill found them insidious.

Isaac was a fortnight shy of his forty-sixth birthday. Since his hair had gone white, his appearance had changed very little; he never stopped working to eat or drink and so he was as slender as he had always been, and the only symptom of age was a deepening translucency of his skin, which brought into view tangles of azure veins strewn around his eyes. Like many College dwellers he found it a great convenience to hide his clothing—which was always in a parlous state, being not only worn and shabby but stained and burnt with diverse spirits—underneath an academic robe; but his robe was scarlet, which made him stand out vividly at the College, and here in London all the more so. He did not wear it in the street, but he was wearing it now. He had not affected a wig, so his white hair fell loose over his shoulders. Someone had been brushing that hair. Probably not Isaac. Daniel guessed Fatio.

For the Earl of Upnor it had been a challenging couple of decades. He'd been banished once or twice for slaying men in duels, which he did as casually as a stevedore picked his nose. He had gambled away the family's great house in London and been chased off to the Continent for a few years during the most operatic excesses of the so-called Popish Plot. He had, accordingly, muted his dress somewhat. To go with his tall black wig and his thin black moustache he was wearing an outfit that was, fundamentally, black: the *de rigueur* three-piece suit of waistcoat, coat, and breeches, all in the same fabric—probably a very fine wool. But the whole outfit was crusted over with embroidery done in silver thread, and thin strips of parchment or something had been involved with the needle-work to lift it off the black wool underneath and give it a three-dimensional quality. The effect was as if an extremely fine network of argent vines had grown round his body and now surrounded him and moved with him. He was wearing riding-boots with silver spurs, and was armed with a Spanish rapier whose guard was a tornadic swirl of gracefully curved steel rods with bulbous ends, like a storm of comets spiraling outwards from the grip.

Fatio's attire was relatively demure: a many-buttoned sort of cassock, a middling brown wig, a linen shirt, a lace cravat

They were only a little surprised to see him, and no more than normally indignant that he'd burst in without knocking. Upnor showed no sign of wanting to run him through with that rapier. Newton did not seem to think that Daniel's appearing here, now, was any more bizarre than any of the other perceptions that presented themselves to Isaac in a normal day (which was probably true), and Fatio, as always, just observed everything.

"Frightfully sorry to burst in," Daniel said, "but I thought you'd like to know that the King's turned up in Sheerness—not above ten miles from Castle Upnor."

The Earl of Upnor now made a visible effort to prevent some strong emotion from assuming control of his face. Daniel couldn't be certain, but he thought it was a sort of incredulous sneer. While Upnor was thus busy, Daniel pressed his advantage: "The Gentleman of the Bedchamber is in the Presence as we speak, and I suppose that other elements of Court will travel down-river tomorrow, but for now he has nothing—food, drink, a bed are being improvised. As I rode past Castle Upnor yesterday evening, it occurred to me that you might have the means, there, to supply some of His Majesty's wants—"

"Oh yes," Upnor said, "I have all."

"Shall I make arrangements for a messenger to be sent out then?"

"I can do it myself," said the Earl.

"Of course I am aware, my lord, that you have the power to dispatch messages. But out of a desire to make myself useful I—"

"No. I mean, I can deliver the orders myself, for I am on my way to Upnor at daybreak."

"I beg your pardon, my lord."

"Is there anything else, Mr. Waterhouse?"

"Not unless I may be of assistance in this house."

Upnor looked at Newton. Newton—who'd been gazing at

Daniel—seemed to detect this in the corner of his eye, and spoke: "In this house, Daniel, a vast repository of alchemical lore has accumulated. Nearly all of it is garbled nonsense. Some of it is true wisdom—secrets that ought rightly to be *kept* secret from them in whose hands they would be dangerous. Our task is to sort out one from the other, and burn what is useless, and see to it that what is good and true is distributed to the libraries and laboratories of the adept. It is difficult for me to see how you could be of any use in this, since you believe that *all* of it is nonsense, and have a well-established history of incendiary behavior in the presence of such writings."

"You continue to view my 1677 actions in the worst possible light."

"Not so, Daniel. I am aware that you thought you were showering favors on me. Nonetheless, I say that what happened in 1677 must be looked on as permanently disqualifying you from being allowed to handle alchemical literature around open flames."

"Very well," said Daniel. "Good night, Isaac. M'Lord. Monsieur." Upnor and Fatio were both looking a bit startled by Isaac's cryptic discourse, so Daniel bowed perfunctorily and backed out of the room.

They resumed their previous conversation as if Daniel were naught more than a servant who'd nipped in to serve tea. Upnor said, "Who can guess what notions have got into his head, living for so many years in that land, over-run with the cabals of crypto-Jews, and Indians sacrificing each other atop Pyramids?"

"You could just write him a letter and ask him," suggested Fatio, in a voice so bright and reasonable that it annoyed even Daniel, who was rapidly backing out of earshot. He could tell, just from this, that Fatio was no alchemist; or if he was, he was new to it, and not yet inculcated to make everything much more obscure and mysterious than it needed to be.

He turned around finally, and nearly bumped into a fellow whom he identified, out of the corner of his eye, as a merry monk who had somehow got grievously lost: it was a robed figure gripping a large stoneware tankard that he had evidently taken out on loan from one of the local drinking establishments. "Have a care, Mr. Waterhouse, you look too little, for listening so well," said Enoch Root affably.

Daniel started away from him. Locke was still standing there embracing his book; Root was the chap he'd been talking to earlier. Daniel was caught off guard for a few moments; Root took advantage of the lull to down a mouthful of ale.

"You are very rude," Daniel said.

"What did you say? Root?"

"*Rude,* to drink alone, when others are present."

"Each man finds his own sort of rudeness. Some burst into houses, and conversations, uninvited."

"I was bearing important news."

"And I am celebrating it."

"Aren't you afraid that drink will shorten your longevity?"

"Is longevity much on your mind, Mr. Waterhouse?"

"It is on the mind of every man. And I am a man. Who or what are *you*?"

Locke's eyes had been going back and forth, as at a tennis match. Now they fixed on Enoch for a while. Enoch had got a look as if he were trying to be patient—which was not the same as being patient.

"There's a certain unexamined arrogance to your question, Daniel. Just as Newton presumes that there is some absolute space by which all things—comets even!—are measured and governed, you presume it is all perfectly natural and pre-ordained that the earth should be populated by men, whose superstitions ought to be the ruler by which all things are judged; but why might I not ask of you, 'Daniel Waterhouse, who or what are you? And why does Creation teem with others like you, and what is your purpose?' "

"I'll remind you, sirrah, that All Hallows' Eve was more than a month since, and I am not of a humour to be baited with hobgoblin-stories."

"Nor am I of a humour to be rated a hobgoblin or any

other figment of the humane imagination; for 'twas God who imagined me, just as He did you, and thereby brought us into being."

"Your tankard brims over with scorn for our superstitions and imaginings; yet here you are, as always, in the company of Alchemists."

"You might have said, 'Here you are in the center of the Glorious Revolution conversing with a noted political philosopher,'" Root returned, glancing at Locke, who flicked his eyes downward in the merest hint of a bow. "But I am never credited thus by you, Daniel."

"I have only seen you in the company of alchemists. Do you deny it?"

"Daniel, I have only seen *you* in the company of alchemists. But I am aware that you do other things. I know you have oft been at Bedlam with Hooke. Perhaps you have seen priests there who go to converse with madmen. Do you suppose those priests to be mad?"

"I'm not sure if I approve of the similitude—" Locke began.

"Stay, 'tis just a figure!" Root laughed rather winningly, reaching out to touch Locke's shoulder.

"A faulty one," Daniel said, "for you *are* an alchemist."

"I am *called* an Alchemist. Within living memory, Daniel, everyone who studied what I—and *you*—study was called by that name. And most persons even today observe no distinction between Alchemy and the younger and more vigorous order of knowledge that is associated with your club."

"I am too exhausted to harry you through all of your evasions. Out of respect for your friends Mr. Locke, and for Leibniz, I shall give you the benefit of the doubt, and wish you well," Daniel said.

"God save you, Mr. Waterhouse."

"And you, Mr. Root. But I say this to you—and you as well, Mr. Locke. As I came in here I saw a map, lately taken from this house, burning in the fire. The map was empty, for it depicted the ocean—most likely, a part of it where no man has ever been. A few lines of latitude were ruled across that vellum void, and some legendary isles drawn in, with great authority, and where the map-maker could not restrain himself he drew phantastickal monsters. That map, to me, is Alchemy. It is good that it burnt, and fitting that it burnt tonight, the eve of a Revolution that I will be so bold as to call my life's work. In a few years Mr. Hooke will learn to make a proper chronometer, finishing what Mr. Huygens began thirty years ago, and then the Royal Society will draw maps with lines of longitude as well as latitude, giving us a grid—what we call a Cartesian grid, though 'twas not his idea—and where there be islands, we will rightly draw them. Where there are none, we will draw none, nor dragons, nor sea-monsters—and that will be the end of Alchemy."

"'Tis a noble pursuit and I wish you Godspeed," Root said, "but remember the poles."

"The poles?"

"The north and south poles, where your meridians will come together—no longer parallel and separate, but converging, and all one."

"That is nothing but a figment of geometry."

"But when you build all your science upon geometry, Mr. Waterhouse, figments become real."

Daniel sighed. "Very well, perhaps we'll get back to Alchemy in the end—but for now, no one can get near the poles—unless you can fly there on a broom, Mr. Root—and I'll put my trust in geometry and not in the books of fables that Mr. Boyle and Sir Elias are sorting through below. 'Twill work for me, for the short time I have remaining. I have not time to-night."

"Further errands await you?"

"I would fain bid a proper farewell to my dear old friend Jeffreys."

"He is an old friend of the Earl of Upnor as well," Enoch Root said, a bit distractedly.

"This I know, for they cover up each other's murders."

"Upnor sent Jeffreys a box a few hours ago."

"Not to his house, I'll wager."

"He sent it in care of the master of a ship in the Pool."

"The name of the ship?"

"I do not know it."

"The name of the messenger, then?"

Enoch Root leaned over the baluster and peered down the middle of the stairwell. "I do not know that, either," he said, then shifted his tankard to the other hand so that he could reach out. He pointed at a young porter who was just on his way out the door, bearing another pile of books to the bonfire. "But it was *him*."

HARE RODE AT ANCHOR, LANTERNS a-blaze, before Wapping: a suburb crooked in an elbow of the Thames just downstream of the Tower. If Jeffreys had already boarded her, there was nothing they could do, short of hiring a pirate-ship to overhaul her when she reached blue water. But a few minutes' conversation with the watermen loitering round the Wapping riverfront told them that no passengers had been conveyed to that ship yet. Jeffreys must be waiting for something; but he would wait close by, within view of *Hare,* so that he could bolt if he had to. And he would choose a place where he could get strong drink, because he was a drunkard. That narrowed it down to some half a dozen taverns, unevenly spaced along the riverbank from the Tower of London down to Shadwell, mostly clustered around the stairs and docks that served as gate-ways 'tween the Wet and the Dry worlds. Dawn was approaching, and any normal business ought to've been closed half a dozen hours ago. But these dockside taverns served an irregular clientele at irregular hours; they told time by the rise and fall of the tides, not by the comings and goings of the sun. And the night before had been as wild as any in England's history. No sane tavernkeeper would have his doors closed now.

"Let's be about it smartly then, guv'nor," said Bob Shaftoe, striding off the boat they'd hired near Charing Cross and lighting on King Henry's Stairs. "This may be nigh on the longest night of the year, but it can't possibly be much longer; and I believe that my Abigail awaits me at Upnor."

This was a gruff way of speaking to a tired sick old Natural Philosopher, yet an improvement on the early days in the Tower, when Bob had been suspicious and chilly, or recent times when he'd been patronizing. When Bob had witnessed John Churchill shaking Daniel's hand on the Tower causeway a few hours earlier, he'd immediately begun addressing him as "guv'nor." But he'd persisted in his annoying habit of asking Daniel whether he was tired or sick until just a quarter of an hour ago, when Daniel had insisted that they shoot one of the flumes under London Bridge rather than take the time to walk around.

It was the first time in Daniel's life that he'd run this risk, the second time for Bob, and the fourth time for the waterman. A hill of water had piled up on the upstream side of the bridge and was finding its way through the arches like a panicked crowd trying to bolt from a burning theatre. The boat's mass was but a millionth part of it, and was of no account whatever; it spun around like a weathercock at the brink of the cataract, bashed against the pilings below Chapel Pier hard enough to stave in the gunwale, spun round the opposite way from the recoil, and accelerated through the flume sideways, rolling toward the downstream side so that it scooped up a ton or so of water. Daniel had imagined doing this since he'd been a boy, and had always wondered what it would be like to look up and see the Bridge from underneath; but by the time he thought to raise his gaze outside the narrow and dire straits of the boat, they'd been thrust half a mile downstream and were passing right by the Traitor's Gate once more.

This act had at last convinced Bob that Daniel was a man determined to kill himself this very night, and so he now dispensed with all of the solicitous offers; he let Daniel jump off the boat under his own power, and did not volunteer to bear him piggy-back up King Henry's Stairs. Up they trudged into Wapping, river-water draining in gallons from their clothes, and the waterman—who'd been well paid— was left to bail his boat.

They tried four taverns before they came to the Red Cow. It was half wrecked from the past night's celebrations, but efforts were underway to shovel it out. This part of the river-front was built up only thinly, with one or two strata of inns and warehouses right along the river, crowding in against a main street running direct to the Tower a mile away. Beyond that 'twas green fields. So the Red Cow offered Daniel juxta-positions nearly as strange as what he'd witnessed in Sheer-ness: viz. one milkmaid, looking fresh and pure as if angels had just borne her in from a dewy Devonshire pasture-ground, carrying a pail of milk in the back door, stepping primly over a peg-legged Portuguese seaman who'd passed out on a heap of straw embracing a drained gin-bottle. This and other particulars, such as the Malay-looking gent smok-ing bhang by the front door, gave Daniel the feeling that the Red Cow merited a thoroughgoing search.

As on a ship when exhausted sailors climb down from the yards and go to hammocks still warm from the men who re-place them, so the late-night drinkers were straggling out, and their seats being taken by men of various watery occu-pations who were nipping in for a drink and a nibble.

But there was one bloke in the back corner who did not move. He was dark, saturnine, a lump of lead on a plank, his face hidden in shadow—either completely unconscious or extremely alert. His hand was curled round a glass on the table in front of him, the pose of one who needs to sit for many hours, and who justifies it by pretending he still nurses his drink. Light fell onto his hand from a candle. His thumb was a-tremble.

Daniel went to the bar at the opposite corner of the room, which was little bigger than a crow's nest. He ordered one dram, and paid for ten. "Yonder bloke," he said, pointing with his eyes, "I'll lay you a quid he is a common man— common as the air."

The tavernkeeper was a fellow of about three score, as pure-English as the milkmaid, white-haired and red-faced. "It'd be thievery for me to take that wager, for you've only seen his clothes—which *are* common—while I've heard his voice—which is anything but."

"Then, a quid says he has a disposition sweet as clotted cream."

The tavernkeeper looked pained. "It slays me to turn your foolish bets away, but again, I have such knowledge to the contrary as would make it an unfair practice."

"I'll bet you a quid he has the most magnificent set of eyebrows you've ever seen—eyebrows that would serve for pot-scrubbers."

"When he came in he kept his hat pulled down low, and his head bowed—I didn't see his eyebrows—I'd say you've got yourself a wager, sir."

"Do you mind?"

"Be at your ease, sir, I'll send my boy round to be the judge of it—if you doubt, you may send a second."

The tavernkeeper turned and caught a lad of ten years or so by the arm, bent down, and spoke to him for a few moments. The boy went directly to the man in the corner and spoke a few words to him, gesturing toward the glass; the man did not even deign to answer, but merely raised one hand as if to cuff the boy. A heavy gold ring caught the light for an instant. The boy came back and said something in slang so thick Daniel couldn't follow.

"Tommy says you owe me a pound then," the tavernkeeper said.

Daniel sagged. "His eyebrows were not bushy?"

"That wasn't the wager. His eyebrows *are* not bushy, that was the wager. *Were* not bushy, that's neither here nor there!"

"I don't follow."

"I've a blackthorn shillelagh behind this counter that was witness to our wager, and it says you owe me that quid, never mind your weasel-words!"

"You may let your shillelagh doze where it is, sir," Daniel said, "I'll let you have that quid. I only ask that you explain yourself."

"Bushy eyebrows he might have had yesterday, for all I know," the tavernkeeper said, calming down a little, "but as we speak, he has no eyebrows at all. Only stubble."

"He cut them off!"

"It is not *my* place to speculate, sir."

"Here's your pound."

"Thank you, sir, but I would prefer one of full weight, made of silver, not this counterfeiter's amalgam . . ."

"Stay. I can give you better."

"A better coin? Let's have it then."

"No, a better circumstance. How would you like this place to be famous, for a hundred years or more, as the place where an infamous murderer was brought to justice?"

Now it was the tavernkeeper's turn to deflate. It was clear from his face that he'd much rather not have any infamous murderers at all in the house. But Daniel spoke encouraging words to him, and got him to send the boy running up the street toward the Tower, and to stand at the back exit with the shillelagh. A look sufficed to get Bob Shaftoe on his feet, near the front door. Then Daniel took a fire-brand out of the hearth and carried it across the room, and finally waved it back and forth so that it flared up and filled the dark corner with light.

"Damned be to Hell, you shit, Daniel Waterhouse! Traitorous, bastard whore, pantaloon-pissing coward! How dare you impose on a nobleman thus! By what authority! I'm a baron, as you are a sniveling turncoat, and William of Orange is no Cromwell, no Republican, but a *prince,* a nobleman like me! He'll show me the respect I merit, and *you* the contempt you deserve, and 'tis *you* who'll feel Jack Ketch's blade on his neck, and die like a whipped bitch in the Tower as you should've done!"

Daniel turned to address the other guests in the tavern— not so much the comatose dregs of last night as the breakfasting sailors and watermen. "I apologize for the disruption," he announced. "You have heard of Jeffreys, the Hanging Judge, the one who decorated trees in Dorset with bodies of ordinary Englishmen, who sold English schoolgirls into chattel slavery?"

Jeffreys got to his feet, knocking his table over, and made for the closest exit, which was at the rear; but the tavernkeeper raised the shillelagh in both hands and wound up like a woodman preparing to swing his axe at a tree. Jeffreys shambled to a stop and reversed direction, heading for the front of the room. Bob Shaftoe let him build to full speed, and let him enjoy a few seconds' hope, before side-stepping in front of the doorway and whipping a dagger out of his boot. It was all Jeffreys could do to stop before impaling himself on it; and the casual look on Bob's face made it clear he would not have turned the point aside.

The men in the tavern had all got to their feet now and begun reaching into their clothes, betraying locations of various daggers, coshes, and other necessaries. But they did this because they were confused, not because they'd formed any clear intentions. For that, they were still looking to Daniel.

"The man I speak of, whose name you have all heard, the man who is responsible for the Bloody Assizes and many other crimes besides—judicial murders, for which he has never dreamed he would be made to pay, until this moment—George Jeffreys, Baron of Wem, is *he*." And Daniel pointed his finger like a pistol into the face of Jeffreys, whose eyebrows would have shot up in horror, if he still had any. As it was, his face was strangely devoid of expression, of its old power to stir Daniel's emotions. Nothing he could do with that face could now make Daniel fear him, or pity him, or be charmed by him. This was attributing more power to a set of eyebrows than was really sensible, and so it had to be something else instead; some change in Jeffreys, or in Daniel.

The daggers and coshes had begun to come out—not to be used, but to keep Jeffreys hemmed in. Jeffreys was speechless for the first time since Daniel had known him. He could not even curse.

Daniel met Bob's eyes, and nodded. "Godspeed, Sergeant Shaftoe, I hope you rescue your princess."

"So do I," Bob said, "but whether I live or die in the attempt, do not forget that I have helped you; but you have not helped me yet."

"I have not forgotten it, nor will I ever. Chasing armed men cross-country is not something I am very good at, or I would come with you now. I await a chance to return the favor."

"It is not a favor, but one side of a contract," Bob reminded him, "and all that remains is for us to choose the coin in which I shall be repaid." He turned and bolted into the street.

Jeffreys looked around, taking a quick census of the men and weapons closing in around him, and finally turned his gaze on Daniel: not fierce any more, but offended, and bewildered—as if asking why? Why go to the trouble? I was running away! What is the point of this?

Daniel looked him in the eye and said the first thing that entered his mind:

"You and I are but earth."

Then he walked out into the city. The sun was coming up now, and soldiers were running down the street from the Tower, led by a boy.

❦

Venice

JULY 1689

❦

The *Venetian* Republick began thus; a despicable Croud of People flying from the Fury of
the *Barbarians* which over-run the *Roman* Empire, took Shelter in a few inaccessible Islands
of the *Adriatic* Gulph . . . THEIR City we see
raised to a prodigious Splendour and Magnificence, and their rich Merchants rank'd
among the ancient Nobility, and all this by
Trade.

—DANIEL DEFOE,
A Plan of the English Commerce

To Eliza, Countess de la Zeur and
Duchess of Qwghlm
From G. W. Leibniz
July 1689
Eliza,
   Your misgivings about the Venetian Post Office
have once again proved unfounded—your letter
reached me quickly and without obvious signs of tam-
pering. Really, I think that you have been spending too
much time in the Hague, for you are becoming as prim
and sanctimonious as a Dutchwoman. You need to
come here and visit me. Then you would see that even

the most debauched people in the world have no difficulty delivering the mail on time, and doing many other difficult things besides.

As I write these words I am seated near a window that looks out over a canal, and two gondoliers, who nearly collided a minute ago, are screaming murderous threats at each other. This sort of thing happens all the time here. The Venetians have even given it a name: "Canal Rage." Some say that it is a new phenomenon—they insist that gondoliers never used to scream at each other in this way. To them it is a symptom of the excessively rapid pace of change in the modern world, and they make an analogy to poisoning by quicksilver, which has turned so many alchemists into shaky, irritable lunatics.

The view from this window has changed very little in hundreds of years (God knows that my room could use some maintenance), but the letters scattered across my table (all delivered punctually by Venetians) tell of changes the like of which the world has not seen since Rome fell and the Vagabond Emperor moved his court to this city. Not only have William and Mary been crowned at Westminster (as you and several others were so kind as to inform me), but in the same post I received word from Sophie Charlotte in Berlin that there is a new Tsar in Russia, named Peter, and that he is as tall as Goliath, as strong as Samson, and as clever as Solomon. The Russians have signed a treaty with the Emperor of China, fixing their common border along some river that does not even appear on the maps—but from all accounts, Russia now extends all the way to the Pacific, or (depending on which set of maps you credit) to America. Perhaps this Peter could march all the way to Massachusetts without getting his feet wet!

But Sophie Charlotte says that the new Tsar's gaze is fixed westwards. She and her incomparable mother are already scheming to invite him to Berlin and Hanover so that they can flirt with him in person. I would not miss that for the world; but Peter has many rivals to crush and Turks to slay before he can even consider such a journey, and so I should have plenty of time to make my way back from Venice.

Meanwhile *this* city looks to the east—the Venetians and the other Christian armies allied with them continue to press the Turks back, and no one here will talk about anything else but the news that came in the latest post, or when the next post is expected. For those of us more interested in philosophy, it makes for tedious dinners! The Holy League have taken Lipova, which as you must know is the gateway to Transylvania, and there is hope of driving the Turks all the way to the Black Sea before long. And in a month I'll be able to write you another letter containing the same sentence with a different set of incomprehensible place names. Woe to the Balkans.

Pardon me if I seem flippant. Venice seems to have that effect on me. She finances her wars the old-fashioned way, by levying taxes on trade, and this naturally limits their scope. By contrast, the reports I hear from England and from France are most disquieting. First you tell me that (according to your sources at Versailles) Louis XIV is melting down the silver furniture in the *Grands Appartements* to pay for the raising of an even vaster army (or perhaps he wanted to redecorate). Next, Huygens writes from London that the Government there has hit upon the idea of financing the Army and Navy by creating a national debt—using all of England as collateral, and levying a special tax that is earmarked for paying it back. I can scarcely picture the upheaval that these innovations must have created in Amsterdam! Huygens also mentioned that the ship he took across the North Sea was crowded with Amsterdam Jews who appeared to be bringing their entire households and estates with them to London. No doubt some of the silver that used to be part of Louis' favorite armchair has by this route made its way via the *ghetto* of Amsterdam to the Tower of London where it has been minted into new coins bearing the likeness of William and Mary, and then been sent out to pay for the building of new warships at Chatham.

Thus far, in these parts, Louis' declaration of war against England seems to have had little effect. The duc d'Arcachon's navy is dominant in the Mediterranean, and is rumored to have taken many Dutch and English merchantmen around Smyrna and Alexandria, but there have not been any pitched sea-battles that I know of. Likewise, James II is said to have landed in Ireland whence he hopes to launch attacks on England, but I have no news thence.

My chief concern is for you, Eliza. Huygens gave me a good description of you. He was touched that you and those royals you have befriended—the Princess Eleanor and little Caroline—went to the trouble of seeing him off on his voyage to London, especially given that you were quite enormously pregnant at the time. He used various astronomical metaphors to convey your roundness, your hugeness, your radiance, and your beauty. His affection for you is obvious, and I believe he is a touch saddened that he is not the father (who *is*, by the way? Remember I am in Venice, you may tell me *anything* and I cannot be shocked by it).

At any rate—knowing how strongly you are attracted to the financial markets, I fret that the recent upheavals have drawn you into the furor of the Damplatz, which would be no place for one in a delicate condition.

But there is little point in my worrying about it now, for by this time you must have entered into your confinement, and you and your baby must have emerged dead or alive, and gone to the nursery or the grave; I pray both of you are in the nursery, and whenever I see a picture of the Madonna and child (which in Venice is about three times a minute) I phant'sy it is a fair portrait of you and yours.

Likewise I send my prayers and best wishes to the Princesses. Their story was pathetic even before they were made into refugees by the war. It is good that in the Hague they have found a safe harbor, and a friend such as you to keep them company. But the news from the Rhine front—Bonn and Mainz changing hands, &c.—suggests that they shall not soon be able to return to that place where they were living out their exile.

You ask me a great many questions about Princess Eleanor, and *your* curiosity has aroused *mine;* you remind me of a merchant who is considering a momentous transaction with someone she does not know very well, and who is casting about for references.

I have not met Princess Eleanor, only heard strangely guarded descriptions of her beauty (e.g., "she is the most beautiful German princess"). I did know her late husband, the Margrave John Frederick of Brandenburg-Ansbach. As a matter of fact I was thinking of him the other day, because the new Tsar in Russia is frequently described in the same terms as were once applied to Eleanor's late husband: forward-thinking, modern-minded, obsessed with securing his country's position in the new economic order.

Caroline's father went out of his way to welcome Huguenots or anyone else he thought had unusual skills, and tried to make Ansbach into a center of what your friend and mine, Daniel Waterhouse, likes to call the Technologickal Arts. But he wrote novels too, did the late John Frederick, and you know of my shameful weakness for those. He loved music and the theatre. It is a shame that smallpox claimed him, and a crime that his own son made Eleanor feel so unwelcome there that she left town with little Caroline.

Beyond those facts, which are known to all, all I can offer you concerning these two Princesses is gossip. However, *my* gossip is copious, and of the most excellent quality. For Eleanor figures into the machinations of Sophie and Sophie Charlotte, and so her name is mentioned from time to time in the letters that fly to and fro between Hanover and Berlin. I do believe that Sophie and Sophie Charlotte are trying to organize some sort of North German super-state. Such a thing can never exist without princes; German Protestant princes and princesses are in short supply, and getting shorter as the war goes on; beautiful princesses who lack husbands are, therefore, exceptionally precious.

If precious Eleanor were rich she could command, or at least influence, her own destiny. But because her falling-out with her stepson has left her penniless, her only assets are her body and her daughter. Because her body has shown the ability to manufacture little princes, it is enfeoffed to larger powers. I shall be surprised if a few years from now, your friend Princess Eleanor is not dwelling in Hanover or Brandenburg, married to some more or less hideous German royal. I would advise her to seek out one of the madly eccentric ones, as this will at least make her life more interesting.

I hope that I do not sound callous, but these are the facts of the matter. It is not as bad as it sounds. They are in the Hague. They will be safe there from the atrocities being committed against Germans by the army of Louvois. More dazzling cities exist, but the Hague is perfectly serviceable, and a great improvement over the rabbit-hutch in the Thüringer Wald where, according to gossip, Eleanor and Caroline have been holed up for the last few years. Best of all, as long as they remain in the Hague, Princess Caroline is being exposed to *you,* Eliza, and learning how to be a great woman. Whatever may befall Eleanor at the hands of those two redoubtable match-makers, Sophie and Sophie Charlotte, Caroline will, I believe, learn from you and from them how to manage her affairs in such a way that, when she reaches a marriageable age, she shall be able to choose whatever Prince and whatever Realm are most suitable to her. And this will provide comfort to Eleanor in her old age.

As for Sophie, she will never be satisfied with Germany alone—her uncle was King of England and she would be its Queen. Did you know she speaks perfect English? So here I am, far away from home, trying to track down every last one of her husband's ancestors among the Guelphs and the Ghibellines. Ah, Venice! Every day I get down on my knees and thank God that Sophie and Ernst August are not descended from people who lived in some place like Lipova.

At any rate, I hope you, Eleanor, Caroline, and, God willing, your baby are all well, and being looked after by officious Dutch nurses. Do write as soon as you feel up to it.

Leibniz

P.S. I am so annoyed by Newton's mystical approach to force that I am developing a new discipline to study that subject alone. I am thinking of calling it "dynamics," which derives from the Greek word for force—what do you think of the name? For I may know Greek backwards and forwards, but *you* have taste.

The Hague

Dear Doctor,

"Dynamics" makes me think not only of force, but of Dynasties, which use forces, frequently concealed, to maintain themselves—as the Sun uses forces of a mysterious nature to make the planets pay court to him. So I think that the name has a good ring to it, especially since you are becoming such an expert on Dynasties new and old, and are so adept at balancing great forces against each other. And insofar as words are names for things, and naming gives a kind of power to the namer, then you are very clever to make your objections to Newton's work a part of the very name of your new discipline. I would only warn you that the frontier between "ingenious" (which is held to be a good quality) and "clever" (which is looked at a-skance) is as ill-defined as most of the boundaries in Christendom are today. Englishmen are particularly distrustful of cleverness, which is odd, because they are so clever, and they are wont to draw the boundary in such a way as to encompass all the works of Newton (or any other Englishman) in the country called "ingenious" while leaving you exiled to "clever." And the English must be attended to because they seem to be drawing all the maps. Huygens went to be among the Royal Society because he felt it was the only place in the world (outside of whatever room *you* happen to be in) where he could have a conversation that would not bore him to death. And despite the never-ending abuse from Mr. Hooke, he never wants to leave.

I have been slow to write about myself. This is partly because the very existence of this letter proves, well enough, that I live. But it is also because I can hardly bring myself to write about the baby—may God have mercy on his little soul. For by now, he is with the angels in Heaven.

After several false starts my labor began in the evening of the 27th of June, which I think was extremely late—certainly I felt as if I had been pregnant for two years! It was early the next morning that my bag of waters broke and poured out like a flood from a broken dam.* Now things became very busy at the Binnenhof as the apparatus of labor and delivery swung into action. Doctors, nurses, midwives, and clergy were summoned, and every gossip within a radius of five miles went to the highest state of alert.

As you have guessed, the incredibly tedious descriptions of labors and deliveries that follow are nothing but the vessel for this encrypted message. But you should read them anyway because it took me several drafts and a gallon of ink to put into words one one-hundredth of the agony, the endless rioting in my viscera as my body tried to rip itself open. Imagine swallowing a melon-seed, feeling it grow in your belly to full size, and then trying to vomit it up through the same small orifice. Thank God the baby is finally out. But pray for God to help me, for I love him.

Yes, I say "love," not "loved." Contrary to what is written in the unencrypted text, the baby lives. But I get ahead of myself.

---

* ䷪ Break-through: Hexagram 43 of the *I Ching,* or 011111.

For reasons that will shortly become obvious, you must destroy this letter.

That is, if I don't destroy it first by dissolving the words with my tears. Sorry about the unsightly blotching.

To the Dutch and the English, I am the Duchess of Qwghlm. To the French, I am the Countess de la Zeur. But neither a Protestant Duchess nor a French Countess can get away with bearing and rearing a child out of wedlock.

My pregnancy I was able to conceal from all but a few, for once I began to show, I ventured out in public only rarely. For the most part I confined myself to the upper storys of the house of Huygens. So it has been a tedious spring and summer. The Princesses of Ansbach, Eleanor and Caroline, have been staying as honored guests of the Prince of Orange at the Binnenhof, which as you know is separated from the Huygens house by only a short distance. Almost every day they strolled across the square to pay a call on me. Or rather Eleanor strolled, and Caroline sprinted ahead. To give a curious six-year-old the run of such a place, cluttered as it is with Huygens's clocks, pendulums, lenses, prisms, and other apparatus, is a joy for the little one and a deadly trial for all adults within the sound of her voice. For she can ask a hundred questions about even the least interesting relic that she digs up from some corner. Eleanor, who knows practically nothing of Natural Philosophy, quickly wearied of saying "I don't know" over and over again, and became reluctant to visit the place. But I had nothing better to do with my time as the baby grew, and was hungry for their company, and so attended closely to Caroline and tried as best I could to give some answer to every one of her questions. Perceiving this, Eleanor got in the habit of withdrawing to a sunny corner to do embroidery or write a letter. Sometimes she would leave Caroline with me and go out riding or attend a soiree. So the arrangement worked out well for all three of us. You mentioned to me, Doctor, that the late Margrave John Frederick, Caroline's father, had a passion for Natural Philosophy and Technologickal Arts. I can now assure you that Caroline has inherited this trait; or perhaps she has dim memories of her father showing off his fossil collection or his latest pendulum-clock, and so feels some communion with his departed soul when I show her the wonders of Huygens's house. If so it is a tale that will seem familiar to you, who knew your father only by exploring his library.

Thus Eliza and Caroline. But too Eliza and Eleanor have been talking, late at night, when Caroline is asleep in her bedchamber in the Binnenhof. We have been talking about Dynamics. Not the dynamics of rolling balls on inclined planes, but the dynamics of royal and noble families. She and I are both a little bit like mice scurrying around on a bowling-green, trying not to be crushed by the rolling and colliding balls. We must understand dynamics in order to survive.

Only a few months before I became pregnant, I visited London. I was at Whitehall Palace with Daniel Waterhouse when the son of James II—now Pretender to the throne—was supposedly born. Was Mary of Modena really pregnant, or only stuffing pillows under her dress? If she was pregnant, was it really by the syphilitic King James II, or was a healthy stud brought in to the royal apartments to father a robust heir? Supposing she was really pregnant, did the baby survive childbirth? Or was the babe brought forth from that room really an orphan, smuggled into Whitehall in a warming-pan, and triumphantly brought forth so that the Stuart line could continue to reign over England?

In one sense it does not matter, since that king is deposed, and that baby is being reared in Paris. But in another sense it matters very much, for the latest news from across the sea is that the father has taken Derry, and is on the march elsewhere in Ireland, trying to win his kingdom back for his son. All because of what did or did not happen in a certain birthing-room at Whitehall.

But I insult your intelligence by belaboring this point. Have you found any changelings or bastards in Sophie's line? Probably. Have you made these facts known? Of course not. But burn this anyway, and sift the ashes into that canal you are always writing about, making sure beforehand that there are no ill-tempered gondoliers beneath your window.

As a Christian noblewoman, never married, I could not be pregnant, and could not have a child. Eleanor knew this as well as I. We talked about it for hours and hours as my belly grew larger and larger.

My pregnancy was hardly a secret—various servants and women of the household knew—but I could deny it later. Gossips would know I was lying, but in the end, they are of no account. If, God forbid, the baby was stillborn, or died in infancy, then it would be as if it had never happened. But if the baby throve, then matters would be complicated.

Those complications did not really daunt me. If there was one thing I learned at Versailles, it was that Persons of Quality have as many ways of lying about their affairs, perversions, pregnancies, miscarriages, births, and bastards as sailors have of tying knots. As the months of my pregnancy clunked past, ponderous but inexorable, like one of Huygens's pendulums, I had some time to consider which lie I would choose to tell when my baby was born.

Early, when my belly was just a bit swollen, I con-

sidered giving the baby away. As you know, there are plenty of well-funded "orphanages" where illegitimate children of the Quality are raised. Or if I searched long enough I might find some decent mother and father who were barren, and would be more than happy to welcome a healthy infant into their house.

But on the first day that the baby began to kick inside of me, the idea of giving him away faded to an abstraction, and shortly vanished from my mind.

When I reached my seventh month, Eleanor sent to Eisenach for a certain Frau Heppner. Frau Heppner arrived some weeks later, claiming to be a nurse who would look after Princess Caroline and teach her the German language. And this she did; but in truth, Frau Heppner is a midwife. She delivered Eleanor, and has delivered many other noble and common babies since then. Eleanor said that she was loyal and that her discretion could be relied on.

The Binnenhof, though far from luxurious by the standards of French palaces, contains several suites of apartments, each appointed in such a way that a royal house guest can dwell there in the company of her ladies-in-waiting, Lady of the Bedchamber, &c. As you will understand from my earlier letters, Princess Eleanor did not have enough of a household to occupy a suite fully; she had a couple of servants who had come out from Eisenach, and two Dutch girls who'd been assigned to her, by William's household staff, as an act of charity. And now she had Frau Heppner. This still left an empty room in her suite. And so, when Frau Heppner was not giving Caroline lessons, she began organizing the bedsheets and other necessaries of the midwife's art, making that extra room into a birthing-chamber.

The plan was that when I went into labor I would be carried across the square into the Binnenhof in a sedan-chair, and taken direct to Eleanor's suite. We

*practiced this, if you can believe such a thing: I hired
a pair of brawny Dutchmen to serve as porters, and
once a day, during the final weeks of my pregnancy,
had them carry me from Huygens's house to the Binnenhof, not stopping or slowing until they had set the
sedan chair down inside Eleanor's bedchamber.*

*These dress rehearsals seemed a good idea at the
time, because I did not know the strength of my enemy,
and the number of his spies in the Binnenhof. In retrospect, I was telling him everything about my plan, and
giving him all he needed to lay a perfect ambush.*

*But again I get ahead of myself. The plan was that
Frau Heppner would preside over the delivery. If the
baby died and I lived, no word of it need ever leave that
chamber. If I died and the infant lived, it would become
a ward of Eleanor, and inherit my wealth. If both I and
the baby survived, then I would recuperate for a few
weeks and then move to London as soon as the obvious
symptoms of childbirth were gone from my body. I
would bring the infant along with me, and pass it off as
an orphaned niece or nephew, the sole survivor of some
massacre in the Palatinate. There is no shortage of
massacres to choose from, and no want of Englishmen
who would be eager to credit such a tale be it never so
patchy—particularly if the tale came from a Duchess
who had been of great service to their new King.*

*Yes, it all sounds absurd. I never would have
dreamed such things went on if I had not gone to
Whitehall and seen (from a distance) the retinue of
high and mighty persons gathered there for no reason
other than to stand in the Queen's bedchamber and
stare fixedly at her vagina all day, like villagers at a
magic-show, determined to catch the magician out in
some sleight-of-hand.*

*I supposed that my own vagina, so humble and com-
mon, would never draw such a large and distinguished
audience. So by making some simple arrangements*

ahead of time, I should be able to adjust matters to my satisfaction after it was over.

You may refer to the plaintext now, doctor, to become acquainted with all of the delightful sensations that preoccupied me during my first several hours of labor (I assume it was several hours; at first 'twas dark outside and then light). When my bag of waters broke, and I knew that the time had come, I sent word for the porters. Between contractions, I made my way carefully downstairs and climbed into the sedan chair, which was kept waiting in a room at the side of the house, at street-level. Once I was inside the box, I closed the door, and drew the curtains across the little windows, so that curious eyes should not look in on me as I was taken across the square. The darkness and confinement did not really trouble me, considering that the baby inside my womb had been living with far worse for many weeks, and had suffered it patiently, aside from a few kicks.

Presently I heard the familiar voices of the porters outside, and felt the sedan being lifted into the air, and rotated around in the street for the short journey to the Binnenhof. This passed without incident. I believe that I may have dozed a little bit. Certainly I lost track of the twists and turns, after a while, as they carried me down the long galleries of the Binnenhof. But soon enough I felt the sedan being set down on a stone floor, and heard the porters walking away.

I reached up, flipped the door-latch, and pushed it open, expecting to see the faces of Frau Heppner, Eleanor, and Caroline.

Instead I was looking at the face of Dr. Alkmaar, the court physician, a man I had seen once or twice, but never spoken to.

I was not in Eleanor's apartment. It was an unfamiliar bedchamber, somewhere else in the Binnenhof. A bed was ready—ready for me!—and a steaming vat of water rested on the floor, and piles of torn sheets had been put *in position. There were some women in the room, whom I knew a little, and a young man I'd never seen at all.*

It was a trap; but so shocking that I did not know what to do. Would that I could tell you, Doctor, that I kept my wits about me, and perceived all that was going on, and jumped out of the sedan chair and ran down the gallery to freedom. But in truth, I was perfectly dumbfounded. And at the moment that I found myself in this unfamiliar room, I was taken by a strong contraction, which made me helpless.

By the time that the pangs had subsided, I was lying in that bed; Dr. Alkmaar and the others had pulled me out of the sedan chair. The porters were long since gone. Whoever had arranged this ambush—and I had a good idea of who it was—had either paid them to take me to the wrong room, or somehow talked them into believing that this was what I wanted. I had no way to send out a message. I could scream for help, but women in labor always scream for help. There was plenty of help already in the room.

Dr. Alkmaar was far from being a warm person, but he was reputed competent and (almost as important) loyal. If he spied on me (which was only to be expected) he would tell my secrets to William of Orange, who knows my secrets anyway. Dr. Alkmaar was assisted by one of his pupils (the young man) and by two girls who had no real business being in this room. When I had arrived in the Hague almost nine months before, in a canal-boat with Eleanor and Caroline, William had tried to furnish me with the rudiments of a household, befitting my exalted rank. The Prince of Orange did this not because I desired it but because it is how things are done, and it seemed absurd to have a Duchess in residence at a royal palace who was bereft of servants and staff. He sent me two young women. Both were daughters of minor nobles, serving time at Court, awaiting husbands, and wishing they were at

Versailles instead. Since being spied on by members of one's household is the staple of palace intrigue, I had been careful to have all of my conversations with Eleanor in places where neither of these two girls could possibly overhear us. Later I had moved to Huygens's house, dismissed them from my service, and forgotten about them. But by some narrow definition of Court protocol, they were still technically members of my household, whether I wanted them or not. My fogged mind, trying to make sense of these events, cast that up as an explanation.

Again refer to plaintext for description of various agonies and indignities. The point, for purposes of this narration, is that when the worst fits came over me, I was not really conscious. If you doubt it, Doctor, eat some bad oysters and then try doing some of your calculus at the moment your insides try to turn themselves inside out.

At the conclusion of one of these fits I gazed down through half-closed eyes at Dr. Alkmaar, who was standing between my thighs with his sleeve rolled up and his armhairs plastered to his skin by some sort of wetness. I inferred that he had been inside me, doing a little exploration."

"It's a boy," he announced, more for the benefit of the spectators than for me—I could tell from the way they looked at me that they thought I was asleep or delirious.

I opened my eyes slightly, thinking that it was all over, wanting to see the baby. But Dr. Alkmaar was empty-handed and he was not smiling.

"How do you know?" asked Brigitte—one of those two girls who made up my household. Brigitte looked like she belonged in a Dutch farm-yard operating a butter churn. In Court dress she looked big and out of place. She was harmless.

"He is trying to come out buttocks-first," Dr. Alkmaar said distractedly.

Brigitte gasped. Despite the bad news, I took comfort from this. I had found Brigitte tedious and stupid because of her sweetness. Now, she was the only person in the room feeling sympathy for me. I wanted to get out of bed and hug her, but it did not seem practical.

Marie—the other girl—said, "That means both of them will die, correct?"

Now, Doctor, since I am writing this letter, there is no point in my trying to keep you in suspense—obviously I did not die. I mention this as a way of conveying something about the character of this girl Marie. In contrast to Brigitte, who was always warm (if thick-seeming), Marie had an icy soul—if a mouse ran into the room, she would stomp it to death. She was the daughter of a baron, with a pedigree pieced together from the dribs, drabs, fag-ends, and candle-stubs of diverse Dutch and German principalities, and she struck me (by your leave) as one who had issued from a family where incest was practiced often and early.

Dr. Alkmaar corrected her: "It means I must reach up and rotate the baby until it is head-down. The danger is that the umbilical cord will squirt out while I am doing this, and get throttled later. The chief difficulty is the contractions of her uterus, which bear down on the infant with more strength than my arms, or any man's, can match. I must wait for her womb to relax and then try it."

So we waited. But even in the intervals between my contractions, my womb was so tense that Dr. Alkmaar could not budge the infant. "I have drugs that might help," he mused, "or I could bleed her to make her weaker. But it would be better to wait for her to become completely exhausted. Then I might have a better chance."

More delay now—for them it was a matter of standing around waiting for time to pass, for me it was to be a victim of bloody murder and then to return to life again, over and over; but a lower form of life each time.

By the time the messenger burst in, I could only lie there like a sack of potatoes and listen to what was said.

"Doctor Alkmaar! I have just come from the bedside of the Chevalier de Montluçon!"

"And why is the new ambassador in bed at four in the afternoon?"

"He has suffered an attack of some sort and urgently requires your assistance to bleed him!"

"I am occupied," said Dr. Alkmaar, after thinking about it. But I found it disturbing that he had to mull it over in this way.

"A midwife is on her way to take over your work here," said the messenger.

As if on cue, there was a knock at the door. Showing more vitality than she had all day, Marie dashed over and flung it open to reveal a certain crone of a midwife, a woman with a very mixed reputation. Peering out through a haze of eyelashes I could see Marie throwing her arms around the midwife's neck with a little cry of simulated joy, and muttering something into her ear. The midwife listened and said something back, listened and said something back, three times before she ever turned her colorless gray eyes towards me, and when she did, I felt death reaching for me.

"Tell me more of the symptoms," said Dr. Alkmaar, beginning to take an interest in this new case. The way he was looking at me—staring without seeing—I sensed he was giving up.

I mustered the strength to lever myself up on one elbow, and reached out to grab the bloody cravat around Dr. Alkmaar's neck. "If you think I am dead, explain this!" I said, giving him a violent jerk.

"It will be hours before you will have become exhausted enough," he said. "I shall have time to go and bleed the Chevalier de Montluçon—"

"Who will then suffer another attack, and then another!" I replied. "I am not a fool. I know that if I become so exhausted that you are able to turn the baby around in my womb, I shall be too weak to push her out. Tell me of the drug you mentioned before!"

"Doctor, the French Ambassador may be dying! The rules of precedence dictate that—" began Marie, but Dr. Alkmaar held up one hand to stay her. To me, he said, "It is but a sample. It relaxes certain muscles for a time, then it wears off."

"Have you experimented with it yet?"

"Yes."

"And?"

"It made me unable to hold in my urine."

"Who gave it to you?"

"A wandering alchemist who came to visit two weeks ago."

"A fraud or—"

"He is well reputed. He remarked that, with so many pregnant women in the house, I might have need of it."

"'Twas the Red?"

Dr. Alkmaar's eyes darted from side to side before he answered with a very slight nod.

"Give me the drug."

It was some sort of plant extract, very bitter, but after about a quarter of an hour it made me go all loose in the joints, and I became light-headed even though I had not lost that much blood yet. So I was not fully conscious when Dr. Alkmaar did the turning, and that suited me, as it was not anything I wanted to be conscious of. My passion for Natural Philosophy has its limits.

I heard him saying to the midwife, "Now the baby is head down, as it should be. God be praised, the cord did not emerge. The baby is crowning now, and when the drug wears off in a few hours, the contractions will resume and, God willing, she will deliver normally.

Know that she is delivering late; the baby is well-
developed; as frequently occurs in such cases, it has
already defecated inside the womb."

"I have seen it before," said the midwife, a little bit
insulted.

Dr. Alkmaar did not care whether she was insulted or
not: "The baby has got some of it into his mouth. There
is danger that when he draws his first breath he shall as-
pirate it into his lungs. If that happens he shall not live
to the end of the week. I was able to get my finger into
the little one's mouth and clear out a good deal of it,
but you must remember to hold him head-down when he
emerges and clear the mouth again before he inhales."

"I am in debt to your wisdom, Doctor," said the
midwife bitterly.

"You felt around in his mouth? The baby's mouth?"
Marie asked him.

"That is what I have just said," Dr. Alkmaar replied.

"Was it . . . normal?"

"What do you mean?"

"The palate . . . the jaw . . . ?"

"Other than being full of baby shit," said Dr. Alkmaar, picking up his bag of lancets and handing it to
his assistant, "it was normal. Now I go to bleed the
French Ambassador."

"Take a few quarts for me, Doctor," I said. Hearing
this weak jest, Marie turned and gave me an indescrib-
ably evil look as she closed the door behind the de-
parting Doctor.

The crone took a seat next to me, used the candle on
the nightstand to light up her clay-pipe, and set to
work replacing the air in the room with curls of smoke.

The words of Marie were an encrypted message that
I had understood as soon as it had reached my ears.
Here is its meaning:

Nine months ago I got into trouble on the banks of

the Meuse. As a means of getting out of this predicament I slept with Étienne d'Arcachon, the scion of a very ancient family that is infamous for passing along its defects as if they were badges and devices on its coat of arms. Anyone who has been to the royal palaces in Versailles, Vienna, or Madrid has seen the cleft lips and palates, the oddly styled jaw-bones, and the gnarled skulls of these people; King Carlos II of Spain, who is a cousin to the Arcachons in three different ways, cannot even eat solid food. Whenever a new baby is born into one of these families, the first thing everyone looks at, practically before they even let it breathe, is the architecture of the mouth and jaw.

I was pleased to hear that my son would be free of these defects. But that Marie had asked proved that she had an opinion as to who the father was. But how could this be possible? "It is obvious," you might say, "this Étienne d'Arcachon must have boasted, to everyone who would listen, of his conquest of the Countess de la Zeur, and nine months was more than enough time for the gossip to have reached the ears of Marie." But you do not know Étienne. He is an odd duck, polite to a fault, and not the sort to boast. And he could not know that the baby in my womb was his. He knew only that he'd had a single opportunity to roger me (as Jack would put it). But I traveled for weeks before and weeks after in the company of other men; and certainly I had not impressed Étienne with my chastity!

The only possible explanation was that Marie—or, much more likely, someone who was controlling her — had read a deciphered version of my personal journal, in which I stated explicitly that I had slept with Étienne and only Étienne.

Clearly Marie and the midwife were working as cat's-paws of some Frenchman or other of high rank. M. le comte d'Avaux had been recalled to Versailles shortly after the Revolution in England, and this Chevalier de Montluçon had been sent out to assume his role. But Montluçon was a nobody, and there was no doubt in my mind that he was a meat marionette whose strings were being pulled by d'Avaux, or some other personage of great power at Versailles.

Suddenly I felt sympathy with James II's queen, for here I was flat on my back in a foreign palace with a lot of strangers gazing fixedly at my vagina.

Who had arranged this? What orders had been given to Marie?

Marie had made it obvious that one of her tasks was to find out whether the baby was sound.

Who would care whether Étienne's bastard child had a well-formed skull?

Étienne had written me a love poem, if you can call it that:

Some ladies boast of ancient pedigrees
And prate about their ancestors a lot
But cankers flourish on old family trees
Whose mossy trunks do oft conceal rot.

My lady's blood runs pure as mountain streams
So I don't care if her high rank was bought
Her beauty lends fresh vigor to my dreams
Of children free of blemish and of blot.

Étienne d'Arcachon wanted healthy children. He knew that his line had been ruined. He needed a wife of pure blood. I had been made a Countess; but everyone knew that my pedigree was fake and that I was really a commoner. Étienne did not care about about that—he had nobility enough in his family to make him a Duke thrice over. And he did not really care about me, either. He cared about one thing only: my ability to breed true, to make children who were not deformed. He, or someone acting on his behalf, was controlling Marie. And Marie was now effectively controlling me.

That explained Marie's unseemly curiosity about what Dr. Alkmaar had felt when he had put his fingers into the baby's mouth. But what other tasks might Marie have been given?

The baby trying to escape from my womb, healthy as he might be, could never be anything other than Éti-enne's bastard: a trivial embarrassment to him (for many men had bastards) but a gross one to me.

I had bred true, and proved my ability to make healthy Arcachon babies. When Étienne heard this news, he would want to marry me, so that I could make other babies who were not bastards. But what did it all portend for today's baby, the inconvenient and embarrassing bastard? Would he be sent to an orphanage? Raised by a cadet branch of the Arcachon family? Or—and forgive me for raising this terrible image, but this is the way my mind was working—had Marie been ordered to make certain that the child was stillborn?

I looked around the room between contractions and thought of the possibilities. I had to get away from these people and deliver my baby among friends. A day of labor had left me too weak to get up, so I could hardly get up and run away from them.

But perhaps I could rely upon the strength of some, and the weakness of others. I have already mentioned that Brigitte was built like a stallion. And I could tell she was good. Sometimes I am not the best judge of character, it is true, but when you are in labor, con-fined with certain people for what seems like a week, you come to know them very well.

"Brigitte," I said, "it would do my heart good if you would get up and find Princess Eleanor."

Brigitte squeezed my sweaty hand and smiled, but

Marie spoke first: "Dr. Alkmaar has strictly forbidden
visitors!"

"Is Eleanor far away?" I asked.

"Just at the other end of the gallery," Brigitte said.

"Then go there quickly and tell her I shall have a
healthy baby boy very soon."

"That is by no means assured yet," Marie pointed
out, as Brigitte stormed out of the room.

Marie and the midwife immediately went into the
corner, turned their backs to me, and began to whisper.
I had not anticipated this, but it suited my purposes. I
reached over to the nightstand and wrenched the candle out of its holder. The nightstand had a lace tablecloth draped over it. When I held the flame of the
candle beneath its fringe, it caught fire like gunpowder. By the time Marie and the midwife had turned
around to see what was happening, the flames had already spread to the fringe of the canopy over my bed.

This is what I meant when I said I must rely on the
weakness of some, for as soon as Marie and the midwife perceived this, it was a sort of wrestling-match
between the two of them to see which would be out the
door first. They did not even bother to cry "Fire!" on
their way out of the building. This was done by a stew-
ard who had been walking up the gallery with a basin
of hot water. When he saw the smoke boiling out of the
open door, he cried out, alerting the whole palace, and
ran into the room. Fortunately he had the presence of
mind to keep the basin of water steady, and he flung its
whole contents at the biggest patch of flames that
caught his eye, which was on the canopy. This scalded
me but did not really affect the most dangerous part of
the fire, which had spread to the curtains.

Mind you, I was lying on my back staring up
through the tattered and flaming canopy, watching a
sort of thunder-storm of smoke-clouds clashing and

gathering against the ceiling. Quickly it progressed downwards, leaving a diminishing space of clear air between it and the floor. All I could do was wait for it to reach my mouth.

Then suddenly Brigitte was filling the doorway. She dropped into a squat so that she could peer under the smoke and lock her eyes on mine. Did I call her stupid before? Then I withdraw the accusation, for after a few heartbeats she got a fierce look on her face, stomped forward, and gripped the end-seam of my mattress—a flat sack of feathers—with both hands. Then she kicked off her shoes, planted her bare feet against the floor, and flung herself backwards towards the door. The mattress was practically ripped out from under me—but I came with it, and shortly felt the foot of the bed sliding under my spine. My buttocks fell to the floor and my head rapped against the bed-frame, both cushioned only a little by the mattress. I felt something giving way inside my womb. But it hardly mattered now. It felt as if my whole body were coming apart like a ship dashed on rocks—each contraction another sea heaving me apart. I have a distinct memory of the stone floor sliding along inches from my eyes, boots of the staff running the other way with buckets and blankets, and—gazing forward, between my upraised knees—the huge bare feet and meaty calves of Brigitte flashing out from under her bloody skirt hem, left-right-left-right, as implacably she dragged me on the mattress down the length of the gallery to where the air was clear enough for me to see the frescoes on the ceiling. We came to a stop underneath a fresco of Minerva, who peered down at me from under the visor of her helmet, looking stern but (as I hoped) approving. Then the door gave way under Brigitte's pounding and she dragged me straight into Eleanor's bedchamber.

Eleanor and Frau Heppner were sitting there drink-

*ing coffee. Princess Caroline was reading a book
aloud. As you might imagine, they were all taken
aback; but Frau Heppner, the midwife, took one look at
me, muttered something in German, and got to her feet.*

*Eleanor's face appeared above me. "Frau Heppner
says, 'At last, the day becomes interesting!'"*

*People who are especially bad, and know that they
are, such as Father Édouard de Gex, may be drawn to
religion because they harbor a desperate hope that it
has some power to make them virtuous—to name their
demons and to cast them out. But if they are as clever
as he is, they can find ways to pervert their own faith
and make it serve whatever bad intentions they had to
begin with. Doctor, I have come to the conclusion that
the true benefit of religion is not to make people virtuous, which is impossible, but to put a sort of bridle on
the worst excesses of their viciousness.*

*I do not know Eleanor well. Not well enough to
know what vices may be lurking in her soul. She does
not disdain religion (as did Jack, who might have ben-
efited from it). Neither does she cling to it morbidly,
like Father Édouard de Gex. This gives me hope that in
her case religion will do what it is supposed to do,
namely, stay her hand when she falls under the sway of
some evil impulse. I have no choice but to believe that,
for I let her take my baby. The child passed straight-
away from the midwife's hands to Eleanor's arms, and
she gathered it to her bosom as if she knew what she
was doing. I did not try to fight this. I was so exhausted
I could scarcely move, and afterwards I slept as if I
did not care whether I ever woke up or not.*

*In the plaintext version of my story of labor and de-
livery, Doctor, I tell the version that everyone at the
Binnenhof believes, which is that because of the disgraceful cowardice of Marie and of that midwife, my
baby died, and that I would have died, too, if brave*

Brigitte had not taken me to the room where the good German nurse, Frau Heppner, saw to it that the afterbirth was removed from my womb so that the bleeding stopped, and thereby saved my life.

That is all nonsense. But one paragraph of it is true, and that is where I speak of the physical joy that comes over one's body when the burden it has borne for nine months is finally let go—only to be replaced a few moments later by a new burden, this one of a spiritual nature. In the plaintext story it is a burden of grief over the death of my child. But in the real story— which is always more complicated—it is a burden of uncertainty, and sadness over tragedies that may never happen. I have gone back to live by myself at the house of Huygens, and the baby remains at the Binnenhof in the care of Frau Heppner and Eleanor. We have already begun to circulate the story that he is an orphan, born to a woman on a canal-boat on the Rhine as she escaped from a massacre in the Palatinate.

It seems likely that I shall live. Then I will take up this baby and try to make my way to London, and build a life for both of us there. If I should sicken and die, Eleanor will take him. But sooner or later, whether tomorrow or twenty years from now, he and I shall be separated in some way, and he shall be out in the world somewhere, living a life known to me only imperfectly. God willing, he will outlive me.

In a few weeks or months, there shall be a parting of ways here at the Hague. The baby and I will go west. Eleanor and Caroline will journey east and enjoy the hospitality, and take part in the schemes of, the women whom you serve.

When, God willing, I reach London I shall write you a letter. If you receive no such letter, it means that while I was recuperating I fell victim to some larger scheme of d'Avaux. He may or may not want the baby dead. He certainly wants me at Versailles, where I shall

*be none the less in his power for being the unwilling
wife of Étienne d'Arcachon. The next few weeks, when
I am too weak to move, are the most dangerous time.*

*There remain only two loose ends to clear up: one,
if Étienne is the father, why is the baby flawless? And
two, if my cypher has been broken, and my private
writings are being read by the* cabinet noir, *why am I
telling you all of these secrets?*

*Actually there is a third loose end, of a sort, which
may have been troubling you: why would I sleep with
Étienne in the first place, when I had my pick of ten
million horny Frenchmen?*

*All three of these loose ends may be neatly tied up
by a single piece of information. During my time at
Versailles I got to know Bonaventure Rossignol, the
King's cryptanalyst. Rossignol, or Bon-bon as I like to
call him (hello, Bon-bon!) was sent out to the Rhine
front last autumn during the build-up to the invasion
of the Palatinate. When I blundered in to the middle of
it all, and got into trouble, Bon-bon became aware of
it within a few hours, for he was reading everyone's
despatches, and came galloping—literally—to my rescue. It is difficult to tell the story right under present
circumstances, and so I'll jump to the end of it, and
admit that his gallantry made my blood hot in a way I
had never known before. It seems very crude and simple when I set it down thus, but at root it is a crude and
simple thing, no? I attacked him. We made love several
times. It was very sweet. But we had to devise a way
out for me. Choices were few. The best plan we could
come up with was that I seduced Étienne d'Arcachon,
or rather stood by numbly in a sort of out-of-body
trance while he seduced me. This I then parlayed into
an escape north. I wrote it all down in a journal. When
I got to the Hague, d'Avaux became aware of the existence of that journal and prevailed upon the King's
cryptanalyst to translate it—which he did, though he*

left out all the best parts, namely, those passages in which he himself played the romantic hero. He could not make me out to be innocent, for d'Avaux already knew too much, and too many Frenchmen had witnessed my deeds. Instead Bon-bon contrived to tell the story in such as way as to make me into the paramour of Étienne: the true-breeding woman of his, and his family's, dreams.

I must stop writing now. My body wants to suckle him, and when at night I hear him cry out from across the square, my breasts let down a thin trickle of milk, which I then wash away with a heavier flood of tears. If I were a man, I'd say I was unmanned. As I am a woman, I'll say I am over-womanned. Good-bye. If when you go back to Hanover you meet a little girl named Caroline, teach her as well as you have taught Sophie and Sophie Charlotte, for I prophesy that she will put both of them in the shade. And if Caroline is accompanied by a little orphan boy, said to have been born on the Rhine, then you shall know his story, and who is his father, and what became of his mother.

Eliza

Bishopsgate

OCTOBER 1689

Thou art too narrow, wretch, to comprehend
Even thy selfe: yea though thou wouldst but
   bend
To know thy body. Have not all soules thought
For many ages, that our body'is wrought
Of Ayre, and Fire, and other Elements?
And now they thinke of new ingredients,
And one Soule thinkes one, and another way
Another thinkes, and 'tis an even lay.
Knowst thou but how the stone doth enter in
The bladders cave, and never break the
   skinne?
       —JOHN DONNE, *Of the Progresse of the Soule,*
                    The Second Anniversarie

THE VISITOR——FIFTY-SIX YEARS old, but a good deal more vigorous than the host—feigned aloofness as he watched his bookish minions fan out among the stacks, boxes, shelves, and barrels that now constituted the personal library of Daniel Waterhouse. One of them strayed towards an open keg. His master warned him away with a barrage of clucking, harrumphing, and finger-snaps. "We must assume that anything Mr. Waterhouse has placed in a barrel, is bound for Boston!"

But when the assistants had all found ways to make them-

selves busy cataloguing and appraising, he turned towards
Daniel and foamed up like a bottle of champagne. "Can't
say what an *immense* pleasure it is to see you, old chap!"

"Really, I do not think my countenance is all that pleasing
at the moment, Mr. Pepys, but it is extraordinarily decent of
you to fake it so vigorously."

Samuel Pepys straightened up, blinked once, and parted
his lips as if to follow up on the *Conversational Opportunity*
Daniel had just handed him. The hand trembled and crept toward the Pocket where the Stone had lurked these thirty
years. But some gentlemanly instinct averted him; he'd not
crash the conversation onto that particular *Hazard* just yet.
"I'd have thought you would be in Massachusetts by now,
from the things the Fellows were saying."

"I should have begun making my preparations immediately following the Revolution," Daniel admitted, "but I de-
layed until after Jeffreys had his enounter with Mr. Jack
Ketch at the Tower—by then, 'twas April, and I discovered
that in order to leave London I should have to liquidate my
life—which has proved much more of a bother than I had
expected. Really, 'tis much more expedient simply to drop
dead and let one's mourners see to all of these tedious dispositions." Daniel waved a hand over his book-stacks, which
were dwindling rapidly as Pepys's corps of librarian-
mercenaries carried them towards their master and piled
them at his feet. Pepys glanced at the cover of each and then
flicked his eyes this way or that to indicate whether they
should be returned, or taken away; the latter went to a hard-
bitten old computer who had set himself up with a lap-desk,
quill, and inkwell, and was scratching out a bill of particulars.

Daniel's remark on the convenience of dropping dead laid
a *second* grievous temptation in the way of Mr. Pepys, who
had to clench his fist to keep it from stabbing into the pocket.
Fortunately he was distracted by an assistant who held before him a large book of engravings of diverse fishes. Pepys
frowned at it for a moment. Then he recognized and rejected

in the same instant, with revulsion. The R.S. had printed too many copies of it several years ago. Ever since, Fellows had been fobbing copies off on each other, trying to use them as legal tender for payment of old debts, employing them as doorstops, table-levelers, flower-presses, *et cetera*.

Daniel was not normally a cruel man, but he had been laid flat by nausea for days, and could not resist tormenting Pepys yet a third time: "Thy judgment is swift and remorseless, Mr. Pepys. Each book goes to thy left hand or thy right. When a ship founders in a hurricano, and Saint Peter is suddenly confronted with a long queue of soggy souls, not even he could despatch 'em to their deserved places as briskly as thee."

"You are toying with me, Mr. Waterhouse; you have penetrated my deception, you know why I have come."

"Not at all. How goes it with you since the Revolution? I have heard nothing of you."

"I am retired, Mr. Waterhouse. Retired to the life of a gentleman scholar. My aims now are to assemble a library to rival Sir Elias Ashmole's, and to try to fill the void that shall be left by your departure from the day-to-day affairs of the Royal Society."

"You must have been tempted to plunge into the new Court, the new Parliament—"

"Not in the slightest."

"Really?"

"To move in those circles is a bit like swimming. Swimming with rocks in one's pockets! It demands ceaseless exertions. To let up is to die. I bequeath that sort of life to younger and more energetic strivers, like your friend the Marquis of Ravenscar. At my age, I am happy to stand on dry land."

"What about those rocks in your pockets?"

"I beg your pardon?"

"I am giving you a cue, Mr. Pepys—the segue you have been looking for."

"Ah, well done!" said Pepys, and in a lunge he was by Daniel's bedside, holding the auld Stone right up in his face.

Daniel had never seen it quite this close before, and he noticed now that it had a pair of symmetrically placed protru-
sions, like little horns, where it had begun growing up into
the ureters leading down from Pepys's kidneys. This made
him queasy and so he shifted his attention to Pepys's face,
which was nearly as close.

"BEHOLD! My Death—premature, senseless, avoidable
Death—mine, and *yours,* Daniel. But I hold mine in my
hand. Yours is lodged thereabouts—do not flinch, I shall not
lay hands on you—I wish only to demonstrate, Daniel, that
thy Stone is only two inches or so from my hand when I hold
it thus. *My* Stone is *in* my hand. A distance of only two
inches! Yet for me that small interval amounts to thirty years
of added life—three decades and God willing one or two
more, of wenching, drinking, singing, and learning. I beg
you to make the necessary arrangements, Daniel, and have
that rock in your bladder moved two inches to your pocket,
where it may lodge for another twenty or thirty years without giving you any trouble."

"They are a very significant two inches, Mr. Pepys."

"Obviously."

"During the Plague Year, when we lodged at Epsom, I
held candles for Mr. Hooke while he dissected the bodies of
diverse creatures—humans included. By then I had enough
skill that I could dissect *most* parts of *most* creatures. But I
was always baffled by necks, and by those few inches around
the bladder. Those parts had to be left to the superior skill of
Mr. Hooke. All those orifices, sphincters, glands, frightfully
important bits of plumbing—"

At the mention of Hooke's name, Pepys brightened as if
he had been put in mind of something to say; but as Daniel's
anatomy lesson drew on, his expression faded and soured.

"I of course *know this,*" Pepys finally said, cutting him off.

"Of course."

"I know it of my own knowledge, and I have had occasion
to review and refresh my mastery of the subject whenever

some dear friend of mine has died of the Stone—John Wilkins comes to mind—"

"That is low, a very low blow, for you to mention him now!"

"He is gazing down on you from Heaven saying, 'Can't wait to see you up here Daniel, but I don't mind waiting another quarter-century or so, by all means take your time, have that Stone out, and finish your work.'"

"I really think you cannot possibly be any more disgraceful now, Mr. Pepys, and I beg you to leave a sick man alone."

"All right . . . let's to the pub then!"

"I am unwell, thank you."

"When's the last time you ate solid food?"

"Can't remember."

"Liquid food, then?"

"I've no incentive to take on liquids, lacking as I do the means of getting rid of 'em."

"Come to the pub anyway, we are having a going-away party for you."

"Call it off, Mr. Pepys. The equinoctial gales have begun. To sail for America now were foolish. I have entered into an arrangement with a Mr. Edmund Palling, an old man of my long acquaintance, who has for many years longed to migrate to Massachusetts with his family. It has been settled that in April of next year we shall board the *Torbay*, a newly built ship, at Southend-on-Sea; and after a voyage of approximately—"

"You'll be dead a week from now."

"I know it."

"Perfect time for a going-away party then." Pepys clapped his hands twice. Somehow this caused loud thumping noises to erupt in the hall outside.

"I cannot walk to your carriage, sir."

"No need," Pepys said, opening the door to reveal two porters carrying a sedan-chair—one of the smallest type, little more than a sarcophagus on sticks, made so that its occupant could be brought from the street all the way into a house before having to climb out, and therefore popular among shy persons, such as prostitutes.

"Ugh, what will people think?"

"That the Fellows of the Royal Society are entertaining someone extremely mysterious—business as usual!" Pepys answered. "Do not think of *our* reputations, Daniel, they cannot sink any lower; and we shall have plenty of time, after you are gone, to sort that out."

Under a flood of mostly non-constructive criticism from Mr. Pepys, the two porters lifted Daniel up out of his bed, turning gray-green as they worked. Daniel remembered the odor that had filled Wilkins's bedchamber during his final weeks, and supposed that he must smell the same way now. His body was as light and stiff as a fish that has been dried on a rack in the sun. They put him into that black box and latched the door on him, and Daniel's nostrils filled with the scent of perfumes and powders left behind by the usual clientele. Or maybe that was what ordinary London air smelt like compared to his bed. His Reference Frame began to tilt and sway as they maneuvered him down-stairs.

They took him north beyond the Roman wall, which was the wrong way. But inasmuch as Daniel was facing his own death, it seemed illogical to fret over something as inconsequential as being kidnapped by a couple of sedan-chair carriers. When he wrenched his rigid neck around to peer out through the screened aperture in the back of the box, he saw Pepys's coach stealing along behind.

As they maneuvered through streets and alleys, diverse views, prospects, and more or less pathetic spectacles presented themselves. But one large, newly-completed, stone building with a cupola kept presenting itself square in their path, closer and closer. It was Bedlam.

Now at this point any other man in London would have commenced screaming and trying to kick his way out, as he'd have realized that he was about to be sent into that place for a stay of unknown duration. But Daniel was nearly unique among Londoners in that he thought of Bedlam not solely as a dumping-ground for lunatics but also as the haunt of his friend and colleague Mr. Robert Hooke. Calmly he allowed himself to be carried in through its front door.

That said, he was a bit relieved when the porters turned away from the locked rooms and conveyed him towards Hooke's office under the cupola. The howls and screams of the inmates faded to a sort of dim background babble, then were drowned out by more cheerful voices coming through a polished door. Pepys scurried round in front of the sedan chair and flung that door open to reveal *everyone:* not only Hooke, but Christiaan Huygens, Isaac Newton, Isaac's little shadow Fatio, Robert Boyle, John Locke, Roger Comstock, Christopher Wren, and twenty others—mostly Royal Society regulars, but a few odd men out such as Edmund Palling and Sterling Waterhouse.

They took him out of his sedan chair like a rare specimen being unpacked from its shipping-crate and held him up to accept several waves of cheers and toasts. Roger Comstock (who, since England's Adult Supervision had all run away to France, was becoming more terribly important every day) stood up on Hooke's lens-grinding table (Hooke became irate, and had to be restrained by Wren) and commanded silence. Then he held up a beaker of some fluid that was more transparent than water.

"We all know of Mr. Daniel Waterhouse's high regard and admiration for Alchemy," Roger began. This was made twice as funny by the exaggerated pomposity of his voice and manner; he was using his speaking-to-Parliament voice. After the laughter and Parliamentary barking noises had died down, he continued, just as gravely: "Alchemy has created many a miracle in our time, and I am assured, by some of its foremost practitioners, that within a few years they will have accomplished what has, for millennia, been the paramount goal of every Alchemist: namely, to bring us *immorality*!"

Roger Comstock now affected a look of extreme astonishment as the room erupted into true Bedlam. Daniel could not help glancing over at Isaac, who was the last man in the world to find anything amusing in a joke about Alchemy or immorality. But Isaac smiled and exchanged a look with Fatio.

Roger cupped a hand to his ear and listened carefully, then appeared taken aback. "What!? You say, instead, *immortality*?" Now he waxed indignant, and pointed a finger at Boyle. "Sirrah, my solicitor will call upon you in the morning to see about getting my money back!"

The audience had now been rendered completely helpless, which was the way Roger liked his audiences. They could only wait for him to continue, which he was only too happy to do: "The Chymists have accomplished smaller miracles along their way. Among those who frequent drinking establishments—or so I am told—it is known, empirically, that spiritous liquors are frequently contaminated by unwanted and unwholesome by-products. Of these, the most offensive by far is *water*, which gorges the bladder and obliges the drinker to step outside, where he is subject to cold, rain, wind, and the disapproving glares of neighbors and passers-by until such time as the bladder has become empty—which in the case of our Guest of Honor may be as long as a fortnight!"

"I can only say in my defense that I have time to sober up during those fortnights," Daniel returned, "and when I go back inside I find that you have left all the glasses empty, my lord."

Roger Comstock answered, "It is true. I give the contents of those glasses to our Alchemical brethren, who use them in their lucubrations. They have learnt how to remove water from wine and produce the pure spirit. But this is beginning to sound like a *theologickal* discourse, and so let me turn to *practical* matters." Roger hoisted the beaker up above his head. "Pray, gentlemen, extinguish all smoking materials! We do not wish to set fire to Mr. Hooke's edifice. The inmates will be so terrified that they will be driven sane, to a man. I hold in my hand the pure spirit I spoke of, and it could burn the place down like Greek fire. It will remain a grave hazard until our Guest of Honor has been so prudent as to sequester it in his belly. Cheers to you, Daniel; and rest assured that this libation will surely go to your head, but not a drop of it will trouble your kidneys!"

Under the center of the cupola they had set up a very stout oaken chair on a platform like a throne, which Daniel thought extremely considerate, as it put his head at or above the level of everyone else's. It was the first time in ages he'd been able to talk to anyone without feeling as if he were being peered down at. Once he was mounted in that chair, and wedged more or less upright by a few pillows, he did not have to move anything save his jaw and his drinking-arm. The others came round in ones and twos to pay court to him.

Wren spoke of the progress building the great Dome of St. Paul's. Edmund Palling related details of the voyage to Massachusetts planned for April. Hooke, when not arguing with Huygens about clocks (and fending off bawdy puns on "horology" from Roger Comstock), discoursed of his work on artificial muscles. He did not say that they were for use in flying machines, but Daniel already knew it. Isaac Newton was living in London now, sharing lodgings with Fatio, and had become Member of Parliament for Cambridge. Roger was bursting with scandalous gossip. Sterling was devising some sort of plot with Sir Richard Apthorp, some colossal scheme for financing the eternal follies of Government. Spain might have mines in America and France might have an infinite supply of taxable peasants, but Sterling and Sir Richard seemed to think that England could overcome her lack of both with some metaphysical sleight-of-hand. Huygens came over and told him the melancholy news that the Countess de la Zeur had got pregnant out of wedlock, then lost her baby. In a way, though, Daniel was pleased to hear that she was getting on with her life. He had dreamed once of proposing marriage to her. Looking at his condition now, it was hard to imagine a worse idea.

But thinking about her put him into a sort of reverie from

which he did not return. He did not lose consciousness at any one certain point; consciousness slowly leaked out of him, rather, over the course of the evening. Every friend who came to greet him raised his glass, and Daniel raised his beaker in return. The liquor did not trickle down his throat but raced like panic across his mucous membranes, burning his eye-sockets and his eustachian tubes, and seeping direct from there into his brain. His vision faded. The babble and roar of the party put him gently to sleep.

The quiet woke him up. The quiet, and the light. He phant'sied for a moment that they had carried him out to face the Sun. But there were several suns ranged about him in a constellation. He tried to raise first one arm, then the other, to shield his eyes from the glare, but neither limb would move. His legs, too, were frozen in place.

"Perhaps you imagine you are having a cerebral anomaly, a near-death, or even a post-death, experience," said a voice quietly. It emanated from down low, between Daniel's knees. "And that several arch-angels are arrayed before you, burning your eyes with their radiance. In that case I would be a shade, a poor gray ghost, and the screams and moans you hear from far off would be the complaints of other departed souls being taken off to Hell."

Hooke was indeed too dim to see clearly, for the lights were behind him. He was sorting through some instruments and tools on a table that had been set in front of the chair.

Now that Daniel had stopped looking into the bright lights, his eyes had adjusted well enough to see what was restraining him: white linen cord, miles of it, spiraled around his arms and legs, and cunningly interwoven into a sort of custom-built web or net. This was clearly the work of the meticulous Hooke, for even Daniel's fingers and thumbs had been individually laced down, knuckle by knuckle, to the arms of this chair, which were as massive as the timbers of a gun-carriage.

His mind went back to Epsom during the Plague Year, when Hooke would sit in the sun for an hour watching through a lens as a spider bound up a horse-fly with whorls of gossamer.

The other detail that caught his eye was the gleaming of the small devices that Hooke was sorting out on the table. In addition to the various magnifiers that Hooke always had with him, there was the crooked probe that would be inserted up the length of the patient's urethra to find and hold the stone. Next to it was the lancet for making the incision through the scrotum and up into the bladder. Then a hook for reaching up through that opening and pulling the stone down and out between the testicles, and an assortment of variously sized and shaped rakes for scraping the inside of the bladder and probing up into the ureters to find and withdraw any smaller stones that might be a-building in the crannies. There was the silver pipe that would be left in his urethra so that the uproar of urine, blood, lymph, and pus would not be dammed up by the inevitable swelling, and there was the fine sheep-gut for sewing him back together, and the curved needles and pliers for drawing it through his flesh. But for some reason none of these sights perturbed him so much as the scale standing by at the end of the table, its polished brass pans flashing inscrutable signals to him as they oscillated on the ends of their gleaming chains. Hooke, ever the empiricist, would of course weigh the stone when it came out.

"In truth you are still alive and will be for many years— more years than I have remaining. There are some who die of shock, it is true, and perhaps that is why all of your friends wished to come and pass time time with you before I started. But, as I recollect, you were shot with a blunderbuss once, and got up and walked away from it. So I am not afraid on that 'count. The bright lights you see are sticks of burning phosphorus. And I am Robert Hooke, than whom no man was ever better suited to perform this work."

"No, Robert."

Hooke took advantage of Daniel's plea to jam a leather strap into his mouth. "You may bite down on that if you wish, or you may spit it out and scream all you like—this is

Bedlam, and no one will object. Neither will anyone take heed, or show mercy. Least of all Robert Hooke. For as you know, Daniel, I am utterly lacking in the quality of mercy. Which is well, as it would render me perfectly incompetent to carry out this operation. I told you a year ago, in the Tower, that I would one day repay your friendship by giving you something—a pearl of great price. Now the time has come for me to make good on that promise. The only question left to answer is how much will that pearl weigh, when I have washed your blood off it and let it clatter onto the pan of yonder scale. I am sorry you woke up. I shall not insult you by suggesting that you relax. Please do not go insane. I will see you on the other side of the Styx."

When he and Hooke and Wilkins had cut open live dogs during the Plague Year, Daniel had looked into their straining brown eyes and tried to fathom what was going on in their minds. He'd decided, in the end, that *nothing* was, that dogs had no conscious minds, no thought of past or future, living purely in the moment, and that this made it worse for them. Because they could neither look forward to the end of the pain, nor remember times when they had chased rabbits across meadows.

Hooke took up his blade and reached for Daniel.

❧

Dramatis Personae

❦

MEMBERS OF THE NOBILITY went by more than one name: their family surnames and Christian names, but also their titles. For example, the younger brother of King Charles II had the family name Stuart and was baptized James, and so might be called James Stuart; but for most of his life he was the Duke of York, and so might also be referred to, in the third person anyway, as "York" (but in the second person as "Your Royal Highness"). Titles frequently changed during a person's lifetime, as it was common during this period for commoners to be ennobled, and nobles of lower rank to be promoted. And so not only might a person have several names at any one moment, but certain of those names might change as he acquired new titles through ennoblement, promotion, conquest, or (what might be considered a combination of all three) marriage.

This multiplicity of names will be familiar to many readers who dwell on the east side of the Atlantic, or who read a lot of books like this. To others it may be confusing or even maddening. The following Dramatis Personae may be of help in resolving ambiguities.

If consulted too early and often, it may let cats out of bags by letting the reader know who is about to die, and who isn't.

The compiler of such a table faces a problem similar to the one that bedeviled Leibniz when trying to organize his patron's library. The entries (books in Leibniz's case, per-

sonages here) must be arranged in a linear fashion according
to some predictable scheme. Below, they are alphabetized by
name. But since more than one name applies to many of the
characters, it is not always obvious where the entry should
be situated. Here I have sacrificed consistency for ease of
use by placing each entry under the name that is most commonly used in the book. So, for example, Louis-François de
Lavardac, duc d'Arcachon, is under "A" rather than "L" because he is almost always called simply the duc d'Arcachon
in the story. But Knott Bolstrood, Count Penistone, is under
"B" because he is usually called Bolstrood. Cross-references
to the main entries are spotted under "L" and "P," respectively.

Entries that are relatively reliable, according to scholarly
sources, are in Roman type. Entries in *italics* contain information that is more likely to produce confusion, misunder-
standing, severe injury, and death if relied upon by time
travelers visiting the time and place in question.

⚭

ANGLESEY, LOUIS: 1648–. *Earl of Upnor. Son of Thomas
More Anglesey. Courtier and friend of the Duke of Monmouth during the Interregnum and, after the Restoration,
at Trinity College, Cambridge.*

ANGLESEY, PHILLIP: 1645–. *Count Sheerness. Son of
Thomas More Anglesey.*

ANGLESEY, THOMAS MORE: 1618–1679. *Duke of Gunfleet.
A leading Cavalier and a member of Charles II's court in
exile during the Interregnum. After the Restoration, one
of the A's in Charles II's CABAL (which see). Relocated
to France during the Popish Plot troubles, died there.*

ANNE I OF ENGLAND: 1665–1714. Daughter of James II by
his first wife, Anne Hyde.

APTHORP, RICHARD: 1631–. *Businessman and banker. One*

of the A's in Charles II's CABAL *(which see)*. *A founder of the Bank of England.*

D'ARCACHON, DUC: 1634–. *Louis-François de Lavardac. A cousin to Louis XIV. Builder, and subsequently Admiral, of the French Navy.*

D'ARCACHON, ÉTIENNE: 1662–. *Étienne de Lavardac. Son and heir of Louis-François de Lavardac, duc d'Arcachon.*

D'ARTAGNAN, CHARLES DE BATZ-CASTELMORE: C. 1620–1673. *French musketeer and memoirist.*

ASHMOLE, SIR ELIAS: 1617–1692. Astrologer, alchemist, autodidact, Comptroller and Auditor of the Excise, collector of curiosities, and founder of Oxford's Ashmolean Museum.

D'AVAUX, JEAN-ANTOINE DE MESMES, COMTE: French ambassador to the Dutch Republic, later an advisor to James II during his campaign in Ireland.

BOLSTROOD, GOMER: 1645–. *Son of Knott. Dissident agitator, later an immigrant to New England and a furniture maker there.*

BOLSTROOD, GREGORY: 1600–1652. *Dissident preacher. Founder of the Puritan sect known as the Barkers.*

BOLSTROOD, KNOTT: 1628–1682. *Son of Gregory. Ennobled as Count Penistone and made Secretary of State by Charles II. The B in Charles II's CABAL (which see).*

BOYLE, ROBERT: 1627–1691. Chemist, member of the Experimental Philosophical Club at Oxford, Fellow of the Royal Society.

VON BOYNEBURG, JOHANN CHRISTIAN: 1622–1672. An early patron of Leibniz in Mainz.

CABAL, THE: unofficial name of Charles II's post-Restoration cabinet, loosely modeled after Louis XIV's Conseil d'en-Haut, which is to say that each member had a general area of responsibility, but the boundaries were vague and overlapping (see table, p. 420).

CAROLINE, PRINCESS OF BRANDENBURG-ANSBACH: 1683–1737. Daughter of Eleanor, Princess of Saxe-Eisenach.

THE CABAL

Responsible party	General area[s] of responsibility	Corresponding roughly to formal position of*
C COMSTOCK, JOHN (EARL OF EPSOM)	(Early in the reign) domestic affairs and justice. Later retired	Lord High Chancellor
A ANGLESEY, LOUIS (DUKE OF GUNFLEET)	(Early) the Exchequer and (covertly) foreign affairs, especially vis-a-vis France. Later Apthorp came to dominate the former. After Comstock's retirement, but before the Popish Plot, domestic affairs, and the Navy.	Various, including Lord High Admiral
B BOLSTROOD, KNOTT (COUNT PENISTONE)	Foreign affairs (ostensibly)	Secretary of State
A APTHORP, SIR RICHARD	Finance	Chancellor of the Exchequer
L LEWIS, HUGH (DUKE OF TWEED)	Army	Marshal, or (though no such position existed at the time) Defense Minister

*But sometimes they formally held these positions and sometimes they didn't.

CASTLEMAINE, LADY: see Villiers, Barbara.
CATHERINE OF BRAGANZA: 1638–1705. Portuguese wife of Charles II of England.
CHARLES I OF ENGLAND: 1600–1649. Stuart king of En-

gland, decapitated at the Banqueting House after the victory of Parliamentary forces under Oliver Cromwell.

CHARLES II OF ENGLAND: 1630–1685. Son of Charles I. Exiled to France and later the Netherlands during the Interregnum. Returned to England 1660 and re-established monarchy (the Restoration).

CHARLES LOUIS, ELECTOR PALATINATE: 1617–1680. Eldest surviving son of the Winter King and Queen, brother of Sophie, father of Liselotte. Re-established his family in the Palatinate following the Thirty Years' War.

CHARLES, ELECTOR PALATINATE: 1651–1685. Son and heir to Charles Louis. War-gaming enthusiast. Died young of disease contracted during a mock siege.

CHESTER, LORD BISHOP OF: see Wilkins, John.

CHURCHILL, JOHN: 1650–1722. Courtier, warrior, duellist, cocksman, hero, later Duke of Marlborough.

CHURCHILL, WINSTON: Royalist, Squire, courtier, early Fellow of the Royal Society, father of John Churchill.

CLEVELAND, DUCHESS OF: see Villiers, Barbara.

COMENIUS, JOHN AMOS (JAN AMOS KOMENSKY): 1592–1670. Moravian Pansophist, an inspiration to Wilkins and Leibniz among many others.

COMSTOCK, CHARLES: 1650–1708. *Son of John. Student of Natural Philosophy. After the retirement of John and the death of his elder brother, Richard, an immigrant to Connecticut.*

COMSTOCK, JOHN: 1607–1685. *Leading Cavalier, and member of Charles II's court in exile in France. Scion of the so-called Silver branch of the Comstock family. Armaments maker. Early patron of the Royal Society. After the Restoration, the C in Charles II's CABAL (which see). Father of Richard and Charles Comstock.*

COMSTOCK, RICHARD: 1638–1673. *Eldest son and heir of John Comstock. Died at naval battle of Sole Bay.*

COMSTOCK, ROGER: 1646–. *Scion of the so-called Golden branch of the Comstock family. Classmate of Newton,*

Daniel Waterhouse, the Duke of Monmouth, the Earl of Upnor, and George Jeffreys at Trinity College, Cambridge, during the early 1660s. Later, a successful developer of real estate, and Marquis of Ravenscar.

DE CRÉPY: *French family of gentlemen and petty nobles until the Wars of Religion in France, during which time they began to pursue a strategy of aggressive upward mobility. They intermarried in two different ways with the older but declining de Gex family. One of them (Anne Marie de Crépy, 1653–) married the much older duc d'Oyonnax and survived him by many years. Her sister (Charlotte Adélaide de Crépy 1656–) married the Marquis d'Ozoir.*

CROMWELL, OLIVER: 1599–1658. Parliamentary leader, general of the anti-Royalist forces during the English Civil War, scourge of Ireland, and leading man of England during the Commonwealth, or Interregnum.

CROMWELL, ROGER: 1626–1712. Son and (until the Restoration) successor of his much more formidable father, Oliver.

EAUZE, CLAUDE: see *d'Ozoir, Marquis.*

ELEANOR, PRINCESS OF SAXE-EISENACH: d. 1696. Mother (by her first husband, the Margrave of Ansbach) of Caroline, Princess of Brandenburg-Ansbach. Late in life, married to the Elector of Saxony.

ELISABETH CHARLOTTE: 1652–1722. Liselotte, *La Palatine.* Known as Madame in the French court. Daughter of Charles Louis, Elector Palatinate, and niece of Sophie. Married Philippe, duc d'Orléans, the younger brother of Louis XIV. Spawned the House of Orléans.

EPSOM, EARL OF: see *Comstock, John.*

FREDERICK V, ELECTOR PALATINATE: 1596–1632. King of Bohemia ("Winter King") briefly in 1618, lived and died in exile during the Thirty Years' War. Father of many princes, electors, duchesses, etc., including Sophie.

FREDERICK WILLIAM, ELECTOR OF BRANDENBURG: 1620–1688. Known as the Great Elector. After the Thirty Years'

War created a standing professional army, small but effective. By playing the great powers of the day (Sweden, France, and the Hapsburgs) against each other, consolidated the scattered Hohenzollern fiefdoms into a coherent state, Brandenburg-Prussia.

DE GEX: *A petty-noble family of Jura, which dwindled until the early seventeenth century, when the two surviving children of Henry, Sieur de Gex (1595–1660), Francis and Louise-Anne, each married a member of the more sanguine family de Crépy. The children of Francis carried on the de Gex name. Their youngest was Édouard de Gex. The children of Louise-Anne included Anne Marie de Crépy (later duchesse d'Oyonnax) and Charlotte Adélaide de Crépy (later marquise d'Ozoir).*

DE GEX, FATHER ÉDOUARD: 1663–. *Youngest offspring of Marguerite Diane de Crépy (who died giving birth to him) and Francis de Gex, who was thirty-eight years old and in declining health. Raised at a school and orphanage in Lyons by Jesuits, who found in him an exceptionally gifted pupil. Became a Jesuit himself at the the age of twenty. Was posted to Versailles, where he became a favorite of Mademoiselle. de Maintenon.*

GREAT ELECTOR: see Frederick William.

GUNFLEET, DUKE OF: see *Anglesey, Thomas More.*

GWYN, NELL: 1650–1687. Fruit retailer and comedienne, one of the mistresses of Charles II.

HAM, THOMAS: 1603–. *Money-goldsmith, husband of Mayflower Waterhouse, leading man of Ham Bros. Goldsmiths. Created Earl of Walbrook by Charles II.*

HAM, WILLIAM: 1662–. *Son of Thomas and Mayflower.*

HENRIETTA ANNE: 1644–1670. Sister of Charles II and James II of England, first wife of Philippe, duc d'Orléans, Louis XIV's brother.

HENRIETTA MARIA: 1609–1669. Sister of King Louis XIII of France, wife of King Charles I of England, mother of Charles II and James II of England.

HOOKE, ROBERT: 1635–1703. Artist, linguist, astronomer,

geometer, microscopist, mechanic, horologist, chemist, optician, inventor, philosopher, botanist, anatomist, etc. Curator of Experiments for the Royal Society, Surveyor of London after the fire. Friend and collaborator of Christopher Wren.

HUYGENS, CHRISTIAAN: 1629–1695. Great Dutch astronomer, horologist, mathematician, and physicist.

HYDE, ANNE: 1637–1671. First wife of James, Duke of York (later James II). Mother of two English queens: Mary (of William and Mary) and Anne.

JAMES I OF ENGLAND: 1566–1625. First Stuart king of England.

JAMES II OF ENGLAND: 1633–1701. Duke of York for much of his early life. Became King of England upon the death of his brother in 1685. Deposed in the Glorious Revolution, late 1688–early 1689.

JAMES VI OF SCOTLAND: see James I of England.

JEFFREYS, GEORGE: 1645–1689. Welsh gentleman, lawyer, solicitor general to the Duke of York, lord chief justice, and later lord chancellor under James II. Created Baron Jeffreys of Wem in 1685.

JOHANN FRIEDRICH: 1620–1679. Duke of Braunschweig-Lüneburg, book collector, a patron of Leibniz.

JOHN FREDERICK: see Johann Friedrich.

KÉROUALLE, LOUISE DE: 1649–1734. Duchess of Portsmouth. One of the mistresses of Charles II.

KETCH, JACK: Name given to executioners.

LAVARDAC: *A branch of the Bourbon family producing various hereditary dukes and peers of France, including the duc d'Arcachon* (see).

LEFEBURE: French alchemist/apothecary who moved to London at the time of the Restoration to provide services to the Court.

LEIBNIZ, GOTTFRIED WILHELM: 1646–1716. Refer to novel.

LESTRANGE, SIR ROGER: 1616–1704. Royalist pamphleteer and (after the Restoration) Surveyor of the Imprimery, hence chief censor for Charles II. Nemesis of Milton. Translator.

LEWIS, HUGH: 1625–. General. Created Duke of Tweed by *Charles II after the Restoration, in recognition of his crossing the River Tweed with his regiment (thenceforth called the Coldstream Guards) in support of the resurgent monarchy. The L in Charles II's CABAL (which see).*

LISELOTTE: *see* Elisabeth Charlotte.

LOCKE, JOHN: 1632–1704. Natural Philosopher, physician, political advisor, philosopher.

DE MAINTENON, MME.: 1635–1719. Mistress, then second and last wife of Louis XIV.

MARY: 1662–1694. Daughter of James II and Anne Hyde. After the Glorious Revolution (1689), Queen of England with her husband, William of Orange.

MARY OF MODENA: 1658–1718. Second and last wife of James II of England. Mother of James Stuart, aka "the Old Pretender."

MAURICE: 1621–1652. One of the numerous princely offspring of the Winter Queen. Active as a Cavalier in the English Civil War.

DE MESMES, JEAN-ANTOINE: see d'Avaux.

MINETTE: see Henrietta Anne.

MONMOUTH, DUKE OF (JAMES SCOTT): 1649–1685. Bastard of Charles II by one Lucy Walter.

MORAY, ROBERT: C. 1608–1673. Scottish soldier, official, and courtier, a favorite of Charles II. Early Royal Society figure, probably instrumental in securing the organization's charter.

NEWTON, ISAAC: 1642–1727. Refer to novel.

OLDENBURG, HENRY: 1615–1677. Emigrant from Bremen. Secretary of the Royal Society, publisher of the *Philosophical Transactions,* prolific correspondent.

D'OYONNAX, ANNE MARIE DE CRÉPY, DUCHESSE: 1653–. *Lady in Waiting to the Dauphine, Satanist, poisoner.*

D'OZOIR, CHARLOTTE ADÉLAIDE DE CRÉPY, MARQUISE: 1656–. *Wife of Claude Eauze, Marquis d'Ozoir.*

D'OZOIR, CLAUDE EAUZE, MARQUIS: 1650–. *Illegitimate son of Louis-François de Lavardac, duc d'Arcachon, by a domestic servant, Luce Eauze. Traveled to India in late 1660s as part of ill-fated French East India Company expedition. In 1674, when noble titles went on sale to raise funds for the Dutch war, he purchased the title Marquis d'Ozoir using a loan from his father secured by revenues from his slaving operations in Africa.*

PENISTONE, COUNT: see *Bolstrood, Knott.*

PEPYS, SAMUEL: 1633–1703. Clerk, Administrator to the Royal Navy, Member of Parliament, Fellow of the Royal Society, diarist, man about town.

PETERS, HUGH: 1598–1660. Fulminant Puritan preacher. Spent time in Holland and Massachusetts, returned to England, became Cromwell's chaplain. Poorly thought of by Irish for his involvement with massacres at Drogheda and Wexford. For his role in the regicide of Charles I, executed by Jack Ketch, using a knife, in 1660.

PHILIPPE, DUC D'ORLÉANS: 1640–1701. Younger brother of King Louis XIV of France. Known as Monsieur to the French Court. Husband first of Henrietta Anne of England, later of Liselotte. Progenitor of the House of Orléans.

PORTSMOUTH, DUCHESS OF: see *Kérouaille, Louise de.*

QWGHLM: *Title bestowed on Eliza by William of Orange.*

RAVENSCAR, MARQUIS OF: see *Comstock, Roger.*

ROSSIGNOL, ANTOINE: 1600–1682. "France's first full-time cryptologist" (David Kahn, *The Codebreakers,* which buy and read). A favorite of Richelieu, Louis XIII, Mazarin, and Louis XIV.

ROSSIGNOL, BONAVENTURE: d. 1705. Cryptanalyst to Louis XIV following the death of his father, teacher, and collaborator Antoine.

RUPERT: 1619–1682. One of the numerous princely offspring of the Winter Queen. Active as a Cavalier in the English Civil War.

DE RUYTER, MICHIEL ADRIAANSZOON: 1607–1676. Exceptionally gifted Dutch admiral. Particularly effective against the English.

VON SCHÖNBORN, JOHANN PHILIPP: 1605–1673. Elector and Archbishop of Mainz, statesman, diplomat, and early patron of Leibniz.

SHEERNESS, COUNT: see *Anglesey, Phillip.*

SOPHIE: 1630–1714. Youngest daughter of the Winter Queen. Married Ernst August, who later became duke of Braunschweig-Lüneburg. Later the name of this principality was changed to Hanover, and Ernst August and Sophie elevated to the status of Elector and Electress. From 1707 onwards, she was first in line to the English throne.

SOPHIE CHARLOTTE: 1668–1705. Eldest daughter of Sophie. Married Frederick III, elector of Brandenburg and son of the Great Elector. In 1701, when Brandenburg-Prussia was elevated to the status of a kingdom by the Holy Roman Emperor, she became the first Queen of Prussia and spawned the House of Prussia.

STUART, ELIZABETH: 1596–1662. Daughter of King James I of England, sister of Charles I. Married Frederick, Elector Palatine. Proclaimed Queen of Bohemia briefly in 1618, hence her sobriquet "the Winter Queen." Lived in exile during the Thirty Years' War, mostly in the Dutch Republic. Outlived her husband by three decades. Mother of many children, including Sophie.

STUART, JAMES: 1688–1766. Controversial but probably legitimate son of James II by his second wife, Mary of Modena. Raised in exile in France. Following the death of his father, styled James III by the Jacobite faction in England and "the Old Pretender" by supporters of the Hanoverian succession.

UPNOR, EARL OF: see *Anglesey, Louis.*

VILLIERS, BARBARA (LADY CASTLEMAINE, DUCHESS OF CLEVELAND): 1641–1709. Indefatigable mistress of many satisfied Englishmen of high rank, including Charles II and John Churchill.

WALBROOK, EARL OF: see *Ham, Thomas.*

WATERHOUSE, ANNE: 1649–. *Née Anne Robertson. English colonist in Massachusetts. Wife of Praise-God Waterhouse.*

WATERHOUSE, BEATRICE: 1642–. *Née Beatrice Durand. Huguenot wife of Sterling.*

WATERHOUSE, CALVIN: 1563–1605. *Son of John, father of Drake.*

WATERHOUSE, DANIEL: 1646–. *Youngest (by far) child of Drake by his second wife, Hortense.*

WATERHOUSE, DRAKE: 1590–1666. *Son of Calvin, father of Raleigh, Sterling, Mayflower, Oliver, and Daniel. Independent trader, political agitator, leader of Pilgrims and Dissidents.*

WATERHOUSE, ELIZABETH: 1621–. *Née Elizabeth Flint. Wife of Raleigh Waterhouse.*

WATERHOUSE, EMMA: 1656–. *Daughter of Raleigh and Elizabeth.*

WATERHOUSE, FAITH: 1689–. *Née Faith Page. English colonist in Massachusetts. (Much younger) wife of Daniel, mother of Godfrey.*

WATERHOUSE, GODFREY WILLIAM: 1708–. *Son of Daniel and Faith in Boston.*

WATERHOUSE, HORTENSE: 1625–1658. *Née Hortense Bowden. Second wife (m. 1645) of Drake Waterhouse, and mother of Daniel.*

WATERHOUSE, JANE: 1599–1643. *Née Jane Wheelwright. A pilgrim in Leiden. First wife (m. 1617) of Drake, mother of Raleigh, Sterling, Oliver, and Mayflower.*

WATERHOUSE, JOHN: 1542–1597. *Devout early English Protestant. Decamped to Geneva during reign of Bloody Mary. Father of Calvin Waterhouse.*

WATERHOUSE, MAYFLOWER: 1621–. *Daughter of Drake and Jane, wife of Thomas Ham, mother of William Ham.*

WATERHOUSE, OLIVER I: 1625–1646. *Son of Drake and Jane. Died in Battle of Newark during English Civil War.*

WATERHOUSE, OLIVER II: 1653–. *Son of Raleigh and Elizabeth.*

WATERHOUSE, PRAISE-GOD: 1649–. *Eldest son of Raleigh and Elizabeth. Immigrated to Massachusetts Bay Colony. Father of Wait Still Waterhouse.*

WATERHOUSE, RALEIGH: 1618–. *Eldest son of Drake, father of Praise-God, Oliver II, and Emma.*

WATERHOUSE, STERLING: 1630–. *Son of Drake. Real estate developer. Later ennobled as Earl of Willesden.*

WATERHOUSE, WAIT STILL: 1675–. *Son of Praise-God in Boston. Graduate of Harvard College. Congregational preacher.*

WEEM, WALTER: 1652–. *Husband of Emma Waterhouse.*

WHEELWRIGHT, JANE: see *Waterhouse, Jane.*

WILHELMINA CAROLINE: see Caroline, Princess of Brandenburg-Ansbach.

WILKINS, JOHN (BISHOP OF CHESTER): 1614–1672. Cryptographer. Science fiction author. Founder, first chairman, and first secretary of the Royal Society. Private chaplain to Charles Louis, Elector Palatinate. Warden of Wadham (Oxford) and Master of Trinity (Cambridge). Prebendary of York, Dean of Ripon, holder of many other ecclesiastical appointments. Friend of Nonconformists, Supporter of Freedom of Conscience.

WILLESDEN, EARL OF: see *Waterhouse, Sterling.*

WILLIAM II OF ORANGE: 1626–1650. Father of the better-known William III of Orange. Died young (of smallpox).

WILLIAM III OF ORANGE: 1650–1702. With Mary, daugher of James II, co-sovereign of England from 1689.

WINTER KING: see Frederick V.

WINTER QUEEN: see Stuart, Elizabeth.

WREN, CHRISTOPHER: 1632–1723. Prodigy, Natural Philosopher, and Architect, a member of the Experimental Philosophical Club and later Fellow of the Royal Society.

YORK, DUKE OF: The traditional title of whomever is next in

line to the English throne. During much of this book, James, brother to Charles II.

DE LA ZEUR: *Eliza was created Countess de la Zeur by Louis XIV.*

Read on for a special sneak preview of THE CONFUSION, PART I: The Baroque Cycle #4, in which a cabal of Barbary galley slaves——including one Jack Shaftoe, aka King of the Vagabonds, aka Half-Cocked Jack—— devises a daring plan to win freedom and fortune, embarking on a perilous race for an enormous prize of legendary gold . . .

. . . while in Europe, the exquisite and resourceful Eliza, Countess de la Zeur, finds herself stripped of her immense personal fortune and caught up in a web of international intrigue, even as she desperately seeks the return of her most precious possession.

"[T]he definitive historical-sci-fi-epic-pirate-comedy-punk-love story. A-."
Entertainment Weekly

Barbary Coast
OCTOBER 1689

HE WAS NOT MERELY *AWAKENED*, but *detonated* out of an uncommonly long and repetitive dream. He could not remember any of the details of the dream now that it was over. But he had the idea that it had entailed much rowing and scraping, and little else; so he did not object to being roused. Even if he *had* been of a mind to object, he'd have had the good sense to hold his tongue, and keep his annoyance well-hid beneath a simpering merry-Vagabond façade. Because what was doing the waking, today, was the most tremendous damned noise he'd ever heard—it was some godlike Force not to be yelled at or complained to, at least not right away.

Cannons were being fired. Never so many, and rarely so large, cannons. Whole batteries of siege-guns and coastal artillery discharging en masse, ranks of 'em ripple-firing along wall-tops. He rolled out from beneath the barnacle-covered hull of a beached ship, where he had apparently been taking an afternoon nap, and found himself pinned to the sand by a downblast of bleak sunlight. At this point a wise man, with experience in matters military, would have belly-crawled to some suitable enfilade. But the beach all round him was planted with hairy ankles and sandaled feet; he was the only one prone or supine.

Lying on his back, he squinted up through the damp, sand-caked hem of a man's garment: a loose robe of open-weave material that laved the wearer's body in a gold glow, so that he could look directly up into the blind eye of the man's penis—which had been curiously modified. Inevitably, he lost this particular stare-down. He rolled back the other way, performing one and a half uphill revolutions, and clambered indignantly to his feet, forgetting about the curve of the hull and therefore barking his scalp on a phalanx of barnacles. Then he screamed as loud as he could, but no one heard him. He didn't even hear *himself*. He experimented with plugging his ears and screaming, but even then he heard naught but the sound of the cannons.

Time to take stock of matters—to bring the situation in hand. The hull was blocking his view. Other than it, all he could see was a sparkling bay, and a stony break-water. He strode into the sea, watched curiously by the man with the mushroom-headed yard, and, once he was out knee-deep, turned around. What he saw *then* made it more or less obligatory to fall right on his arse.

This bay was spattered with bony islets, close to shore. Rising from one of them was a squat round fortress that (if he was any judge of matters architectural) had been built at grand expense by Spaniards in desperate fear of their lives. And apparently those fears had been well founded because the top of that fort was all fluttery with green banners bearing silver crescent moons. The fort had three tiers of guns on it (more correctly, the fort *was* three tiers of guns) and every one of 'em looked, and sounded, like a sixty-pounder, meaning that it flung a cannonball the size of a melon for several miles. This fort was mostly shrouded in powder-smoke, with long bolts of flame jabbing out here and there, giving it the appearance of a thunderstorm that had been rammed and tamped into a barrel.

A white stone breakwater connected this fort to the mainland, which, at first glance, impressed him as a sheer stone wall rising forty or so feet from this narrow strip of muddy beach, and crowded with a great many more huge cannons, all being fired just as fast as they could be swabbed out and stuffed with powder.

Beyond the wall rose a white city. Being as he was at the

base of a rather high wall, he wouldn't normally expect to be able to see anything on the opposite side thereof, save the odd cathedral-spire poking out above the battlements. But this city appeared to've been laboriously spackled onto the side of a precipitous mountain whose slopes rose directly from the high-tide mark. It looked a bit like a wedge of Paris tilted upwards by some tidy God who wanted to make all the shit finally run out of it. At the apex, where one would look for whatever crowbar or grapple the hypothetical God would've used to accomplish this prodigy, was, instead, another fortress—this one of a queer Moorish design, surrounded with its own eight-sided wall that was, inevitably, a-bristle with even more colossal cannons, as well as mortars for heaving bombs out to sea. All of *those* were being fired, too—as were all of the guns spraying from the several additional fortresses, bastions, and gun-platforms distributed around the city's walls.

During rare intervals between the crushing thuds of the sixty-pounders, he could hear peppery waves of pistol- and musket-fire rolling around the place, and now (beginning to advert on smaller things) he saw a sort of smoky, crowded lawn growing out of the wall-tops—save instead of grass-blades this lawn was made up of men. Some were dressed in black, and some in white, but most wore more colorful costumes: baggy white trousers belted with brilliantly hued swathes of silk, and brightly embroidered vests—frequently, several such vests nested—and turbans or red cylindrical hats. Most of those who were dressed after this fashion had a pistol in each hand and were firing them into the air or reloading.

The man with the outlandish johnson—swarthy, with wavy black hair in a curious 'do, and a knit skullcap—hitched up his robe, and sloshed out to see if he was all right. For he still had both hands clamped over the sides of his head, partly to stanch the bleeding of the barnacle-gashes, and partly to keep the sound from blowing the top of his skull out to sea. The man peered down and looked into his eyes and moved his lips. The look on his face was serious, but ever so slightly amused.

He reached up and grabbed this fellow's hand and used it to haul himself up to his feet. Both men's hands were so heavily callused that they could practically catch musket-balls out of the air, and their knuckles were either bleeding, or else recently scabbed over.

He had stood up because he wanted to see what was the target of all of this shooting, and how it could possibly continue to exist. A fleet of three or four dozen ships was arrayed in the harbor, and (no surprise here) *they* were all firing their guns. But the ones that looked like Dutch frigates were not firing at the ones that looked like heathen galleys, nor vice versa, and none of them seemed to be firing at the vertiginous white city. *All* of the ships, even the ones that were of European design, flew crescent-moon banners.

Finally his eye settled on *one* ship, which was unique in that she was the only vessel or building in sight that was not vomiting smoke and spitting flame in all directions. This one was a galley, very much in the Mohametan style, but extraordinarily fine, at least to anyone who found whorish decoration appealing—her non-functioning bits were a mess of gold-leafed gewgaws that glowed in the sun, even through drifting banks of powder-smoke. Her lateen sail had been struck and she was proceeding under oar-power, but in a stately manner. He found himself examining the movements of her oars just a bit too closely, and admiring the uniformity of the strokes more than was healthy for a Vagabond in his right mind: leading to the questions, *was* he still a Vagabond, and *was* he in his right mind? He recalled—dimly—that he had lived in Christendom during one part of his sorry life, and had been well advanced in the losing of his mind to the French Pox—but he seemed all right now, save that he couldn't recall where he was, how he'd gotten there, or anything at all of recent events. And the very meaning of that word "recent" was called into question by the length of his beard, which reached down to his stomach.

The intensity of the cannonade waxed, if such a thing were possible, and reached a climax as the gold-plated galley drew up alongside a stone pier that projected into the harbor not awfully far away. Then, all of a sudden, the noise stopped.

"What in Christ's name—" he began, but the rest of his utterance was drowned out by a sound that—compared to hundreds of cannons firing at once—made up in *shrillness* what it lacked in *volume*. Listening to it in amazement, he began to detect certain resemblances between it and *musick*. Rhythm was there, albeit of an overly complicated and rambunctious nature, and *melody*, too, though it was not cast in any civilized mode, but had the wild keening intonations of Irish tunes—and then some. Harmony, sweetness of tone, and other qualities normally associated with musick, were absent. For these Turks or Moors or whatever they were had no interest in flutes, viols, theorbos, nor anything else that made a pleasing sound. Their orchestra consisted of drums, cymbals, and a hideous swarm of giant war-oboes hammered out of brass and fitted with screeching, buzzing reeds, the result sounding like nothing so much as an armed assault on a belfry infested with starlings.

"I owe an 'umble apology to every Scotsman I've ever met," he shouted, "for it isn't true, after all, that their music is the most despicable in the world." His companion cocked an ear in his direction but heard little, and understood less.

Now, essentially all of the city was protected within that wall, which shamed any in Christendom. But on this side of it there were various breakwaters, piers, gun-emplacements, and traces of mucky beach, and everything that was capable of bearing a man's weight, or a horse's, was doing so—covered by ranks of men in divers magnificent and outlandish uniforms. In other words, all the makings of a parade were laid out here. And indeed, after a lot of bellowing back and forth and playing of hellish musicks and firing of yet more guns, various important Turks (he was growingly certain that these were Turks) began to ride or march through a large gate let into the mighty Wall, disappearing into the city. First went an impossibly magnificent and fearsome warrior on a black charger, flanked by a couple of kettledrum-pounding "musicians." The beat of their drums filled him with an unaccountable craving to reach out and grope for an oar.

"That, Jack, is the Agha of the Janissaries," said the circumcised one.

This handle of "Jack" struck him as familiar and, in any case, serviceable. So Jack he was.

Behind the kettledrums rode a graybeard, almost as magnificent to look at as the Agha of the Janissaries, but not so heavily be-weaponed. "The First Secretary," said Jack's companion. Next, following on foot, a couple of dozen more or less resplendent officers ("the aghabashis") and then a whole crowd of fellows with magnificent turbans adorned with first-rate ostrich plumes—"the bolukbashis," it was explained.

Now it had become plain enough that this fellow standing next to Jack was the sort who never tired of showing off his great knowledge, and of trying to edify lowlives such as Jack. Jack was about to say that he neither wanted nor needed edification, but something stopped him. It might've been the vague, inescapable sense that he *knew* this fellow, and had for quite a while—which, if true, might mean that the other was only trying to make conversation. And it might've been that Jack didn't know quite where to begin, language-wise. He *knew* somehow that the bolukbashis were equivalent to captains, and that the aghabashis were one rank above the bolukbashis, and that the Agha of the Janissaries was a General. But he was not sure *why* he should know the meanings of such heathen words. So Jack shut up, long enough for various echelons of odabashis (lieutenants) and vekilhardjis (sergeants-major) to form up and concatenate themselves onto the end of the parade. Then diverse hocas such as the salt-hoca, customs-hoca, and weights-and-measures-hoca, all following the hoca-in-chief, then the sixteen causes in their long emerald robes with crimson cummerbunds, their white leather caps, their fantastickal upturned moustaches, and their red hobnailed boots tromping fearsomely over the stones of the quay. Then the kadis, muftis, and imams had to do their bit. Finally a troop of gorgeous Janissaries marched off the deck of the golden galley, followed by a solitary man swathed in many yards of chalk-white fabric that had been gathered by means of diverse massive golden jeweled brooches into a coherent garment, though it probably would've fallen off of him if he hadn't been riding on a white war-horse with pink eyes, bridled and saddled with as much in the way of silver and gems as it could carry without tripping over the finery.

"The new Pasha—straight from Constantinople!"

"I'll be damned—is that why they were firing all those guns?"

"It is traditional to greet a new Pasha with a salute of fifteen hundred guns."

"Traditional *where*?"

"Here."

"And *here* is—?"

"Forgive me, I forget you have not been right in the head. The city that rises up on yonder mountain is the Invincible Bastion of Islam—the Place of Everlasting Vigil and Combat against the Infidel—the Whip of Christendom, Terror of the Seas, Bridle of Italy and Spain, Scourge of the Islands: who holds the sea under her laws and makes all nations her righteous and lawful prey."

"Bit of a mouthful, isn't it?"

"The English name is Algiers."

"Well, in Christendom I have seen entire wars prosecuted with less expenditure of gunpowder than Algiers uses to say hello to a Pasha—so perhaps your words are not mere bravado. What language are we speaking, by the way?"

"It is called variously Franco, or Sabir, which in Spanish means 'to know.' Some of it comes from Provençe, Spain, and Italy, some from Arabic and Turkish. *Your* Sabir has much French in it, Jack, mine has more Spanish."

"Surely you're no Spaniard—!"

The man bowed, albeit without doffing his skullcap, and his forelocks tumbled from his shoulders and dangled in space. "Moseh de la Cruz, at your service."

" 'Moses of the Cross?' What the hell kind of name is *that*?"

Moseh did not appear to find it especially funny. "It is a long story—even by *your* standards, Jack. Suffice it to say that the Iberian Peninsula is a complicated place to be Jewish."

"How'd you end up here?" Jack began to ask; but he was interrupted by a large Turk, armed with a bull's penis, who was waving at Jack and Moseh, commanding them to get out of the surf and return to work—the *siesta* was *finis* and it was time for *trabajo* now that the *Pasha* had ridden through the *Beb* and entered into the *citê*.

The *trabajo* consisted of scraping the barnacles from the hull of the adjacent galley, which had been beached and rolled over to expose its keel. Jack, Moseh, and a few dozen other slaves (for there was no getting round the fact that they were slaves) got to work with various rude iron tools while the Turk prowled up and down the length of the hull brandishing that ox-pizzle. High above them, behind the wall, they could hear a sort of rolling fusillade wandering around the city as the parade continued; the thump of the kettledrums, and the outcry of the siege-oboes and assault-bassoons was, mercifully, deflected heavenwards by the city walls.

"It is true, I think—you are cured."

"Never mind what your Alchemists and Chirurgeons will tell you—there is no cure for the French Pox. I'm having a brief interval of sanity, nothing more."

"On the contrary—it is claimed, by certain Arab and Jewish doctors of great distinction, that the aforesaid Pox may be purged from the body, completely and permanently, if the patient is suffered to run an extremely high fever for several consecutive days."

"I don't feel *good*, mind you, but I don't feel *feverish*."

"But a few weeks ago, you and several others came down with violent cases of *la suette anglaise*."

"Never heard of any such disease—and I'm English, mind you."

Moseh de la Cruz shrugged, as best a man could when hacking at a cluster of barnacles with a pitted and rusted iron hoe. "It is a well-known disease, hereabouts—whole neigh borhoods were laid low with it in the spring."

"Perhaps they'd made the mistake of listening to too much musick—?"

Moseh shrugged again. "It is a real enough disease— perhaps not as fearsome as some of the others, such as Rising of the Lights, or Ring-Booger, or the Laughing Kidney, or Letters-from-Venice . . ."

"Avast!"

"In any event, you came down with it, Jack, and had such a fever that all the other *tutsaklars* in the *banyolar* were roasting kebabs over your brow for a fortnight. Finally one morning you were pronounced dead, and carried out of the *banyolar* and thrown into a wain. Our owner sent me round to the Treasury to notify the *hoca el-pencik* so that your title deed could be marked as 'deceased,' which is a necessary step in filing an insurance claim. But the *hoca el-pencik* knew that a new Pasha was on his way, and wanted to make sure that all the records were in order, lest some irregularity be discovered during an audit, which would cause him to fall under the *bastinado* at the very least."

"May I infer, from this, that insurance fraud is a common failing of slave-owners?"

"Some of them are *completely unethical*," Moseh confided. "So I was ordered to lead the *hoca el-pencik* back to the *banyolar* and show him your body—but not before I was made to wait for hours and hours in his courtyard, as midday came and went, and the *hoca el-pencik* took a siesta under the lime-tree there. Finally we went to the *banyolar*—but in the meantime your wagon had been moved to the burial-ground of the Janissaries."

"Why!? I'm no more a Janissary than you are."

"Sssh! So I had gathered, Jack, from several years of being chained up next to you, and hearing your autobiographical ravings: stories that, at first, were simply too grotesque to believe—then, entertaining after a fashion—then, after the hundredth or thousandth repetition—"

"Stay. No doubt *you* have tedious and insufferable qualities of your own, Moseh de la Cruz, but you have me at a disadvantage, as I cannot remember them. What I want to know is, why did they think I was a Janissary?"

"The first clew was that you carried a Janissary-sword when you were captured."

"Proceeds of routine military corpse-looting, nothing more."

"The second: you fought with such *valor* that your want of *skill* was quite overlooked."

"I was trying to get myself killed, or else would've shown less of the former, and more of the latter."

"Third: the unnatural state of your penis was interpreted as a mark of strict chastity—"

"Correct, perforce!"

"—and assumed to've been self-administered."

"Haw! That's not how it happened at all—"

"Stay," Moseh said, shielding his face behind both hands. "I forgot, you've heard."

"Fourth: the Arabic numeral seven branded on the back of your hand."

"I'll have you know that's a letter V, for Vagabond."

"But sideways it could be taken for a seven."

"How does that make me a Janissary?"

"When a new recruit takes the oath and becomes *yeni yoldash*, which is the lowliest rank, his barrack number is tattooed onto the back of his hand, so it can be known which *seffara* he belongs to, and which *bash yoldash* is responsible for him."

"All right—so 'twas assumed I'd come up from barracks number seven in some Ottoman garrison-town somewhere."

"Just so. And yet you were clearly out of your mind, and not good for much besides pulling on an oar, so it was decided you'd remain *tutsaklar* until you died, or regained your senses. If the former, you'd receive a Janissary funeral."

"What about the latter?"

"*That* remains to be seen. As it was, we thought it was the former. So we went to the high ground outside the city-walls, to the burial-ground of the *ocak*—"

"Come again?"

"*Ocak*: a Turkish order of Janissaries, modeled after the Knights of Rhodes. They rule over Algiers, and are a law and society unto themselves here."

"Is that man coming over to hit us with the bull's penis a part of this *ocak*?"

"No. He works for the corsair-captain who owns the galley. The corsairs are yet another completely different society unto themselves."

After the Turk had finished giving Jack and Moseh several bracing strokes of the bull's penis, and had wandered away to go beat up on some *other* barnacle-scrapers, Jack invited Moseh to continue the story.

"The *hoca el-pencik* and several of his aides and I went to that place. And a bleak place it was, Jack, with its countless tombs, mostly shaped like half-eggshells, meant to evoke a village of *yurts* on the Transoxianan Steppe—the ancestral homeland for which Turks are forever homesick—though, if it bears the slightest resemblance to that burying-ground, I cannot imagine why. At any rate, we roamed up and down among these stone yurts for an hour, searching for your corpse, and were about to give up, for the sun was going down, when we heard a muffled, echoing voice repeating some strange incantation, or prophecy, in an outlandish tongue. Now the *hoca el-pencik* was on edge to begin with, as this interminable stroll through the graveyard had put him in mind of daimons and *ifrits* and other horrors. When he heard this voice, coming (as we soon realized) from a great mausoleum where a murdered *agha* had been entombed, he was about to bolt for the city gates. So were his aides. But as they had with them one who was not only a slave, but a Jew to boot, they sent me into that tomb to see what would happen."

"And what did happen?"

"I found you, Jack, standing upright in that ghastly, but delightfully cool space, pounding on the lid of the *agha*'s sarcophagus and repeating certain English words. I knew not what they meant, but they went something like this: 'Be a good fellow there, sirrah, and bring me a pint of your best bitter!' "

"I *must* have been out of my head," Jack muttered, "for the light lagers of Pilsen are much better suited to *this* climate."

"You were still daft, but there was a certain spark about you that I had not seen in a year or two—certainly not since we were traded to Algiers. I suspected that the heat of your fever, compounded with the broiling radiance of the midday sun, under which you'd lain for many hours, had driven the French Pox out of your body. And indeed you have been a little more lucid every day since."

"What did the *hoca-el-pencik* think of this?"

"When you walked out, you were naked, and sunburnt as red as a boiled crab, and there was speculation that you might be some species of *ifrit*. I have to tell you that the Turks have superstitions about everything, and most especially about Jews—they believe we have occult powers, and of late the Cabbalists have done much to foster such phant'sies. In any event, matters were soon enough sorted out. Our owner received one hundred strokes, with a cane the size of my thumb, on the soles of his feet, and vinegar was poured over the resulting wounds."

"Eeyeh, give me the bull's penis any day!"

"It's expected he may be able to stand up again in a month or two. In the meanwhile, as we wait out the equinoctial storms, we are careening and refitting our galley, as is obvious enough."